"This ~~~~~~~~~~~~~~~~~~~~ *uttered.*

12/05

Daffyd looked at his new roommate. She was pacing. "It has to," he said. "Tell you what. Toss me a coverlet, I'll sleep on the floor. You'll be as safe as a nun. I won't touch you." He grinned. "Unless you want me to."

She stopped and stared at him.

He flung up his hands. "An attempt at humor, nothing else. It's been a hard night. So it wasn't very funny. Of course I won't bother you. Especially after what happened yesterday. Fine way to thank you, that would be."

"But if people hear we stayed together, my reputation will be ruined!"

"So will mine. Don't worry. No one knows us. You're safe, and so am I. See, I really am grateful to you and would do almost anything to thank you," he said sincerely. "But not marry you. I'd hate to have to do that."

Her eyes flashed, then narrowed. "I do *not* want to marry you!" she said in a violent whisper.

Other **AVON ROMANCES**

EDITH LAYTON

GYPSY LOVER

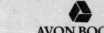

AVON BOOKS
An Imprint of HarperCollinsPublishers

AVON BOOKS
An Imprint of HarperCollins*Publishers*
10 East 53rd Street
New York, New York 10022-5299

Copyright © 2005 by Edith Felber
ISBN-13: 978-0-06-075784-7
ISBN-10: 0-06-075784-1
www.avonromance.com

First Avon Books paperback printing: November 2005

Avon Trademark Reg. U.S. Pat. Off. and in Other Countries, Marca Registrada, Hecho en U.S.A.
HarperCollins® is a registered trademark of HarperCollins Publishers Inc.

Printed in the U.S.A.

10 9 8 7 6 5 4 3 2 1

For Diane and Gene Armyn:
good neighbors and good friends.

FIC
326-6254

An English lord came home one night,
Inquir-ring for his lady,
The servants said on every hand,
She's gone with the Gypsy Laddie.

Go saddle up my milk-white steed,
Go saddle me up my brownie
And I will ride both night and day,
Till I overtake my bonnie.

Oh he rode East and he rode West,
And at last he found her,
She was lying on the green, green grass,
And the Gypsy's arms all around her.

How can you leave your house and land,
How can you leave your baby,
How can you leave your rich young lord,
To be a gypsy's lady.

It's I can leave my house and land,
And I can leave my baby,
I'm a-goin' to roam this world around
And be a gypsy's lady.

Child Ballad

Prologue

He sat in the shadows, waiting. A wedge of lamplight from the hallway fell into the dimly lit bedchamber, widening as the door opened further and the woman came in. And still, the man in the shadows didn't move. It amused him to wait to be noticed. He wondered if the lady would even see him before she got into bed, because she was obviously preoccupied with her thoughts. He'd let her know he was there long before that, of course. But he was pleased. He liked the element of surprise. Especially in this case.

She was a slender woman of a certain age, dressed to the best effect that taste and money could achieve. The three snowy egret plumes nested in her hair band complemented her pale hair and the light gold of her gown. The soft light in the room also flattered her, hiding the evidence of time's passage. Her profile was perhaps the most beautiful thing about her, except, the man in the shadows thought with professional interest, for the exquisite diamonds at her white throat, on her hands, and in her ears.

She went to the chair by her dressing table, and sat. The lamp that had been left lit on the table showed a flash of blue as her eyes met her reflection in the looking glass. She began to remove an earring. Most women of fashion had their maids wait up for them to help them undress after a party, but the man in the shadows knew she'd sent hers to bed hours earlier. Fashionable parties lasted until nearly dawn, and she'd need the services of a wide-awake maid more at noon, when she awoke. After all, she wasn't expecting company now. He smiled.

That white smile was what she saw reflected in her looking glass. Her narrow shoulders raised a fraction, but she didn't cry out. Her expression went from alarm, to mere surprise, then rueful recognition . . . and sorrow? He wasn't sure, because in a second, she was composed again.

"You," she said with a twisted smile.

He sketched a bow from where he sat on her window seat, but didn't stand. "Me," he agreed.

It was difficult to see him clearly in the half-light he sat in, but she saw him well enough to recognize his brilliant mocking smile.

"You sent for me," he said.

"So I did," she said as she removed her other earring. "But I didn't expect to find you here."

"Exactly," he said and then stood. He roamed her bedchamber, as though pricing every ornate item of furniture, including her satin bedcovers.

She watched him in her glass as he wandered her room. He was a lean, dark, dangerously attractive, restless young man of middle height. She frowned. He wore a laboring man's clothes. A shapeless hat sat low on his forehead, shadowing his face; he had on a long, dark, baggy coat and ugly scarred and misshapen boots. "They'd have you clapped in prison if they caught you entering my house as you are," she commented and went back to stripping off her jewelry.

"But they wouldn't. Catch me, that is."

She shrugged. "Perhaps not. But they did once."

"They caught me mate," he said in one of the rough accents he sometimes used. "Not me. They only got me because I stayed by 'im." He looked up, and she saw a flash of his blue eyes in his dark face as it lit in a devilish grin. "They'll not catch me again, my lady," he drawled in aristocratic tones. "You may make book on it."

She shrugged again. "I don't know why you must always be so dramatic," she said. "You might have come see me below stairs."

"Where I belong?" he asked sweetly.

Her eyes flew open, her composure cracked. "I never meant that!"

"I know," he said. He ran a finger lightly along the porcelain skirts of a Dresden shepherdess on the mantel over her hearth. "Just checking to see if your heart was beating, my lady. After all, you wouldn't want to anger the lad you've summoned to do work for you. What is it you want, then?"

"How did you get in?" she asked curiously, ignoring his question.

"By the window."

"But it is two stories up. How could you? There are no trellises, ledges, or handholds. Did no one see you?"

"Then not by the window," he said with a shrug. "No troubles. I'm here as you asked, aren't I?"

"I want to know . . ." she began to say.

". . . if anyone saw me?"

". . . *if* I must tell Mr. Fitch you are here so the servants don't try to apprehend you as a trespasser when you leave," she finished.

"Ah," he said. "Well, no worries there." He pulled off his disreputable hat, and she saw that his shining black hair had been expertly barbered. It was a bit overlong, but that was obviously his preference and not lack of style. He took off his long bulky coat. She suddenly saw a fashionable gentleman before her; his fitted blue jacket bore the mark of a master tailor, his spotless neckcloth had seen the hands of a valet, his dun breeches fit without a wrinkle. He slipped a foot out of a boot and exposed a shining black shoe. "Again," he said, as she stared. "What is it you want of me?"

"You were at my party!" she exclaimed.

He smiled. "I thought you invited me. Not to worry. I wasn't seduced by any of your lady guests. Nor by any of the gents, either. Nor do any of them know who I was. Nice party, by the way. Crowded to the doors. The lobster patties were a bit dry, I thought, but the wine was fine. I'll leave by the window though, in my old coat and with my hat on, so I can be invisible, or as good as. There *are* handholds out there, by the way. No need to stir up old Fitch. You wouldn't want anyone knowing I was in your rooms, would you? Well, I wouldn't care for it even if you don't mind. Now, will you tell what it is you want, or should I go?"

She kept looking at him, hunger as well as sorrow in her intent expression. Then she looked away. In a moment she sat abruptly upright again. She pulled off a ring and placed it in her jewelry box. "I need your special talents," she said as curtly as he had.

His head came up. "Someone snabbled something from you?"

"No. I need someone I can trust to be discreet to find something else for me."

He approached her. But when he got to her side he ignored her and lifted the ring she'd just put down. He inspected it, turning it around and around in his long fingers. " 'Discreet,' is it? Aye, well, so I can be."

"Discreet," she repeated with a nod, "and practiced in stealth, as well as adept at finding things gone astray. By which I mean, I need someone who would know the mind of an impetuous and troubled youth, and know to where such a person might stray."

He frowned, obviously pretending to be thinking hard. "Oh. Aye, took me a while, but I figured it out," he finally said. "You mean, knowing criminals and runaways. But, my lady, it's sure you know the latter as well as me."

She might have winced. It might have been the flame in her lamp flickering. In a moment, her expression was serene again. "Yes. But the world has changed since I was young. You would know it now. I do not."

"Who's gone missing?" he asked as he put down her ring and picked up the diamond bracelet she had discarded, weighing it in his hand. "And did he run away, or was he kidnapped?"

"*She* ran away. She left a note saying she had. No one disputes it."

He looked up at that. "How old is she, and where did she run from, and what's it to you? Or me?"

"She's seventeen, and the daughter of a friend. I am, in fact, her godmother. I should hate to see her come to ruin."

"If she ran off, and they told you," he said, "it means they haven't found her. She has already come to ruin. I can't help. What else do you want of me? Need her fortune told? I might oblige, but she isn't here."

She made an impatient sound. "Don't play games, Daffyd. She isn't ruined, because few others know and her family has the money and position to keep her misadventure secret at least a little while longer. They asked me precisely because they thought I might have some ideas."

"She run off with a gypsy lad?" he asked in surprise.

Now he could see she winced. "No. That is to say, they're not sure. There were gypsies in the neighborhood, but it's spring and there would be, wouldn't there? She ran away from her fiancé. She was visiting at his country estate and they discovered her gone in the morning. Her note said she'd be safe, but had to get away for a spell."

"Arranged marriage?"

She nodded. "But they've known each other since childhood. She seemed well pleased with the match."

"Were you?"

"They seemed to suit," she said carefully.

He grew still. "Tell me about her."

"Young, pretty, blond with blue eyes. She is perhaps a bit headstrong. But I don't doubt she'll settle down when she matures, because she is by no means stupid. She does have a charming lisp that might give that impression. But she tries to correct it. That is to say, she doesn't lisp because it's a fashionable affectation. She actually has a delightfully refreshing personality."

"Family got money and position?" he asked slowly.

"They are wealthy. Her father is a landed baron."

"Ah," he said with what might have been relief, "then you're not matchmaking. Don't stare. I thought it possible. Might be the chit was already ruined, and you were trying to get a husband, any husband for her because of a debt you owe. It isn't like you to trouble yourself about other people's misfortunes."

She stiffened. "It is, but I can't expect you to know that."

"Aye," he said, putting her bracelet down. "You can't. So. Why should I help you?"

"She's alone in a strange world now, and I hoped you might be sympathetic."

"Where's her father? And the fiancé?"

"Her father has hired a Runner to trace her."

Her guest's low laughter was mocking.

"Yes, exactly," she said. "I have as little confidence in them finding her as you do. Her fiancé has gone in search of her himself as well, but he's also young, inexperienced, and hotheaded. So who knows what danger he will get into himself?"

"I do," he said.

"Yes. So will you look for her? If not as a favor to me, then at least to help another young person who has put herself in jeopardy? The world's a dangerous place for those who have no experience with it."

He looked directly at her then. For once, there was no humor in his expression. She saw all the rebuttals he wanted to make in his eyes: dark blue eyes that were an echo of her own. She lowered her gaze because of the intensity of his.

But, "Aye, why not?" he finally said. "I live to oblige you, my dear mama."

"There's a lie," she said bitterly.

"Is it?" he asked. "Well, that's something neither of us knows, isn't it? And we haven't known each other long enough to even guess. But I surprise myself. I have sympathy for her. So I'll do it. I'll find the wench and return her to you."

"You won't . . . that is to say, when you find her . . ." she paused.

"I won't take her, in any way, and to no place but back to her home," he said with a wry, humorless smile. "Not every gypsy lad lusts for well-bred flesh, Mama. Some of us prefer any lass who wants us for ourselves, not just for the novelty of a tumble with a rough lad, for a taste of forbidden fruit, even if it's rotten."

"I thought I loved your father," she said, raising her chin.

"The more fool you," he murmured. "But that's past. Talking about it won't profit either of us now. As for now, I'm here and strangely enough, at your service, just as my da was, if in a different fashion. No matter," he said, waving a hand. "I know that was a vile thing to say."

He walked back to the chair where he'd left his hat and coat. He clapped on his hat and shrugged into his coat. "Give me the chit's name and her father's direction, and I'll be gone. I'll bring her back if I can, untouched by me, at least. That's a promise."

She handed him a slip of paper. "I've written it all out."

"I'll get someone to read it to me," he assured her with grave mockery, his hand on his heart.

"You don't like me, do you?" she asked suddenly.

"What's that to do with anything?" he said in surprise as he pocketed the paper and moved toward the window. He threw it open, looked out, smiled back at her, and then stepped out into the darkness of the night.

"Everything," she finally answered softly to the breeze that blew in through the empty window after he'd gone.

Chapter 1

After a hurried stop for refreshment, the Brighton-bound coach, the last coach of the night, left the muddy courtyard of the *Ruddy Rooster* and splashed off and down the main road again.

The flurry of excitement over, the guests at the *Rooster* prepared to settle in until morning. Most stayed at the tap, and most were locals, because the *Rooster* wasn't luxurious enough to attract many strangers apart from those on the public coaches. There were finer inns along the busy Brighton Road.

Still, it was crowded enough this night, maybe because of the rain, or maybe because there seemed to be some sort of entertainment going on.

"And so now that I've beguiled you," a smooth

11

male voice was saying to the attentive listeners clustered around him at the long bar in front of the tap. "*And* bought you all another pint . . ."

This was met with a rush of laughter.

"Maybe some of you will loosen your lips?" the voice asked.

The speaker was a young man, dark as a gypsy, but dressed neatly and soberly, like a fellow with ambitions. He was certainly attractive. Of medium height, lean and trim, he wore clean linen and a devilish smile. He had ink black hair, regular features, an aristocratic nose, and in the light of the leaping hearth, his dark eyes sparked blue.

"After all," he went on smoothly, "I'm not asking after your grannies or your sisters, this is my fiancée I'm looking for. I think she may have passed this way this week. She's blond and shapely, with big blue eyes. The only man among you who could have missed her would be a blind one. Even if he was, he'd know her, because she speaks with a lisp like a highborn lady, though her father isn't any better born than mine, and mine's only as close to Quality as the bills he keeps sending them for their boots.

"I know she doesn't deserve my time after the trick she played me," the dark man continued, shrugging his shoulders, "running off on the eve of our wedding. But I forgive her because she's young and I love her madly. I do," he swore theatrically, his hand on his chest. "And so I only want to be sure she's safe. If she doesn't want me she doesn't have to take me, but I have to know she's not come to harm.

"Now," he said in a wheedling voice, "if you don't take pity on me, or her, is there anyone here who wants to earn a golden guinea? It's yours for a hint. Where is she, or have you seen her?"

The other guests at the *Rooster* shook their heads and shuffled their feet.

The dark young man looked around the room, and then his gaze sharpened. He saw a young woman at the back of the crowd, prim as a Puritan and just as shocked as one might have been if she'd seen the devil.

Daffyd was used to women staring at him, but not in obvious terror. His interest was caught. It would have been caught anyway. Once a man looked past her drab clothing, she was a charming little thing, with big brown eyes, a pretty face, and a neat little shape. Her only ornament was that flower face of hers; she was dressed all in gray, plain as a nun, and looked respectable as one. Not the sort of female who usually ogled him, at least not openly. He was definitely interested. And she was decidedly horrified. That interested him even more. So he looked away from her immediately, and turned his attention back to the locals he'd met at the tap.

"Not seen such a miss such as you're seeking, lad," one old fellow told him. "Leastways not here, and not of late. Blond, blue eyed, and talking like a lady? Be sure I'd remember that."

The others rumbled agreement.

"Here now," another fellow said, laughing, "You're

not taking your pint back just because we can't help, are you?"

"Well you can't have mine," an old woman cackled, and then gulped down the contents of her mug. She plunked down the empty mug, wiped her mouth with the back of her hand and added, "Can't see as how any miss in her right mind would leave you, anyways. Bad cess to her. Could I interest you in a female of experience, instead?" she asked, with an enormous wink.

"You could, love," Daffyd said, "if I wasn't so afraid of all your gentleman friends."

That was met with laughter, and he remained at the tap, joking with them. He took expressions of sympathy on his bad luck as well as advice on how to mend a broken heart with the same good humor. No one had any information for him; he hadn't really thought they would. The trail was growing cold. But so was he, and it had been time for dinner when that trail brought him to the inn.

Still, he reasoned, the track he was on wasn't completely without promise. If a female looked at him with horror, there had to be a reason. Could the baron's daughter have a confidante? A maid? A friend? Someone getting the lay of the land for her before she set foot in a place? Could the runaway then be close by? That made sense. Even more reason to keep his eye on the gray-clad woman.

So, of course, he pretended he'd never seen her while watching her from the corner of his eye as she was shown to a table in a far corner. Even more interesting, he thought. She wasn't running away from him. Good, he didn't feel like leaving. He was hungry and the rain was going to be an all-night affair.

"And so now, thank you all," he finally told his audience, "but even though my heart is breaking, my stomach's growling. I must have dinner. I'll stay the night and leave in the morning. So if anyone thinks of anything to tell me about my missing fiancée, I'm here until dawn and would be grateful for any information. Thank you all." He bowed, to please them, and then winked at the serving girl.

"A table in the corner, luv?" he asked her. "I'm tired of talking. How about that one—there?" He gestured toward a table in the gray lady's lonely corner.

"Right, it's yours," the serving girl said, and whispered, with a wink of her own. "And if you get tired of not talking, sir, I'm here until the place closes. After it does," she added, "I'm here all night too—so if you still don't want to talk, I'm sure we can find other things to do."

She was plump and passably fair, and looked clean. And an intimate assignation wouldn't be out of character for an abandoned fiancé. Daffyd started to smile, but paused. He was bemused to discover that this time, the thought of free fun with no obligations didn't cause his flesh to rise. He was surprised at himself. Was it age or experience that killed his desire? But he wasn't yet thirty, and his previous intimate experiences with females had always brought pleasure.

It could have been a good way to while away a chilly night in an unfamiliar place. He wasn't feeling sick, only tired. But he wasn't interested. Something was definitely changing in him as well as in his world.

Could it possibly be because his two adopted brothers had recently married? It might be that in comparing his bachelor's rakings with their obviously deeper and more satisfying matings his looked like the empty pleasures they were. But he'd never minded empty pleasures. He tucked the thought away for future consideration.

Still, because a gracious offer ought to be accepted as such, he tipped a smile to the serving wench. "I'll keep it in mind, luv," he told her; although he already believed his mind was the only place he'd have it.

There were two tables available in the corner of the room he'd indicated: one to the back of the gray lady, and one in front of her. Daffyd took the one in front. She'd be too nervous with him behind her, and he didn't want her to take flight. Besides, she probably thought he couldn't see her. But a seemingly casual repositioning of his dinnerware gave him her reflection in a knife's edge, and she showed very nicely on the side of the smooth silver match safe he set in front of his plate.

He ordered his meal. Then he sat back and waited for his dinner, amusing himself by watching the waitress roll her hips as she strolled away with his order. And all the while he tried to read the gray lady's expressions as she decided what to do next.

She peeped at him from time to time. Sometimes she frowned. Sometimes she bit her lip. But she stayed where she was, and though he could see her nibbling at her dinner, she paid more attention to him than to her plate.

Of course, Daffyd thought as he tucked into the fine mutton chop that had been put in front of him, it might only be that she'd mistaken him for some other villain. His dark gypsy looks had always made females shiver, and men look askance. Even when he'd been a boy, if anything was discovered stolen in his vicinity, people always looked at him. Which was why he'd been caught holding goods rather than stealing them. He'd been a good thief, but a bad risk. His dark looks made him resemble every Englishman's notion of a villain, from a Frenchie to a gypsy to any unknown foreigner. That was why he wore good clothes and spoke in flowery accents tonight.

He was by nature short spoken, but could ape anyone, and had found people liked speaking to people who sounded like themselves, or just a bit better. He always mimicked his betters among strangers. Otherwise he might be turned away at the door, mistaken for a tinker or a traitor, or the gypsy that he was.

The woman in gray might have been afraid of him simply because of his looks. He'd certainly never seen her before, and he remembered faces. But in that moment when their eyes had met she'd thought she recognized him, he'd swear it. She could be addled, of course, he'd met females who were. But she didn't look it. She looked sober, proper, and apprehensive. Still, though she kept studying him, she didn't move from her table.

No one from the tap came to talk to him either.

So much for hoping that he'd be able to find the runaway heiress on the Brighton Road. He wondered where to go next, because he wasn't ready to give up the search. He disliked his errand, but disliked having to report failure at it even more. The thought of rescuing his mother from anxiety and then waving off her thanks and disappearing from her life had pleased him very much. But he could live without that pleasure. He'd lived without her for so long anyway. However, the thought of telling his adopted father he'd failed at the task bothered him much more.

"I think it's a good thing for you to do, Daffyd," the earl had said just days ago when he'd told him about the mission. "For too many reasons to enumerate. Although I'm sure you're aware of them all."

"If you think I'm going to retrieve the wench, sit at the viscountess's feet and wallow in her praise, you're wrong," Daffyd had answered.

They'd been sitting in the new earl of Egremont's study at Egremont, his magnificent manor house, after a lavish dinner, drinking excellent port wine together. Everything at Egremont was excellent, most of all, to Daffyd's mind, the fact that Geoffrey Sauvage, eleventh earl of Egremont, was in his rightful place at last.

He said so then.

Geoffrey had looked amused. He'd been dressed

casually that night, at least for a man of such power and wealth. He'd taken off his beautifully fitted jacket and unwound his elaborate neckcloth and discarded it, as he always did when he wasn't in company. The fine linen shirt he wore showed he was still muscular, if a bit thicker around the waist then when Daffyd had met him. But he was fit, and though a few gray hairs now showed in his brown hair, his dark blue eyes were as keen as ever.

"Avoiding the subject doesn't change it, Daffyd," he'd said softly. "She came to you for a favor and you elected to try to do it for her. That's good, and I'm proud of you for it."

Daffyd had grunted something, and reached for his glass of port. He didn't want to discuss the matter and so focused instead on his host.

Geoffrey hadn't looked much like an earl when they'd met, but he hadn't been one then, or thought there was much chance he'd ever be. No place on earth could have been further from where they sat that night either. Because they'd met in Newgate prison. Familiar territory for Daffyd, but Geoffrey Sauvage had never seen anything like it. That had formed the basis for their association. Not much else could have.

Their situations couldn't have been more different, though their fates would be the same. Both had committed crimes the Crown punished by death. But Geoffrey had all unknowing been accused and convicted of a crime committed by a relative who wanted his title and estate. Daffyd had actually committed his crime, and many others besides. Geoffrey was said to have stolen a silver snuffbox, but he hadn't even known where it was hidden when the Runner found it in his house. Daffyd definitely had plans for the stolen pound note he'd been arrested with in his pocket. Geoffrey had been a sober man of business, Daffyd a petty thief from the streets of London. Geoffrey was university educated. Daffyd was ignorant of most things except for those that would get him food and a place to sleep out of the rain.

And most of all, Geoffrey had been a grown man with a son Daffyd's age, imprisoned with him for the same crime. Daffyd had been a boy with less than a dozen years to his name.

But Daffyd had known one thing Geoffrey and his son didn't: how to survive in prison. After all, he'd done it many times before. And so then, for that brief time, he and his adopted brother in crime, Amyas, had been able to help Geoffrey and his son. In return, they'd gotten the one thing they didn't have: the power and protection of a grown man in a place where muscle meant survival as much as cunning did.

It had been a better bargain for them than that. A noble relative of Geoffrey's had influence that spared him the hangman's noose. He'd gotten that pardon for Daffyd and Amyas, too. They'd been transported to Botany Bay instead of dancing on air at the end of a rope. And though that fate could have been just as lethal, they'd defied the odds. They'd survived and prospered just as their partnership did.

They became rich and returned to England again: Geoffrey to become earl of Egremont, Daffyd and his brother to become young men about town.

They'd arrived in England only the year before. Daffyd's world had changed once again. Now, he was wealthy and free, but for the first time in his life, alone. Oh, he had a suite in this great palace of a manor house reserved for him, and another one in Geoffrey's London townhouse. He had his own flat in London as well. What he didn't have were his two boon companions: the earl's son, Christian, and his first "adopted" brother and fellow street rat, Amyas St. Ives. He'd lost them both to marriage. They were still his brothers indeed. But their lives belonged to their lovely wives now, and Daffyd wouldn't have wanted it any other way—except on nights when he was especially at loose ends.

The earl had leaned forward and held Daffyd's gaze. "Your mother wants to mend matters with you," he'd said gently. "I don't think it matters if you succeed so much as that you try."

Daffyd had kept his expression and his voice bland. "It isn't the lady I'm trying to please. The run-away wench interests me."

"You've never met her," the earl had reminded him.

"Lookee, your lordship," Daffyd had said in a growl, his voice taking on old slum cadences, as it often did when he was upset, "I'm not doing it for the old bitch. I'm doing it because I choose to."

The earl winced, and put up one hand.

"Your ears grown as tender as your feelings?"

Daffyd had asked sourly. He'd ducked his head and swept out one hand in a mockery of an elaborate bow, though he didn't rise from his chair. "Excuse me. Didn't know you'd put on new airs with your new clothes, my lord."

"I'm not saying what your mother is, or is not," the earl said mildly. "I am saying that she is your mother, and even if she tried to throttle you at birth, a well-bred man never calls his mother that."

"But I'm not well-bred, as you well know," Daffyd said on a strained but wide white smile. "You taught me my letters, my numbers, everything I know that isn't illegal, in fact. Before you met me, I wasn't bred, I was only begot. Or should I say: misbegot? You did teach me how to speak too," he added, when he saw the earl's slight smile. "But aye—you taught me my manners, too. So I beg your pardon. I didn't mean to offend you, and I did. What I said wasn't right."

"Oh, it may have been right," the earl commented dryly, "it just was not polite."

They'd laughed together then, and with the atmosphere eased, Daffyd told the earl about his quest.

"I don't know if I can find the chit," he'd finally admitted. "She's been gone for days. I'm definitely going to be sniffing a cold trail. But if she's in England I'll find her, if only because runaways always go to ground. And I have so many friends on the ground, and in the fields, and the gutters. Being a gypsy as well as a convict has its uses."

"A half gypsy and an ex convict," he'd been corrected.

"The half is enough for most people. And the convict never leaves, even when you leave prison."

"As well I know," the earl had sighed. "But a man is much more than the sum of his parts."

"Aha! Belittling my parts, are you?" Daffyd joked, to lighten the mood. "I never had any complaints. They're always admired in all the right places. Or rather, in the wrong places when they're in the right places."

He'd smiled, but Geoffrey hadn't. "I have faith in you," the earl had said seriously. "That's why I told your mother you were the man to ask for help."

"*You!*" Daffyd had exclaimed, rising from his chair. "You were the one who turned her on me? So she never wanted me in the first place!" He'd tried to suppress the ridiculous flash of pain he felt. "Well, that makes sense, at least. It's only habit with her. Well, damn you for such courtesies, my lord. I thought you knew me better."

"Softly, softly," the earl had said. "And please sit down. I do know you. She did come to me first, but only to ask whom I might know that could help her find her goddaughter. There was no flattery or honor in that for me. I'm an old lag too, you know, and all she wanted was someone with criminal connections. She wouldn't have dared ask you on her own. She's as nervous about you as you are about her, and you'll agree, with even better cause."

"I see," Daffyd said stiffly, though he sat again. "Well, she's a fine-looking woman. I congratulate you."

"You know," the earl had said, keeping his voice even, "if I didn't like you so much I'd thrash you for that, or try to; I'm not sure I could anymore. But hear this: I do not desire your mother. She *is* fine-looking, but though she's my age, she is not my sort. Not now, not then, nor ever. I won't traduce her, but I'm too much of a gentleman to tell you all the reasons why I could if I wanted to. Suffice it to say, she's not for me. Remove the thought from your mind. But speaking of which, you've been in England for a year. Have you found the right woman yet?"

"Nice try at changing the subject," Daffyd had laughed. "Yes, I have, many times, and I hope many times more, thank you."

"I mean, a woman to marry. Any chance we'll have another wedding soon? We can have it here, I've got the hang of it now."

Daffyd had thrown up his hands in horror. "Married, me? Never!"

"I know you've got a poor opinion of the institution," the earl had said. "With good reason, considering your history. But surely by now, seeing the happiness the other boys have found, you've changed your mind? I tell you straightly, I was married and I loved the state I found myself in."

"Yes," Daffyd had said sourly. "Which is why you've remarried, isn't it?"

The earl had sighed. "You joke, but, yes, you're right, in a way. The only reason I'm not married now is that I've decided to not marry again unless I think my new union won't shame my old one. I'd prefer to live on what I had rather than spoil that memory with a bad, hasty union for the sake of companionship. Companionship, I can find. Sex, as you know, is easily found, too. Love's another thing altogether. But then I can afford to refuse marriage because I'm not alone, I have three children—no, five, counting my two new daughters. But you, Daffyd, don't you want children, one day?"

"Lord, no! I want to be an uncle. I look forward to it!"

The earl groaned and put one hand over his face, but Daffyd had seen his smile under it. "Oh, Gods, what have I done? I forgot. Spare me the famous 'uncle' speech, please."

"But it's true," Daffyd had said, grinning. "That's why it's famous. Uncles have the best of it. I didn't have one who'd speak to me, but I've seen it and heard it from others. Peasant or nob, it's always the same. Uncles are fun, uncles are generous: uncles have much better reputations than parents do. They don't have to raise kids. When they see their nieces and nephews, the brats are trotted out for them, all cleaned up and polite, because they've been threatened with death unless they behave.

"One shiny coin flipped to a niece or nephew once in a while by an uncle— especially a rich one, which I plan to remain—is good as years of patient parenting. And when the brats grow into people, they cater to their uncles, however eccentric or crabby they are.

Because they want to inherit their fortunes. Oh, no, I leave the joys of parenthood to others. It's the uncle's life for me!"

"Done?" the earl had asked, lifting his hand from his eyes so he could see Daffyd again.

"Not really, I could go on. But you know the rest, so I'll spare you."

The earl had laughed. "Thank you. Now, down to business. Tell me what you'll be doing and where you're going, so that I can get word to you if I must, and so I can find you should you not return on time. I have to keep track of all my boys, you know."

And for that, because Daffyd was no more really Geoffrey Sauvage's boy than he'd been all those years ago, but because he'd always been treated as such, Daffyd told him everything he planned.

Now Daffyd sat in a nondescript inn on the Brighton Road, digesting his meal. He was done with watching the woman in gray at the table behind him. It was getting late, the room was emptying, and she hadn't done anything new. Watching a pretty female could be interesting, but watching a blurred reflection of one grew boring. Whatever her problem was with him, it wasn't a thing he'd likely ever know.

He stifled a yawn. Just as well. There was only so long a fellow could linger over dessert. This stop had yielded nothing but an excellent dinner. It was time for bed, so he could be on the trail again at first light. Again, he debated the wisdom of seeking the serving wench's company until then. And again, he tended to think such sport was hardly worth his time or effort. . . .

"Excuse me?" a soft voice asked, breaking into his thoughts.

Daffyd's eyes went wide. He only kept himself from leaping to his feet by steely self-control. But one hand slid inside his waistcoat to grasp the pistol he had secreted there. He looked up.

The woman in gray stood directly in front of his table. He took a steadying breath. She'd done what no woman had done in years. She'd surprised him.

"Yes?" he asked, rising, cocking his head to the side, watching her.

"Oh, please sit," she begged him. "Don't let me ruin your dinner."

Since his dinner was a memory and they both knew it, he could only wait for her to tell him what she wanted of him.

"I mean," she said, looking flustered, "I don't wish to disturb you. Only I couldn't help hearing you ask about your fiancée, the blond lady with the lisp? And after much consideration, I decided I ought to tell you . . . I have seen her, I think."

He bowed, suddenly calm as a dead man. He smiled at her, fascinated. "Sit down, please," he said, holding out a chair, but keeping his eyes locked on hers. "And tell me more."

Chapter 2

"**H**eartsease," that's what they were, Daffyd suddenly remembered. He didn't know much about flowers, but he thought that was what they called those velvety things that popped up in meadows every spring. Yellow, they were, or violet, with brown markings, their arrangement of petals making them look like winsome little faces. This woman had such a face. He was more used to full-blown roses, but had to admit she was very taking.

He listened to her soft voice and thought about what she was saying. Her face was much better than her tale. He didn't believe a word of it.

"And so," she concluded, "although I never thought I'd do something so bold as to approach a strange man, I felt so sorry for you I had to speak up, even though we are not acquainted. You see, I overheard your telling everyone about how you're searching for your runaway fiancée: a blond girl with blue eyes who speaks with a lisp, like a lady. I'm traveling down south, and did hear about such a woman."

She paused, flushed, and in the absolutely worst recover of a slip that he'd ever heard, added, "That is to say, the maid cleaning my room was chatting with me and said she'd just had another lady stay over in the same chamber, and thought it unusual, because they didn't have many ladies traveling without maids. . . . My maid became ill and will join me soon," she added quickly. "The point is," she went on doggedly, "I heard about a pretty young lady who lisped. But she had black hair."

"That could be a wig," he said. "My love is fond of masquerading."

Her big brown eyes snapped wide and looked far less innocent as she studied him. "I don't wish to pry," she said. "But I also heard she was in the company of a dark man. Which would of course, have been you, sir. Unless she met another such man, but that's improbable, wouldn't you say? Except there are many dark gentlemen . . . To be sure we're speaking of the same woman, when did you last see her?"

The turning of tables was done so awkwardly that he was amused. Whatever she was, this woman was not only a bad liar, but also a terrible interrogator. He relaxed, marginally. She could also be a superb liar who knew how to act like a novice.

"I last saw her at her home, when I called on her," he said. "That was just the other week."

Her expression said the triumphant "aha!" she was obviously suppressing. That wasn't all she suppressed. She sat straight upright on the edge of her chair, like a bird that might fly off at any minute. He smelled soap and a trace of lemon. She smelled like good furniture, he thought, repressing his own smile. Prim, proper, not his sort at all. Or was she?

Now it was clear she thought she'd caught him in a lie. Her eyes narrowed as she studied him again. He could almost see her thoughts as she decided what to say next. Whether she was a professional or an innocent, he hadn't been so entertained in days.

"And her name is . . . ?" she finally asked.

She seemed to have forgotten that it wasn't her business to question him. By doing so she was letting him know she wasn't a casual traveler who had simply heard about the runaway.

"Her name is Rosalind," he said, making his voice sound lover-like, and his eyes distant and dreamy. "Rosalind Osbourne."

He heard her sharp intake of breath. Her eyes grew wide again. He could see the invisible wheels of her thoughts turning, and waited, politely, for them to arrive at their destination.

"She wasn't your fiancée," the woman finally blurted. "I advise you to tell me why you're looking for her, this minute! I'll have you know the Bow Street Runners are looking for her, too . . ." Her voice dwindled. "Oh," she asked. "Are you a Runner? Is that it?"

"God forbid," he said honestly.

She bit her lip. He realized they were beautifully shaped. In fact the closer he looked, the better she looked. She had pale, fine-grained skin and a faultless complexion. Her hair was thick, brown as hazelnuts, and looked lovely even though it was ruthlessly tied back. Her nose was insignificant, her eyes, her best feature: they spoke, they glowed. Everything else about her was understated. She talked softly and stepped lightly. He was charmed. She wasn't the sort of female he usually noticed, but now he was glad that she'd cropped up in his path, whatever her motives.

He watched as those honey brown eyes widened again, and she took in a deep breath. "Then—did you abduct . . . No, that's wrong of me," she corrected herself. "Forgive me. Did she run off with you, and then change her mind and run away? Is that why you're searching for her? If so, I implore you to let her go. She's young and foolish; surely you know that. Her father will doubtless pay a great deal to get her back safely, but it would be much safer for you to give the information and let someone else find her. The Osbournes are honest, they'll see you get your reward."

"They'll pay a gypsy lad for luring her away, and not clap him in irons?" he asked in rougher accents, to see what she would say. "Ho! Try pulling the other one, it's got bells on."

She frowned. Then she put her head to the side. "You're a gypsy?"

"Half," he said abruptly. "But half's as good as a whole in the eyes of the world."

"But how could you have done it?" she murmured almost to herself. "It's not possible. I knew where she was every moment. And if she'd met a gypsy. . . ." She sat bolt upright. "You're making a May game of me."

"It's September," he said. "Now, my turn. Who are you?"

The serving wench saved her from replying. "Anything else, sir?" the girl asked, staring with disdain at the woman at his table. "Or are you satisfied? I thought you were the sort of man who needed more than what I see you got."

He smiled. The woman at the table was turning scarlet. "I'll have another round of your excellent home brew, and bring one for the lady. I should celebrate. This gentlewoman may have heard about my runaway bride," he told the serving girl. "She's being kind enough to tell me about it. Please," he said to his crimson companion, "will you join me?"

She murmured something. With a suspicious glance and a decided flounce, the serving girl went off to fill his order.

"Now," he said, leaning forward on his elbows, "your name, and the reason you're involved in this. Don't try to lie. You're either a bad liar, in which case, I'll know if you do; or you're an adventuress, in which case I won't let you go so easily."

She looked around wildly. Then, though white-faced, she shook her head. "You can't do anything to me. This is a public place."

"Yes. But it's a long night and a longer way to get anywhere else from here. A long, lonely way. I advise you not to lie," he said coldly. "Because you'll pay for it, and eventually tell the truth, too."

He sounded like a bully, and disliked himself for it. But the time for amusement was over. He needed to know who she was and why she was here.

She scowled. "How do I know you aren't the dark man she was with? How do I know she isn't running away from you?"

"Because if I'd got my hands on her, she'd only be going in one direction: home. And she would not get away."

She believed it; he could see it in her eyes. She let out a breath, and sat up straighter. "I am Margaret Shaw," she announced.

He waited.

The fact that he hadn't reacted to her name seemed to make her relax a little. "I am Rosalind Osborne's companion. And now I think I'd be surprised to find out you ever met her."

He smiled. "Right. I haven't. So, where is she?"

"I haven't the faintest idea."

"Right," he said again, in bored tones. "So what are you doing here?"

"Looking for her."

"Alone?"

"Yes. Well, the Bow Street Runners are looking,

too, but I'm not with them, and I don't think they're following me."

He paused. That was foolish of her to tell him. Unless of course she knew where the runaway was. And that, at last, made sense.

"So where is she? You might as well tell me," he said, sitting back and stretching out his legs. "Her godmother sent me to find her. I'm very good at finding things. So why not tell me now, save time, and possibly her reputation?"

"Her godmother?" she asked slowly.

"A lady born, who doesn't want her name brought into this," he answered in a bored voice. Then he leaned forward again. "Listen. I'm on the square, in this, at least. The lady asked me because I know all the bad places a young chit might find herself after pulling a caper like that. Running off in the night looks good in books. It's bad in real life. Really bad. I'm here to save your Rosalind from herself and whatever she picked up on the way. Believe me, a girl on her own will pick up a lot worse than fleas. I've never met her. So if she was with a dark man, it wasn't me. I aim to find out who it was, though. I'll save the wench from herself or whomever she got involved with. Now, tell me what you know, and you can go home."

He didn't expect her to answer right away. She surprised him.

"I won't go home until I find her!" she declared. Then looking uneasily around the room, she lowered her voice. "I'll come with you."

"No," he said. "Tell me where she is and I'll bring her back to you. Even if she's just down the road, it might be dangerous. Who knows what rig the man she's with is running? I don't want a female along. So, spill it. Where's the girl?"

Her gaze fell to the tabletop. "Well, that's just it. I'm not sure."

"Oh, wonderful," he said. Then he studied her. "S'truth?" he asked.

She nodded, and examined her fingers.

"Then what the devil are you doing here?"

"I think I know where she's going," she said softly.

He waited.

"Why should I trust you?" she asked, looking at him as though judging his worth, hoping to find he was a good bargain.

"Good question. How about because the lady who sent me did so on request from the baron Osbourne? And," he added as she took that in, "because I want to get this over and done. Now, if you don't tell me, it's too bad for you, because I'll follow you like a burr on a dog's tail from now on. And there goes your reputation, right? So you may as well."

He looked up to see the serving wench coming. He gave her a gold coin and a wink, and let her leave laughing. Then he turned to Margaret Shaw again. She was staring into her mug of ale.

She lifted eyes the same color of the amber brew, and just as wet, to his. "I have no reputation," she said sadly. "I'm only a companion, and that's only a

glorified servant. And if I don't get Rosie back, I'll
have no livelihood either." She raised an imploring
gaze to his.

"Forget it," he said roughly. "I don't travel with females, not even for my comfort. I take that as it
comes." His gaze went boldly to her breasts.

She stiffened and rose to her feet, one hand going
to the top of her gown as though to block his view. "I
see," she said coldly. "I also see you're right about
one thing. I'm obviously in far over my head. But I
don't think it wise to tell a stranger I met in a tavern
anything about my charge, not even my wildest
guesses. And that, I see now, is all that I had. Except
I've also had enough. I'll be writing to the baron, but
I'm going home now. Good evening," she said, in-
clining her head in a slight bow. "Mr. . . ." she hesitated, "I don't even know your name."

"Daffy," he said without thinking, coming up
with the name the earl and his brothers jokingly
called him.

"Well then," she said, "Good night, Mr. Daffeigh,
and good-bye. I'll trouble you no more, and will
thank you to do the same for me."

Meg went up to her room, bolted the door, and
sank to the bed. She was trembling like a tuning fork.
That man!

He was the most unusual fellow she'd ever met, by
turns charming and threatening. There had been moments when she would have sworn he was a gentleman. And then he spoke like a man pushing a barrow

in the street. And those eyes! Deep dark blue, and always searching. He was a gypsy, he'd said it. Where did a gypsy get such eyes?

She frowned. What did she know of gypsies, really? For all she knew they might have eyes all the colors of the rainbow. She reviewed what she did know: Gypsies did dress like rainbows. They told fortunes and stole chickens and babies, mended pots and pans and worked at traveling carnivals. Their women were stout and wore dozens of skirts. Their men were swarthy and had Roman noses. This man had an impressive nose, but it could as easily be considered aristocratic, since it was narrow and elegant, as were his other features. He had high cheekbones and a severe and shapely mouth.

His skin *was* olive, and his hair was jet black. Still, he dressed soberly and well. But clothes, after all, didn't make the man.

Yet surely he'd been joking. Even if he were really Romany, what connection did a gypsy have to a viscountess, or the baron Osbourne? She didn't believe him.

She could believe he'd find Rosalind though. There'd been an air of competence about him, of surety. He wasn't a muscular man, like a laborer, or even like the dashing Corinthians she'd seen in London, fellows who rode to an inch, boxed and fenced, and lived the active outdoor life. But he was lean and fit, and emanated an aura of power.

He didn't wear a fob or a quizzing glass, and his boots, though clean, were serviceable, not polished like looking glasses and hung with tassels. But he could act like a Bond Street beau when it pleased him. He was also manipulative: glib and pleasant, fierce and menacing, as it suited him. And when he looked into a person's eyes it was impossible to look away. It was like looking down from a high cliff and feeling pulled down to the dark sea far below.

Meg rubbed her hands along her upper arms, and then hugged herself. What had she gotten herself into? It was too late to turn back. She, Margaret Shaw, companion, had taken to the road to find her missing charge, and ought to be prepared to face the dangers she met along the way.

The danger she faced if she didn't find Rosalind was clear enough. At first she'd been accused of helping Rosalind run off. Who knew what would have happened to her if the baron and his wife hadn't eventually decided she wasn't in league with their runaway daughter? Thank heavens Rosalind had left merry little notes for everyone, including Meg, saying she was in no danger, and promising to write and tell them all about her adventure when she got where she was going.

So the baron and his wife hadn't accused Meg of anything but stupidity and carelessness. But they did that constantly. Everyone else in the house looked at her with suspicion, too, and no one but the Bow Street Runner would talk to her. It had become unendurable.

Meg decided she wouldn't endure it. She was no adventuress, but she couldn't just sit and wait for Rosalind to return or send word. She had to take action the way Rosie's childhood friend, and fiancé, young Tom Rackham, immediately had. He'd leaped on a horse and rode off to find her. That was simpler for a hotheaded, rich young gentleman than it was for a paid servant. But Meg had once had independence. And she wasn't going to give up what little of it she had left without a fight.

The Runner had been kinder to her. He'd given her permission to leave an unpleasant situation and stay with her retired governess for the duration—as long as she left her direction with him. Meg did more. She also sent a letter to her old governess, swearing her to secrecy, begging that she tell anyone who asked that she *was* there, or would be arriving soon. Because Meg wasn't going there. The only way to prove her innocence and ensure a bearable future was to strike out on her own and find Rosalind.

The thought of Rosie leaving her redheaded, mischief-loving Thomas for another man was ridiculous. They'd been a well-matched pair, always playing like a pair of puppies. She also couldn't believe Rosie could have kept such a secret from her. After all, Rosie was seventeen and Meg three and twenty, so they'd been more like friends than mistress and servant . . . or so Meg had thought.

But there had been that one night when Meg had wondered why Rosie wasn't in bed and had gone looking for her. She'd found Rosie standing in the library, studying one of her father's folding canvas-backed traveling maps, a finger paused on a spot

amongst the roads and routes. Rosie had been startled when she'd seen Meg appear in the doorway.

"What is it?" Rosie had said as she hurriedly
folded up the map again.

"I only wondered why you weren't in bed," Meg
had said.

"Oh," Rosie had said with a forced giggle, "I thup-
pose I couldn't thleep I wath thinking tho much
about my honeymoon trip. Tom theth we'll thee a bit
of England before we leave. We'll travel down to
Brighton. No . . . no, Penthance? Bother, thome-
thing with a 'B' or a 'P' in it, anyway. Then we'll get
board a packet for the Continent. Thuth fun! I can
hardly wait!"

"Well, you'd better, because that's months away!"
Meg had told her. "Come to bed, silly. We've almost
a year to get through before you leave. You don't
have to memorize maps now."

So, laughing, the two had gone up the stairs again.

Meg had told the Runner about it. But she hadn't
remembered anything else until the night before she
herself had left. Then she'd wandered back to the library, trying to recreate that moment, if only because it was the only time she'd felt Rosie had lied to
her. Meg had found the map and unfolded it. And
then in a flare of lamp light, she'd noticed a pock, an
indentation, only that, but just exactly where Rosie
had put her finger that night, she'd swear it. Meg
stared: *Plymouth*.

That was where Meg was going now. She had to
believe that was the right direction. It was never

pleasant traveling alone, but she'd been on her own before. Servants after all, even jumped-up ones, didn't need chaperones when going from one position to another. But it was daunting. She had two weeks in which to find Rosie. Dressed in gray or brown like a servant, eyes downcast, she'd thought she could be as much as invisible as she traveled. But the clock was ticking and it was proving more difficult than she'd imagined.

Rosie could have gone off on a lark and gotten herself into trouble, and she herself was in trouble now. If she didn't find Rosie, she'd be dismissed without a reference.

That would mean she'd have to go back to live with the two maiden aunts who'd taken her in when she'd been orphaned at thirteen. When she'd left them six years later she'd vowed she'd never again live on their charity. Not that they were cruel, or couldn't afford her upkeep. They were only frugal, insular, and totally lacking laughter. Their house in the Lake District was remote, and exquisitely lonely. If Meg returned there, it would probably be where she'd spend the rest of her life.

She was too wellborn for her aunts to allow her to be courted by local lads, and they wouldn't sponsor her in Society, even such as there was there. There were few single men of any kind near her aunts' house; it was difficult enough finding women friends. That was why Meg had gone for a position when she'd turned nineteen: to find company. She'd found work, and little else, but at least that little had been interesting. She'd had two positions in London that showed her how the upper class lived, even if she only lived on the edges of their privileged world. Then she'd gone to the countryside to stay with Rosie, where she'd felt like a guest, not a servant.

Now she was three and twenty and if she didn't find silly little Rosie, her whole future would be past.

She'd been traveling down from the baron's house for two days now, with many an alarm and a few starts to frighten her, but no real danger. Meeting a dangerous man was only something else she had to face, and get over. The feelings the fellow had awakened in her were troubling, though. He seemed to be considering more than the truth of what she was saying. He seemed to be thinking about how she'd feel in his arms, and that made her consider it as well.

She was wise enough to know those were feelings she couldn't afford to have. With great luck she might someday meet a man she could marry. She couldn't tarry with any other kind. Anyway, she knew very well that she wasn't the sort of female that appealed to such a man. His apparent interest in her body was only another way to threaten or coerce her. As though such a man would be lusting for a nondescript female in cheap, drab, concealing clothes, with not a shred of coquetry in her!

Meg scowled. She'd be damned if he'd fool her. Literally. She shivered again. It wasn't only the sexual allure of the man. He positively radiated danger of all sorts. It was only too bad that they were traveling the same road.

Meg's expression brightened. But since he was going her way it meant he'd gotten his information from the Runners. And she was the one who had given the Runners that information. That gave her an edge. She smiled. "Stick like a burr," indeed! He believed she was headed for Brighton. Good. When she could, she'd leave the Brighton Road. She'd head for Plymouth and, hopefully, Rosie. Her wild guess might find Rosie, and then she could go on with her life as though nothing had happened.

Meg took off her gown and folded it. She washed in the cool water from the pitcher and basin on the table, brushed her teeth, slipped on a nightshift, went to the bed and sat to brush and braid her hair for the night.

She hated to get a late start in the morning, but she had to leave the inn after he did, so he'd think she'd gone home. Her fingers stilled on her night braid. Her spirits lifted. The gypsy didn't know where her home was. So it didn't matter where he saw her going. She finished braiding her hair and pulled back the bedcovers.

She stopped. She felt a tickling in her bladder that told her she'd forgotten to do one last thing before going to bed. Drat the man for rattling her so much as to make her forget it!

Meg peered under the bed and saw the cracked thunder mug left for her use. Her nose wrinkled. She hated to sleep with that smell in her nostrils, especially since it always got stronger as the night went on.

So it was off to the Jericho then. It was located out back of the inn, in the garden. The trip would have been easier when she'd been dressed. But she had a night robe, and she had a cape, so she didn't have to get dressed again.

Meg went down the stair and peered around. The tap was closed, the room was empty, but the inn wasn't entirely still. The serving wench came clomping out of the room, empty mugs in her hands. She gave Meg a cold, haughty stare.

"The Jericho is out back?" Meg asked, with equal friendliness.

"Where else?" the wench said, and marched into the kitchens.

Well, so the dark man hadn't taken company to his bed tonight, Meg thought. She was a little surprised, but more annoyed when she found herself relieved. She stepped out into the night and made her way into the garden, and then into the vine-covered outhouse.

Her mission didn't take long. The rain had stopped. It was a cool, damp, misty night; the only light came from the inn and the two lanterns burning in front of it. Meg began to wend her way back to the light, and stopped, her hand flying to her throat, as she saw a dark figure standing in the path before her.

"No worries!" the dark man said, throwing up his hands. "I mean you no harm. Just came out to blow a cloud."

Meg waited until her heart stopped hammering enough for her to speak. She looked around to see she was close enough to the inn to be heard if she screamed. "You came out to smoke a cheroot in front of the privy?"

"Why not? Some folks say it smells the same."

"That's vulgar," she said.

"Aye, what else did you expect from me?"

She didn't deign to reply.

"I didn't expect anyone to be out and about at this hour, either," he added.

She didn't believe him. "Well, but I am, and I should like to be inside now. So if you'd be so kind as to let me pass?"

"Oh. Sorry," he said, stepping aside and sweeping her a mocking bow.

She picked up her head and marched toward the inn. Her cheeks burned. Ridiculous to be uncomfortable about being seen leaving a privy, but she was.

"So, you're leaving me tomorrow?" she heard him ask.

"I am going home," she snapped, "as soon as I may."

"Good night," he said. "Godspeed."

She didn't reply. She still had almost two weeks of the absence granted by the Runner before she had to go back to the baron and face the consequences of Rosie's disappearance. She'd use them well. And so if she ran into the gypsy again, if he somehow chose her path, she'd watch him as carefully as he was obviously watching her now.

The back of her neck crawled as she walked to the inn, but she forbade herself to turn around. She was sure he hadn't moved. She was equally sure he'd come out to see where she was going. She was relieved he hadn't accepted the insane bargain she'd offered earlier: It would have been impossible to travel with him. He was deceptive, and much too aware of his attraction. She'd been lucky, because her offer had been made out of fear and cowardice and she was ashamed of herself for it. She had to behave rationally. She would, from now on.

She didn't trust the dark man, but she believed him, in that he was determined to find Rosalind. But so was she.

Chapter 3

"Oh, but miss," the innkeeper's wife said, "I already told the poor young man I didn't know anything about his fiancée. Isn't it shocking, though? Why would a girl leave such a well set up and nice-spoken young fellow at the altar? Although I heard it wasn't exactly the altar, since he said she run off in the night. Bride nerves, that's all it was," she declared, putting her elbows on the desk as she warmed to the subject. "So I told him, and so it was! She'll be back, never fear, says I."

Meg sighed. "And when did you tell him this?"

"Why just this morning, miss."

"But I thought mine was the first coach to arrive today."

"So it is," the innkeeper's wife said comfortably.

"But the young man, he came on horseback, even earlier."

Horseback! Meg felt as though she'd been struck in the face with the news. She'd never thought about that. So that was why he'd been a step ahead of her all day yesterday. Well, good. That meant he wasn't following her. But it also meant that she might just as well save her breath to cool her porridge for this last leg she'd take on the Brighton Road. Except, she reasoned slowly, if he *had* found out anything, she could discover what it was, too. There was a lot to be said for following the gypsy, actually.

"And now it turns out the girl was your cousin!" the innkeeper's wife marveled. "Wonders will never cease. Well, if I find out anything, be sure I'll send the news on ahead to where you're bound. Where are you going next, miss?" she asked eagerly.

"I'm on my way to . . ." Meg paused. There was a jot too much eagerness in the woman's tone, a touch too much excitement. "To Brighton," she said.

She'd better not trust anyone. Who was to say that the gypsy hadn't promised the woman payment for information about where she was bound? "Thank you," she added. "I'll be stopping where the coach does along the way, so if you hear of anything and can send on information I'll be grateful." And surprised, she thought.

Meg swallowed her tea, and hopped back up into the coach again when the guard signaled it was time to move on. There was a long way to travel before she'd leave the road and strike out on her own. When she found the place where the road diverged and went east and west, she wouldn't get on the Brighton stage again. There was a junction where passengers could continue on to Brighton or go west along the coast road toward Plymouth. That was where she'd make her move.

And if she didn't find a shadow of Rosie in all her travels, in Plymouth or anywhere along the way?

Meg sighed, closed her eyes and laid her head on the back of her seat as the coach rocked on down the long road. Well, then, she'd have wasted her time and her money. So what? She wouldn't need either when she was back with the aunts, after all.

The *Stoned Crow* wasn't as tidy an inn as the *Old Fancy* across the street, where the coaches stopped, nor as famous for its menu as the *Rose and Bull*, a little way from there. But it wasn't as crowded either, and that suited Meg's purposes exactly. The fewer people who saw her come and go from this crossroads, the better. She got a room at the top of the stairs, looked out the window, and saw the Brighton coach leave the *Old Fancy*'s busy inn yard a half hour later. She planned to get on the next coach headed toward Plymouth at first light.

But there was dinner to be had first, and a night to get through. Meg went downstairs. The *Stoned Crow* had a separate taproom and a small dining parlor. The tap was dark, thick with smoke, noisy, and filled with men. The parlor's air was fresher, but it was half empty. Meg could see why. The bits of carpet on the floor were threadbare and stained, the floor itself in little better state. A fitful fire was slowly strangling in the sooty hearth, and the tables were battered and dented. But no one from the coach she'd arrived on was here, and that was what mattered most. Meg seated herself and waited to have her dinner.

But first, as always, as soon she gave the serving woman her order, she asked her usual question.

"A runaway heiress?" the woman asked with interest when she was done.

"I didn't say heiress," Meg said, "but she might be considered such." She sighed, accepting the inevitable. "I suppose her fiancé told you that, did he? When did you speak with him?"

The woman cocked her head to the side. Her hair was untidy, her round face shiny from running to the tap, the kitchens, and back to the tables. Meg hoped her hands were cleaner than her apron. Service was not only cheaper here than at the two more popular inns, it was definitely more casual.

"I never talked to no fiancée," the woman said. She focused on Meg as though seeing her for the first time. Meg put up her chin, hoping a well-bred air of affront at being evaluated so openly would make up for her being alone and in such plain, unfashionable clothing.

It must have done, the woman's face grew a poorly concealed look of cunning, as she asked, "So he's after her, too? I suppose there's a reward?"

Meg's hopes rose. "Yes, there is. Have you heard about her?"

"I may have," the woman said evasively. "Not like I know nothing exactly, o'course. But I hear things. Lemme think on a bit. I'll be back with your soup, and by then mebbe—who knows?—I'll have some information for you, too."

By the time the woman returned, Meg was more starved for news than for her dinner.

"Uh huh," the woman said quietly as she put the bowl of soup down in front of Meg. "I heared something. Not saying as to how I'm disobliging, miss, but I gotta see the color of your coin first, if you know what I mean." She gave Meg a look that showed she wondered if she could pay for her dinner, much less information.

"Oh, yes," Meg said. "And wouldn't I be the fool to show my money before getting anything for it? I lost quite a bit on the way down here by doing just that," she added in her loftiest accents. "But I am, you might say, a downier pigeon than that now, thank you. I do learn from my mistakes. I pay when I'm convinced there's something to pay for. So. What can you tell me?"

She fell still, hoping she'd be taken for a wealthy eccentric. She had some money to pay for information, but never much.

The woman frowned, then shrugged. She leaned down as if rearranging Meg's tableware and lowered her voice, "Well, see, right after I talked to you, I heared these three fellas at the tap talking about a runaway heiress and suchlike. So I just went and asked them a thing or two, and they got shifty. Meaning they won't tell me nothing, 'cause they know I got nothing, so they got nothing to gain from it, see? But then I told them you was looking to know more, and that you offered money, too. So what I can do is show you who they are and you can ask them yourself. But not for nothing." She straightened, and waited.

Meg dug into her purse and produced a coin, large enough for her to regret, small enough to make the serving woman frown.

But the woman took it and dropped it into her apron pocket. "Listen," she said. "I gotta work now. I'll pass the word, and come back and tell you when they're ready for you."

The soup was salty and thin. The roast that came next was tough and stringy, and the gray lumps accompanying it might have been vegetables before they were cooked into total submission. Meg didn't notice. She was too busy trying to peer into the corners of the taproom. If she got a hint of Rosie's whereabouts she could leave this dismal place as the sun rose and get on with her hunt.

The parlor slowly emptied of diners. Meg could see men straggling out of the tap, too. The hour was growing late; she was tired from a day of traveling. But she couldn't leave the room, much less close an eye, if there were a chance she'd learn more about Rosalind.

When everyone had left the parlor, and when Meg was about to march upstairs, convinced she'd been fleeced, the serving woman appeared again. She looked furtive. Meg's hopes rose again.

"All right," the woman said. "Go on in to the tap. Them is the three at the table toward the corner by the window. Ain't many left in there now, you can't miss them." She hurried away.

Meg went into the tap and looked around. It had been less inviting than the parlor. It was more so now. The smell of ale was thick as the air, which was heavy with coal and pipe smoke. There was only a handful of men left in the dim room—and three of them sat shoulder to shoulder at a table by the window. Meg straightened her own shoulders and advanced.

She stopped when she got to their table and plucked up her courage. They were not the sort of men she was accustomed to speaking to.

One was dark, but the darkness of that face wasn't his natural complexion, the irregular streaks on it showed it came from grime. His hair wasn't visible beneath his battered hat, but the calculation in his narrowed eyes was. The man in the middle was cleaner, or at least pink faced. He wore clothes that showed his attempt at playing the peacock, because he had a soiled red kerchief tied around his plump neck. The third man was thick, and looked thick-witted too, as he gave her a wide and broken-toothed smile that had no humor in it.

"Gentlemen," she said as calmly as she could. "I've been told you might know something about my cousin. She's a very pretty blond, blue-eyed young

woman who dresses like a lady." She paused, because she realized she hated to so much as describe
pretty Rosalind to this foul-looking trio. Still, not
only in spite of, but because of the way they looked,
she reasoned they must have their ears to the ground.

Knowing that she had to, she added, "She speaks
with a lisp, as well, and it's unmistakable. I've reason to believe she's traveling this road. I'm looking
for her, and I've missed her at all turns. I—I'll pay
for information about her, if you have any."

The men gave each other significant looks. Then
the plump one spoke up. "Might be we have, at that,
little lady. Could be. What do you think, men?"

"What?" the filthy one grunted. "How do we know
she ain't playing at something, eh? Got a man or two
behind that there door, Missy? And him with an eye
on robbing decent folk, someways?"

The thickset man giggled.

"Aye, right," the plump one said. "She don't look
like she's running a rig, but who knows? After all,
there are dark forces afoot here, and don't we know
it?"

"No, no one's with me," Meg said quickly. "I vow
it. I was separated from my cousin, and that's why I
must find her."

"Well . . ." The grimy man looked at the others,
and then they all stared at her.

"Aye, she'll do," the plump one said. "But not
here! Listen, Missy. What we say could get us in
some trouble, y'see. So, best we don't spill it here

where anyone can overhear. Want us to come up to your room?"

Meg took a step back. She didn't even want to be in the same inn with them. She shook her head and managed to say, "No, that would be most improper!"

The plump man grinned. "Aye, so it would. Where's my head? We ain't used to Quality like you, miss. Begging your pardon. So then, if not here or there, how about you meet us 'round back? It's dark enough to cover us, and quiet enough so's we can hear anyone coming. Just out back. You go now. We'll meet you soon's as we see the coast's clear."

Meg hesitated.

"Blimey!" the grimy man said. "Look, she's scart to even talk to us. So then why did you come 'round bothering with us, Missy, eh?"

"C'mon, miss," the plump one said, with a smile. "You want to know about your cousin, right? Well, we know a thing or two. But we ain't putting our necks on the line, not for any money. Though we do like money. And I hear you got some for us, in exchange for what we know. So meet us halfway, just 'round back." He spread his hands wide. "Why not? What's there? The stables. A Jericho. But leastways that way we can see anyone coming, and we can be gone if we do. What we have to say might make some folks mad at us, and that we don't need. Y'see?"

She nodded. But stayed where she was.

"Well, then," the plump one said with an elaborate

shrug, "if you don't care about your cousin, so be it. Though, from what I heard about what's happening to her, if she was my woman, I'd care something terrible, I can tell you."

That did it. Meg nodded, and slowly backed away. "Out back," she whispered. "I'll be there."

It was both darker and quieter behind the inn than Meg had realized. The place had been bustling only hours before, now even the better inns across the street were still. Coaches came early; travelers went to bed early too. The *Stoned Crow* had fewer guests to begin with, so the back of the inn was as quiet as a graveyard and just as full of life. The *Stoned Crow* didn't spend money where it could be seen. There were no lamps or lanterns lit behind the inn. Meg could only see by the light of the half moon above.

Though it was too dark to see more than an outline of the stables, Meg could smell the horses. Unfortunately, she could also smell the Jericho. She vowed to use the hated basin under her bed tonight; she'd gagged when she'd entered the noxious outbuilding during the day. Nothing would induce her to go in there at night.

Meg stood and waited for the trio of men to appear. She had three sizeable coins in her purse, one to give each man. She hoped it would be enough. She was just beginning to wonder why they hadn't asked her how much money she would reward them with, when she was distracted by a soft, but clear "*Hist!*" coming from the stable yard.

She squinted, and then made out three figures standing at the side of the stables. A very dark side of it. She shivered and fought back a desire to run right back to the inn. They said they knew something about Rosalind. She wanted to believe it. But she wasn't a fool, and she was suddenly too uneasy here. Still, she reasoned she was within shouting distance of the inn. And she was so very tired of traveling an increasingly cold trail. And more than all that, they'd implied that Rosie was in danger.

She forced herself to stand erect, and walked toward the men.

"Yes?" she whispered. "I'm here. What have you to tell me?"

The plump man gestured frantically. "Closer," he said huskily. "Dunno who might be coming out to use the privy, y'know. Don't want to wake no one in the stables, neither."

She didn't want to go closer, the men smelled bad enough from where she stood. But she edged a step nearer.

"Yes. Well, then. So, about my cousin," she said, aware that she was too nervous to be talking clearly, and suddenly even more aware that she'd possibly done a very stupid thing.

A moment later, she couldn't talk at all. A big hand whipped out from behind her and clapped over her mouth. It tasted rancid, and held her fast as another hand clamped around her waist. She was pulled back against a hard body. She struggled, biting and hissing, but she could hardly breathe, much less make a sound. She couldn't land a kick either, her legs were held still, captured between her assailants'. She was silently and inexorably dragged into the shadows behind the stables.

"You was right," she heard the filthy man from the inn say softly from behind her. He fumbled at her, and squeezed a breast hard. "Pretty and plump in all the right places. I goes first."

"Damned if you do!" the plump man said in a fierce whisper. "Whose idea was it, eh?"

Meg felt her stomach grow cold and her legs weak.

The plump man began to unbutton his breeches. "I found her," he said. "I get her first, that's the way of it."

"Damned if you do," the man behind her growled. "You got the last one. It's my turn."

"No," breathed the big thick man as he stared at Meg. "This time, it's me."

"Now, listen to me," the plump man said in a hoarse whisper. "I made the game, and I make the rules. This one is mine first. Then, you two decide who goes next. But make it fast, and be quiet, and then cosh her and leave her. We're out of here and gone right after. We take her, and then her purse, and then we go. Understood?"

There was a moment of grudging silence.

Meg felt hot tears and cold shame as she strained to break free. She wasn't a big woman, but she thought herself fit, and was shocked to find she couldn't even move. She'd never had her strength tested against a grown man before. It felt as though she were caught in a vise. The man behind her clamped down hard to stop her struggles. She felt his rising excitement against her back. For the first time in her life she knew what it was to be utterly powerless. There was no argument that she could make, no appeal she could utter, no strength to break free. She refused to believe what was happening.

She could only stare at the plump man in horror as, smiling, he strolled toward her.

And then she saw him stop, look over her shoulder, and stare.

The hard hand left her mouth, the crushing pressure on her arms eased abruptly, she suddenly found herself freed. She stumbled, then righted herself and pulled away, looking frantically for a place to run to, terrified that this was only a new game. But when she glanced behind her she saw the man who had caught her slumped on the ground.

She spun around and saw the plump man's lips open, but no words came out. They were stopped by the fist that struck him square in the mouth. Meg stood, astounded, as his attacker rushed in, knocked the plump man to the ground, dragged him up by his bandana and struck him down again, until he lay still.

The thickset man stood watching, dumbfounded. Then he closed his opened mouth. He shook himself out of his astonishment and came lumbering forward. And went reeling back, as the man who had struck down the other two came hurtling at him head bent, and rammed him in the stomach. While the thick man staggered, the other man landed one, two, three more blows, not stopping until his opponent was laid out on the ground.

The inn yard was quiet again, except for Meg's ragged gasping, and the rough breathing of the man who stood, hands on his hips, facing her.

She steeled herself. She hadn't fought before. Now, she'd run. Scream the rooftops down; she'd attack with her nails and her teeth, she'd fight to her death if she had to. She would not be captured again. She raised her chin.

"Lord, woman, have you no sense at all?" the gypsy asked in exasperation.

Chapter 4

❧

"**N**o. It could *not* have happened to anyone," Daffyd said, cutting off Meg's stammered explanation. "It could only happen to someone too stupid to be left out by herself in the rain, much less the dark. Now, go inside. I'll talk to you later. I have to see to these beauties." He poked one of the men in the ribs with the tip of his boot.

"What are you going to do with them?" Meg asked nervously, taking a tiny step back. The shock of seeing that it was the gypsy, Mr. Daffeigh, who had come to her rescue had eased somewhat, but she was still wondering if he was somehow in league with the vile trio.

He raised an eyebrow. "I'm going to take them home and nurse them. What do you think I'm going to do? . . . Oho," he said, seeing her expression, "You think they're my mates, do you? Could be. Maybe I always let them abduct women, and then after I beat the cra . . . stuffing out of them, it's my turn to menace the female. But since I like my comforts, I take my women in their beds instead of inn yards."

It sounded ridiculous, but the horror of what had happened was so fresh in her mind it also sounded weirdly plausible to Meg. She stepped back another pace.

"Oh, go away," he said in disgust. "You don't have to see me again. It had nothing to do with you. I just don't like rapists. Don't worry. You won't see them again either. Well?" he asked angrily, when she just stood there. "Are you going?"

"I *do* want to see you again," she said, knotting her hands together. "I need to talk to you."

"Then you will," he said, looking at the villain by his feet. The man was stirring. "But not now. Go!"

Meg fled. She ran into the inn, up the stairs, into her room, bolted the door, and sat on her bed. After a moment, she rose, lit her lamp, and then sat down on the one chair. She sat, shivering, wondering what to do next. What she most wanted to do was hide.

But she waited. By the time she became aware that she was cold, it was growing late, and the night was passing. It was dead silent, and for the first time she began thinking about what to do next. She wouldn't go to bed. Sleep would make her vulnerable. But when first light appeared, she'd watch from her window, be sure that the villains were nowhere in sight, then creep down the stair, avoid the treacherous serving maid, and get on the first coach going in any direction.

That decided, Meg breathed normally for the first time in a very long time.

A clattering at her window made her shoot to her feet, and begin to edge back toward the door. Then she froze, wondering if someone was throwing things at her window precisely so she *would* leave her room, so they could grab her when she did. She looked around wildly, but saw no weapon with which she could defend herself. The lamp by the bedside might catch her sleeves on fire if she hurled it. The bag she traveled with was too soft to hurt anyone. There wasn't a hearth in the wretched little room, so there wasn't even a fire poker to defend herself with.

She suddenly thought of the only possible lethal weapon at her command. She snatched it up. Then she edged away until she stood with her back to the door. She raised her weapon and looked at the window, breathing rapidly, waiting for the inevitable, whatever it might be.

The shutters flew inward. A dark shape slipped inside, and stooped when it saw her.

"Is that for me?" Daffyd asked, gesturing toward the heavy chamber pot she'd raised over her head. "Thankee. Considerate of you. But I don't need it. I had the whole outdoors to use just now."

"Why didn't you come in the door?" she demanded, still holding the chamber pot over her head.

"Oh. And I suppose you'd have let me in if I knocked?" he asked sweetly.

"If you said who you were."

"Right. And since I didn't want anyone to know, I'd have whispered. So if you didn't hear me, I'd have had to shout. Then the world would know you had a man coming to your room." He cocked his head to the side. "Or did you want that?"

"No," she said, "Of course not, no."

"You might as well put it down," he said conversationally, eyeing the way her arms were wavering under the weight of the chamber pot. "If it slips you'll have the mother of all headaches. Is it full, by the way?"

"Oh," Meg said, lowering her arms and looking at what she held. "No, of course not, no."

He noted her pallor, her breathless, repetitive speech. He frowned. Then his voice changed, grew softer, gentler. "Put it on the floor," he told her. "Things get heavier the longer you hold them. Then sit down. The men who bothered you won't be back. I won't hurt you. You're safe. Really." He reached out a hand. "If you can't put it down, give it to me. No sense hanging on to it. Or is there?"

"No, of course not, no," she said, and held the chamber pot out to him.

He took it, put it on the floor, and studied her. Her eyes were wide, her face was white, and her breathing was quick and shallow. He'd seen this before. "Just sit," he said. "We'll talk. When you feel like it. You're fine, it's fine, nothing will hurt you now."

She stood still.

He sighed. "I promise," he said quietly. "I won't hurt you."

She believed him. She suddenly realized that what he said was true. It was over. She was safe. He hadn't attacked her, he'd saved her. She made a queer little sound, like a stifled sob, and looked at him directly for the first time since he'd come into her room. "Thank you," she said. "Did I say thank you?"

"You're welcome," he said gravely. "Now, will you sit down?"

She went to the chair and sat, drawing her skirts primly around her ankles.

He nodded, and leaned against the wall by the window. "Now," he said. "Want to tell me the real reason you're chasing the heiress?"

She took a deep shuddering breath. "What happened to them? The men, I mean."

"Oh, them. No worries. They're gone. Not free," he added quickly, when he saw her eyes widen. "In custody, you could say."

"The Runners?"

He laughed. "No. Nor with the local justice of the peace. The Runners are too far off and there was no reason to wake the justice. No, I've friends. They're taking care of those nasty blokes. For a profit, so I know it's being done right. That's how everything gets done in this world. A man can be any kind of evil and get away with it. But not if he interferes with business. Money is God in most civilized places.

Matters more than life, actually. That's why a fellow can get his neck stretched for stealing a man's snuffbox, same as for taking his life. Blood and money comes to the same thing in the world of justice."

"They're not coming back?" she asked.

"Never. They're being delivered to those who'll appreciate their company the most, and come down heavy for it. See, I heard about them before I met up with them. Those dirty guts have been preying on people up and down the Brighton road. There's a reward out. Coaching companies don't like someone spoiling their business. Of course, His Majesty's Royal Mail would be interested in them, too." His voice curled with irony as he added, "But though there's little justice for the wicked in this land, there are loopholes, now and then. I didn't want them to find any. Bribes, blackmail, luck—oh, there are ways a villain can escape his fate. So I thought it best they never got even so far as Tyburn tree. They won't. The gents that run the coaching lines will see to that. Don't trouble yourself. It's over. They're gone."

He straightened and stared at her. "Now, why the devil are you chasing after the chit? And why were you such a fool as to meet those devils alone, in the dark? Or were you meeting them for the first time? Are you as innocent as you pretend, after all?"

"I met them because I was a fool," she said sadly. Her eyes widened. "But the serving girl? Is she in league with them?"

"She's in league with whoever's got coins in their pocket. Forget her. More. Tell me more."

"I told you, I'm Rosalind's companion, or was. When she disappeared they blamed me for not keeping closer watch on her. I couldn't bear the way they were looking at me. The Runner in charge, Mr. Murchison, suggested I leave for a spell." She raised one hand. "I know. I think he might have wanted me to leave so someone could follow to see where I was going. But I changed coaches and believe I fooled whoever that was several miles back on the road, and he lost my trail."

"Now, why would you do a thing like that?" he asked softly, but with new interest.

Her temper flared. "Because if you'd been accused, if not in so many words, of being in league with a runaway heiress, and then, when you were already packed and ready to go visit with your old governess, and then, and only then, remembered your charge might have given you a hint of where she was off to"—she drew in a much needed breath—"would you have changed your story?"

He laughed. "I wouldn't be doing any of that, so I couldn't say. But I can sympathize. I'm not fond of Runners, though I've met one of two who are decent enough. Murchison is, by the way."

She stared. "You know him?"

"Yes," he said and finally moved. He began to pace her little room. "So where is she going?"

She hesitated. "What is your interest in this, sir? You said you're a gypsy, but you don't sound or look like one. You said you were asked to find her, but how can I believe you?"

He stopped his pacing and cocked his dark head again. She saw his white teeth glint in the growing light in the room. "Because," he said, "who else are you going to believe?"

He waited until she'd taken that in, and added, "I told you. I'm looking for her as a favor to her god-mother. I'll find her and take her home. That's all there is to it. Now, again. Where do you think she's gone?"

She knew when she'd come to the end of one road. She'd acted like a fool, but she wasn't one. Her experience tonight had showed her that this pursuit was filled with dangers she hadn't foreseen. She needed help. This man, whoever he was, had a still, sure certainty about him. And he'd saved her from a terrible fate. For whatever reason, she trusted him, and though he was rough spoken at times, and certainly mysterious, she believed she could work with him.

"I think," Meg finally admitted, "she's going to Plymouth." She raised her eyes to his. "At least, I think I remember she had her finger on the map and it was on Plymouth."

She didn't expect his reaction. He threw back his head and laughed. "Listen, Miss Margaret, I already knew that," he said, on a last chuckle. "And you risked your pretty neck—and other pretty parts—for that? Folly." He shook his head. "Why else do you think I'm here? I've followed you all the way, but I didn't mean to. I saw you in passing and kept seeing you, and then I got interested. Nice work, the way you shook off the Runner Murchison sent after you. But I haven't stuck to the main road. I met you by chance today. I've been on and off the road all the way down, asking questions of those who know answers. Your Rosalind is probably on her way to Plymouth. Or so I'd bet. And I'm on her trail. So go home. Or back to the baron's, or to that governess of yours, if she even exists. Just go and leave this chase. All you can do is get hurt."

"No," she said. "I can find her, exonerate myself, and be free. I won't work for her family again, but I will be able to find work elsewhere and get on with my life, and I won't be able to do that if I just give up and go away, and wait on events. So," she said, pulling herself upright, "I have a bargain for you."

He stared.

She nodded. "Yes. I can be invaluable to you. I know one thing you don't. I know what she looks like." She sat back and looked at him triumphantly.

He smiled. "So you do. And so what? I have her description, and if she's got a brain in her head, she doesn't look like that anymore. I'm not just relying on her looks. I know other things about her, and her companion. Aye, I doubt she was abducted. It doesn't look like she's eager to give him the slip either, I'm told. Believe me, I'm on their trail."

"But I can make your work easier," she argued.

"Listen, my girl," he said, shaking his head, "I understand your interest. But you can't come with me. It's a long road, maybe with danger ahead. Even if there isn't, I'll be sleeping in wagons and barns, when I'm lucky, and under hedgerows when I'm not. There's no room for a female in my plans."

"But you must make room for me," she insisted. "I can be of use to you. You'll see."

"Oh," he said thoughtfully. "Well, it ain't the first time I've misread a wench. So no wonder you didn't fear those villains." His smile grew wider. He took a step toward her. "I'm flattered. I'm also willing and able. All right. I'll oblige you now, but I'm leaving at dawn. So, I'm sorry, but it will have to be a quick one."

She stared.

He came closer, his smile becoming a leer. "On the bed? Or where you are? I'm adaptable, too."

She shot to her feet. "I did not mean *that*!" she gasped.

He laughed. "Didn't really think so. You've got prim written all over you and that ain't my sort at all. But what other use would I have for a female on my journey?"

"I can help," she said, ashamed to discover she was almost pleading. She gathered her wits, with effort. There he stood, implacable, untouchable: a man in a world of men, free to do exactly as he pleased. She had to face danger at every turn, and yet if she didn't, she might have no future at all.

She steadied her voice and herself. "I may have made a mistake this evening," she said. "But I'm not buffle-headed. There are some places where having a female along may help you—places I can go where you can't, questions I can ask that you may not."

"Yes," he agreed. "But I don't want a woman with me. Look, Miss Margaret, helpful as you are, and I'm sure you are, I'd find you more of an anchor than a sail. I have to travel light and fast. Women can't. I like to change my direction with the wind, and not have to explain myself."

"Not every wench you interview can be bought or charmed," she said desperately. "Sometimes only a woman can get an answer from another female." She hesitated, wondering how sensitive he was about being a gypsy and then dared to add, "That's especially true if she's respectable."

That amused him. "True," he said. "And there couldn't be a more respectable miss than you, I agree. But that also makes you bane to me. See, if you were caught traveling with me, I'd either be arrested for it, or have a pack of your relatives after me demanding my life—or my name, such as it is. Traveling with an unmarried female is an offense punishable by marriage in this country. Now, if I were all gypsy, it wouldn't be so bad. They'd only want my death. But I'm half respectable, and so there's always a chance your family would think that half worth marrying. That frightens me more than death."

She stamped her foot. "That's nonsense! My family, such as it is, wouldn't care . . ." Her voice trailed off. She couldn't honestly say what the aunts would think if she were found in the company of a gypsy, or a half gypsy, or any kind of male. They'd think her a slut, whomever she was found with. "Well, they'd cast me off," she finally said, "but they wouldn't care who he was, or if I married him."

"That's too bad. You have my sympathy," he said. "But I don't want you on my conscience either. I do have one. It isn't enough to make me offer you a wedding, but it would put me off my food for a while—at least until I found a safe harbor for you. And that's trouble I don't need. Look, leave off. My mind's set. You'd be a liability and a responsibility, and I want and need neither. I'm going. And you're not coming with me. Understood?"

"You can't be that sure of yourself," she cried. But as she said it, she knew he was.

He stood there smiling—no, smirking, she thought: a lean young man, attractive, clean and well made, well dressed, too. He was an assured man who could act the gentleman or the rogue, and be as charming or violent as the occasion suited, or as suited him. He was also everything she was not and never could be. He was strong, self-sufficient, and free. And so in that moment, as she gazed at him, in spite of what he'd done for her, she hated him.

"I see," she said. She blinked back tears and swallowed her disappointment. She drew herself up. "Then Godspeed and good luck. We shall not meet again, Mr. Daffeigh. I cannot belabor the issue, it's clear your mind is made up. I don't agree, but that matters little, doesn't it? Oh, and again, my thanks.

I'm not unaware of what you saved me from this evening, and for that I am truly grateful and always will be. If ever I can repay you, please let me know. Don't laugh, please."

"I'm not."

She nodded. "Good, because life has strange twists and turns to it, so one never knows what lies ahead. It may be that some day I can do you a good turn, too. So." She took a deep, painful breath. "Whatever the outcome of my charge's adventure and my employment with baron Osbourne, I know he's a decent man. I'm sure that if you need me and sent word to him, he'll forward your note wherever I may be. Now, if you please, would you leave?"

He frowned. Then, when she didn't say anything else, but only stood stick straight, waiting, he shrugged. He bowed. And then, without another word, he climbed out the window, and was gone.

The morning dawned cool, bright and beautiful. Daffyd had his breakfast. He chatted with the servants, and put a word in the innkeeper's ear about his serving wench and how cheaply her loyalty to his patrons could be bought. Then he strolled over to the *Old Fancy*, lingered in the taproom there, and watched as four coaches arrived and then pulled away. He waited until the *Brighton Beacon* collected Miss Margaret Shaw. Then he stayed watching from the shadows until it bore her down the road, and away.

Only then did he allow himself to feel a little regret. She was a pretty piece, although too prim for his tastes. Yet if she loosed her hair and her manner, wore different clothes, and smiled more, he'd wager she'd turn a head or two. That hair was thick and soft; that mouth was made for laughter. Yes, he'd bet a man with patience and time could find what he needed under all that civilization. He could see hints of it in her flashes of anger, and in the vaunting spirit that had sent her off alone down an unknown road on her dangerous, ill-advised mission.

She was a contradiction, because she was clearly educated and intelligent. But she was also dim when it came to judging strangers, gullible as a sheltered child, and vulnerable as a shucked oyster. She was well out of it. And doubly well off away from him.

The truth was that prim as she was, he had to admit she attracted him. He liked women with clean, sweet-smelling hair, clear complexions, shapely figures, and real smiles. He liked women with soft, alluring mouths. He especially liked those who had something to say with those mouths. He was fascinated by a woman who had something in her eyes apart from desire, and he dearly loved a good argument. No question, Miss Margaret Shaw was a challenge.

Still, she would slow him down, get in his way, divert him too much. He was on his way to Plymouth with a few interesting stops along the way. He'd find the runaway. He'd fling his success in his mother's face and leave without her getting so much as a chance to say thanks. He'd pay a debt he didn't owe. Because after all the hard times in his life, and all the ways he'd paid back hurt, this time he planned to inflict a pain that had no payback. The bitch who'd borne him would finally see that she'd thrown away something far more valuable than she'd known. And then he'd be able to ignore her forever after, the same way she'd ignored him.

And then he'd get on with his life.

Whenever he found out what that was supposed to be.

Chapter 5

Daffyd arrived at the inn at dusk, tired but pleased with himself and his day's and night's work. He'd ridden far and learned much. He could finally afford a good night's sleep. Not only would exhaustion make him clumsy in his search, but now he was certain the runaway heiress was only a few days ahead of him. She wasn't in any difficulty, at least so far as he'd been told.

Miss Rosalind Osbourne was in the company of a gent, and they were having the time of their lives. Or so it seemed to everyone who'd seen them. She giggled, the fellow guffawed; they'd left a trail of merriment behind them as they headed toward the coast. That both calmed and annoyed Daffyd, because it was now clear the girl was a runaway, not a victim.

There were many ways a captor could influence and subdue his captive, but however clever he was, Daffyd had never heard of one who could make his prisoner collapse into hilarity every other minute.

They were having a fine game of it, complete with wigs and costumes. Because sometimes the heiress was seen to be blond, sometimes she was dark, her hair could be straight or curled, and she'd even been sighted with bright red tresses. Her companion's hair color changed as often as hers did, as did his hats. But she was always charming and lovely, and always lisped her thanks for favors received from the shopkeepers, maids, ostlers and innkeepers who served her. And her escort always looked at her lovingly and held her hand—and it wasn't to keep her from straying, because all said she looked like she never wanted to leave his side.

Of course, her hotheaded fiancé was also always seen riding after them, missing them by moments every time, coursing like the wind down their backs after they'd left. Or so Daffyd was told.

Half of what he heard he disregarded. Some people would say anything for money, and he'd spent a good deal of it in the inns and stables, coach yards, taverns, and shops where he'd stopped. But the people in the fields and on the roads that he knew were as careful with their reports as they were with their true identities, and them, he believed. Half of them were his own people—in every sense of the word.

It was hard chasing after a bubble-headed chit and her illicit lover, or at least he felt it keenly when he was tired, cold, or wet. But then Daffyd would think of the expression on his mother's face when he returned her idiot goddaughter, and that made it better.

Now it was evening again, and Daffyd felt he could afford a night of rest. He left his horse at the stables, picked up his bags, and went into the *Thieving Magpie,* across the road from a coaching stop and another inn. Since the *Magpie* wasn't always crammed with travelers eager to stop at the first place they found themselves deposited at after a long grueling coach ride, its table and accommodations had to be that much better for it to survive.

Daffyd spoke for a room, went up and inspected it. It was small but adequate, with a window overlooking the front so he could see what was coming and going down the road. Best of all, the bed looked soft and deep. He washed, brushed the dust of the road from his coat and boots, and then went back downstairs for a drink to clear it from his throat.

The taproom was dim but not musty, and was filled with local men.

"We've a table for you in our private parlor," the innkeeper told Daffyd when he saw him looking into the taproom.

"I'll take one in here," Daffyd said, with a smile. "Been by myself too long as it is. A horse's conversation gets tedious after a while."

"As you will, sir," the innkeeper said, and showed him to a table. Daffyd sat, sniffed, and smiled. He smelled roast beef and duck, and pie, and though anything tasted good when eaten around a campfire, the *Magpie*'s menu smelled better than anything he'd tasted in days.

But as always, he had more than the menu on his mind.

"So then: the soup, the duck, and the ragout, and a bottle of our best claret," the serving girl said, repeating his order. She showed him a dimple in her cheek as she smiled, and another more intimate one as she bent down low in front of him to fuss with his tableware. "Anything else, sir?"

"Just a question," he said softly.

Her eyes brightened.

"I'm looking for a girl."

Her smiled curled; she was about to speak, when he put up a hand. "It's a sad story," he told her, looking at her earnestly. "But you see, my fiancé ran off the night before our wedding day."

She gasped.

He nodded, hunched his shoulders, stared at his locked hands on the tabletop, and added, "That's her right, and my sorrow. I ought to just let her go and forget. I tried. But when the liquor cleared from my head I realized I couldn't. I have to hear it from her own lips before I can go on. So I've been looking for her. She's been seen on this road. I think she's headed toward the coast, to leave England, I suppose before the autumn storms prevent her." He heaved a sigh. "I heard there's a man in her company. It could be my best friend, George. That would be worse."

He shrugged. "But I have to find them. She's blond, with blue eyes." He gazed up into the serving girl's own sympathetic eyes as he added, "I also heard she's been wearing wigs, kerchiefs, and suchlike to throw pursuers off her trail. Her family's not best pleased either. She's very beautiful, whatever colors she chooses to sport. She talks with a lisp. Have you seen her?"

"Oh, sir!" she sighed, one hand to her bosom. "How terrible! If I knowed I'd tell you for certain. But I don't know nothing. I'll ask 'round the inn, if you'd like. A fine gent like you—left in the lurch! It's a dirty shame, no female with a bit of Quality would never of done it, I'm sure. I'm that sure you're better off, too!" she added indignantly.

Daffyd sat with a sad smile as she went on about how badly his fiancé had acted. He tried to look oblivious as her sympathy turned to not too subtle hints about how some other girl would be glad to help him mend his broken heart—or at least tend to another more intact organ—in the meanwhile.

"I'll just get your dinner now," she said. "Don't worry. I'll find out what I can whilst you wait."

When she'd bustled off, Daffyd sat back and stretched out his legs. It never hurt to ask. He was thinking about how weary he was, and deciding that though the serving girl was kindness itself, he wanted that big warm bed upstairs all to himself, when he became aware of someone standing in front of his table. Several someones, in fact.

There were at least six men standing staring down

at him. Or rather, he realized, as his muscles involuntarily tensed, glowering down at him. Six local fellows, with a few more standing behind them. They were hard men with weather-bitten faces who obviously worked with their backs and hands. It was their minds that concerned him. He knew danger when he ran into it.

Daffyd slowly rose to his feet. A sitting man was only at an advantage when he had power. Otherwise, a man should face another as an equal. He was acutely aware that he was at a disadvantage now. He was in a strange place with no mates to see to his back. And these men meant him no good.

"Aye," one of them muttered. "Dressed up like a Christmas goose, but he's a filthy gypsy, anyone can see it."

Daffyd went still. He was dressed for traveling, neither well nor poorly, because he'd had to speak to all kinds of people on this journey. But to these men, he was dressed like a nob. Because a man couldn't do a decent day's work loading, or plowing, in a tight-fitted jacket, breeches and good boots.

"Black hair, black heart, skin's dark as an olive," another said, eyeing him carefully. "I thought they wasn't allowed in decent places. Old Thomas out of his mind letting him in here?"

"His gold must have blinded Old Thomas. Business at the *Magpie* ain't been good," another said.

"They been seen in the woods," a harsh faced man added. "Like I said. We was going to go see if they was still there tomorrow. This saves us the trouble.

Gypsy," he said, staring at Daffyd, "tell us where the girl is, and we'll let you go, maybe."

Daffyd kept his face expressionless, and thought fast. Had someone said he was the one who had kidnapped the Osbourne girl? The prim pansy-faced miss he'd met last night had thought so. Well, then, he'd only have to give them a few good names, and they could verify his story. But these didn't look like men in the mood for verifying. He'd met their sort before, too many times, in too many places. They wanted justice and injury to whomever did the injustice, whichever came faster.

Daffyd took swift inventory. He carried two knives and a pistol, and was good with his feet and hands. But still: at least nine of them to his one. He decided on tact, and luck, and a swift silent prayer.

"The girl," he said calmly. "I was just asking after her. I'm her fiancé. I've been tracking her from her home, all the way down the Brighton Road. She ran away the night before our wedding day. I wish I did know where she was. I'm trying to find her myself."

This was met with a silence so stony that Daffyd's heart began to race.

"Aye," the first man said with a sick caricature of a smile. "You was engaged to a six-year-old, was you? And one you never seen afore you came here? Well, maybe a filthy gypsy would've thought a little mite's laughter was fetching. And maybe you dirty dogs think nothing of stealing a child—we all know that. But bedding one? Fah." He spat. "You're among decent men now. You won't be doing that no more." He snorted. "Ah—let's string him right up," he told the others. "We'll get his story out afore we cut him down."

Daffyd's eyes widened and he moved. But it was much too late. They seized him, smothering him in their onslaught. One man took his arm and grabbed hard before Daffyd could grasp the hilt of his pistol inside his jacket. Someone else grabbed his other arm before he could get to the knife in his boot. He couldn't kick because there was no room to raise a knee or foot. Worst of all, someone seized his neck from behind and held it in the crook of an elbow, cutting off his last and best weapon: his voice.

"Now then!" one of them said, triumphant, "The old oak, in front. It were good enough for traitors in good King Charles's day, it'll do for him. Let's take him there."

"But we got to find out about the little girl," another protested.

"We will. When we hang him up and let him down often enough, he'll cough it out. We just got to take care we don't haul him up too long afore he does, but we can after, that's certain."

They tried to frog march him out the door, but he had fury enough to resist. So they picked him up and held him fast, and carried him, head first, as though he was a battering ram and they were going to charge an enemy's gates with him.

The blood throbbed in Daffyd's ears, his breathing became difficult. He became aware that for all the certain deaths he'd managed to elude, this time, incredibly enough, he would die. But this time, for someone else's sin. He'd survived beatings and prisons, been sentenced to death, and been sent halfway around the world instead of being hanged so he could die more slowly but just as surely now. He'd been left for dead many times and come back to health each time, too.

He was a fighter, a street rat, sly and slick and quick to take advantage, otherwise he wouldn't have gotten to the age he was now. He'd cheated death at every turn.

Now, here in his homeland, in England, rich at last and free from prison, it seemed his luck had at last run out. He'd die without judge or jury at the hands of angry men, merely because of what he looked like. He thought of the irony, the injustice of it. But that was the way of his life, after all. So it would be the way of his ending.

A tilted world passed under his gaze, and then he saw darkness and felt night air on his face. He could only hope he died bravely, without pleading, without kicking too long or strangling too slow, as so many brave lads had, dangling on the ropes on Tyburn Hill.

He was roughly turned. Now the starry night sky was all he could see. That, and the bulky bodies of his captors and their angry faces above him. But he could hear.

"Wait!" a woman's voice cried.

The men paused.

"What are you doing with my man?" the shrill female voice shouted. "Oh, my love, my dear, what are you doing to him?"

The men all turned to the sound of that frantic voice.

"Let him go!" it cried.

"Lissen, ma'am," one of the men holding him said, "See, he's . . ."

"Let him go!" the voice cried imperiously. "What can you be thinking? I leave for a moment, simply to nap, and you *abduct* him? Where were you taking him? Why? Is this not England? Where's the law? I shall have the law down upon you, you villains!"

Daffyd felt himself lowered to the ground. A moment later, he was released, and then covered by the soft weight of a slight female form, as a woman flung herself on top of him. Gentle hands cradled his head. He looked up to see Miss Margaret Shaw. But she ignored him. She glowered up at the men who stood in a ring around them.

"I demand to know the reason for this!" she shouted.

"Well, see, we thought he . . ." one of them muttered.

"See, ma'am, your man," another ventured to say, "he was asking after a girl, and see, we got one gone and went missing all day . . ."

"We was looking in the fields and hedgerows," the first man said, "and we seen a gypsy camp, or what was one . . ."

"And he looks like a gypsy . . . beggin' your pardon, ma'am," another man said quickly, "I mean, what with his skin and hair and all."

"A *gypsy*!" she shrieked, "Wherever have you seen a gypsy with such eyes? Blue as bonny English bluebells, like his mama's," she said, her voice momentarily softening. "His grandfather was consul in Spain, which is where he met his grandmother—Oh! I have no time for such nonsense." She rose to her knees. "Where is the law? I'll have you clapped in irons, the lot of you! And don't dare even think of laying a hand on me, my buckos," she announced, as she rose to her feet. She shook a finger at them, "My parents know our direction, and be sure—if we go missing His Majesty will hear of it! To think," she marveled, "we attempt to travel as any ordinary young couple might, and it comes to this."

Daffyd lay on his back, getting his wind back, stunned, disbelieving, and bizarrely enough, vastly entertained by his rescuer's dramatic abilities.

"Well?" she demanded, her hands on her hips. "Are none of you going to help him to his feet? Oh, it will go badly for you if you have hurt any part of him," she said angrily.

The men scrambled to help Daffyd up. One dusted off his jacket, another awkwardly patted his shoulder. One somehow produced his hat, which had been left at the inn.

"Are you all right, my dear?" Meg asked Daffyd with such solicitousness he almost believed every word she'd said was true.

"I am well enough," he said with hard-won calm.

"Thank you, my dear." He took her hand and raised it to his lips.

She colored, and looked away. He hoped it was dark enough, because no man would believe a well-loved female could blush at such a trifle. But from the corner of his eyes he saw that these louts were impressed by her shyness and his gesture. Only a highborn fellow would salute a woman who'd just saved his life in such a trifling way. Only a lady would be so moved by it, too.

"I think, however," he said, mastering understatement, "that we should not rest here this night."

The innkeeper had come hurrying out of the inn to join the growing crowd and see what the fuss was all about. Now he pushed through the throng. "Oh, sir. Lady," he said, bowing low. "Please, stay on. Let me make it up to you. Didn't know you two were together, sir, seeing as how you arrived separate. I'd have given you a better room. I will!" he added, on inspiration. "Free, too. Can't have folk thinking we're savages here. The *Magpie*'s got a reputation for comfort. Quality used to stop here all the time. Please, let us show you we still got the touch. And don't be feared of being disturbed! These knot heads come within an inch of you again, and I'll shoot them myself, I will!"

The serving girl had pressed forward too. But she was staring at Daffyd and frowning. "But what about your fiancée?" she asked him. "I mean, you said you was looking for your fiancée: a blond who lisps. And so, who is this lady?"

The crowd grew still.

Meg turned to Daffyd, newborn fear in her wide eyes.

"Oh, that," he said, in his most refined accents. "Well, my dear," he told the serving girl, "If I'd asked after my sister, would you have been so quick to help me? No, I don't think so. Or so I have found it to be in these past days. You might have thought I was chasing my sister to force her to marry against her wishes. That's what I hear she's been telling people all along the road so they'll help her and I won't find her. But I must. In truth, she's a rich young girl besotted by a very bad man who wants her fortune. So it's much easier to say she's my love, and get answers, then say she's my relative and have people try to protect her. Women are soft hearted, brothers can be painted as villains. Come, my dear, don't you agree?"

The girl smiled.

"Now, my lady here," Daffyd went on, "is helping me in my quest, and since there are questions only a woman can ask, she travels a bit apart from me until nightfall. She says my sister is her cousin. Because after all, I ask you: Who in the world has any sympathy for in-laws?"

There were nods and chuckles. The men who had held him began backing away. At last Daffyd could breathe easily again. He turned his head and put his lips against Meg's ear as though he were brushing a kiss there. He felt her stiffen, and quickly whispered, "We have to stay here, if only for the night. It's too late to travel on with any safety tonight."

She swallowed hard. He could hear it. Then she nodded. "We have to talk," she whispered back.

"Oh, never doubt it," he said.

The room they were led to was sumptuous, by the *Magpie*'s standards. It was large, there was a fire in a hearth: two chairs, a table, a wardrobe, and a huge, high bed. Daffyd wondered if the sheets on the bed were still warm. He was certain someone had been turfed out so he and Margaret Shaw could be put in. His calm in the face of disaster and her histrionics had convinced the innkeeper they were Quality. The Quality were famous for their queer habits and mad starts. And whatever else they were, the Quality were needed for the prosperity of any inn.

The men who had almost hanged him had each apologized humbly and then vanished into the night. The innkeeper had bowed so much he looked like a Mandarin. The servants rushed to make sure their every need was met. But their only need now was for the night to pass.

Daffyd looked at his new roommate. She was pacing.

"This will never do," she muttered.

"It has to," he said, leaning back against the wall. "Tell you what: toss me a coverlet, I'll sleep on the floor. You'll be safe as a nun. I won't touch you—unless you want me to."

She stopped and stared at him.

He flung up his hands. "An attempt at humor. Nothing else. It's been a hard night. So it wasn't very funny. I can't help it. My humor was bruised, too. Of course I won't bother you. Especially after what happened yesterday. Fine way to thank you, that would be. I owe you, you know."

She spoke through gritted teeth. "But if people hear we stayed together, my reputation will be ruined."

"So will mine. Don't worry. No one knows us. I didn't use my real name. Did you? Even if you did, it doesn't matter. Here, they believe you're my wife. We'll never see them again. Who else would see you or know you if they did?"

"Well, the Runner," she said slowly.

"But he's not here. So no one knows. Right?"

She nodded.

"So you're safe. And so am I. See, I really am grateful to you and would do almost anything to thank you," he said sincerely. "But not marry you. I'd hate to have to do that."

Her eyes flashed, then narrowed. "I do *not* want to marry you!" she said in a violent whisper. "I saved you because I knew you were innocent of kidnapping that child. Any Christian woman would have done the same. But I don't want to marry you. I don't know you; I don't particularly like you, and so why would I want to marry you? I don't. Can't you get that through your head?"

He sat on a chair. "Understood," he said simply.

"But . . ." she said, stopping and thinking deeply. "There *is* something you can do for me."

"I'm listening."

"Take me with you. In for a penny, in for a pound.

You just said no one will know about tonight, so how will they know about any other nights? I have eight days left to find Rosie and I can do that better with you. And more safely, you said that, too. We can stay in separate rooms at the next inn. But let me come along to find Rosalind! That's what you can do for me."

"No," he said.

"I can help. You saw that tonight. Let me come along. Then if I fail I can at least know I tried everything."

He looked exasperated. "Why endanger yourself and your reputation? I know it's no pleasure to sit and wait. I sympathize. I'd hate to do it. But you're a female, and gently bred, at that. There are dangers and discomforts on the road apart from the possibility of rape. I said I was good at finding things. Just go home and wait."

Her face was white. But her fists were clenched and her head was high. It was as if now that she'd found courage and anger, she refused to let them go.

"Why not?" she asked, her eyes bright, her voice forceful. "Because I *have* no real home. If I fail to find Rosie, I'll only have a place with my aunts. A proper place. A remote one, as far from humanity as Napoleon in exile on his island. I'd be like a prisoner too, only I committed no crime except for having no home of my own. Oh, I'd be taken care of. I'd have food and shelter and clothing. And I'd live under my aunts' feet and their rules for the rest of my life with no will of my own, less than a servant, not even free as one. Servants at least earn money and have half days off once a week. I know, I had that as a companion.

"But if I go to live with my aunts, I won't have anything but a place to sleep and eat, though I will work for my keep. And I won't be thanked for it. I'll be suffered, and made sure I know it. I'll be fenced in and hemmed 'round; I'll have no freedom, no say in my future. That's why. I know. I've lived with them, and vowed never to do so again. But if Rosie is gone and I'm blamed for it . . ."

She turned her head so he wouldn't see the furious tears rushing to her eyes. "Ah, why am I bothering to tell you? You can't understand, how could you? You're a man, you've always been free."

He stayed absolutely still. Then he shrugged. "Why didn't you say that from the first? All right. If you want, you can come with me."

She spun around to face him, her face alight.

He held up a hand. "But no whining. No complaining. No special favors for you. Because all I'll say is, 'I told you so.' And you have to keep up with my pace. Agreed?"

She smiled in rapturous dawning belief, and absolute relief.

"Agreed!"

Chapter 6

~~~❦~~~

"Are you really half gypsy?"

The voice came out of the darkness. Daffyd shifted on his pallet on the floor. It wasn't as comfortable as the bed would have been, but Miss Margaret Shaw had generously given him two coverlets to sleep with, one for under his body, and one for over it. He had a soft down pillow, and the hearth still radiated warmth. She had the bed, and he the floor next to it, under the window and nearer to the door, in case anyone hadn't gotten the innkeeper's warning.

Daffyd stretched and gave a soft sigh of pleasure. It wasn't the prime accommodation he'd been expecting. But he'd been comfortable with far less in his time. The room was filled with a warm darkness, and most of all, it wasn't a permanent darkness. He'd been saved from death. And as always when that happened, just the mere act of breathing felt good. He even felt kindly towards his unwanted charge, where she lay on the big, high bed that was supposed to have been his.

After he'd agreed to take her along, her smile had faded away, and she'd just stood, watching him nervously. It took him a moment to understand the problem. When he had, he'd left the room, used the time to go to the convenience, and then loitered in the night air long enough for her to prepare for bed. He'd guessed she'd have slept fully clothed if he hadn't given her time to undress. When he returned the room was dark except for one lamp. She was tucked into bed, and his improvised pallet was waiting for him. He'd murmured a "thanks," she'd murmured a "you're welcome." Then she'd blown out the lamp. All he'd seen of her before the light went out was a vague shape beneath her coverlets.

He'd undressed in total darkness, at least, taken off his jacket, neckcloth and boots, and laid himself down. He closed his eyes, and she spoke. It didn't surprise him. In his experience, darkness always made a man feel like loving and a woman feel like talking. He was sure, though, that all he'd get was talk tonight.

"Yes," he answered. "My father was a gypsy. My mother isn't. She's a lady. But why bother asking? Everyone knows gypsies are liars."

"I don't think you're lying," she said in a soft, sleepy voice that suddenly made him think he could be much more comfortable if he were in that bed with her. "I think you would lie if it benefited you, but what would be the point of lying to me? Oh," she said, and he could tell she was smiling. "Actually there would be a point, wouldn't there? If your grandfather had actually been a consul in Spain, you'd be afraid I'd try to marry you." She giggled.

"I don't think *everyone* is trying to marry me," he said, sounding a little defensive. "Still, it's a trap women have tried to spring. Mind you, I know I'm not prime goods. But I come from a land where women badly need husbands of any sort. Not just for a fellow's looks, name or fortune. They need his protection, too."

"What land?" she asked curiously.

"The Antipodes," he said.

She didn't answer. The room was still and dark.

"Botany Bay," he went on. "Actually, Port Jackson. The penal colony. Well, the whole place is one. I was one too. A convict, that is."

The only sound was that of a last log ticking into embers in the hearth.

He felt the usual twist of sour amusement deep in his gut. Only this time he also felt a curious sense of disappointment. "You don't have to leave right away," he remarked conversationally. "For one thing, it's too dark. There are worse things out there now than me. You're safe enough. You can go in the morning. Remember, I tried to warn you. But you said, 'In for a penny, in for a pound.' Don't worry about the pound, at least, of flesh. I said I wouldn't harm you and I won't. So go to sleep."

"I wasn't thinking about running away," she said. "I was just thinking about what you said. Why were you sent to the Antipodes?"

"Because they decided not to hang me. Don't bolt. I didn't kill anyone. I was a boy, a street rat, when they sentenced me. I had my hands on a pound note my mate had dipped, and it was my bad luck the beaks found it there when they burst into our lay. They nabbed me and my mate and we were sent to Newgate. Wasn't the first time. But in the past we'd been caught for trifles. A pound means the rope, and we were for it. We found our luck there, though. We met up with a gent—a real one—and his son, and made a bargain. The man would look after us boys, in return we'd teach him how to get on in the jail. It's an art, you know, or rather, don't. But it is.

"It helped them, and got us a voyage to the Antipodes instead of swinging, because the gent had a family with influence. They didn't want their name involved, and a hanging gets attention. Transportation gets rid of a fellow just as well, but it's quieter. He got a trip to the Antipodes for himself and his son instead of the noose, and he got us in on the bargain. We became a family. He made us his wards, treated us square as he did his own son. He didn't have anything to give us but the shirt off his back then, though it was in tatters, and he needed it. We lived to get through the voyage there. We worked out our sentences, made ourselves rich, and came home again. Only last year, in fact."

He heard movement, and looked up. He thought he'd see her flinging on her cape and rushing out into the night. Instead, she sat bolt upright and stared down at him.

"No!" she breathed in excitement. "I heard about you! I was in London with Miss Fisher, as her companion, last year. She traveled in a fashionable set. You and your brothers were the talk of the town. The gentleman was the Earl of Egremont rightfully returned to his estate! And you were one of his two wards? People could speak of nothing else. What a story! And so you were the gypsy lad! I *am* impressed. . . ." Her voice dwindled. "That is, if you're telling the truth now?"

"Why should I lie? Forget that, a gypsy doesn't need a reason. But I'm not. Lying, that is."

"So what are you doing tracking down Rosalind . . . ? Oh! Now it makes sense. Your mother is her godmother, she's the lady you spoke of. That's wonderful! I wish you'd told me straight away, I wouldn't have been wary of you. I feel as though I know you now."

He flung off his coverlet and marched, stocking-foot, over to her bedside. He towered over her in her bed. "You," he said angrily, "are the greatest fool in the world, even if you are smart! You *don't* know me.

Notoriety is not acquaintance. You trust too much and think too little. I could be a rapist, a murderer, a thoroughgoing villain. And yet here you sit crowing because you know me? You should be locked up somewhere and the key thrown away. For your own good."

She shrank from him. That was satisfying, but it made him feel like a bully. Then she rallied, and stared him down—or rather, up, lifting her chin and facing him squarely. That made him feel much better.

"I am perhaps too trusting," she retorted. "And I don't always make good judgments, but only because though I've encountered meanness of spirit, it's always been the socially acceptable sort, if you know what I mean. I have no experience of crime and criminals, that's true. But I learn quickly, and I have good instincts . . . most of the time. Yes, it was foolish of me to think you can be trusted simply because I had heard about you."

She paused, then added, "But I had confidence in you before I did. Because you've always treated me with, if not civility, then at least decency. You saved me from villains when there was nothing for you in it. So that's why I trust you, and if that's no reason to, then how can anyone know when to trust anyone?"

Though it was too dark to be sure, he knew she was looking him straight in the eye.

"Aye," he said in a lower voice. "There's that. A person has to take risks. And trust their own judgment, or else they'd never be able to take a step out the door. All right. But don't trust me too far, and make up your own mind when it comes to important things. I'll take you along with me, but I won't be your papa, understand?"

"*'Papa'*?" she asked, amazed. "I never thought so!"

"Or brother, or whatever," he grumbled as he went back to his pallet on the floor.

"Of course not," she said.

"Of course," he said softly, thoughtfully, after a moment, "There are other masculine roles I can play aside from papa and brother, especially on such a wakeful night. There are things I can do to help you relax, for example, help send you off to sweet and easy sleep. Eventually."

There was a silence. It went on. It was definitely waiting. And listening. He suddenly had expectations for the long night ahead. But he thought of the quiet pansy-faced girl in the bed, and took his time before going on.

"You don't have to worry," he finally added in a lower, softer voice. "I won't compromise you. Promise! No, honestly, that's a fact. You might not know, but there are things that can be done between a man and a woman that are sweet, enjoyable; things that won't endanger you in any way, to get you through a long and lonely night. Things your governess never told you. Intimate, yes, but never the final intimacy that could jeopardize your future. After all," he said with indignation, "life's hard enough for a female, so it would be a selfish careless lout who leaves a babe in his wake each time he seeks pleasure! Pleasure can be given and gotten with no one but us ever the wiser."

"I do not love you," she said in a stiff little voice.

He stifled a snort of surprised laughter. "Love has nothing to do with it. I'm talking about pleasure, a good way to pass dreary time. Rich folk are always looking for sport and thrills. Poor folk don't have the time or money for that. But they're just as good at finding pleasure. I've seen it in slums and prisons, everywhere. See, if you don't have anything to pleasure yourself with except for your body, you learn how to use it. You don't have to love to love what we can do."

The silence was deafening.

"I mean," he said with a little more force. "I know my way about. Well, you know us gypsies, we can steal the egg out from under a hen without ruffling a feather." He winced, realizing, too late, what a bad analogy that was. He also knew she wouldn't be seduced by words alone, no matter how tender. And his, he admitted, were not.

She knew that, too.

"I do not have an egg," she snapped. "Nor would I want it stolen if I did. And if you so much as lay a finger on me, I shall . . . I'll . . ."

"Oh, I know, I know," he said grumpily. "Forget it, it was a mad start brought on by a late night. I'm more tired than I know. Go to sleep, alone and untouched. Don't worry. I didn't say I was mad with desire, did I? But think about it. What sort of a man would I be if I didn't even ask?"

"A nicer one," she said.

He had no answer. So he just turned his back on her.

He heard her settle down in her coverlets again. It took him longer to do that in his own makeshift bed. He hadn't seen her, but she'd smelled of faint flowers, and her voice had sounded sweet and sleepy and warm. Until he'd offered to share that warm bed of hers.

Daffyd turned over again with a thump that made his hip feel the floor beneath his blankets. He winced and thought, *Good!* The last thing he needed was to feel randy now. She wasn't his sort. Even if she were, he never let himself become entangled with any female who wanted more than a joyous night with him. And since that was decidedly not what he'd get from her this night, he closed his eyes and forced himself to think about nothing, until there were nothing but dreams on his mind.

She ate like a hawk. A fastidious hawk. But then, all hawks were fastidious. He'd seen one take down a songbird once: pluck it from the sky, land in a meadow, shuck it out of its feathers, and leave nothing but a neat pile of feathers and fluff behind when it was done eating. But he'd never seen a human female engulf and devour a meal with similar rapacity and delicacy until he'd seen Miss Margaret Shaw eat her breakfast. Daffyd was charmed.

She was full of surprises this morning. He sat

across the table from her and watched her demolish a trencherman's meal of eggs, steak, ham, sausage, bacon, fried tomatoes, biscuits, butter and honey. She used her fork and knife like a surgeon and didn't get one speck of food or sauce on her chin or her gown. And she made polite conversation all the while.

Her plate was finally empty when she looked up and saw his expression. Her cheeks flushed. She put down her fork. "I was very hungry this morning," she said. "The food's delicious, the country air must be the spice I needed."

He smiled.

She blushed more. "Truth is," she admitted. "I do like a good breakfast."

"Nothing to apologize for. You'll need it. We're going to be doing some hard traveling. Are you ready?"

She blinked. Lovely eyes, he thought, golden in the sunlight, like the hawk he'd been thinking about. It was an odd comparison. She was nothing like a bird of prey, she was the most helpless female he'd ever spent a night with. But then he thought about how she'd thrown herself on him and saved him from being hanged. Not so helpless, then. But inexperienced. He doubted she'd stay with him long enough to get much more experience of the world.

Daffyd rose from the table. "I'll pay the reckoning, get our horses ready, and we'll go in a half hour." He saw her horrified expression and frowned. She wasn't ready to travel? But she'd been on fire to accompany him last night. Maybe she'd had second thoughts. Or maybe it was a difficult time of the month for her? Surely she didn't expect him to wait on her moon cycles? Whatever it was, it freed him of all obligations. He ought to have been overjoyed, but found himself disappointed in her.

"What?" he asked abruptly. "Change your mind? I have to leave before noon. If you can't, I'll see you safely on the next stage out."

"Oh, no. I'll be ready. It was just unexpected. But how foolish of me," she said, rallying. "I ought to have known we'd leave at first light. Thank you for letting me sleep on as long as you did."

He nodded. He hadn't been monster enough to wake her at dawn. She'd looked so vulnerable, sleeping. Without her bright eyes to distract him, or her usual gray gowns to disguise her, he'd seen how defenseless she looked. He'd been able to stand over her and study her, seeing her hair braided like a girl, the slight shape of her beneath the covers. Like a girl, indeed, he'd thought. Most women he had experience with would have woken as he approached them. The females he knew always slept with one eye open. Seeing him approaching their bed, they'd either have reached out their arms to him or come at him with a knife. Miss Margaret Shaw just dreamed on, her cheeks flushed, her lips parted in sleep.

He doubted she'd last an hour with him today. He expected to have to waste another half day seeing her off in a coach. But he'd promised she could try,

and he'd give her at least that. That—and the extra
hour of sleep.

"In a half hour, then," he said, and strode away.

Her horse was golden, and tall. That was the first
thing Meg saw. The last time she'd ridden, the horse
had seemed even taller. That was because she'd been
a girl then. Now she was a woman. She gritted her
teeth. She'd done it then, she could do it now. If she
didn't, she was sure she'd be left behind. And if she
wasn't in on the discovery of Rosalind's whereabouts, she might as well bid her future good-bye
and go back to the aunts. There, the only way she'd
ever ride would be behind the old horse pulling the
cart she was allowed to take into town once a week to
pick up supplies. That was, if she'd finished all her
chores.

"Well, then," she said brightly. "I'm ready."

She was glad he was occupied with paying the
ostler, because that way no one but the stable boy
who helped her mount saw her struggle to get on the
horse and arrange herself and her skirts.

Her foot went there—yes, and the other, there.
She remembered. She could do it, and she would.
But the ground was very far away when she was
done. She took a deep breath and closed her eyes.
She felt her stomach heave as the horse shifted. She
clung to the saddle and breathed deep.

"Something you ate?" she heard Mr. Daffeigh ask
curiously.

"What?"

"You're green. Too much breakfast or too soon after?"

She opened her eyes. He was sitting astride a white horse, beside her.

She shook her head. "No. It's been a while since I rode. I'm merely—getting acc—" Her heart lurched as the horse stepped forward. She reined in her emotions hard. "—accustomed again," she said, as she grasped her horse's reins.

"How long has it been since you were on a horse?" he asked bluntly.

She thought a moment. "Fifteen years . . . or so. But one never forgets," she tried to chirp brightly. Her voice came out disappointingly breathless and faint.

He frowned.

"Look, Mr. Daffeigh," she said with effort, "I will ride, and I won't complain, and I'll get used to it again. So we might as well start."

Daffyd watched her closely. She was pale, her forehead shiny and damp. Her lovely mouth was compressed into a thin line; her eyes were wide with poorly concealed terror. The little hawk was flagging. Well, he thought, but she was only a songbird, pretending. At any rate, she'd given him the perfect reason to leave her behind. They had to ride far today.

But seeing her gallantry moved him. He decided to give her more rope. If she could hold on, so be it. If she couldn't, she'd hang herself and ditch her own chances.

"Fine," he said. "Just follow me. We're going on

the main road until after luncheon. Then we cut across country and head east. And by the way, the name isn't 'Mr. Daffeigh.' That's only what old friends call me. My name's Daffyd. Or if you need to be more formal: Mr. Reynard. Now, let's go." He kneed his horse, and rode out to the road, but slowly, far more slowly than he usually did. She'd follow, or try to, and there was no sense letting her break her neck right off.

They rode until noon. Daffyd was shocked at his companion's tenacity. After the first half hour, she was actually riding and not just hanging on for dear life. After the next half hour, she was actually smiling as she moved with the horse instead of against it. But as the sun rose directly overhead, he noticed her smile becoming strained and her conversation faltering.

He noticed, because she talked. Oh lord, he thought, how the woman talked! She started out by commenting on the weather and the countryside they were passing through. Though it was through gritted teeth, she persevered. Then as her confidence grew and her fear of falling off her horse eased, she went on to chat, asking him about his feelings about the weather and the countryside. Soon Daffyd found himself telling her about the Antipodes. He edited his comments.

He spoke at first to set her at her ease, then found himself actually enjoying the conversation. That surprised him. He wasn't good at small talk. His brothers said that was because his talk was really very small. It was true he wasn't a flowery speaker. He said what needed saying, and seldom elaborated. That always made him feel a little challenged at the social affairs his two glib brothers shone at.

But Miss Margaret, or Meg, as she soon asked him to call her, didn't seem to mind. It only made her ask more questions, which he always answered. That made him forget that he was not good at conversation. He supposed if she spliced all his answers together, she got a fair idea of what she wanted to hear.

He was surprised when he realized it was already noon.

"We're right on time," he said as they rode up to the courtyard of the *Rose and Thistle*, a modest inn on the main road. He halted, slid off his horse, and began unbuckling his saddlebags. "We'll stop here, change horses, rest, and eat. And then move on."

"Fine," she said brightly, and sat where she was.

He glanced up at her curiously. She sat upright, and smiled. But she didn't move. Then she looked down at him, and her lips curved in a real smile, an apologetic one. "I forget how to get off," she said.

He held up his arms, and she slid down into them. Warm, he thought as he received her slight weight in his arms, and curved, he realized, and fragrant, he thought as she bent her head and her soft hair brushed against his lips. He held her a moment longer than he'd planned to. And was relieved when he realized it was necessary, because she was having a hard time regaining her feet. "All right?" he asked softly.

She nodded, head down. "I'm fine. It was just new to me."

"You'll be sore by nightfall," he warned her.

She nodded again. "Likely. But I'll be that much closer to Rosalind, won't I?"

He was surprised to discover he'd forgotten the runaway heiress. "Aye," he said gruffly. "You'll be right on her trail."

They lunched on fresh bread, game pie, and mutton, ale for him and lemonade for her. She fell upon her lunch as she had on her breakfast, and again, he marveled at her appetite, the fact that it didn't seem to add an ounce to her neat shape, and her endless supply of conversation. The most amazing thing was that her talking didn't annoy him. She said interesting things, had a good eye for detail and a lively imagination. She had the same eagerness about new experiences that she showed when food was brought to her. And she made her companion feel her joy in each. He marveled. She was like a woman who'd never seen anything, been anywhere, or eaten anything good. But unlike the women he'd known who had never done or been anything, she rejoiced in each new thing.

"What was it like there, with your aunts?" he asked, while she finished off her cream-drenched apple tart. "I mean, in the countryside."

She looked at him and put down her fork, for once ignoring food on her plate. "It was . . . the same," she said thoughtfully. "Day after day. Please understand, my aunts aren't cruel. They only seemed that way after my parents. I mean, my father was a sportsman, a jolly fellow who always told stories, and laughed at his own jests, or so I recall. My mama was warm and easygoing. I was ten when they died. They were riding home from a day in London. There were two young bloods racing on the same road. Their carriage was overturned. Too bad," she said in a bleak little voice, "that my father fancied driving his high wheeled phaeton. They look lovely, but aren't safe.

"Well, in any event," she said, attacking the last of her pie crust, "I was lucky the aunts took me in. I didn't think so then. They aren't wicked, just satisfied with their lives, and don't understand why I'm not. Aunt Edna rules the roost, and Aunt Ruth doesn't seem to mind. But I do. So as I said, they aren't bad, they're just . . . Oh, Daffyd," she said, looking up at him, her eyes wide and sad, "They're not good with people. And it's as if they forgot they were ever young. Maybe they weren't. I would do *anything* to avoid going back to them."

"Well, you have," he said, signaling to the serving girl for his bill. "You've decided to come along with me."

"But you've been wonderful," she protested, her eyes kindling with emotion. "You've been kinder and better to me than I could have believed."

He rose to his feet. "You've only been with me a day. Wait," he said with a bitter smile. "We've a long road ahead. Wait."

Chapter 7

As daylight began to fail, so did Meg's attempts at keeping up a conversation. She needed all her attention on her horse as she followed Daffyd down long, strange, winding paths.

They'd gone off the main road and taken back ways through forests and across fields. They'd ridden alongside fences and pastures full of sheep, but stayed far from human eyes. There was a dark earthy smell of autumn on the wind, but it was warm enough. Daffyd seemed to know where he was going. He only paused every now and again to scan the landscape before moving on. Now it was dusk, that time when shapes shift in violet shadows, and trees and fences grow into each other in changing contours that fool the eye. Meg was afraid the horse wouldn't be able to see the way any better than she could. But she followed in Daffyd's wake.

He astonished her.

He'd warned her not to rely on him, but had made concessions to her all through the day. He slowed when he saw her falter, told jokes when her spirits flagged, and always made sure she was able to keep up. Now it also amazed her that she'd been so intimidated by him at first. Of course, he had been a stranger, and she'd never made an acquaintance, much less a friend, of a strange man before. He was also devilishly attractive in a dangerous sort of way. And he had an admittedly criminal past. But now she'd follow him without hesitation.

She realized she was well on her way from one extreme to another. Because now she was awed by him. She could, and did, watch him for hours. He rode as though to the saddle born, but she also liked seeing him walk. He made every motion seem effortless. She could believe he'd been a pickpocket. He was agile, alert, and quick-witted as he was deft. And he knew his way around the world.

The bad part of it was that she began to find herself drawn to him, even though she knew nothing good could come of it. She supposed the aunts had been right: Strange things happened when a female marched away from everyone she knew and dared to confront the world on her own. There were more dangers than she'd imagined, and not just from evil strangers with mayhem on their minds. Sometimes, danger wore a much more pleasant face.

Before she'd gone on this mad quest she'd only wanted an agreeable job and a comfortable place to live, maybe spiced by a chance to meet new friends, so she'd have someone to go with on her half days off.

Now, she wanted much more, impossibly more. She couldn't stop thinking about Daffyd, how capable and kind he was, how masculine and how attractive. She thought about the expressions in his dark blue eyes, and found it impossible to forget how light his touch had been as he'd held her when he'd helped her off her horse. Such a little thing; an impossibly trivial thing, she knew that. What had so delighted her was only a small thing made large by a life that had no life in it. But now she knew such trifling things had spoiled her hopes of future content.

Because he'd made her think about men for the first time in a long time. Not the sort of men who had threatened to hurt her—a wise female always worried about those men. And not even the respectable men she'd sometimes met, men who also had little to offer and were looking for the best, most advantageous marriages they could find. No, Daffyd didn't make her think about either violent or cold-blooded men.

He made her think about males, what they could do, and how they could make a woman desire them.

Not that a man who confessed he'd been a street rat and a convict was any kind of man for her, of course. But it was too easy to forget that when she was with him. . . . She longed to touch his ebony hair, and wondered if it would feel cool, and flow through her fingers the way it did when he turned his head and it brushed against his cheeks. . . .

"Meg," he said.

He woke her from her reveries. She reined in before her horse walked right past him. He'd stopped and was half turned around, looking back at her. His voice was pitched low, but she heard him well enough. The sun had set, the birds had finished their evening songs, and the only other sounds were that of the wind rustling through the trees and their horses' breathing.

"Yes?" she whispered.

"We're going to meet some friends and relatives of mine now," he said softly. "Stay with me. Let me do the talking. These relatives don't care for women who aren't family. They really wouldn't like one who put herself forward. They have odd habits, but bear with me. We're only staying the night and traveling on with them for a while tomorrow. They can help in our search. Just follow me and do as I say. You'll be safe enough. My word on it."

He hesitated, then spoke briskly. "No blushes—I must know: Is it your time of the month? Or anytime soon?"

Meg gasped, then whispered, "No."

"Good. It would present difficulties; they wouldn't welcome you if it were. One other thing: Never walk in front of me. Stay behind me at all the time, and don't go anywhere without my permission. Can you do that? Just for a day?"

She breathed a tiny, shaky, "Yes," and steeled herself for whatever would come next.

* * *

They rode out of the forest onto a hilltop that over-
looked a long rolling meadow. That was when Meg
smelled the smoke, and then, a moment later, saw
the fires. Campfires, lit like small beacons against
the oncoming night, lay spread out on the meadow
below, adding to the growing autumn twilight haze.
Still she made out the shapes of wagons and
horses . . . a gypsy camp!

Meg felt dread and excitement in equal parts as
they rode up to the camp. All she'd ever heard about
the gypsies came flooding back: they stole, they lied,
they cheated. They spoke to horses, fixed pots and
pans, and told fortunes. They also stole babies, though
why they'd do that, she had no idea, since she'd heard
they had enough of their own. She wished she'd had
the time to ask Daffyd more about himself.

Well, she had, she admitted, but he was closemouthed when it came to personal things, and she'd
tried to hard to be polite.

No, she thought sadly. She'd been cowardly.

Daffyd halted his horse at the edge of the meadow,
near one small campfire that was set apart at the edge
of the encampment, far from the others. He called
out into the glare of the dancing flames: "Tante
Keja—it is I, Daffyd, returned. And I have brought a
stranger."

Meg saw someone squatting by the campfire rise.
She squinted to try to see the figure as it slowly came
toward them. But then the man ran up to them and
danced around their horses, laughing.

"By God!" the man cried. "It *is* Daffy, himself. And look what you've brought! A woman. Yours?"

"Yes," Daffyd said sourly. "For now. I didn't expect to see you, Johnny. Where's Keja?"

"What a welcome. Well, I didn't expect to see you either. How long has it been? Too short a time for you, eh? But what a pretty lady. What's your name, sweetheart?" the man Daffyd had called Johnny asked Meg, as he stared up into her face.

"Her name is my business, brother," Daffyd said curtly.

Johnny flung two hands in the air. "Softly, softly! I won't bite her, though she's pretty as a pippin. Hello, luv," he said, still eyeing Meg.

Meg stared down at him, but his back was to the fire and she couldn't make out his face. It was embarrassing and awkward because obviously he was a gypsy, part of Daffyd's family, or tribe. He had on a white shirt, but no jacket, and dark breeches and boots. But she didn't say a word, just as Daffyd had asked.

"Well trained," Johnny said with approval. "You always were a lucky lad, Daffy."

"Aye, fortune always smiles on me," Daffyd said sourly. "As you know."

"Yes, lucky," Johnny said, with irrepressible good spirits. "You fooled Old Reynard. Got away from him slick as a whistle. That's a first, they still talk about it. True, you spent some time in a rat's castle in the Rookeries, got done in the start, did your bit in the Hulks, and then lagged. But you're back! And look at you now! Rich as you can stare, with influential friends. Or are you still? Come to think on, brother, what are you doing here now?"

"I'm well enough," Daffyd said. "Where's Aunt?"

"Out on a mission of mercy. Some local girl's popping out a babe, and having a hard time of it. Though they wouldn't let Tante Keja in their front door during the day, they begged her to go in through the back door tonight. So, she'll be a while. Come on, I'll see you settled in."

Johnny grasped the reins of Daffyd's horse and led him into the firelight. Meg followed. Daffyd slid from his horse when he got to the caravan near the fire, and looped the reins over a peg in the earth. Johnny went to Meg's horse and looked up at her.

Meg tried to stifle her gasp. Because the man looking up at her shared the same face as Daffyd. It hadn't been a turn of speech. Johnny had to be Daffyd's real brother.

"Go in," Johnny said, as Daffyd came round to help Meg down. "I'll get some food. We'll have a feast."

Meg followed Daffyd up the short back stair into the caravan. She ducked her head, stopped, and looked around. The interior of the wagon was neat and clean, more like a well-furnished room than a vehicle of any sort she'd ever seen. The place smelled of wood smoke, sandalwood, and delicious spices. It was bright even in the low light of one lamp, because of the riot of colors everywhere. There were dozens of hues to catch the eye, yet they all seemed to complement each other.

The high bed against one wall was covered with a spread that was gold and red, green and blue, all pieced together. But that was hard to see because there were pillows of all sizes and hues strewn over it. A bright fringed shawl was thrown over the one table. The only plain wall had pots and pans hanging from it, as well as chairs on pegs that held them high off the variously carpeted wood floor. A gold and green curtain was drawn across half the room; Meg got a glimpse of another table with a washbasin, and a cabinet with dishes behind it.

In all, though not large, it was a cozy, jolly-looking place, much more comfortable than many rooms Meg had been given by her employers in their stately homes.

"I'll get some water," Daffyd said, seizing the basin. "I'll be right back. Stay."

When he returned, he set the basin on the table, and tossed her a bit of cloth. "Wash," he said. "But never tell anyone I let you go first. I'll be back." He drew the curtain behind him and left the caravan.

Meg washed quickly, loving the feel of the cool water. She began to hurry when she realized there was no door for him to knock on when he returned, and she didn't want to be caught with her bodice down. But she'd been done for a while, and was waiting with impatience and a little anxiety when he finally returned. And when he did, he stopped, waited outside the curtain, and asked in a low voice, "Ready?"

"Oh, yes," she said.

He pulled the curtain aside. She noted his dark hair was damp. "I washed at the pump," he explained. "Now," he said, pulling a chair down from the wall for her and taking the other for himself. "What are your questions?"

"Is he your brother?" she asked eagerly. "What did he say?"

"He's my half brother. And you heard him."

"I heard him, but what was it he said? I mean, about you living in a rat's castle and being lagged and such."

"Oh." Daffyd smiled. "A rat's castle is a flash ken in the Rookeries, which are London slums. A thieves' ken," he explained, "is where all the rum coves and divers . . ." He paused. "I mean, young thieves and pickpockets and the like—it's where they kip at night. Kip," he said to her uncomprehending stare. "Sleep. And also eat, and plan. Not a good place, but safer than the streets for a homeless boy. Then I was sent to Newgate. That's being 'done in the start.' Then I went to the Hulks, which are the prison ships they send you to when the prisons are full, especially if you're bound for Botany Bay. Then I was sent to the Antipodes, or 'lagged.' I told you all that in English. Johnny spoke thieves' cant. Which is what Johnny is, whatever he calls himself this week."

Meg hesitated, then asked, "But who was this 'Old Reynard' you were so lucky to run away from?"

"My father," Daffyd said briskly.

"And his, too?"

"Yes," Daffyd said. "Different mothers. Same sire. Now, we'll eat. One warning. Do not leave my sight. Not even with my brother. Especially not with him. He's not dangerous, in the usual sense. But he'll have you out of your gown and off with your virginity before you can whistle. And it wouldn't be rape."

"Oh!" she gasped. Then she became outraged, and shot to her feet. "How dare you!"

"I don't. He might. That's what I said." He walked to the entrance of the caravan and looked back at her. "Come, let's go."

She followed, silently fuming. Then she paused again on the top step of the caravan. From that vantage point she could see all the fires of the encampment brightly burning for all the people she could now see milling about or sitting in groups in the tight circle of the many tents and wagons.

"We stay here," Daffyd said, as he looked up at her.

Meg couldn't see why Daffyd thought his half brother was so seductive. Johnny was merry and funny, actually charming, in a raffish fashion. But he didn't have half of Daffyd's dark, effortless appeal.

The three of them sat before the fire, sated with the spicy stew that simmered in a huge pot, suspended on the tripod over their cook fire.

Now that she could see Johnny clear in the fire-

light, Meg saw he wasn't really that much like
Daffyd. He was darker, which might be because of
hours spent in the sun, but he also looked sturdier,
more muscular. Daffyd was slender, with long, well-
knit musculature. Johnny's nose was higher at the
bridge, his face a jot wider, his chin more determined, and his eyes were brown, not blue. He did
have the same straight black hair and engaging
smile, but on balance, she now could see more differ-
ences than similarities between the brothers.

Daffyd frowned more. His smile was as charming,
if less frequent, and so, being hard won, more exciting. At least, so it seemed to Meg. Daffyd was altogether a stiller person, in that he watched more than
he spoke. Johnny never stopped talking, but he
watched as he did. He especially watched Meg, playing for her smiles and, she realized, for his brother's
wrath.

Meg shifted; her back was growing stiff and starting to ache. It had been a hard day's riding, and trying to sit upright with her skirts tucked securely
around her ankles was hard. That was probably why
gypsy women wore layers of skirts, she realized. Her
own slender gown was much more difficult to ma-
nipulate in order to keep her dignity while sitting on
the ground.

"Here, have a drink," Johnny said, passing her a
wineskin. "You look tense. This will ease your day's
woes."

Meg looked at Daffyd. He shook his head. "She
can't drink from our wineskin, you know that."

"So old-fashioned?" Johnny jeered.

"So worried about Tante. She'd have our heads for it. Worse, she'd ban us from her caravan. And then where would we be? If you want, and she does too, you can pour some into her cup. Meg, you can drink that. But there's coffee, too. Johnny's brew is lethal stuff, just take a little."

Johnny poured Meg another jot of the clear liquid. She drank it cautiously. It smelled like flowers and made her throat burn, yet after a moment she found it eased her cramped limbs.

"So, why are you here, brother?" Johnny asked again.

"I might ask the same of you," Daffyd said. "And I will."

"Me?" Johnny said with a laugh. "The usual. I'm resting up before I leave again. I had a good rig running up north, that is, until it went bad. I thought I'd make myself vanish for a while. There aren't any emeralds in Yorkshire, but there's gold in having folks believe it. And you? Come, why are you suddenly here among us again?"

Daffyd laughed derisively. "*Us*? Coming it strong, Johnny. You're only one of 'us' when the law's on your trail. It isn't after me. The fine lady asked a favor and I need to find out more than the law knows."

Johnny whistled. "Thought you weren't going to have anything to do with her?"

"Aye," Daffyd said. "So did I. But I reckon a favor done by me will be like a mote in her eye. Anyway, the earl asked me, too, and I'd never say no to him."

"Never going to forgive her, are you?"

"Not likely," Daffyd agreed. "So. She's asked me to find a young chit; an heiress who ran away and is trying to ship out with a lover in tow. There's a fiancé, a hothead youth, pursuing. Redbreasts, too. Heard anything about it?"

"I have," Johnny said simply. "What's in it for me?"

"Gelt," Daffyd said simply, and then added, with a grin, "and my undying thanks."

"Oh, that will buy me an abbey," Johnny said. "But I'll take the money, and thanks."

"The information first," Daffyd said decisively.

"Of course. It's yours when we leave tomorrow."

"Leaving?" Daffyd asked, one eyebrow going up.

"Have to. Folk hereabouts are getting the wind up their tails. We been here for a fortnight, and that's too long. Any chicken wanders off and it's our fault, you know the way of it. They'll be coming to turf us out soon, so we're moving on tomorrow.

"We know about the runaways," he went on. "Well, who better? If anyone takes a path off the beaten one, we'd notice. The pair you want have been seen. And used. They've paid good money for bad advice, and would be at sea already if they hadn't been sent wrong so often. There's more money in running them in circles than steering them straight. I'll set you straight on their trail though, when we leave tomorrow. For tonight, rest, relax. So, pretty maid," Johnny said, turning to Meg, leaning on an elbow and looking up at her. "You a mute? Or just shy?"

She looked at Daffyd.

He tilted a shoulder in a shrug. "Here, and now, you can talk as much as you like, if you want. Johnny knows what's good for him," he added enigmatically.

"I wouldn't vex my little brother," Johnny said. "No more than I'd trouble you, miss," he added in an upper-class accent. "I just wanted a little decent conversation to while away the night. And yes," he said, noting her expression, "my brother isn't the only one who can talk posh. So, my dear, who are you?"

She looked at Daffyd again. He seemed exquisitely uninterested. He sat a little apart; his arms locked around his knees, as though in his own private world.

"I'm Margaret Shaw," she said. "The runaway was my charge. I was her companion. So I want to find her. If I don't, I'll never get a reference, and will lose my employment."

"Ah, damnation," Johnny said with a sigh, rolling over on his back. "And here I thought you'd brought me a woman of fortune, Daffy. Still," he added, with a brilliant smile, "you did bring me one of beauty and intelligence, so I won't complain."

"I was not brought for you!" Meg said in annoyance. "And so you can save the honey for your breakfast biscuits."

"And spirit," Johnny said with admiration. "Well done. Peace, Miss Shaw. Let's just have a nice evening together. Here, have another jot of juniper to keep off the dew. And don't sip. It's made to go down quick."

Meg took a swallow, and found warmth spreading through her stomach. It made her feel warmer and more comfortable immediately. She took another swallow and felt even better. And then she heard music. Lively, bright, and enticing music. Her head shot up.

"You're in for a treat, Miss Margaret," Johnny said. "We're having a *patshiv*, celebrating the gathering of families. There's dancing tonight because we'll be off on the road tomorrow, and who knows when there'll be such a meeting again? So, we've the fiddles, guitars, tambours, a squeezebox, and a man who's a treat with the flute."

Meg craned her neck to see what was happening at the other campfires. The music was winding through the night, making her feel restless and excited all at once.

"Sorry, but we're not welcome at their fire, Margaret," Johnny said from her elbow, as he filled her cup again. "You, certainly not. You're an outsider. Daffy isn't all Rom. And me, because I've been a bad lad, by their lights. But why worry? They can't fence in music. Enjoy, Miss Maggie, enjoy."

"That stuff is strong," Daffyd remarked from out of the dark. "Not for ladies. You'd be wise to ask for some coffee instead, Meg."

"Are you going to let my brother decide everything for you, Miss Meg?" Johnny asked her.

"He is my host," Meg said in what she thought was politic fashion. "I don't feel like having coffee now. May I drink this?" she asked Daffyd.

"I wouldn't."

"Why not?"

"Because I offer it," Johnny said. "But see?" He took a large swallow and grinned. "Why be such a kill sport, brother?"

"That's only my advice, not an order," Daffyd said.

"So, be merry, Miss Meggie," Johnny said. "Don't think you can trust me, brother?" he asked Daffyd with a wide grin as he poured some more for Meg. "Or don't think you can trust her with me?"

"She can do as she pleases in this," Daffyd said. "I trust her instincts."

"Well, then!" Johnny said merrily, "Let's have some fun, Miss Meggie."

She did. She drank more, sat back, listened to the music and Johnny's banter, and laughed, often. The firelight was warm, the night was cool, and she was enjoying herself. She wasn't used to much company and not at all to such merry male companionship. She wished Daffyd would join in, and then became a little annoyed when he did not. She was obeying his wishes, after all. She wasn't walking in front of him, or talking without being spoken to, and didn't know why he was so silent, and why his silence seemed so disapproving.

She began to sip more of the lovely juniper drink because it didn't feel hot going down anymore. She laughed at every amusing thing Johnny said. Occasionally, she'd look over at Daffyd. But he sat still as a stone, and all she ever saw was the firelight reflecting in his eyes as he looked at the campfire where the music and dancing was. She began to resent it.

"Come," Johnny finally said.

She looked up to see him standing before her, holding out a hand. He'd discarded his bandana and she saw his strong tanned neck as the night breeze blew his night black hair back from his lean, dark face. His teeth were startling white as his billowy shirt as he smiled down at her. He looked, she thought, exactly as a handsome young gypsy should.

"Where?" she asked.

"Nowhere," he said. "Only dance with me. Here."

"But I can't dance like a gypsy," she said, suddenly feeling very sorry for herself. "I can waltz, though I've never been asked to, but I've taught it to girls in my charge. I can do the minuet, and the polonaise, and the Sir Roger de Coverly, and any number of country-dances. But I can't dance like a gypsy. Well," she said sadly, plucking at her plain gray skirt, "I haven't got yards and yards and . . ." She shook her head, aware there were too many "yards" in her sentence and managed to go on. ". . . yards of red and yellow and green skirts, like a gypsy lass has, either."

"No matter," he said, holding out his hand.

She took it, and was pulled, and was surprised to find herself suddenly standing, dizzy, feeling empty and light and little sick to her stomach all at the same time.

"Here!" Johnny said, and began clapping his hands in time to the gypsy music, while stepping lightly all around her.

She couldn't keep track of his movements as he circled her, laughing and dancing. She suddenly wanted nothing more than to sit down again.

"Come, Maggie," Johnny said, and pulled her into his arms.

She also didn't feel so very merry anymore. Johnny's body was too hot against her, his smile was too bright and too close, and he held her much too close. She tried to pull away.

"What's this?" he asked, looking down at her, holding her even tighter as she struggled. "Faint-hearted at the last minute?"

"Faint stomach, I think," she heard Daffyd say in a dry voice. She suddenly saw him beside her, and wondered where he'd been for so long. "She isn't used to drinking, brother. I'd let her go, and step back, if I were you. Because if she doesn't dirty your shirt in a minute, I'll flatten your nose instead."

Johnny let her go.

"Oh, Daffyd," Meg moaned, one hand on her forehead, as she tried to keep the world from spinning around her, the other on her stomach to keep it in place. "I'm going to be so sick."

"Of course you are," he said, as he led her to a darker spot, away from the caravan.

"Why didn't you stop me?" she groaned.

"Can't learn anything if you're stopped before you try it, can you?"

She had no reply. She was too busy being sick.

Chapter 8

Meg opened her eyes, and wished she hadn't. She closed them, but it was too late. The light was too bright, the colors too vivid, and her head and stomach protested too much. She lay still, caught between shame and sickness. Then she opened her eyes again and discovered she was not alone.

She shot upright. Her stomach protested. She gasped. That made the woman standing by her bed scowl. She was a short, squat, middle-aged woman with a round face, olive skin, gold earrings, and a ferocious frown. Her garments were more colorful than Meg's eyes could bear. That, and the frown directed at her, made Meg close her eyes again.

But her brain began working. It was morning light.

She was in bed in the gypsy caravan, so this must be the gypsy woman whose caravan it was.

Meg forced herself to sit up. "I beg your pardon," she said immediately. "You must be Daffyd's aunt. I am Margaret Shaw. I didn't mean to take your bed, but you weren't here and I wasn't thinking when I was put to bed . . . that is to say, I didn't know when I was put here . . ."

The woman's eyes opened wide, to show they were fine, dark, intelligent, and appalled.

"No!" Meg said at once, waving her hands in denial because her head hurt too much to shake. "I didn't *do* anything. That is, except for drinking that juniper drink Johnny offered me. But then I got very sick. I remember that . . . and yes, I remember Daffyd steering me in here." She stopped, appalled, realizing how that sounded.

She looked down at herself with fearful trepidation. "See?" she said in triumph. "I'm fully dressed! Not even unbuttoned."

The woman's dour expression hadn't changed.

"I know things can be done with gowns on," Meg went on desperately. "At least, so I've heard. But I didn't! I'd know it. I haven't forgotten anything, I wish I could. I was so sick. But I didn't do anything immoral. Just stupid. I drank too much juniper. Please forgive me."

The woman sniffed, turned her back, and walked away.

Meg scrambled out of bed, the aftereffects of the juniper forgotten in the embarrassment of the moment. "Please forgive me," she babbled. "I never meant to disturb you, or to be here at all."

The woman didn't turn around. Meg realized she probably didn't speak English.

"I'll just go out and wash up, and be gone," Meg mumbled anyway, looking around for her slippers.

"No," the woman said in clear English accents. "Stay here. There's water in the basin. If you have to make any, wait for dark or use the pot under the bed. Don't put your head out the door. There is shame enough."

"But Daffyd said we'd be on our way this morning," Meg protested.

"Daffyd," the woman said without turning around, "does not know everything."

"Well, that will be news to him," Meg grumbled as she got to her knees to search for her slippers.

"So, you are not in love with him?" the woman asked with interest.

"No," Meg said. She fished beneath the bed, and found her fingers didn't encounter anything but the cool sides of a porcelain chamber pot.

"But you are his woman?"

"No!" Meg said, and shot upright. She suppressed a groan at the stab of pain she felt, and insisted, "I'm not! I'm merely traveling with him in order to find the whereabouts of my charge, who ran away. That way I can get my position back, or failing that, at least be able to get another. I'm a governess-companion, you see. Daffyd's looking for her, too. We joined forces, but nothing else."

She felt her face grow hot as she added, "He told Johnny I was his woman, and I didn't protest because he said I was to say nothing. But I'm not. And I tell you, if it weren't for the fact that I've only days left in which to find my charge, I'd have walked off and left him right after he said it. If," she added meticulously, "I hadn't been so weary after riding all day. And if it hadn't been nighttime. And if I knew where I was and where I was going. I've done a rash thing, but I'm not a fool."

The woman stared at her. Then she smiled. "Good. To be *that* one's woman is to be a fool. He isn't fully Rom, but he is in his desires. He's a rover. You don't look like the sort he'd take up with anyway."

Meg didn't know whether to be flattered or hurt, but before she could decide, the woman continued, "Wash," she said. "I'll give you something to drink to set your head straight. Then you may talk with him. But not in here. There are always eyes watching and he may not visit with you. It would ruin his reputation entirely. Taking up with a *gaje* is bad enough, bringing her here and showing her off would be worse. I'll take you into the wood, you can talk there."

"Thank you," Meg said, wondering what reputation Daffyd had left to lose. "And then, whatever comes, I want to leave. Not that I don't appreciate your hospitality, but I don't belong here."

The woman smiled. "That's true. But neither does he."

"You just said he was like a Rom."

"Because he wishes to be. He doesn't know what he is," the woman said. "Nor can I tell him, because it is not yet decided. Your slippers are at the foot of the bed. Wash. You will see him when the time is right."

The gypsy woman put her finger to her lips and grasped Meg's hand. "Come, and move fast," she whispered. She poked her head out her caravan door, and quickly stepped down the stair.

Meg followed. It was a warm morning. She heard birdsong, the sound of voices, the jingling of harnesses and traces, horses moving in the distance. But she didn't dare look anywhere but at the woman she followed. They paced quickly into the nearby wood, and then walked on the leaf-strewn forest floor for what seemed like a half hour.

They stopped only once, at Meg's urgent request. She saw a likely looking copse of bushes, and asked the gypsy woman if she could have a moment of privacy.

"You sick?" the woman asked.

"No," Meg said. "I just don't like chamber pots."

The woman seemed amused. She waited. When Meg returned, they marched on.

Finally, the woman stopped. She looked around, listened, and finally nodded. "Good," she said in a low voice. "No one is watching. The camp's breaking, no one has time for spying. Stay here. He'll find you." Then she turned and hurried back the way she'd come, leaving Meg alone in a cool, green glade, feeling lost, like a child in a fairy story who had wandered too far from home.

The glade was a small clearing in a wood filled with trees, their leaves showing only the faintest flush of autumnal rust. The day was blooming summer warm, intensifying the scent of acorns, leaf mold and late brambleberries defying the calendar. Blue asters flourished on a sunny slope nearby, but the place where Meg waited was floored with thick, soft moss. It was altogether a beautiful place, she'd have appreciated it more if it weren't far from anyplace she wanted or needed to be.

"You're better this morning," Daffyd said.

Meg whirled around. The moss had muffled his approach. He stood in his shirtsleeves, as his half brother had been last night. But Johnny had been laughing. Daffyd looked calm and enigmatic, and as wickedly handsome as ever. He didn't need starlight or firelight to enhance his looks, Meg thought with a little sigh.

She'd washed her face and brushed her hair, but still wore her crumpled, worn gray gown. Last night he'd seen her most vilely ill. Life was, she thought, sadly, not very fair.

"I'm better," she said. "But that's not a hard thing to be."

"Jug bitten was all you were. You had enough blue ruin to make any man stagger. It just took a while to get to you."

"Blue ruin?" she asked. Her eyes widened. "That was *Geneva*?"

He nodded. "Sky blue, Mother's milk, clap of thunder, flash of lightning, strip me naked. Cheap homemade Geneva, the stuff of dizzy dreams and a worse stomach. But you seemed to like it."

"It tasted like flowers," she said bleakly, "hot flowers."

He smiled.

"Why didn't you warn me?"

He shrugged. "I thought it might be what you wanted. Johnny's a beguiling devil."

"What? It was the taste of the gin, not your half brother's urging that made me drink it." She paled. "Did you think otherwise?" Her voice went up, "Did *he*?"

Daffyd leaned against a tree trunk, crossed his ankles, and snatched a leaf off the tree overhead. "Aye."

"Aye to what?"

"Both," he said, looking down at the leaf. "I thought you knew he was trying to seduce you. I thought you were cooperating."

"*Cooperating*?" she gasped.

"Laughing at everything he said, drinking his liquor like it was nectar. Why shouldn't I think so?"

"Because . . ." She sputtered. "Because I wouldn't. I didn't. I don't. So you let me drink myself silly because you thought I wanted to . . . be with Johnny?"

He nodded. "It was a possibility. Nothing against your morals, Miss Shaw, but I don't really know you, do I? And Johnny's a very seductive lad."

"Well, know this," she said, her hands clenching to fists at her side. "I would *not* do that. And . . . and filling a woman with liquor and grabbing her? That's not seduction!"

He cocked his head to the side and studied her, his eyes catching the tint of the asters behind him. "No? It's true I don't know that many proper females. What's your idea of seduction, then?"

"Well . . ." She hesitated. She knew, of course. She went to church. She'd read novels. She had a vague idea of situations involving soft music and sweet words, false promises, delicate touches . . . and liquor. Her cheeks colored. That seemed to amuse him. It infuriated her. "Never mind," she said. "I just do."

He was far too amused for her comfort. "Who is that woman who took me here? Is she your aunt?" she asked quickly.

"No. My grandmother."

"She looks too young to be that."

"Not to me. Gypsies marry young."

"But why didn't she introduce herself to me? Oh," Meg said, abashed. "She thinks the worst of me and doesn't want to know me, I suppose. I don't blame her. Can we leave, please?"

"We will, in time. She doesn't think the worst of you. She just doesn't want to think of you at all."

"Why didn't she let you come into the caravan to talk with me?" Meg asked curiously. "She said something about you not being able to because of your reputation. Preserving it, I mean."

He nodded. "She spoke true. It's not the time I
spent in the clutches of His Majesty she worries
about. Even an honest gypsy is considered criminal
by the good folk of England. But I'm barely toler-
ated here because of my mixed blood. Poor Keja is
shunned now, too, though she's gypsy back to the
Ark. She's only allowed to travel with the family because she's a healer and they need her. Even so, she
has to keep to the rear of their train. That's because
of her son: my father. He disgraced the family, and
now his sons continue to. Me, because I'm a half
blood and a bastard. Johnny, because he chooses to
walk his own path and it's often a crooked one.
Criminals bring too much attention to the camp for
comfort."

"But I don't understand. If you're already in disgrace, why does she worry about your reputation?"

"Because she still has hopes for me. That's why
she doesn't want me seen with a *gaje*, a non-gypsy
woman, here in camp. That would sink me once and
for all. She wants me to marry. She thinks if I marry
a good gypsy girl, I'll be taken back to the heart of
the family."

"Oh," Meg said, feeling a little deflated. "Well,
that makes sense. Why don't you?"

"Because I don't want to be taken back into the
heart of the family. And because I don't want a
fourteen-year-old bride."

"What?"

"The best ones are taken by the time they're fifteen," he explained. "I told you. They believe in mar-

rying young. And forever. My father didn't, the forever part, that is. He liked the young well enough. Actually, he liked any female well enough. He betrayed Johnny's mother long before he met my mother, and so she left him. A hard man on mothers, my father. Keja was the best thing that happened to me. Because of her, with all that's happened to me, I still appreciate women. But my father returned to the caravan when I was seven, and so I had to leave her. I ran away."

He snatched another leaf from the tree and paid attention to it as he spoke. "Men are the law here. I suppose they are everywhere in England. So Keja had no say in my punishments when I was a boy. My father was a hard man on his sons, too. I saw him dole out punishment to Keja when she stood up for me one day. If he'd done it again, I'd have had to kill him. So I left, and took my chances in London. I survived."

"But didn't your mother have any say in the matter?"

"My mother left me soon after I was born."

Meg struggled for the right words for what she hoped wouldn't be the wrong question.

He understood. Because she hadn't asked, he could tell her. "My mother was—is—as I said, a lady born. She ran away with my father like the lady in that old song. Gypsies know that song, too, but they sing it differently. Their version is the true version. It has the gypsy beheaded by the nobleman. They don't blame the lord for what he did. Only they'd not have only beheaded the rascal who stole the wife, they'd have tossed the straying bitch out if she dared try to crawl back home.

"My mother must have known her husband wouldn't do anything to her. When she decided she had enough of my father she left him and returned to her highborn lord. He took her back. I suppose my gypsy half is stronger, because that shocks me. I'll never understand the nobility."

"And you?" Meg asked quietly. "Why didn't she take you with her?"

He shrugged one shoulder. "I was too much baggage for her. I don't blame her. After all, she knew her husband would let her come back. Whether that was because he was a fool, or in love, or didn't want scandal, I'll never know. He's long dead. But he wasn't a capon. He had some ballocks. He wouldn't have also taken her bastard by another man, and a gypsy, at that. I doubt she ever told him I existed."

He looked up to see Meg looking anguished. He scowled. "But don't weep for me. I prospered, like the wicked usually do."

"I'm sorry I asked you," she said truthfully.

"I'm sorry I answered," he said as truthfully.

They stood in the soft, shifting sun-dappled shadows and looked at each other.

"I don't know what got into me," he finally murmured. He threw away the leaf he'd pleated in his fingers and lifted his shoulders from the tree he'd been leaning against. "Enough of me. What are you going to do now?"

"Me?" she asked, surprised at his sudden change

of subject. "Why, I'll go on with my search for Rosie," she said. She lifted her chin, though her heart sank. It sounded as though he was through with her. "With you or without you."

"Without me?"

"You said your family would help us. If they won't, and you won't, I have to try on my own again. You should understand that."

"And you don't think you'll be plucked like a pigeon? I'd say that was unwise of you."

He walked toward her, stopping when he was only inches away. "I let Johnny ply you with liquor last night because I wasn't going anywhere. I made sure that if you didn't want him you wouldn't have to take him. But whatever happened, at least you'd at last understand why you can't be trusted on your own, and why you don't belong on this chase. Look at you, Meg. I've known a lot of women in my time, and not all of them in what my friend the earl calls the biblical sense, either. I've known tough ones, of course. No other kind survives the slums and prisons, or gypsy camps, for that matter. But highborn females can be as strong. My mother is. If I thought you were like them, I'd agree with your scheme. But you're not. You're not cut out for it."

She stared up into his eyes, her own blazing. "I saved you," she reminded him. "I can think quickly, and act, as well."

He nodded. "True."

"I'm sorry about last night," she said. "But I still must find Rosalind."

"And you still feel competent to do that?"

"I've done some foolish things," she admitted. "But I learn. I shouldn't have gone off with those vile men. I'll never do anything like that again, believe me. I shouldn't have trusted your brother. I certainly won't do anything like that again either. Come to think of it," she said bitterly, "my only problems have come from trusting men. I certainly won't do that again."

His eyes grew sad. "I see. So that's how you came to know so much about seduction."

"What?" She blinked. "Oh, no. You mistake me."

"Then how do you know so much about it?"

She couldn't look in his eyes. He was too close, and her feelings were too jumbled. Instead, she looked past his shoulder.

"Who doesn't know?" she asked. "It's preached from every pulpit. Seduction is when someone makes you want to do something even though you know you shouldn't." She dared to look at him because now she felt on firmer ground. He was watching her quizzically. "Getting a woman drunk and seducing her is making her do something she ordinarily wouldn't, that's true. But that's doing it by unfair means, and that is not seduction. A seducer addles a girl's brains, but not with liquor. He does it with words and gestures and . . . such."

"Oh, I'd say the 'such' is heart of it," he said with a smile in his voice. "I see. You have personal experience of this?"

"Of course not!" she snapped.

He didn't say anything. He just stepped closer. She used every last shred of courage to stand firm, though he was so close she had to lower her eyes because if she'd tried to look at him she was sure her eyes would cross.

"Coward," she felt him whisper into her ear. Her skin thrilled at the slight touch of his breath.

"No," she murmured, still not daring to look.

"No?" he asked, his hand lightly caressing her cheek. "No to what? To this? Or to being a coward?"

"I'm sensible," she said with desperation, opening her eyes and looking directly at him. "Not cowardly. I know you're just trying to make a point. I can protect myself, and you, too, for that matter. But of course I wouldn't strike out at you. Oh, what am I to do with you?"

"Oh, this," he said, bent his head, and covered her lips with his.

She'd been kissed in her time. But not like this. His mouth was soft and firm, warm velvet. It made her own mouth tingle; it made her whole body tingle. Now she could feel his smile.

"Open to me," he whispered against her lips. "You're not a child."

She opened her mouth to tell him she wouldn't, and she wasn't, and she was lost.

His kiss had been warm, now it was hot. She felt the touch of his tongue on her lips, and gasped, and gasped again when she felt it on her own tongue. It was alarming, and thrilling and delicious in ways she'd never imagined. He touched her breast. She wanted to pull away, and stepped toward him. He pulled her closer to his lean, warm body, and kissed her again.

All she could do was follow.

He was all tensile strength, gentle and yet sure, all knowing, too, because he knew just what pleased her. And that was everything he did and was. He tasted of sunlight and forest. He kissed her cheek, her neck, his kisses light and teasing. He only left off so he could kiss her lips again, and then his kisses didn't tease, but were slow and dark and full of darker promises. He slowly lowered her gown so he could move his warm seeking mouth to her breast. All she could do was sigh, and hope he'd stop and pray he wouldn't, all the while promising herself she'd stop, and soon, if he didn't.

He didn't.

Somehow, he'd turned her so her back now rested against the tree. She didn't feel it, she only felt him. One of his hands cupped her bottom so she moved with his body as she clung to him. Though his movements were slow and calculated, she knew he was as excited as she was. She'd never felt anything so wonderful and so terrifying, so perfectly right and utterly wrong. Her heart pounded but she didn't want to stop. Not when he lowered her gown further, not even when he pulled up his shirt so her naked breasts could peak against his smooth, warm, hard chest as his other hand raised her skirts, and stroked her, and moved higher.

But with all it was, it was all new to her, and however delicious it was, it was daylight. And when she opened her eyes she realized who he was and where they were and who she was.

"Daffyd," she said when he moved his mouth to her other breast. She looked down at the dark rainbows spun by the sunlight in his clean soft, inky hair. "Daffyd," she said with a sigh. "Stop."

And he did.

He stood back and looked at her, his eyes darker than the night sky, bluer than asters.

"Stop?"

"Yes," she said. "Of course." She put a hand over her breasts.

He took another step back.

"We can't do this," she said, her eyes on his. "I can't do that. You make it so hard to say so. But it's not right, at least, not for me. I have to go on. I have only this time and these days, and then a whole eternity of days and nights by myself for the rest of my life." She forgot her rumpled state, she was still too linked with him, too involved in what she had to explain to worry about what she would later regret. She wished she dared reach out and touch him, to elicit an expression, any expression she could read. But she was afraid he'd take her hand in his and she'd be lost again.

"I suppose I didn't understand what seduction was," she said, her eyes searching his. "Was that your point?"

He looked at her, his eyes unreadable.

"Well, even if it wasn't, now I understand," she said in a shaky voice. "It has nothing to do with liquor and music, or maybe it does, but it can happen anywhere at any time, can't it? I didn't know. Now I do. You're . . . very good at teaching. But I can't tumble in the moss with a handsome lad. That's not my path, that's not my way. Though I'll confess that now I wish it was and I could. But I have to be realistic. I know the world as it is, and where I fit in it. I have to be above reproach."

One of Daffyd's thin dark eyebrows lifted. "And yet you ran off with me, on your own?"

She bit her lip. "That's a thing I gambled on, hoping no one would find out. So far, no one has."

"Ah," he said. "Right. After all, my grandmother and my brother don't count."

She looked stricken. "That's not what I meant!"

"Still, it's true," he said blandly. "You've been lucky."

"No," she said sadly. "That, I've never been. But as for what just happened . . . Oh, Daffyd, I'm a respectable creature with a long, dull life before me—if luck finally smiles on me. I *must* be this way; I can't make life more difficult than it is. Surely you see that?"

He stepped further back. And at last, he smiled again. "Bravo," he said. "You do learn."

Chapter 9

Daffyd and Meg walked in silence until they came to a clearing near the camp. Then, with no parting word, he stayed in the shadows while she ran to his grandmother's caravan. He waited until she disappeared inside it, and then finally paced away.

He didn't go far, only behind the caravan to tend to his horse.

He curried and brushed until the horse's coat gleamed, and the horse itself was transported to some kind of equine ecstasy.

Daffyd worked until he felt his muscles begin to relax. But his mind didn't. He'd confused himself; he seldom did that. His life had always literally depended on his knowing what he was doing, and why. Had money and good living changed him that much?

Last night he'd been shocked and surprised, and that itself was a huge surprise to him. Today he'd surprised himself again.

He hadn't meant to kiss Miss Margaret Shaw. Yes, she'd looked lovely. And yes, he was a man. And it was also true that she somehow got under his guard, and made him say things he seldom did. But whatever he'd intended, and he was still unsure of that, he hadn't meant to let her surrender carry him away. It had been a long time since he'd been a greedy boy, but the shocking truth was that he'd come within seconds of losing control of himself. If she hadn't stopped him he'd have pleasured her on the soft moss of the forest floor. And he'd never intended that.

Yes, she was delicious, and her tentative, then willing, response had delighted him. But there was more to it than that. There had to be. He never did anything without a reason, and desire had never been reason enough for him to jeopardize his freedom. She was still too well-bred for him to attempt, and he knew that very well.

He'd expected her to pull away sooner. He'd been drawn to her, of course. But he'd allowed himself the embrace because in the back of his mind he supposed he was also trying to teach her a lesson, showing her what could happen to incautious females. And that, because of the uneasy night she'd given him.

It had been hard to sit and watch Johnny spin his web around her. Harder still to see the so proper Miss Margaret Shaw slowly being pulled into that finely woven web of laughter and teasing. But as he'd watched, dumbfounded, she'd taken Johnny's liquor and his jests, and enjoyed them both. She had to have seen the invitation in Johnny's eyes. Still, Daffyd had been unwilling to leave until he knew what she intended to do. It was her choice, after all. So he'd watched and listened. He'd heard her laughter, seen her eyes in the firelight, recognized her fascination, and finally saw her willingly pulled up into his brother's eager arms.

Daffyd had believed everything she'd told him until then, and that was rare enough for him. But she'd always been proper with him. She'd worn those god-awful gray gowns and behaved as if she didn't know or care how attractive she was or could be. Last night he'd finally seen the shape of her young, firm body as she'd stood silhouetted against the leaping firelight, her soft brown hair coming unloosed, her lips parted, staring up into Johnny's sparkling eyes.

Daffyd had gotten to his feet. He'd had enough. He'd appointed himself her protector, but he wasn't a voyeur. He'd felt his gut curdling, and not just because she'd proven herself just another well-born slut out for an adventure. And yet, he'd hesitated.

Should he just walk away if Johnny wanted to bed her and she wanted it, too? He was only responsible for her safety, after all. Sex might be unsafe for a single female, but if she wanted sex with his brother, what should he do? So he'd stood, irresolute. Did she know what she was doing? Had she done it before? And what business was it of his?

And why hadn't she wanted *him*?

Then he'd seen her try to struggle away from Johnny. He'd seen her expression, her sickly pallor, and her confusion. He'd been delighted. It hadn't been so delightful holding her head while she'd been sick. But even that had pleased him last night.

Damned fool of a woman.

But wasn't he a damned fool of a man for caring? Worse, for touching her this morning?

The horse heaved a great, long, gusty sigh of pure bliss as it was curried within an inch of its mortal life again.

Meg stared unseeing at the kaleidoscope of colors inside the gypsy wagon, and wished she could leave. She'd sat alone all morning, growing more morose. But running away without a plan or an idea of how to do it was as stupid as . . . *kissing a man you'd asked to help you*, she thought unhappily.

Because now she couldn't travel on with him, at least not from the gypsy camp. Once she was on the main road she thought she could get back on Rosalind's trail again. But now the thought of traveling anywhere without him was painful, because against all odds, he'd been a thoughtful, knowledgeable companion . . . and because she had grown to like him much too much for her good.

Because when he'd touched her she'd forgotten about her safety. She'd had kisses pressed on her in her time by demanding males: relatives or friends of her various employers. She'd always responded to them with a slap, or with a swift, silent escape if the one who'd stolen the kiss was in a position to harm her reputation. She'd kissed a few fellows of her own free will a few times, too, just so she could know if that made it different from what had been forced on her. Those kisses had been interesting, nothing more. She'd noted the texture of the fellow's lips, the scent of the man, the way he reacted to her. Her mind had been engaged but her body hadn't responded.

Daffyd's kisses bypassed her brain and went straight to her senses. They'd intoxicated her more than Johnny's gin.

Her own reaction to Daffyd's embraces had been harder to fight than any man who'd ever tried to force his kisses on her. She felt threatened and thrilled and loved, all at the same time. But it hadn't been love on his part or hers. It was, she suspected, sheer sensation. She tingled, just remembering.

He hadn't attacked her. She could have resisted, because as soon as she had, he'd let her go. But she hadn't wanted to.

She was no better than he'd thought she was. That was a surprise, one she didn't know how to deal with. Best not to deal with it at all. She knew what she had to do now. The only cure for excess was to remove oneself from the source of desire for it. The aunts had taught her that.

Still, a gypsy and *Margaret Shaw*? Making love? The thought was preposterous. A thief, a pickpocket, an ex convict, and a gypsy, such a man *coupling* with Margaret Shaw? She'd wanted that. She couldn't evade it. It had to be animal passion and base desire, but she hadn't known she had either until he'd kissed her. Still, Meg thought miserably, though she might be a wanton at heart, at least she was an honest one. She admitted that actual lovemaking was what she and Daffyd had been on their way to doing this morning. The thought was appalling, doubly so because she realized how much she'd wanted him this hateful, fateful morning, when she'd discovered her true nature.

However high she'd thought her morals, when Daffyd had put his hands on her body and she'd felt his mouth on hers, the warm, clean, sunny taste and feel of him had amazed her as much as it had dismayed her. And that was considerably. Everything he'd done had felt right, even though, thank God, she'd realized in time how wrong it would be.

To be alone in the world and at the mercy of the aunts would be terrible enough. To not be alone in the world, but saddled with the bastard child of a gypsy thief and at their mercy was something beyond horrible to contemplate. Not every mating ended in pregnancy. But enough did. The world was full of bastard children and fallen females. It was a gamble she could never take.

Few couplings led to declarations of love and fidelity. Those kinds of protestations were usually made before the act. Daffyd had never made any before he'd touched her. He was honest about that. For men, sex was something apart from love. The aunts had told her that, too. She hadn't believed them. It was depressing how right they'd been.

Now it was afternoon and Meg was hours older and felt years wiser. She had to leave here, and fast. But she couldn't leave the caravan, nor could she wander the forest looking for a way back to the road. She had to wait until someone appeared to show her. So when she heard someone entering the caravan she shot to her feet.

"He wants to talk with you," Keja said as she came in a whirl of skirts, bringing the scents of the autumn day as well as a vivid new collection of colors into the caravan.

"Yes," Meg said, snatching up a scarf to throw over her shoulders. "I'm ready to leave."

"Wait," Keja said, easing herself down in a chair. She waved a hand. "Sit. We must first talk."

Meg sat, folded her hands in her lap, and looked at the older woman.

Keja looked back at her. "So," she said, her dark eyes intent. "What do you think of my grandson Johnny?"

Meg blinked. "Oh. Johnny. Well, he seems very nice . . ."

"Yes, nice. Handsome as a ripe blackberry, and jolly too. The girls all think so. You liked his company last night."

Meg's face flushed. "I found him to be very hospitable," she said carefully. "But I didn't understand that what he pressed on me was actually Geneva. That's no excuse, I should have known anything that made me feel so good was spirits, and I ought to have stopped drinking sooner. It made me vilely ill. If it weren't for Daffyd, I suspect it would have been worse." She stopped, her face heating as she wondered how much worse it might have been in so many ways if Daffyd hadn't been there.

"Johnny's a rogue. But there's no great harm in him," his grandmother said, as though reading her thoughts. "Who knows what was intended? Wickedness? Or sport? Men often don't know the difference. It's up to a woman to know. Whatever was meant, no harm was done. But harm could come." She watched Meg for another long moment, and then sighed. "You are not Daffyd's woman. I think that if you go away with him again that may change."

Meg ducked her head. She didn't know how the gypsy knew what had happened in the glade, but didn't doubt she did. When she looked up her eyes filled with more misery than she knew. "That's not his fault. I'm not degenerate," she added, lifting her chin. "But he's right, I know very little of the world."

"Yet you trusted a stranger enough to go with him, alone. No decent gypsy woman would have."

"Neither would any decent female I know," Meg whispered. "But I was desperate. I had to, and he turned out to be worthy of my trust. He's never offered me insult. He's a man of his word, and never lied to me."

"No, he's not a liar when he doesn't have to be." Keja leaned forward. "But you knew he is half gypsy, which is half too much for your people, and he is a criminal, or was one, which is the same in the eyes of your world. So why did you go with him?"

"My future depended on it."

Keja nodded. "Daffyd said you were well-born. You are a lady?"

Meg laughed. "Oh, no. My father and mother were connected to some titled persons, back along the line. I have an education because of that, but no funds at all. My father didn't have much and my mother's jointure stopped when she passed on. My aunts own property and have position in their community, but no, I'm not a 'lady.'" She smiled. "Ladies don't work for their supper. Still, I suppose my name wouldn't be sneered at in places where such things matter."

"If all that is so, why did you ask to accompany my Daffyd?"

Meg sat very still.

"You say you are a good woman," Keja persisted, "so how can this be?"

"Because he's also a good man," Meg said. "And I had no choice. No. I suppose I did. I trusted him. And I did well, because he's never let me down."

Keja grunted. "No, he would not. You are wise in some ways if not others. My Daffyd *is* a good man. He was a good boy, too. Life has never been fair to him. His mother left her husband to run off with my son. She *was* a highborn lady, married to a great nobleman. She was rich and spoiled, like a child. When she saw Daffyd's father, she had to have him. She was not used to not having her way. Neither was he."

"I am not rich or spoiled," Meg protested.

"Did I say so? This is not about you. I thought it

might be, but it is different. I'm telling you about
Daffyd. The lady came to live with me. It was a great
shame, and a disgrace for me, because she was an
outsider and my son already had a wife. It made us
marhime, unclean. You understand? Whatever you
gajes say about the Rom, we have strict rules of behavior. And so we were banished. . . .

"But the gypsy is also compassionate. There was
an infant coming. A gypsy alone is never safe in any
land. And I had a certain standing with my people.
Still, we had to leave the caravan and follow along
far behind it, like whipped dogs hoping for forgive-
ness. Just as well. There was to be more disgrace.
When the lady whelped she ran off and left Daffyd
with his father. I wish his father had run off, too. He
was not a good man—even I do not say he was."

The older woman sighed. "Johnny, at least, had
his mother's clan to escape to. Daffyd only had me
and his father. I could only try to stop things from
getting worse. When I couldn't anymore, and I saw
Daffyd had grown wit and strength enough to fend
for himself, I packed his bag and told him to go, and
made sure that he could, in safety. He'd never have
gotten far without my help."

"But he was only seven years old!" Meg protested.

"Old enough to be hanged for killing his father,"
Keja said coldly. "And he would have. Someone else
did that, with a knife, years later, and it was deserved. But at least Daffyd does not have that on his
head or heart." She pulled back her hair to show Meg
the long scar on her forehead. "I earned that for tak-

ing Daffyd's part against his father. That was when I knew Daffyd had to go. I saw it in his eyes when he looked at his father. Sometimes we must throw our treasure away so we can save it."

Meg didn't know what to say.

Keja nodded. "I heard from Daffyd through the years. He did badly, and then he did well. He can still go down either path. But you're right. He is not a bad man; and he is a man of his word. A woman could do worse than to trust him. But I would not trust any man too far. Well," she said, slapping her knees as she got to her feet. "Are you ready for company?"

"Oh, yes," Meg said, rising as well.

The woman turned. "Stay. Most of the caravan has gone, the others are too busy preparing to leave to care about what happens here. I will send him to you."

Meg paced, preparing herself, trying to think of how to act with Daffyd. She refused to act shamed; she wouldn't try to excuse herself. She wouldn't mention their embraces at all. She'd simply ask him to escort her to the nearest coaching stop, and then be on her way. Wherever that was.

"Miss Shaw?" a deep voice asked.

She wheeled around to see Johnny standing in the doorway.

He was dressed as decently as any young man she might see strolling along a country lane, in a long jacket, breeches, and half boots. He had a white neckcloth, not a colorful scarf, tied round his neck, and wore a soft floppy hat on his head.

"Keja said I owe you an apology," he said, bowing.

"And so I do. I didn't know you had no experience of jacky-gin," he explained with a grin. "But I meant no harm . . . although it's true I hoped it might soften your heart because I was very taken with you." He clapped his hat to his chest, as though smitten. His eyes sparkled as he added, "And I am very particular when it comes to the ladies."

She had to laugh, because he was already laughing at himself.

He was pleased. "Oh, I'm of no account and up to no good, and all of that's true. But I wouldn't have so much as offered you my hand if I'd thought you were Daffyd's woman."

"I'm not!" she yelped.

He shrugged. "As you will. Anyway, I'm glad you don't bear a grudge."

"It would hardly matter if I did," she said simply. "I doubt we'll meet again."

"I wouldn't bet on that, Miss Shaw. And I'll bet on almost anything. But I wish you well, and hope I see you again, and again. Please, to spare me my grandmother's cane on my back, kindly say you forgive me."

She smiled. "I do."

His dark face suddenly grew serious. "I'm still at your service, you know. Why not? You're sweet and very lovely, and no fool. And you're a lady even if not a lady born, which is interesting. I'm your man if you're looking for fun, because I don't take much seriously. Now, Daffy, well, he's had a hard time of it, and it's made him a hard man. But he's come out of it generous, and fair, and you can't ask more of any-one. He was a good boy and could be a good man. So, if you're looking for excitement the way his mother was, or wanting an adventure with a rogue of a gypsy lad, then take me, because I have no heart to lose and can show you a good time, with no regrets."

She stared, then stammered, "But no . . . that's not what I'm after . . ."

"Then good or bad, let the fates decide, and I hope they're on your side. Travel easy and swiftly, and with luck," he said, bowed again, and left the caravan.

Meg stood thinking. Johnny had exerted himself for her. He was bright, handsome in his own way, and like his brother, he could be charming when he wished. But unlike his brother, she sensed no hidden depths to him. More important, she didn't find her-self wanting to look for any. When he left she found it hard to remember him. Looking at Daffyd was like staring into the fire or a bright lamp. When she looked away, she found he always left his afterimage burned into her mind.

She was still standing, frowning, as Daffyd ducked into the caravan.

His expression was dark. "He apologized to you?" he asked.

"Johnny? Oh, yes, though it wasn't necessary."

"It was. You want me to apologize, too?"

"No," she said quickly, not pretending to misun-derstand. "It was my fault as much as yours."

He nodded. "So, what do you want to do?"

He was dressed for riding, immaculate and cool as any gentleman out for a morning's canter. But his dark blue eyes were guarded, and he wore no expression.

She took a deep breath. "I have seven days left. Actually, six and a half now. I want to find Rosalind. That hasn't changed. I was hoping you could still help me, that is, if what happened this morning can be forgotten."

His teeth were a sudden slash of white in his dark face. "No, it can't be forgotten. How could it? Come, Meg, seriously. Can you forget how it was?"

She bit her lip. "No. But it can't happen again. Surely you see that? Can we go on as we were?"

"Of course not."

She nodded. "Then can you take me to the next coaching stop so I can go on by myself?"

"That would be folly," he said. "All right. How about we go on, if not as we were, then with the knowledge of what happened as well as what could happen? That is to say, we go on carefully. I don't want to be compromised any more than you do, Meg."

"But no one will fight for my honor," she said. "I wouldn't tell a soul, and even if I did, no one would force you into anything."

"Oh," he said coldly. "Then you think *I* have no honor?"

She fell silent.

"Look you, Meg. I want to find your runaway too. Remember? You made some good points when you argued to come with me. Now it occurs to me that you *are* the only one who could recognize her no matter how she disguises herself. You're still valuable to me. I've gotten some interesting news and some new paths to follow. So. Shall we resume our quest? That is, if you can keep your hands off me?"

Her eyes flew wide. "I certainly can!" she cried. "I, after all, was *not* the one who approached you, I only . . . agreed to what you proposed . . . silently," she added meticulously.

"All right then, we'll go on, warily. There's nothing like an added degree of difficulty to add spice to a chase. Be ready to ride in a half hour," he said, and grinning, left the caravan.

Leaving Meg to pack her meager belongings again, and wonder just exactly which chase he meant.

Chapter 10

An hour later, Daffyd said good-bye to Keja and Johnny. Meg thanked them for their hospitality. Then Meg and Daffyd got on their horses and rode away from the gypsy caravan. They rode across the long meadow, up a low hill, and then down back to the main road. The path seemed so simple now by daylight that Meg was embarrassed for the hours she'd sat waiting for an escort back to the world again. But she was glad of it. Though they didn't speak this morning, there was comfort in having Daffyd with her.

There wasn't much traffic on the road. She could turn her face up to the pale sunlight, listen to the birdsong, and breathe deep of the clean fresh air without worrying. Night would come and she thought that then she might worry about where she was going and especially about who she was going with, but that was hours away.

"We'll keep going south, by southwest," Daffyd finally said.

Meg looked at him.

"Rumor has the runaway going that way. And gypsy rumor is as good as *gaje* fact," he added.

"So we're close?" she asked eagerly.

"I don't know. Maybe. But the closer we come to the coast, the farther away they could be. Once they go to sea, we've lost them. I'll track them to the shore, but I won't go farther." He looked at her curiously. "Will you follow them over the water?"

"Oh, no! That would be folly."

"And this isn't?" he asked with a crooked smile.

"No. I still have a chance of keeping my journey secret. If I shipped out, that chance would be gone. And what good would it do? It would be weeks before I could get word to her father, and by then the damage would be well and truly done. And what would become of me? I know I acted rashly coming this far. Any farther would be absolute folly."

His smile faded. He slowed his horse. "Meg," he said. "Listen. We're coming to an inn just up the road. We'll stop for luncheon there. Then, if I hear what I expect, I may go somewhere else. But this time, if you came with me you'd be noticed. So you have two choices. You can come to the inn and wait for me to return. But I can't promise when that will be. So you can choose not to wait and go on by yourself, wherever you wish. You're in your world now. It's your decision."

"You mean where you're going, there may be people I know?"

He stopped. "I doubt it. But your name may be recognized."

"So, can't you call me something else? I mean, tell them I have a different name?"

"No. This is a place where I tell the truth. Anyway, how else could I introduce you?"

He looked at her. She wore her usual gray gown. It was crumpled from hours of riding. She'd loosed her bonnet; it hung from its strings on her back. Her soft brown hair was escaping its ribbon. Her cheeks were rosy in the sunlight, and he saw tracings of a few faint new freckles on the bridge of her nose. She looked like a recently ravaged puritan. He smiled.

"You're not dressed like a fancy piece," he said. "No self-respecting bar wench would wear that gown. You don't look like a gypsy. So why would you be traveling with me?"

She looked down at herself, and colored up. "I could borrow a flat iron at the inn, and freshen up," she said quickly.

He shook his head. "And so you'd be a respectable lady's companion with a false name? Traveling with *me*? Why? Believe me, if you lie, much worse would be thought of you than if you tell the truth. I trust the man we'll be seeing. But he has servants and may have guests, so I can't promise you absolute secrecy. So?"

She thought for a long moment. "Is it that you think you might have to ride on immediately after you see him?"

"I don't know."

"I see." She looked at him steadily. "Or are you telling me you don't want me along? You can come right out and say it, you know." Her lips curved up in a smile. "You've done it before. I'm not saying I'd accept that now either. But you could tell me."

"I am," he said. "In fact, it's just the opposite. There's a slight—only a slight—chance your Rosalind might be staying with him, and if so, I'd want you there to identify her. But you have to know that if you do, you might be ruined. Really ruined. Word might get out. Traveling with any man would sink you. Being with me isn't something that would impress the baron even if you found her."

She sighed. "I know. But I've made my bed. Let's eat," she said. "And then let's go find her."

The inn was small and very old, but it was clean and the landlord pleased to have them. Meg was happy to get off the horse, and happier still to find a maid willing to go over her gown with a flat iron. She paid for the use of a room to wash and change in, gave her good gown to the maid, and came down to luncheon in it, feeling better about her appearance than she had in days.

A small anteroom to the side of the common room served as the inn's dining parlor. It had a low ceiling and a tilted floor, but it was bright. Small, ancient diamond-paned windows, too warped with age to show anything but the light from outside, made the room glow. And Daffyd was there, and just the sight of him made Meg glow.

He rose from the table when she appeared, and though it was only a small courtesy, it did a lot to make her feel better. He, too, had changed his clothes. He'd brushed his jetty hair, and wore a well-tied neckcloth, fitted jacket, clean linen, buff breeches, and shining half boots.

Meg took her seat, her pleasure suddenly diminished. She realized she looked like a poor relation or a servant that he was accompanying. His attitude had changed with his clothing. He acted the complete gentleman now. He seemed more distant, languid, both more civil and cooler. He wore the subtly amused expression of a man of taste and fortune. Nothing about him reminded her of the man who'd held her in his arms this very morning and kissed the wits from her. Nothing, except for that finely shaped mouth, and those dark blue eyes set in his grave, handsome face. So she looked down at the table instead of at him, lest he see that memory in her own eyes.

Daffyd wondered at her uncharacteristic silence. He hoped she wasn't getting sick. She looked fine to him. She'd brushed her hair until it gleamed and tied it up at the back of her head. She looked neat and clean and entirely respectable. But she didn't look like any respectable female he'd ever seen. Because she hadn't been able to scrub away the peach tint the sun had kissed onto her cheeks, and nothing could dim the glow in her big brown eyes as she parted those plump pink lips in a shy smile at last when she looked up to see him watching her. She was dressed dry and dull as a prune, with no ornament at all, but she looked delicious.

He frowned. What was he thinking? She was well enough, but no temptress. Yes, she was a charming young woman; but he'd known exquisite ones. She was refreshing, but he'd had exotic and erotic lovers and companions. Obviously, he'd passed too much time alone in her company. The truth was, they had nothing in common but the needs of their bodies, and his need was growing stronger every day. Just as well they were bound for a change. It would clear his head and put the little governess-companion in the proper—and he did mean proper—perspective for him.

She nodded at everything the landlord suggested for their luncheon, from soup to fish, beef, mutton, fowl, and at last, tarts and cheese.

"The riding sharpened my appetite," she explained when the landlord left them. "I'm famished." Her eyes widened. She sat upright and corrected herself quickly. "Which is not to say that I didn't enjoy your grandmother's food. It was very good, and so generous of her to share it."

"She could do no less," Daffyd said with a shrug. "She's Rom."

"And I'm grateful for it," Meg said. "It was wonderful to taste new things, too. But I also do like a traditional luncheon."

Traditional for a field worker, Daffyd thought, remembering her order. But, "I don't blame you," he said. "The Rom have so little that they excel at spicing up their lives and menus. Herbs and spices can make anything taste good, and many can be found in the forest. But there's much to be said for plain English cooking. Myself, I eat everything. I didn't have any choice for too many years. But I have my preferences, too."

"What did they serve in prison?" Meg asked curiously. "What did you eat in New South Wales?"

"Whatever I could get," he said abruptly.

Meg grimaced and hoped she hadn't offended him. "The aunts say I eat like a biblical locust," she said quickly, trying to lighten the subject and his expression. "I expect they're right. I know the rest of what they say is true: I'll start to get so fat I'll have to spend the rest of my days sipping tea and daring to eat a bit of toast," she added with what she hoped was a contagious laugh.

He didn't laugh with her. "I'm sorry," she said softly. "I oughtn't to have asked. It must be a painful subject for you."

He looked at her. "What?"

"I mean, those days you spent in the slums and prisons."

He laughed. "No. Why should it bother me? That's most of my life. I was only thinking it's sad that a woman has to defend her appetites, while a man can brag about them. So. What was it you wanted to know?"

"Just about what you ate. You never talk about those days. But if you don't want to, I quite understand."

"Which days?" he asked. "When I lived in the slums? The prisons? When I was in Newgate, or the Hulks? On the ship to Botany Bay? In Port Jackson? I can tell you all of it. In the slums, we ate what we could afford to buy or be lucky enough to steal. Street food, meaning meat pasties and cakes, things that can be boiled in tubs of water or oil that are hot and cheap and filling, can be very good. Sometimes I find myself hungry for all those fried bits and pieces of anything anyone with money would throw away. Speaking of that, street food, meaning things found in gutters or behind shops, can either be nourishing or poisonous. If you eat them you have to be wise, or lucky.

"In the prisons, we ate whatever the guards gave us and guessed even they didn't know what it was. On the ships, we ate whatever we could hold down. In new South Wales? Worse than that, at first. But the menu improved with our fortunes."

"I'm sorry I brought it up if it makes you uneasy," she said sincerely.

"It doesn't."

"But you never talk about what you went through," she persisted.

"I suppose I don't. What's the point? I don't want to go back even in my imagination. I'll tell you one thing: you learn to store good memories and feed off them in bad times, not the reverse, if you want to survive."

"What were the good memories?"

He laughed. "That's what I'm looking for now. Don't look so sad, Meg. I'll find them. Now these," he added, as a serving girl came in bearing a basket heaped with fragrant hot breads, "will certainly be some of them."

They dined. Daffyd watched Meg and was as entertained by her as he was by what the landlord brought out. Once again, she ate steadily and neatly. He'd seen starving women eat, and that wasn't a thing he liked to remember. He'd seen fine ladies deign to dine, and had grown impatient with the way they picked at good food. But Meg ate with manners and gusto, and continued to amuse him with polite chatter. He found himself wondering if she would make love with the same civility, grace, and zest. The thought made him turn his attention to his roast beef, because he knew there were some hungers best left unsatisfied.

Meg reveled in the luncheon, but only partly because the food was so good. She found it even more delicious to share a meal with someone who could hold up a conversation. Daffyd might be short spoken, but what he said was to the point, and he seemed genuinely interested in what she was saying. But she concentrated on her plate and his answers, and not his expressions. Because what she sometimes saw in his dark blue eyes took her breath and her appetite away, replacing them with a need for things she'd never be served this day.

"That," Meg finally said, when she'd finished, "was wonderful. But I don't think I'll be able to ride for at least an hour."

"We have no choice," Daffyd said, rising from his chair. "We have to go. Don't worry. It's not far, and not difficult. We'll be on the main road most of the way, and there long before dinner, so you won't have to starve, either."

Meg suppressed a sigh as she got up. She didn't feel like bucketing onward on a horse now; she felt like sitting in the sunlight and basking like a lizard. But she said nothing as she went out the door with him.

A curricle stood waiting behind a team of horses in the front yard. Daffyd gave a coin to the lad who had brought it around, and held out his hand to Meg. "Ready?" he asked her.

"But where are the horses?"

"We travel by carriage now," he said. "I rented this one. I prefer to arrive where we're going in some style. We can get horses later—if we need them."

Her eyes grew wider. "You mean, we may be *that* close to Rosalind?"

"We may."

She took his hand and stepped up into the curricle, swept her skirt around her legs and sat up straight. "Then hurry, please!"

"That eager to be rid of me?" he asked as he settled beside her and picked up the whip.

She turned a troubled face to his. "I didn't mean

that. I just want to find her and be done with this, and get on with my life again."

And then she fell still, thinking of that life. If all went as she hoped, she'd soon be back at the baron's house, cleared of all guilt, maybe even rewarded. She'd be able to go on in her position as companion—until Rosalind married. Then she'd go on to a new position.

She'd find a new job, then another, and so on until she grew too old, and then if she were lucky, she'd retire to a cottage. If she was very lucky, she might meet a decent man with small expectations and make a home with him before that. But she suddenly knew that wherever she went and whatever she found, none of it would be as strange, exciting, dangerous, and unexpectedly sweet as these last few days had been. Her chance-met gypsy had helped her. But he'd also poisoned her dreams, forever.

"Change your mind?" he asked, seeing her expression. "Want to wait here?"

"Oh, no."

"Then why so sad?"

She turned her eyes to his. "Not sad. It's just that I realized that our search may really be over."

His expression didn't change. True, he thought. So, they'd part. He wouldn't see her again. How could he? Why should he? "Let's go," he said, touched the horses with a whip, and they were off down the road.

They rode quietly for a half hour, Daffyd obviously deep in thought. But a half hour was as long as Meg could maintain silence.

"This is better than riding horseback," she finally said. "And the carriage is well sprung, so I can't complain. But I'm starting to worry. Can you tell me anything about where we're going?"

"No place to worry about."

"But you said there may be people there who would know me."

"Maybe. My brother may or may not have company. He's a sociable sort, so you never know."

"Oh!" she said with relief, only a little annoyed at his idea of a jest. "So, we're meeting up with the caravan again?"

"No," he said. "I won't be seeing Johnny for a while. But he gave me some news. Your Rosalind surfaced recently. She left the fields and haymows and is traveling in plain sight. I suppose the closer she gets to the sea the safer she feels. There's reason to believe she may have stopped off at my brother's place. He entertains anyone who amuses him."

"Oh," Meg said nervously. "You mean we're going to see one of your adopted brothers? One of the earl's three . . ." She paused and bit her tongue.

Daffyd laughed. "One of the earl's 'three disgraces,' as the nobs in the *ton* named us when we first appeared on the scene with enough money to make them turn green? No. We're not so lucky today. Both my adopted brothers are recently married. My brother Christian lives near the earl's estate; my old mate and brother Amyas, in Cornwall. They're both building their nests. This is a different relative. A blood relative."

"Oh," Meg said, and felt relieved, yet curiously cheated. So they'd go to another gypsy camp. At least, she knew how to behave in one now.

"Yes," Daffyd said, as he turned the carriage off the road and down a long tree-lined drive. "Another person who won't turn us away."

They drove on. Meg tried to relax and not anticipate the future. Finally, Daffyd came to a fork in the road. He turned right and went down a pebbled drive until they came to a small stone cottage. It sat by an iron gate that cut off access to the rest of the drive.

He stopped the carriage. "Ho!" Daffyd called, "Gateman!"

It was a charming cottage, Meg thought, with a small garden bursting with flowers in front, and a rolling meadow in back where cows grazed. She sat still and hoped she looked demure and presentable. A young man came loping out of the cottage and approached the carriage.

He didn't look much like Daffyd, or Johnny, for that matter. He wasn't very attractive, with a shock of sandy hair, jug ears, and spots. Though his complexion was dark, it was ruddy, obviously from the sun. Meg pasted a smile on her lips. Johnny's father must have ranged far.

"Open the gate," Daffyd said.

"Says who?" the young man asked.

Meg decided it was an old joke with them.

"Says Daffyd," Daffyd said in bored tones. "Daffyd, the gypsy. Go tell his lordship, and be quick about it."

The young man gave him a sulky look, but nonetheless went back to the cottage.

"So he's not your brother?" Meg dared whisper.

"Lord, no!" Daffyd said.

The young man emerged a few minutes later. "I sent word to the main house," he said grudgingly, then disappeared into the cottage again.

"We're going to visit your sponsor, the earl?" Meg asked Daffyd fearfully. The earl of Egremont was reputed to be wise, if eccentric. But any man falsely sent to prison, exiled, and then restored to his title and riches and lauded for it, had reason to be odd. Still, an *earl*!

She'd counted herself lucky to have been taken into a baron's household. Not for the first time, she wished she had a better gown to wear, and looked more presentable. She also suddenly wished she'd never embarked on this mad adventure. All her rationalizations for being here came crumbling down. It was one thing to explain herself to a gypsy. How would she look to an earl?

They waited in silence, Meg thinking of a dozen ways to try to make herself seem respectable.

The young gatekeeper appeared again. He scowled as he marched to the winch at the side of the gates. "You're to go straight in," he said, bending to the wheel and straining at the winch until the great gate began to rise. "His lordship says as to how he was expecting you."

"He always is," Daffyd commented, and flipped a coin to the gatekeeper as he drove through.

Whatever the man had thought of his visitor, he plucked the coin from the air quickly enough.

Meg was awed to silence as Daffyd drove down the long, twisting drive. A great architect had obviously engineered it; she'd read about such. The estates near the aunts' had such roads leading to them, although she'd never walked or driven very far up them. This, like other such grand entrances, was a road that curved and snaked, and doubled back so as to keep showing an estate's most spectacular views. Such roads weren't constructed for easy access; they were for visitors who always had time to spare.

They passed huge walls of rhododendron, got glimpses of fountains in the distance, passed a waterfall that spewed into a stream that twisted and chuckled beside the road until it ran beneath a bridge they crossed and then left them altogether. They went over another bridge, this one Oriental, and up a hill, and then under an arch, then straight and then sideways. Then Meg got her first view of a great red house with wings to either side surrounding a shining white oval of a front drive. She lost sight of it a few times more, and then the carriage drove straight up the drive, and stopped.

Meg's breath did, too.

The manor house was more elegant than any

home she'd ever seen up close. And home it was, because as they stopped, the front door opened, and servants in green-and-white livery came spilling down the stairs.

But all her attention was on the man who emerged, stood in front of the door, then came running lightly down the stairs to greet them. He was dressed exquisitely, like a beau on the strut in London, not a gentleman in the countryside. His tightly fitted green jacket was opened to show an exquisitely tied high white neckcloth with an emerald at his throat. He also had on a shirt of fine white linen, a gold embroidered waistcoat, dark breeches covering his long legs without a wrinkle, and high shining boots. A quizzing glass hung from a golden chain around his neck.

He was tall and very thin, and his light brown hair shone silver in the afternoon sun. His face was lean, his skin pale, his nose long and elegant, and he wore a smile on his long, curling mouth. He was much too young to be the earl of Egremont, though clearly he was master here. Still, Meg thought, such a man would seem to be master anywhere he was.

She'd never seen him before, but his eyes were familiar. They were dark and amused. As he neared and looked up at them, the sunlight showed them to also be dark blue.

"Daffyd! Welcome to my humble abode," he said in a purring drawl.

"Humble, my Romany bottom," Daffyd scoffed. "If it gets any more humble, Prinny will try to take it from you. Good to see you, your lordship. May I present my traveling companion?"

"You certainly must!" the gentleman said.

"This is my traveling companion Miss Margaret Shaw. And Margaret, here is Leland Grant, the Viscount Haye."

"Margaret? Such a strict name. But you must let me call you Meg," the gentleman said, smiling up into Meg's astonished eyes.

"No, she mustn't," Daffyd said as he jumped down from the curricle. "She's not my fancy piece, or anyone's, for that matter. She really is just a traveling companion."

"There's a story behind this. I adore it!" the viscount said. "Trust you, Daffyd, to liven up my humdrum existence."

He embraced Daffyd. And to Meg's shock, Daffyd went willingly into that embrace, and returned it, before he thumped the viscount's back and stepped away.

"Well met," Daffyd told him, with a genuine smile.

"And about time, you utter rogue," the viscount said. "I've been perishing from *ennui*, you dog. So if you love me, my dear brother, tell me all!"

Chapter 11

$\sim\!\!\infty\!\!\sim$

"*Half* brother," Daffyd corrected the viscount.

Meg still sat in the carriage, staring down at the two men in shock. One brother was tall and fair, relaxed and obviously amused. The other was lean and dark, tense as an oncoming storm.

"Half is as good as a whole," the viscount told Daffyd. "Better, in fact. Because I'm pleased to call you brother and cannot feel that way about my other wretched sibling, as you well know."

"Don't say that in front of your mama," Daffyd said.

"*Our* mama," the viscount said. "And why ever not? It's not as though she doesn't know."

"Knowing, and being reminded again and again,

are two different things," Daffyd said. "One's truth, the other's spite."

"True," the viscount said. "Your point. But since when are you so compassionate toward her? Is there something I don't know?"

"No. It's just that I don't like being reminded of my connection to her anymore than she does. I thought you were in her good graces."

"No more than you, Daffy, my dear. I've told you that. How tiresome to repeat oneself. You're quite right about that."

"My apologies," Daffyd said without a hint of apology in his voice.

Meg was too busy trying to assimilate the fact that these two men were related to listen to their banter. *Brothers?* she thought, as she saw the lean and languid viscount beaming at Daffyd. This was Daffyd's *brother*? Not only did they not look alike, but the viscount was as foppish as a fashionable fellow from her grandfather's day.

"Do come down from your high perch, my dear Miss Shaw," the viscount said, as though he'd heard her thoughts. "I promise I'm not so wicked as whatever my brother told you."

"She's no fool. If I'd told her anything about you she wouldn't have come this far," Daffyd said, and held his hand out to her.

Meg took it and stepped down from the curricle in a daze.

The viscount noted it. "You didn't tell her everything, you monster. Because she obviously didn't even know we were related. Such a clever little face she has, but every thought and emotion is writ clear on it. You'll have to guard her here. Or else," he added with a wicked smile, "I'll be forced to do it. My dear," he told Meg, "welcome." He swept her a courtly bow. "I am Daffyd's older, and so very much wiser, brother."

She sketched a curtsy. "I didn't know," she said.

"No, how should you?" the viscount said, taking her hand and putting it on his arm. "Daffyd's a clam. *So* unlike me. I wear my heart and my history on my sleeve. Which makes him all the more fascinating, don't you agree? I wish I could master the art of being uncommunicative and gruff. It captivates the ladies. Ah well, I must do what I can with what I am: a merry Andrew. Come," he said, as he began walking her to the stairs that led to his front door, "I've the most charming room for you."

He paused, and looked over her head at Daffyd, who was pacing along beside her. "You *do* want separate rooms? Or should I just dust off a suite for the two of you?"

"Separate," Daffyd said curtly. "As I sent to you. She and I are cooperating on a hunt. Nothing else."

"You disappoint me, brother. And here I thought you had exquisite taste," the viscount said with a curling smile.

"I do," Daffyd said. "But so does she. Unfortunately for me."

That tickled the viscount. He was very merry as he led Meg up the stairs. He told her about her room, and promised her a delightful visit. He was urbane and charming, and made her feel that she was an equal, even in her horrid gown. He was light-natured and full of jests. She wondered if he was always so amused. And then, remembering whose brother he was, she wondered if he was really amused at all.

Her room was exquisite. But then, everything in the viscount's house was. What Meg had seen of the place was as elegant as any stately home she'd ever seen, although, admittedly, she'd seen most of them in books. And yet she'd heard the viscount refer to it as his "little country nest." It took a great many birds to feather this nest, she thought. She'd seen beautiful furniture and valuable curios, it seemed to her there were servants everywhere: all smiling, all ready and willing to run to do her bidding.

It was too bad, Meg thought grumpily, as she sat on the cushioned window seat in her room, that she had no bidding to do.

She washed and refreshed herself as best she could. She had nothing better to wear, nothing that suited any place in this house outside of the servants' quarters. No, not even there, she thought glumly, because the maids' uniforms were prettier.

Now, gazing out the window, looking down at the long swathe of lawn, she could see formal flower gardens to the right, with trellises and arches over the lanes that ran through it, all covered with late roses in full bloom. There was a knot garden to the left, looking like a bit of green tapestry from a medieval manuscript.

And in the distance straight ahead, she could see a huge dark green maze. It staggered her when she realized what it was. She'd read about them, but had never encountered one in reality. She couldn't see the heart of it even from her high window, but it was clearly a living, growing, symmetrical, intricate maze.

Meg had seen the rich at play in theaters and at balls. She'd seen their fine clothes, expensive carriages, and hordes of servants. But she envied none of it so much as she did the very idea of a maze. That seemed to her to be the ultimate luxury. She was boggled at the thought of anyone having enough money and free time to devote themselves to constructing a living game, a giant puzzle, on their grounds for their visitors to play in. The maze could have been built generations ago, but it took time and money to maintain, and wasn't a thing one would likely ever use more than once or twice. After all, if you knew the secret of your own maze, why would you go into it again? It was a perfectly glorious and absolute waste of money, done to show the world you could do it.

She'd have loved to go downstairs and lose herself in the maze, just once. But she didn't budge. Because she could also see people strolling in the gardens below. She saw the tops of ladies' parasols looking like fantastic pastel blooms bobbing on their shoulders as they meandered through the gardens. She saw gentlemen in high beaver hats, swinging their walking sticks as they picked their way down the crushed shell pathways.

She knew she looked as much like the viscount's other company as his strolling peacocks looked like the sparrows that squabbled in the trees outside her window.

So she waited, because Daffyd had said he'd find out more about Rosalind here. She didn't know why he'd say such a thing, but in the brief time she'd known him she'd learned not to doubt him. And whatever he learned here might bring her closer to the end of their journey. Meg rested her forehead against the windowpane. Well, if Daffyd was right, Rosie might be near, Meg thought. And if she was, she'd write to the baron, tell him where his runaway daughter was, and then . . . and then? He'd want to know how she knew.

She'd have to swear Rosie to secrecy when she found her.

But what if Rosie wanted to stay with her lover, and never planned to return? Well, then she'd leave immediately, go to her old governess's cottage as she'd said she'd done, and write to Rosalind's parents from there, saying she'd heard where Rosie was.

But maybe Rosie had had enough and wanted to go home. Then she'd be something of a heroine for finding her, and they could surely invent something to save the day for both of them.

But that wouldn't be likely.

And so now, sitting in a nobleman's gracious estate miles from her home, and worlds away from where she belonged, with only a few days left to pursue Rosalind, Meg finally admitted that she'd gone on this mad quest for reasons other than the one she'd told Daffyd, and herself.

Because now she saw that from the moment Rosalind had disappeared, she'd known her days of relative freedom were over. And so she'd run away as surely as Rosie had done. Only she'd done it because she'd wanted some adventure in her life before her inevitable retirement to the aunts'.

Meg swallowed hard. That didn't remove the cold lump blocking her throat, or the one sitting on her heart. The revelation hurt, but it didn't come as a shock. She supposed she'd known it all along in the back of her mind. Once Rosalind had run away, Meg had seen her own future running down the drain. She'd pursued because she'd wanted to wrest something from life before it all ended, in so many ways, for her.

Daffyd's kisses had opened her eyes in more ways than one. They made her see that there was only so far she could go, and only so much freedom she could enjoy. That had opened the door to her admitting the rest. And so now, here in the lap of luxury, where she didn't belong, Meg finally admitted that she hadn't belonged anyplace she'd been since the moment she'd left the baron's house.

And so it was no wonder that when the maidservants came to her door, they found the viscount's newest guest to be more morose and defeated-looking than any guest they'd ever met before.

"Oh, miss," one of them cried, as she curtsied to her. "Never you mind about your lost bags! The master, he sent to the village and got you some fine new gowns, although not half so fine as you're used to, being as how they're village made, but they'll do until we can get better—you'll see, they'll do. We'll help make sure they will."

The other maid grinned, and held out her arms to show Meg what she carried. She had three gowns neatly draped over her outstretched arms. One was deep coral, another celestial blue, and the third was leaf green. From what Meg could see they were simply styled, but so all gowns were these days: muslin or cotton, either short- or long-sleeved, with skirts that drifted down from high, ribbon-bound waists. But as with most things, taste and money made their presence felt. These gowns showed their line and style, even laid out as they were. Simple the gowns might be, but even Meg could tell they were expensive.

"Oh, no," Meg said. "I couldn't."

"Oh, miss," the first maid said. "You must! The master says so, and so does your friend, Mr. Daffyd. They want you to come down to join them for tea, and you can't in what you're wearing. I mean, begging your pardon, miss, but it's not your fault that your bags were lost on the coach. And it won't be the first time we've had to scurry to fit out a guest when that happened, will it?"

Meg hesitated. It was social death for a woman to accept any item of clothing from a man that was larger or more intimate than a lady's fan. But she wasn't a lady. And it wasn't as if Daffyd was the one giving clothes to her. The viscount wasn't a beau, only her host. And most of all, she'd be gone from here in a matter of hours. So just this once . . .

"Well," Meg said, eyeing the coral gown with longing. "I suppose, if it's made clear that I'm only borrowing until my bags are found . . ."

"Oh, good!" the maids said in unison.

"Miss Shaw!" the viscount exclaimed as he rose to his feet when Meg entered the room. "Behold me ravished."

"Or so you wish," Daffyd muttered to him, as he, too, stood.

"Naughty," his half brother said. "But look at our Miss Shaw. She blooms. Pray do not go into my gardens today, my dear, lest all the roses wilt from pure shame."

"It's a lovely gown," Meg said. The maids had stitched her into it and now it fit to perfection. It was only muslin, but she'd never felt so stylish. "Thank you for the use of it. If you would kindly submit a bill to me, I will see you reimbursed."

"Oh, never!" the viscount said, a hand up in mock alarm.

"Oh, yes," Meg said sternly. "I pay my way in this world, my lord. Please understand it's important for me to do so." She hoped her meager savings would cover the expense. Though the dress was village made, it was more elegant than many she'd seen. She hoped the seamstress's village wasn't really London, after all.

"As you will," the viscount said with a bow.

Daffyd smiled.

"But I do appreciate it," Meg went on. "I had nothing better with me. My other gowns didn't suit your lovely home," she said as she gazed around, taking in her surroundings.

The room they were in was clearly done by Adams; he'd used his favorite colors. The walls were blue, their borders gold, and the ceiling high above was painted with pastoral scenes of happy half-dressed peasants, all done in rose and green and gold, against a brilliantly azure sky.

Daffyd looked only at Meg. He knew what her body felt like next to his. He'd seen her figure silhouetted against the firelight. But now at last he saw what she looked like without her usual drab coverings.

Her arms, the skin at her neck and breast, every part of her shapely body that emerged from the flimsy gown, was smooth and pearlescent. She wore no locket at that white breast, but she didn't need any adornment. Her figure was perfect for the style, as well as for any man he'd ever known. She had firm, high breasts, a slender waist, and—for a small woman—legs that looked long as well. At least, long enough to suit him.

She'd never looked better. It was the color, or the gown, or being in his half brother's house, but now she carried herself with more confidence. He realized she must know how the coral color made her eyes glow amber brown and showed how subtly the sunlight had blushed her cheeks.

Or was she actually blushing? He didn't blame her, he thought with a sudden frown. Lee was eyeing her as though she was one of those scantily clad maidens on the ceiling above them.

"Tea will be in a bit, my dear," the viscount said. "So should you like a tour of my gardens until then?"

Meg looked at Daffyd. His face seemed to darken with some lowering mood, but he didn't say anything. She remembered how he'd left her to his other brother's mercies, and almost said no, though she really did want to see the grounds. Then she recalled that Daffyd had left her in spirit but never in body, because quiet as he'd been, he'd never actually left her alone with Johnny.

"A tour of the gardens? I'd like that," she said simply. "But please, first, can you tell me anything about my search?" She looked at Daffyd. "You did ask?" she asked him.

He nodded. "There's news. She's not here now. But she may have been."

"Indeed," his brother commented. "We're looking into it."

"May have been?" Meg asked with a frown, looking at the viscount.

"I'm told she's a master of disguise," the viscount said with a shrug. "And if she was occupied with her own gentleman . . ." He let the sentence linger before he added, "I have so many guests coming and going. It's amusing for me but troublesome for you, I expect. No matter, I'll know soon enough. My staff is ever alert, even if I am not."

"We can leave in the morning, if we get word," Daffyd said. "But there's nothing we can do now."

"Nothing?" his brother asked, looking shocked. "But I insist you enjoy yourselves in the meanwhile. So since it's conveniently not raining, shall we go for a stroll while the weather holds?" He crooked an arm and offered it to Meg.

She looked at Daffyd. He shrugged. So she took the viscount's arm. An attentive footman handed the viscount his silver-topped walking stick, and then Meg let her host lead her out the door.

"Coming?" the viscount asked Daffyd.

Daffyd didn't answer. But, Meg noted with relief, he was there. He'd come with them. She honestly didn't know what she'd have done if he hadn't.

It was a rare mild autumn day that felt like summer. They strolled along the paths, which, being only wide enough for two, made Daffyd follow behind, silent and dark, like their cast shadow.

The viscount noticed Daffyd's silence, of course, and Meg detected even more amusement in his face and voice. But he didn't try to exclude his brother; in fact, he spoke loudly enough for both of them to hear as he pointed out the flowers and others features of his grounds.

He spoke with self-depreciating wit, and punctuated his comments with graceful flourishes of his hands, in a way that Meg found affected at first, and then amusing. He was theatrical in his every gesture—casual, friendly and loquacious, everything Daffyd was not. But he did know a lot about what grew on his estate, and told them of his hopes for future plantings. A bevy of gardeners tended the flowers as assiduously as the bees and butterflies did. If a gardener caught sight of them, the fellow would bow and touch his hat. The viscount had a gentle word for each who did. Meg had never felt so privileged.

She enjoyed herself enormously—until they came to a turn in the walk, and almost ran into another couple. Then Meg felt her heart leap into her throat.

The gentleman was tall and heavyset, and dressed like a man of money and taste. He was considerably older than the fair young woman he walked with. She was so beautiful that Meg stared. It took a moment for Meg to realize the sunlight showed the lady had augmented her beauty with powder and rouge, and that because she did, she was obviously no lady.

The woman inclined her head in a bow, and the gentleman did, too. Both looked at the viscount and then pointedly at Meg and Daffyd.

"Sir Laycock, Miss Delilah," the viscount purred. "May I give you my long lost, but happily finally found, relative: Mr. Daffyd Reynard? And his cousin, Miss Kovert. They're collaborating on research about seventeenth-century mazes, and pay me the great honor of wishing to see mine for possible inclusion in the book. I am, as you can see, all a-twitter."

"Yes, because you always like to show yours," Miss Delilah said with a giggle and an enormous wink of one kohl-blackened eyelash.

"Indeed," the viscount said with less humor. "Shall I see you at dinner, Laycock?"

"Any reason why not?" the gentleman asked jokingly.

"Think on," the viscount answered in cool tones. He waved his hand to indicate Meg and Daffyd. "These *are* my relatives, sir."

Sir Laycock bowed again. "Then thank you for your hospitality, Haye. But we'll be leaving before dark. I'll see you in London."

The viscount nodded. "You're welcome," he said, and without giving them time to reply, moved on.

"You've gotten very puritanical since I saw you last," Daffyd commented.

"Have I? I don't think so," the viscount said thoughtfully. "But I did want you and especially Miss Shaw to know there's no need to worry. You won't be seeing that pair again. So Miss Shaw need not concern herself about them, or indeed anyone she meets here. She'll never see any of my other guests in any proper places. And you told me that those are the only places she goes. When she's not with you, of course."

"So I said," Daffyd said.

The viscount smiled, and continued with his tour. But eventually, he stopped. "Would you like to see the maze, my dear?" he asked Meg.

"Oh!" she gasped. She was only prevented from

clapping her hands together because she had one hand on her host's arm. "I would! I've read about them, but never been in one."

"You'll *love* this one," her host said comfortably. "It's over two hundred years old. Come along."

They walked across the lawn until Meg saw the maze looming up in front of them. It was even taller than it had looked from the window. It was fully twelve feet high, and made of ancient green shrubs that had knitted together to form dense dark green walls. They stepped in through a doorway cut into the hedge and found themselves in a cool, dark, narrow, green shadowed path. The sun was still overhead, but there was little illumination where they stood. Even the air seemed damp and vegetative.

The viscount stopped. "There's a surprise at the center, a pearl embedded in the great green oyster, as it were. But if you don't know the way it might take you two hundred years to find it. So much as I'd adore having you here as the centuries roll on, I'd never distress you so cruelly. We can see it and have plenty of time left for teatime. I inherited the secret to its heart as well as the estate. But Daffy, my dear," he said, suddenly turning to look at his brother, "with all you've come to know of me in the year since we've met, it occurs to me that you've never visited my maze."

"No," Daffyd said. "Whenever I visited here, the entertainments offered were at night."

"What a lovely idea!" his brother exclaimed. "I shall have to bring torches, and try it." He frowned.

"Fie. No, some bibulous fool would set the place alight. We shall have to leave it for daylight. And so it is! So there's no time like the present for you to see it. But let's make a game of it, as it was meant to be. Are you game, Daffy?"

"Up for anything," Daffyd commented.

"Good," the viscount said. "Now, there are actually two ways to go in order to get to the secret center. Dear brother, you take the left road, and we'll go by the right one. The distances are equal, and of course, I have the advantage because I've been there before. So I'll let you go first and give you a full five-minute start. That should equalize things. I *do* try to play fairly. Winning's not much fun if one doesn't.

"Now, listen carefully. There are many turns, but only eleven you must take in sequence that will get you to the center. The key is Master Shakespeare's immortal sonnet.

" 'Shall I compare thee to a summer's day?' " he recited. " 'Thou art more lovely and more temperate: Rough winds do shake the darling buds of May, and summer's lease hath all too short a date: Sometime too hot the eye of heaven shines, and often is his gold complexion dimm'd; and every fair from fair sometime declines, By chance, or nature's changing course untrimm'd . . .'

"I'm sure you know the rest," he went on with a wave of his hand. "It was popular when the maze was first planned. So if you scan the verse in your mind, it's simple. Note the line number and the letter

number, and if they're even, go right. If the line
number and letter number are odd, go left. Simple.
You see?"

Meg lifted her hand from the viscount's arm, feeling chilled. That surely was a cruel thing to expect
Daffyd to know.

"And if the last line is odd, and the next is the
same?" Daffyd asked.

His brother smiled. "If the last turn is odd or even,
and the next is the same, don't turn at all. Now, even
with the key, I suspect I've given you a hard task. Do
you think you can do it?"

"No reason not to," Daffyd said. "I may only be a
poor illiterate gypsy lad, but we Roms have super-
natural ways of foreseeing the future. I'll be there
waiting for you. If you played fair."

His brother gasped, and clutched his heart. "Me,
cheat? Oh, fie, Daffy. I faint, I fall, I'm wounded!"

"You'll recover," Daffyd said. "See you soon." He
raised a finger to his forehead in mocking mimicry
of the way the gardeners had saluted his brother,
smiled at Meg, turned, walked a few paces, turned
again, and was gone from sight.

The viscount stood chatting with Meg, telling her
about the history of his hedged maze. Then he
looked up at the sun, and pulled a golden watch from
his waistcoat pocket. He glanced at it and nodded.
"Time's up. Onward," he said, and picked his way,
tapping with his walking stick, down the narrow bor-
dered lane with Meg. They turned left, and right, the

viscount chatting so pleasantly that Meg soon forgot trying to solve the puzzle, and simply strolled along with him.

"Now," he finally said, as he stopped at the end of a dark green tunnel. "Close your eyes. Come, trust me. No peeking, please. Walk on with me, and then on my command, open your eyes."

Meg did as he said.

She felt the change. The air suddenly felt clearer, it was definitely easier to breathe, and she saw red against her closed eyelids and felt warmth on her shoulders, meaning that she stood in sunlight again.

"Open!" her host caroled.

She opened her eyes to see that they were in the center of the maze. A huge marble statue of a nude Venus being caressed by an equally nude and obviously enthusiastic Mars, applauded by a bevy of salacious frolicking cherubs, stood in the middle. Meg stared. It was beautiful. And possibly the lewdest thing she'd ever seen.

A quartet of curved marble benches framed the ornate sculpture. And the tall, dense hedges surrounded the whole.

"We won," the viscount said. "Poor Daffy. Now then, my dear Miss Shaw, we have some much-needed privacy at last. He won't join us for some time."

"Didn't you tell him the way?" Meg asked nervously.

He smiled down at her, mischief and something else in his suddenly ardent deep blue gaze. "Oh, I did. Some of it. He's a resourceful fellow. He'll join us eventually. But not for some time. So, my dear Miss Shaw, my so very lovely Miss Shaw. What shall we do to amuse ourselves during our precious stolen hours?"

Chapter 12

Meg blinked, and took a step back. Her eyes flew wide, she stared up at the viscount in dismay.

He didn't seem to notice. "No sense in our standing here until Daffyd finds us," he said in his usual cool amused tones. "We'd put you in danger of exhaustion and that will never do. Pray have a seat, my dear." He motioned to one of the marble benches.

She hesitated.

He misunderstood. "You're right to be cautious," he assured her. "We try to keep everything in perfect order here but my servants can't account for birds that fly overhead." He swept a spotless handkerchief from an inner pocket and dusted it across the spotless white marble of the bench. "But see? The bench is immaculate. Come, sit, my dear."

So it seemed she had been the one to misunderstand. Meg calmed herself, and as carefully as a woman lowering herself into a pot of boiling water, she sat. Her host then sat beside her, threw one long leg over the over, one arm over the back of the bench, and smiled down at her.

He was sitting too close, she thought in sudden alarm. But short of insulting him by moving away, there was nothing she could do. So she pretended not to notice. He certainly didn't seem to.

He inspected his shining boots, and then brushed an invisible spot off one long thigh. That made Meg notice that although he was thin, he was not gaunt. His gray breeches were fashionably tight and she could see that his thighs were well muscled. She looked away, embarrassed. But now she realized he was altogether fit, and his clothes were tailored to show it. In all, he was, if not a handsome man, then certainly an attractive one. His dark blue eyes reminded Meg of Daffyd, but his long, clever face reminded her of someone else. It nagged at her. She searched her brain to find the resemblance. His pale complexion and brown hair, cut in the fashionable windswept style, made it harder, because she had the vagrant nagging notion that the viscount looked like someone she knew who was dark as Daffyd himself.

Meg sat up straighter. She suddenly recognized that curling smile. She'd seen it in pictures of

Charles the Second: England's wittiest, most charming, and most dissolute and licentious king.

She got the scent of lemon and lavender water as her host casually stretched, and used the motion to put his other arm on the bench in back of her and move a jot closer. She dared look at him. He was looking back at her, his eyes intent, his smile at its most winsome. His head began to lower toward hers.

Meg's heart began to race, her reaction was as swift. She leaped to her feet.

He rose as well, looking at her curiously.

She blushed, feeling stupid and childish. He probably had only been trying to whisper something into her ear, because perhaps he knew Daffyd was near. What a gauche fool she was! It well might be because the elegant new gown she had on was giving her airs.

After all, the man was Daffyd's half brother: a lord of the realm, sophisticated, educated, and rich as Croesus. She just wasn't used to the attentions of such a gentleman. The problem was she wasn't sure his behavior was what he might show any guest, or if they were *attentions*, such as she'd had from other men.

But she'd made too many mistakes on her journey so far. She'd trusted a trio of felons and probable rapists. She'd trusted Daffyd's other brother too. She couldn't, wouldn't risk another blunder.

"My lord," she said carefully, looking down at the ground as though she'd find a solution to her predicament there if she looked hard enough. "What I think we should do with that hour is to go back, or find Daffyd straightaway. If we stay here, we could talk about the weather, I suppose. But I . . ."

He was still.

She swallowed hard and went on doggedly. "Please forgive me for what I'm about to say. Put it down to me being totally unused to dealing with suave and worldly gentlemen such as yourself. I fear I'm being presumptuous. I'm probably being vain as well, and very foolish to boot. And so I won't say anything else, except that I do *not* want to do anything but talk with you, you see."

"I do see," he said. He smiled. "And you're not being a bit presumptuous or vain or foolish, Miss Shaw. You *are* lovely, I *am* a rogue, and you read my motives perfectly. I did have lovemaking in mind."

She looked up at him with something like horror.

He shrugged. "Well, at least we got that out of the way," he said. He sat again, and indicated the empty space beside him. "So sit. I won't presume again. You have my word on that."

She sat, careful to keep distance between them.

He stretched out his legs, and sighed. "I do think you're adorable, but I also have a care for Daffyd. For all his air of invulnerability, the fellow is susceptible to pity, and like any man, to charm. So one has to be sure of a female's intentions toward him, especially this one. Speaking of which," he added, eyeing her sidewise, "are you sure?"

She stared at him.

He shrugged. "So be it. At least tell me, is it anything in particular about me that puts you off? Something you dislike?"

"No, my lord," she said, wishing she hadn't sat again. "It's nothing personal at all."

He sighed, this time, theatrically. "Well, it wouldn't be the first time. No accounting for taste. Though, mind, I'm not faulting your taste. He *is* a likely lad. You *do* know his history?"

"I don't know what you mean," she lied.

"You disappoint me," he said mildly. "Come. Don't give up now, courage suits you. Of course you know what I mean. All I asked was if you knew my brother's sad history."

She nodded. "He told me. I met his grandmother and his half brother Johnny, too."

"Ah yes, the formidable Keja and wicked Johnny. Daffy told me all about your quest. I meant the rest of it."

"Yes, I know about the rookeries and Newgate Prison, the Hulks, and the Antipodes."

"But so does anyone who takes the trouble to ask," the viscount said in bored tones. "He positively delights in telling people about that. The proper ones are horrified, the improper show him due respect. He claims that's what separates the wheat from the chaff. I believe he does it to shock those he doesn't like, and avoid the pain of being discovered later and rejected by those he does. That's not what I meant. No, I wanted to know if you knew the rest."

Her eyes opened wider. There was more?

"Don't worry. There are no other criminal charges

pending against him," the viscount said. "I wanted to know if he'd told you his entire history. Do you know why I'm so delighted to have him here? How I discovered he was my brother?"

She shook her head. She couldn't answer outright because she found herself curiously disloyal discussing secrets about Daffyd behind his back.

Again, the languid nobleman read her mind. "It's no secret, at least, not Daffy's, or mine." His smile curled even more. "It would, however, give our mama the pip to know that others know. So *do* let me tell you about it. Our mama," he said, "was greatly daring in her youth. She actually did run off with a rag-tag gypsy, just like in the old song. Only in the song the noblewoman's husband came thundering after her, promptly chopped off her gypsy lover's head, and took her back home."

The viscount cocked his own head to the side. "That was in the earliest ballad, from 1524. The other song comes later. That one's said to be about the gypsy Johnny Faa, of Dunbar. In that song, the cuckolded nobleman rode in, killed the gypsy and hanged his seven brothers, too. It's supposed to be about the sixth earl of Cassilis and his lady. But some say it never happened, the earl just had political enemies who wanted to blacken his lady's name. Still, you can bet something like that happened to someone once, because there are so many songs about it. Gypsy lads have had a certain allure down through the ages, you know.

"Our dear mama, mine and Daffy's, didn't follow

any of the old stories. Her lord didn't come thundering after her or kill her gypsy lover. In fact, he never
saw him. The whole affair ended rather flatly. Our
mama left her gypsy and crawled back to her lord,
and that—until Daffyd appeared, or rather re-
appeared, in London a generation later—was that."

"I see," Meg said softly.

"Not quite," her host said. "Because you see, or
rather, don't, our mama left a son as well as her husband in order to go a-roving with her gypsy. My
brother Martin doesn't remember, of course. He was
born after she returned. Long enough after to ensure
his legitimacy, but I overheard the whispers about
Mama's adventure. You can't lock gossip out of the
nursery and kitchens. Now, mind, I know that hers
was an arranged marriage and that my father was a
martinet, cold as a fish and rather stupid, to boot. So
it's difficult to blame dear Mama for her escapade.
It's much easier to fault her for not mentioning she'd
borne another babe while she was gone with the
gypsy rover."

"She never told anyone?"

"Not so far as I know. But I knew about her adventure. She left when I had a bit more than three years
on my plate, and returned when I was rising five. I
was furious with her for leaving me. In fact, I've
never really forgiven her for it. Still, I think I'd have
been entranced to know I had a half brother rattling
around the world. I didn't. She never said a word.

"At any rate," he went on, "her adventure must

have exhausted her, because Mama settled down. Circumstances made that easier for her. Soon after she brought forth my brother Martin, my father passed away and troubled her no more. She never spoke of the year with her gypsy rover. I never mentioned it—outright—to her again.

"But then, last year, the earl of Egremont returned to England to take his rightful place, and brought with him his terrible trio, straight from exile in the Antipodes. He had his son and the two lads they'd met in prison in tow, one said to be a half-wild, half-gypsy lad, and the other an attractive rogue from nowhere. The *ton* was enthralled with their story. Handsome young convicts who looked and spoke like gentlemen, and were rich as they could hold together? They were invited everywhere, and be-damned if they didn't brazen it out, and go everywhere, too."

Meg sat up when she heard that, her eyes glowing at the mention of Daffyd's bold behavior.

"Of course I heard about them," the viscount said, "as did my mama. In fact, I was there when she first clapped eyes on Daffyd, at the Swansons' ball. One look told her what had become of the son she'd abandoned. She actually grew pale, and staggered. I had only to see my own eyes looking back at me from his face to know there was a reason for it. Later, my mother had to admit it. Daffyd was perfectly forthcoming with me after he discovered the truth from her. The best part was that I discovered I liked him very well indeed. In fact, I'm proud to call him brother."

Meg sat silent. Then she looked at him directly. "But if you like him so well, why did you try to . . . not that I matter to him, in that way, but I came here under his protection and you just . . ."

She paused. She couldn't utter the words, "tried to seduce me."

"Tried to seduce you?" he asked merrily. "Because I do like Daffy and didn't want him embroiled with some wild young chit with the same proclivities as our mama. He deserves more than that, more than a woman just looking for excitement with a handsome gypsy. I thought I might be able to divert you and spare him becoming involved with such another as our mother. Actually, I'm not sure I'd have been that self-sacrificing if you hadn't been quite so pretty. The chore might have been a delight. Alas, I'll never know, will I?" he asked with a charming smile.

Meg's nostrils flared. She forgot her place. "I came along with your brother because I realized I'd been a fool to go off by myself," she told him hotly, "and because I believed he had the best chance of finding Miss Osbourne! It's true," she added in more muted tones, "that it was folly for me to have set out on my adventure at all. But I did, and I enlisted Daffyd's help, and so here I am. And that's all I want from him!"

He smiled. She wanted to slap that curling smile from his mouth.

"Really?" he asked bemusedly. "That well may

have been all there was to it, *then*. Trivial I may be, my dear, and trifling I may wish to be, but I note more than changing fashions. Strange things occur on journeys; people change even as the scenery around them does. They tend to see themselves differently when they're cut loose from their anchors. They certainly see their companions in a different light. I remember an Italian girl I met on my first grand tour, we were snowbound in the Alps . . .

"Be that as it may," he said, "I don't blame you if your emotions changed. Daffyd is clever and perceptive. He wouldn't have survived to this day if he weren't. He's also wily and courageous, which I imagine he also had to be. But strangely enough, he's honest, when he wishes to be, and when he is, he's honest to a fault. He's loyal to a fault as well.

"Oh, I can easily see why constant exposure to my brother Daffyd might change a person. After all," he added with a sly grin, "all the songs say that the Gypsy Davy was exceptionally seductive. Surely you know the tune? One of my favorites."

And then, to Meg's surprise, he sang the rest of what he had to say, in a clear, ringing voice:

> *"I know where I'm going,*
> *and I know who's going with me,*
> *I know who I love,*
> *but the dear knows who I'll marry.*
> *I have stockings of silk,*
> *and shoes of fine green leather,*

Combs to buckle my hair
and a ring for every finger.
Feather beds are soft,
and painted rooms are bonny;
but I would leave them all
to go with my love Johnny."

He stopped and smiled at her. Then he spun around as another voice rang out to finish the lyric for him.

"*Some say he's dark, I say he's bonny,*" the deep masculine voice sang. "*The flower of them all is my handsome, winsome Johnny.*"

Daffyd stood at the entrance to the maze, leaning against the wall of hedges, one ankle crossed over the other. "Nice tune," he said when he was done singing. "But wrong Gypsy laddie. Johnny's my brother. I'm Daffyd. The name was my father's choice. He traveled in Wales once, met up with a man with it, and liked the cut of him, or so he said. He probably only swindled a heavy purse from the poor fellow and never forgot his good luck in doing it. My father scorned gypsy names and wouldn't let my grandmother give me one. Just as well, she wanted to call me 'Luca' and if not, then 'Vesh.' My father did at least one good thing for me in his life.

"My mother . . . your pardon," Daffyd said with a slight bow to his brother. "*Our* mother, didn't give a damn about my name. She left before I got one. Your pardon for my language," he added with a real bow to Meg.

His brother looked at him with something like amusement before he asked, in puzzlement, "But how did you get here so fast?"

"I'm a Rom. I carry a knife," Daffyd said, with an elaborate shrug. "I thought you knew that."

"A knife? I see. Bother the sonnet, is that it? You heard voices and sliced your way here?" The viscount gasped. "You *did*?" He shuddered. "Ah, well," he finally said. "It will only take another generation or two to get the maze in proper shape again. So be it. It will keep my gardeners busy. That was very hasty of you, brother. Still, I applaud you. It was so in character, direct and to the point, literally. Like Alexander and the Gordian knot."

"Alexander?" Daffyd asked. "Did he have a lying, cheating brother too?"

The viscount's smile slipped. "Much is amusing, my dear Daffyd. *That*, I fear, is not. Would you care to explain or rephrase?"

"Would you care to rethink this afternoon?" Daffyd asked as seriously. He uncrossed his ankles, and stood, legs apart, looking straight at his brother, all hint of humor gone. "I don't need a protector, or an apologist. I certainly don't need one who's also a seducer."

"Not a very successful one," the viscount said, as he too rose to his feet. "Rather say, I was looking after your interests."

"Looking down a bodice for them, were you?" Daffyd asked.

"I find that insulting, as well you know I would," his brother said coldly. "I don't carry a knife, but I'd be glad to oblige you with a sword."

"Knife, sword, or pistol," Daffyd answered grimly. "Or bare hands. Which are you asking me to?"

Meg rose to her feet. The brothers weren't joking anymore. She saw it in their tense postures, heard it in their voices. She didn't want to see them fight, didn't want bloodshed. Most of all, she was aware this was the viscount's house and Daffyd was only a guest here, and one with a criminal past. Even if he won any dispute he had with his brother, he'd lose.

"Gentlemen!" she cried. "If you please."

They turned and looked at her.

She stood tall as she could. "I don't like feeling like a bone two curs are squabbling over," she announced. "If you're angry at each other, fine and good and it's no business of mine. But don't make me the reason for it, because then it is my concern. I was not seduced. And I can fight my own battles. And you know? I find I don't want the company of either of you now, because now I can clearly see what I couldn't before. You two are truly brothers—if not apparently on the surface, then certainly under the skin. You're two of a kind. And *not* a kind I care for!"

She stormed out of the circle. She saw a doorway in the hedge, and went through it. She stalked down the narrow path she stepped into, her heart pounding—with exultation. Because it was hard to tell which of them had looked more surprised, and then insulted, by what she'd flung at them before she stomped off. Whatever else she'd done, she'd certainly diverted their anger.

She marched on, praying they wouldn't kill each other and hoping she'd find her way out of the maze before the sun set so she could call for help to stop them. Moments later she heard running footfalls, and then found Daffyd pacing at her side.

"You don't know the way out," he said.

"I do, and I will *not* have more holes poked in my maze," the viscount said as he came up behind them.

"Then make peace," Meg said. "I can't bear to see fighting."

"Oh that," Daffyd said with a negligent shrug. "He knows I didn't mean it."

"I do now. I cry peace, brother," the viscount said. "I cheated, but in a good cause—only as a test, and for your sake. Miss Shaw passed the test, as she would any I could fashion, because she's pure in heart and without artifice, as I, alas, am not. I had to be sure because I do care for you. And I don't confide in those I don't deem fit to hear confidences. As for the seduction, it got nowhere. She simply can't see me."

"She sees well enough," Daffyd said. "But it's past, and done, and forgotten."

"Yes. By me," his brother said. "And so at least, I hope it is for you. As well as for you, Miss Shaw."

"It's forgotten," Meg said, though she was privately surprised that the lofty gentleman apologized to her. She decided to capitalize on it before he regretted it. She stopped and turned to confront the pair. It was dim in the narrow passage and hard to read either of the brothers' expressions. That made it easier for her.

"I may only be a guest here, and not for long, at that," she said. "So, please, if either of you know, tell me—where do you think Rosalind Osbourne is? Am I near, or ought I to give up hope of finding her?"

"She was here," the viscount said. "Thanks to my admirable staff, that much I now know. I didn't know who she was at the time, though. Many wayward travelers find their way here. My hospitality is well known, as is my boredom and penchant for wanting diversion without asking questions. I don't think she's coming back. She was a bird in flight. Still, I may know where she's flying off to. We'll discuss it at tea. Even if you want to leave immediately, it would be foolish to travel at dusk. We can have at least this one night together.

"That is, if it's really peace, brother?" he asked Daffyd. "I find that matters quite a lot to me. With all I have, I haven't enough relatives I trust. In point of fact, you're the only one. Will you stay to reassure me of your friendship?"

Daffyd bowed. "I will. I'm honored. Peace, brother."

They shook hands. Then they strolled back to the house, retracing the way they'd come, this time in comfortable silence. Only now the viscount walked in front of Meg, leaving Daffyd to be at her side.

But when they finally exited the maze, the viscount stopped. He looked back, and frowned. "There are no holes in my hedges. Not a one. You're lean, brother," he said, "but I don't see any slice or wedge big enough for you to squeeze through. Even a squirrel couldn't."

Daffyd grinned. "Learning's a tool, or at least that's what the earl said when he taught me my letters while we were in Newgate. He kept saying it as he kept up my lessons as we shipped out on our long passage to the Antipodes. 'Knowledge is a tool,' he always said. 'Sometimes it's a hammer, sometimes it's a knife.' I prefer to use mine like a knife, because it can cut through anything, like Alexander's blade.

"We prisoners often recited poems to each other on our trip to New South Wales," he went on. "It whiled away the hours at night when we were locked in the hold until dawn. It's amazing how trying to remember poetry can take up all your concentration even when a storm's rocking your world, and especially when you begin to think you'll have to finish the rhyme with bubbles, not words.

" 'Shall I compare thee to a summer's day' is one I remember. You gave me a head start with the first part," he told his brother. "Lucky I remembered the rest:

" 'But thy eternal summer shall not fade,' " Daffyd quoted. " 'Nor lose possession of that fair thou ow'st, Nor shall death brag thou wander'st in his shade, when in eternal lines to time thou grow'st; So long as men can breathe, or eyes can see, So long lives this, and this gives life to thee.' It's a poem about love and how it can help a man transcend time and death. It's one of my favorites."

The viscount clapped his hands, and laughed with glee.

Daffyd didn't notice. He was reciting to Meg, and too intent on watching her brilliant blossoming smile to pay attention to anything else.

Chapter 13

The guests at the viscount's pleasure house re- treat, as Meg quickly came to think of it, found Daffyd's dark good looks and aloof manner fascinat- ing. This included the straying countess, the youthful dowager, the baronet's silly mistress, and half the staff, most but not all of them female. Meg noted it, but watched Daffyd's reactions even more closely. So far as she could tell he was amused by all the at- tention he received, and nothing more. But then, she thought darkly, he was brilliant at concealing his feelings.

As now, after dinner, in the dim light of the vis- count's study, where the three of them were alone at last. Their tea that afternoon had been constantly in- terrupted by too many wandering guests for them to

have a private conversation. The dinner they'd just
had was spent in the thick of the viscount's fashionable and forever chattering company. But now they'd
gone off by themselves. The viscount had given or-
ders not to be disturbed. Meg sat at the edge of her
chair, anxiously waiting for news of Rosalind at last,
so she could decide what to do and where to go next.

Daffyd, looking as handsome as the devil in his
dark evening dress, wandered the study, his movements fluid, restless, and soft as shadows as he
paced, waiting for his brother to speak.

The viscount sat back in a deep red chair by the
fireside. He cradled a goblet of brandy, and stared
into it as though what he had to say was printed
there.

"Nice pose, brother," Daffyd commented from the
side of a mantelpiece where he'd paused. "Very noble. Get a goggle-eyed spaniel to sit at your feet and
have it painted for posterity. But first tell us about the
Osbourne chit, or else Meg will burst with curiosity
and that will make a mess of your study."

Meg couldn't smile. It was too true. She leaned
forward.

"Well," the viscount said, "it appears I had a visitor last week who may well have been the girl you're
looking for. She wasn't fair-haired. In fact, she was
dark as you are, brother, but not half so pretty. That
was because she wore a truly ghastly wig, a cheap,
dead-looking, lank black thing a servant girl would
wear for her Cleopatra costume at a public masquer-
ade." He shuddered. "I don't rely on my own obser-

vations, though they're usually acute. Nor did I much care about the wench, since she had eyes for only her attentive male companion. But the maidservants who attended to her now confirm that the wretched mess on her head was indeed a wig, and that she was fair as the dawn beneath it.

"Still, she was, in spite of her appalling disguise, a taking little creature. At least so her companion thought. He was a redheaded fellow, but I wouldn't swear he was born one either. She spoke with a lisp and everything she said was obviously a lie. They were a genteel pair, or so I believe, because they were mannered and accustomed to command, and they knew about my hospitality, which proves it."

"So you're never invaded by barbarians?" Daffyd asked in disbelief. "How can that be? This place is famous to the rich and noble who want a comfortable, rustic spot where they can sport. This very evening I was invited to play billiards, try my hand at hazard, whist, vingt-et-un, and . . ." He glanced at Meg and changed whatever he was about to say to, ". . . more intimate pastimes. And that was *before* dinner. Don't tell me you don't get commoners in disguise here, not to mention Captain Sharps out to pluck a pigeon."

The viscount waved his hand. "Of course that sort find their way to my gates, but they seldom get in, or stay long if they do. I'm not a fool and neither is my staff. Those two were runaways; anyone could see that. But they were also wellbred, used to money and being waited on, and inexperienced. Anyone would be able to see that too. I've no doubt they were more plucked than pluckers," he added with a grin, "because she was uneasy about accepting my hospitality, and he was apologetic to her and to me. They'd come to the bottom of their purses, I think, and were on their way to the coast, and out of the country."

Meg started. "Did they say so?" she asked.

"Yes, and no," the viscount said. "They asked directions to Plymouth, and the best, though most reasonably priced inns to stop at on the way. They claimed that wasn't because they didn't want to spend the money, but because they wanted to see the 'real England.' I doubt they'd have asked that if they'd been bound for London, as they later remembered to claim they were."

"What did the man look like?" Meg asked.

"A well enough looking youth, for all that the red hair didn't suit him. That's all I recall. I fear men aren't usually my focus of attention," the viscount said.

"And this was how long ago?" Daffyd asked from the window seat where he'd momentarily perched.

"Three days before you arrived. So if they're bound for sea I doubt they've boarded ship yet. It would take them that long to get to Plymouth if they went straightaway after they left here, and they didn't seem in any particular hurry. They seemed like a pair of honeymooners, forgetful of the passing hours. Are you going after them?"

Meg blinked. The question was addressed to her. "I don't know," she said. "I suppose so. I don't see how I can quit the quest now when I'm so close."

Both men studied her. Tonight she wore the green gown, and the color gave life to her fair complexion and showed the whiskey-colored glow in her eyes. The gown did even more for her shape. It was lower at the neck than any gown she'd worn so far, and the material that fell from the high waist clung to her supple young body, outlining her curving hips and rounded bottom.

And so while famous beauties and professional courtesans were well represented tonight at the manor house, both men privately thought that Miss Margaret Shaw certainly could hold her own against them. And each privately thought the other fellow wanted her to hold that body against his own as much as he himself did.

"You realize," the viscount told her, "that whatever secrecy your quest had in the beginning may have been sacrificed here today? My guests are rackety, with nothing more than their own pleasures on their minds. But because of that they have a lot of time, and yards of room even in those shallow brains for trivial information. Your face, form, and I fear, soon your name itself will be part of their gossip."

"I gave a false name," Meg said.

"So you did," the viscount answered. "It's expected here. They can unearth the right one in no time." He shrugged and took a sip of brandy. "Or maybe not."

"They might," Daffyd said. He leaned his shoulders against the wall at the side of door, where he'd paused again. "They have money for bribes and can put two and two together even if they can't count much higher. The gossip about the runaway Osbourne chit's already out. News of her runaway governess will spread just as fast. You're supposed to surface again in a few days, Meg. If you don't, someone will twig to your scheme. Going on down this road is a bigger risk for you now than it was before." He glanced at his brother.

The viscount nodded. "Yes," he said, looking at Meg. "And so that's why I'd suggest you let Daffyd take over now so you can find a safer harbor. I'd love it if you stayed on with me. But I'm being noble tonight and so will tell you the truth: That's the worst thing you could do if you want to preserve your reputation. I can offer you fine food, diversion, amusement, and comfortable shelter, but my brother's right. My guests are scandalous, and since you haven't a chaperone you can imagine what people will think of you if you stay on here."

He shrugged. "But what if gossip and speculation about you gets out while you're blamelessly traveling back to the baron's house? Or even when you're on your way to the Lake District, where I understand your aunts abide? Or while you're snugged in your ex-governess's cottage as you told the Runner you'd be? You could say your trip was interrupted because your carriage broke a wheel, or you were delayed on the road, or even that you or your governess fell ill. You'd be where a good sensible governess companion ought to be. You could deny anything and be able to laugh any rumor off as spite or nonsense.

"If not?" He spread his hands. "I'm very impressed by you, Miss Meg. In fact, I've been taken with you in such a short time that I'm astonished at myself. You're bright and lovely—and courageous, which is a scarcer commodity than the other two, believe me. And so I'd like to help, and not just for Daffyd's sake. I'm willing to do whatever I can for you. But even I can't promise what will eventually become of you if your adventure is made public. I have the feeling that a life as a demimondaine wouldn't be to your liking. But I honestly can't think of any other profession you'd be suitable for if it was discovered that you'd stayed on here with me, or traveled the length of England with no one but Daffyd as your chaperone."

He sighed. "The nobility can be as immoral as they please and still live relatively happy lives. As witness Daffyd's and my erring mama. She doesn't suffer for her youthful folly. Nor, you'll have noted, did most of the runaway ladies in those morose folksongs. Their errant gypsy lovers did. The difference lies in their titles. The sad truth is that the less noble suffer for the merest misadventures. Even a well-paid courtesan isn't precisely free to do as she wishes, you know."

"I know!" Meg said through gritted teeth, "I don't *want* to be one of them, and I don't plan to. But I have three more days. I'd like to use them as best I can." She raised her head high.

"I know everything you say is true," she told them both. "I also know that those last days are all I'll have of freedom for the rest of my life if Rosie Osbourne doesn't go home. What would you do if you were me? That is, if you can even imagine being a female without money or connections? Would you be content to sit back and hope someone else will solve a problem that would affect the rest of your life? I don't think so.

"I know I'm a woman and supposed to wait and pray for a solution. And I certainly know what I risk by not doing that. But if Rosie vanishes and my future life is spent in a kind of bondage because of it, how could I ever forgive myself for not having tried my best to find her? Could you, if you were me?"

She sank to the chair again, and shook her head. "Stupid of me to even ask. You're men. How could either of you ever imagine how it is to be a woman? I suppose even asking you is insulting. Forgive me."

The viscount fell still.

But Daffyd spoke up from where he'd paused, by the side of her chair. "I know what imprisonment is," he said. "And what loss of free will is, too. I've helped you because of that and I'd help more if I could. But your time is running out. It may be time to run away home, Meg."

She ducked her head, and sniffled.

The viscount leaned forward and handed her a handkerchief. As she dabbed her eyes and then her nose, Daffyd reached out a hand to touch her shoulder. He realized what he was doing at the last second, dropped his hand and quickly paced away. Meg saw none of it.

His brother did.

"Still, three more days," the viscount mused. "And considering you're only three days from Plymouth? And that you might even meet up with the runaways on the road as you go there? I don't know. Maybe one last desperate attempt *is* in order."

Meg looked up.

"Consider," the viscount told a frowning Daffyd, "her reputation is almost in tatters as it is. Even if she escapes gossip, the fact remains that her charge ran away with her none the wiser. She'll never get a recommendation from the baron if his daughter successfully elopes."

"You could find someone with some kind of reputation to write her a commendation," Daffyd said.

"*I*?" his brother asked in disbelief, one hand going to his heart as though he'd been stricken. "I couldn't find anyone to write a recommendation that would be believed by anyone remotely respectable, not even if they were recommending someone for the position of rat catcher."

"There's our mother . . ." Daffyd stopped, and scowled. "All right then, there's my friend, the earl . . ." He frowned again. "Surely there's someone we know whose recommendation would be unexceptional!"

"Perhaps we do, maybe we could think of someone . . . eventually," his brother said. "And what should Miss Shaw do in the meantime? Even if we got a bishop to recommend her, there'll always be the possibility of doubt about her culpability in all this. That will cloud her future. But what if she finds the runaway within her three days, persuades the chit to go home, and returns to the baron in triumph? That would mend all, wouldn't it?"

Meg looked up with sudden hope.

"Can you keep her safe for those three days?" the viscount asked Daffyd.

Daffyd paced the room for long moments.

The viscount's eyebrow went up. Meg sat stock-still.

Then Daffyd grudgingly answered. "Yes."

Meg leaped from her chair. "Oh, thank you. I mean, you will come with me to find Rosie?"

"Aye," Daffyd said gruffly.

The viscount smiled.

Daffyd did not.

It wasn't until later, when Meg was asleep and the viscount's other guests were all tucked into each other's beds, and the house was dark, that the viscount broached the subject again.

"Having doubts?" he asked Daffyd as they sat alone in the study after planning out the next day's journey.

"Aye," Daffyd said.

"Then cancel the plan and send her home."

"It would undo her. I can't."

"But you think you can't keep her safe?"

Daffyd placed his empty wine goblet on a table,

rose, and stretched. "I'm to bed. I leave at dawn and need some sleep." He paused. "If I forget in the flurry of leaving, thank you again, brother. I can count on you, and I do, and I want you to know I appreciate it."

"It's nothing you wouldn't do for me. And who knows? One day I may have need of you, too."

"You'll have me," Daffyd said.

"I know it. But, Daffyd, I'm somewhat distressed. I've come to like the chit. You *really* think you can't keep her safe?"

"Depends on what you mean by that," Daffyd said over his shoulder, as he left the room. "From discovery, aye. Probably. But from me? Now that's a different story."

His brother sat alone after he'd left, wearing a faint but growing smile. "Why, Daffyd," he whispered to the empty room, "who would have believed it?"

Meg smiled at Daffyd when she saw him waiting in the main hall as she came down the stair at first light.

This morning he looked like one of his brother's noble houseguests. He wore a neat white neckcloth and a tan jacket, obviously cut by a master's hand. It went wonderfully well with his apricot-colored waistcoat, buff breeches, and shining gold-tassel-topped brown boots.

But he didn't smile back at her. "Change," he ordered the moment he clapped eyes on her.

She looked down at herself. She wore one of her old gray gowns. But it had been ironed and looked respectable again. "This is for traveling," she said in confusion.

"Not today," he said. "Put on one of the gowns my brother sent you. Today we take the main road. We also take the loan of my brother's carriage, his coachman, and a post boy. We'll be traveling fast and asking questions, and for that we need an impressive vehicle and an aura of respectability."

She frowned.

"What if we do find the Osbourne chit?" he demanded. "What if we have to rescue her? Or what if we have to drag her away from her lover? Fine chance we'd have to do anything like that looking like a gypsy and a drab. The locals would call for the militia. They'd toss us in jail—if we were lucky. No. It won't do. I'm dressed to the teeth and so should you be. Ladies wear flimsy fashionable stuff no matter how hard or long they're going to travel."

She nodded. "I won't be a second," she said, turned, and secretly delighted, ran back up the stairs.

It had given her a twinge last night when she'd left the beautiful gowns she'd been given and packed only her own. She'd sighed especially hard when she'd abandoned two other new gowns, along with the bonnets and matching slippers that had magically appeared in her wardrobe as well. She'd never owned so many new clothes at once, not to mention so many beautiful ones.

When she returned to her room she saw the maids

had been in. The new gowns and their accessories had already been packed in her bag.

Meg was smiling when she came down the stair again, wearing a sunny yellow gown, sprigged all over with tiny pink flowers and tied with a pink ribbon at the waist. She wore a dashing pink straw bonnet, and carried a folded parasol. She couldn't help but be pleased to see her new pink slippers peeping out from under her hem with every step she took. She felt she looked like the lady Daffyd asked her to be.

For a moment, she thought he thought so, too. Then his expression became impassive. "We have to eat breakfast and then go," he said.

Two sleepy footmen leaped to attention in the morning dining parlor when Meg and Daffyd entered. They offered a sumptuous breakfast selection from the plates, tureens, and chafing dishes set out on the sideboards. The viscount's guests always found food waiting when they arose, at whatever hour. But no one else joined them.

Meg and Daffyd ate quickly and silently, and then got up to go.

Daffyd paused, reached into his waistcoat pocket and handed Meg a paper. "My brother left a note for you."

My dear Miss Shaw, the note said in firm dark cursive script.

> *Godspeed and good fortune. Forgive me for not seeing you off, but I hate tearful farewells, es-*

*pecially when they are my own tears. I wish
you joy and luck, and hope you return to me
one day.*

Take care of my brother, please.

Your obedient,

Haye

"He left me a note, too," Daffyd said when he saw
her bemused expression as she read it, and then
noted how she carefully folded it afterward. "He said
he didn't want to get up and join us this early because that would cause talk. His servants are used to
people coming and going at all hours. But they aren't
used to seeing him up at what he called 'this un-
godly' hour, unless they're putting him to bed."

She smiled. "He tries to conceal all his better
qualities, doesn't he?"

Daffyd was about to answer when she added, with
a shy smile, "Just the way you do."

There was nothing he could say to that, so he
frowned, and asked, "Ready?"

"Never readier," Meg said. "Let's go."

Chapter 14

⟨✦⟩

It rained a chill, dank rain. It poured in the morning, mizzled at midday, and then came down in torrents by afternoon. The horses made slow going of it. By the time night fell, even the fine-sprung coach Meg and Daffyd were in pitched and swayed and slogged along the road like a galleon breasting rough seas.

"We lost a lot of time today, didn't we?" Meg finally asked as she stared out the window at nothing but rain.

"So did they," Daffyd said from his side of the coach, as he opened his eyes. He stretched, yawned, and looked out the window. "I mean, your Rosalind and her lover. Don't doubt it. They're probably tucked up warm somewhere waiting for the weather to clear. So we didn't lose time at all."

"I did," she said softly. "I only had three days, and now, it's two."

He didn't answer right away. "Again," he finally said, "you can go now and leave it to me. Two days is long enough to get you to your governess's house. I'll let you know what I find as soon as I do."

"Again," she said wearily, "you might not recognize her. I will, immediately. Anyway . . . I've made my bed. You know?" she asked in a little voice, "I suppose I'm glad for the delay today. The weather's been too fine, almost supernaturally so. Who ever heard of such balmy English weather? It deceived me. Being forced to sit here and think has been good. I left in a mad rush and followed Rosie willy-nilly. Now, I can see how foolish that was—but at the same time, how inevitable. I had no choice. So if I fail at the last, what's the worst that can happen? I return to what I escaped from, that's all."

Daffyd frowned. "I can't think of anything worse than returning to what I escaped from. But I've been in places the devil would be ashamed of. Still, I know what a blow that would be to you. No need to give up yet. Two days is forty-eight hours, a lot can happen in that time. She might even be at the inn we stop at tonight."

He smiled at her so broadly she could see his teeth gleam white in the dim light. "The rain's got your soul soggy, is all it is. I know what. Let me try to make love to you so you can flare up at me. It will do you a world of good and take your mind off your troubles."

She didn't smile.

"I won't lay a hand on you until you ask me to," he said piously. "And you will. You'll see. I've never really tried my gypsy wiles on you. You'll be helpless in no time. I'll do it all without putting one paw on you. I'll do it with the music of my words, a little Romany magic, and the purity of my heart's deepest desires."

He thought he detected a flickering of her lips, quickly suppressed.

"Yes, a good game," he said comfortably as he settled back. "Now, where should I begin? Your body? It's always on my mind, but if I talk about it you'll think I'm just being lewd. We'll save that for later, after you see how impressed I am with the rest of you. Now, let's see.

"Your face? That's where everyone starts, but it's too comprehensive. So let's take your face in parts, as they appeal. What tempts me most right now? The light's dim, but I can see your smile. Yes, that definitely lures me. Should I tell you that you have the most enticing lips? No, really, you do. Fashionable females purse their lips to make them look like rosebuds, or at least that's the idea. I think it makes them look like carp in a fishpond. Have you ever gone to a *ton* party? I almost expect to see air bubbles rising from their mouths. I think it would be like kissing a carp. Not appealing.

"Mind," he added, "I don't kiss every available female even if she has nice lips. I wouldn't have time for anything else if I did. And I do have standards.

Speaking of mouths, I hear some girls bite their lips to make them look swollen. I think it looks as though they've been punched in the mouth. Even if it doesn't, having a fat mouth makes a female look lustful or greedy. Nothing wrong with either thing, understand, but it's not my cup of tea.

"By the way," he commented, "did you ever notice that some people have the reverse—hardly any lips at all? Men, usually, and it gets worse as they get older. It's as though their lips decided to leave their faces and are drawing in. That's usually the case with mean men, as though they've been so busy trying not to smile that their lips just quit. But some females have hardly any lips to speak of as well. I imagine that would feel like kissing a seal. Nice animals, but not kissable."

He saw her smile.

"Yes, definitely," he said. "Lips are a barometer of the soul."

She looked at him.

He grinned wider. "Not my quote. I'm not given to thinking about souls. But I heard a fellow say that once. It's true. Laughter and pain make your face what it is as much as your mama and papa did. It shows in the eyes, of course, and everyone talks about that. Don't worry, we'll get around to your eyes soon, I've got lots to say about them. Still, it's interesting that people always say they can read a person by the eyes. They ought to have a look at the lips, too.

"Now, your lips!" he said enthusiastically. "Yours

are pink and plush, and best of all, they bow up in the middle as though they were etched like a face on a cameo ring. Makes a man want to know how they'd feel against his own . . ."

"You know already," she said quietly.

He hesitated. "Yes, I do. But I want to know more."

"Daffyd?" she said in a queer little voice, "You know, if the world were different, I would want to make love to you, too."

He sat absolutely still.

"I imagine you do know how to make love, and beautifully," she said. "And I'm not dead. But I am—me. And so I can't. I've thought about it. Did you know that? You *are* attractive. You have the most amazing dark good looks. Speaking of faces, yours is not soon forgotten. You move with grace, you're quick of mind, and so very charming—that is, when you want to be. You've educated yourself far above others who had better beginnings. I admire you tremendously for raising yourself from such a sad and desperate childhood, and in such dire circumstances. Your brothers adore you, as does your grandmother. I can see why, you have so many good qualities. You are, in your fashion, honest, and you're compassionate, which is amazing, considering what you've had to go through.

"I *do* like you, too," she said sadly, "But I'm wary of you because you're dangerous to me without even meaning to be—sometimes," she added with a smile in her voice. "Other times I think you mean to be, but then, you warn me. Still, I don't think we could be friends, and certainly not lovers.

"We *are* from different worlds. I'm no fine lady looking for sport with a gypsy lad. I can't sport at all. I'm simply not able to fly free. What constrains me? I've thought about it. I guess it's habit and upbringing, as well as reality. You see, if we were friends, there would always be that urge to be lovers. If we made love, however safely, however charmingly—*especially* if it was wonderful, as I suspect it would be, I'd never forget. Long after you were gone on your way, I'd pine for you. I know I'd never find your like again. And I'd ruin myself for a proper husband. Because apart from having an experience I'd have to explain away one day, I know that as time moved on I'd forget the joy and only remember the shame. So, please, if you care for me, at all, in any way, don't ask me again. It's too tempting."

He sat stunned, and said nothing. There was nothing he could think of to say.

She nodded, and then turned her face to the streaming window again. "Will we be there soon?" she asked.

The inn where they at last stopped was old, and cold, because there was a problem with the chimneys. It was being worked on, the landlord assured them. But the dinner was hot, and the landlord apologetic, and every bed was heaped high with blankets.

Daffyd and Meg sat in a private dining chamber after dinner, because the hearth in that room had the one flue that drew perfectly. The blaze in the fireplace sent out light and some heat, and the draperies were closed tight across shutters drawn against the slashing rain. But the fire didn't seem to lighten either of their moods.

"I'm sorry," Daffyd finally said, to the walnut he held in his fingers.

Meg looked up. "About what?"

"About teasing you, pursuing you, even when I knew that a lass like you isn't for me." He scowled. "Listen, Miss Meg. I haven't a good opinion of marriage, or of fidelity, or of love itself. I've seen too many things called love, and little of the real thing. And though I've loved some people in my time, most of that love wasn't a physical sort. I spent a lot of time in the company of men, and there's a kind of love involved, that's true enough, but it's . . . ah, what's that word I learned? Yes—it's platonic love. As for females? Well, I love my grandmother, admire many women, and desire a whole lot more. But I have a hard time finding a woman to trust as I would a man, and still want to love as I would a woman."

He stared down at the walnut turning in his hand. "The earl bemoans that. But that's how I'm made. I enjoy females but I don't think I could be tied down to any particular one of them. You're smart and sweet and a treat to look at, game as a pebble, and full of unexpected laughter. And you need a husband. Truth for truth: I find I'd like to be him. Aye, really. But it would be folly. I'd be the devil of a husband, and no kind of father, and matrimony hasn't ever been in my plans."

"I don't want you to marry me!" she cried.

He shrugged. "I'm not saying you want *me*. I'm thinking about what you need. You need a husband and that's the bald truth. The world's no place for a female alone. It isn't much of one for a man alone either, but at least we have the law on our side—if we have money enough to call on it. We have the ability to earn a wage anywhere. Our safety lies in our muscles, and we can train to protect ourselves. Now, a female, unless she's either wellborn or a Billingsgate fishwife, has none of that. I know, I've seen too many lasses unprotected. I've been in places where women had to trade themselves in order to live, and it's not a thing you'd want to see."

He shook his head. "But that's not to the point. What is, is that you need a husband. You need one who'll be faithful to you. What with my mother and my father, I don't know if that's bred into me. I doubt it. And I've seen how it hurts if a fellow swears constancy and then cheats. Seen it in a man when a wench does the same, and I'm not just talking about my mother."

He looked down into his hand, as though the walnut held the mystery of life within it.

"I'd like to help you. But I wouldn't want to try to do good and do evil instead. I can't swear to constancy, and I don't think you're a lass willing to put up with a rover. You need a man with a serious mind. That's definitely not me. I've had too much seriousness in my time. I plan to live my life lightly from now on.

"Even so," he went on as she stared at him, aghast, "if I thought I could help you by marrying you, I would. So I think what we ought to do is to find your wretched chit Rosie. Then, soon as we do, you come with me to the earl's house, and we'll let him find you a likely lad."

She rose to her feet, her hands clenched. "I'm not a difficult parcel that you're trying to see where to deliver. Whatever I've done, however foolish or misguided I've been, I did it all myself, and I'll take the responsibility for it. If worse comes to worst, what will happen? I won't starve; I won't be thrown out into the cold to fend for myself. There's no workhouse in my future, only my aunts' house. Even if my reputation is gone, well, especially if it is, my aunts will take me in. They're not good company, but they're terribly responsible, and . . ." she paused and permitted herself a ghostly little smile, "I think they'd actually love the chance to tell me how good and sacrificing they're being by taking me back."

Her lips trembled, and she turned to leave.

He was at her side in a moment. He put an arm around her shoulder, and held her. "You're not a parcel," he said, as she turned her head away from him. "You're not an obligation. By now, you're a friend of mine, and if I were a better man, you'd be more than that. In fact," he added on a whisper, "If I was a worse man, you'd be more than that, too. But I'm not. So, sit down. We'll work it all out. Anyway," he added as he steered her to the settee by the fireside. "Why run off to an icy bed? Time enough to do that. For now, come sit by me. Don't despair. We might bump right into the runaways tomorrow morning at breakfast."

He guided her to the settee, and then sat himself beside her. He never took his arm from around her shoulder. And he never stopped talking, slow and low. "Sit back, breathe deep, put your head on my shoulder. Loosen up; I won't do anything but sit beside you. I've been in your place too often to betray you. Come, lean on me and let the fear flow away," he said softly.

It wasn't hard for him to do. He told her the truth. He knew the way of this, he'd done it many times in the darkness of prison cells, in the rocking dark on prison ships, in the darkest of bleak nights in the face of impending disaster. If there was one thing a prisoner knew it was how to help another against despair, especially if he'd been so helped in his own past.

He didn't stroke her soft scented hair, though it tickled his nose, he didn't touch her in any other way. He didn't move his hand at all. He just sat beside her and let her absorb the warmth of his body and feel his slow, deep, even breathing, so she could unknowingly match hers to his.

"Hush," Daffyd said as she finally let her head lean against him. He settled her more comfortably. "Here, rest against my chest. They say 'lean on my shoulder,' but they don't know what they're talking about. Shoulders are hard and bony. A chest's like a pillow, however rocky. There. Comfortable?"

She nodded. But he could still feel how stiffly she held herself.

"Breathe in and out, think of nothing but the breathing," he said. "Of course, you're upset. It's worse at night. That's the way of problems in the night. They grow, because the dark magnifies fear and terror. It's a natural fact. Makes sense, because night is the opposite of day. Well, you know that if you hold a glass to the sun on a fine bright day you can start a fire in dry grass underneath it? You can. That's because the sun sends heat and light and the glass magnifies it. The night does the same, only in reverse. See? It makes everything dark bigger. Instead of starting a fire, the magnification of the night starts to suck out your soul, and it empties you of energy, it makes your thoughts darker than they were to start with. If you remember that, you can stop it from happening. Remember, by morning light, your problems and fears shrink back to size again."

He felt her lips curve in a smile against his chest.

"So, let's fool the night. I'll keep talking. It'll keep raining, but we'll hold back the night. Yes, you did do a silly thing. And you've had a mad adventure. But you know? One day, soon, when you look back, all of this—me included, will seem like some strange dream. Oh, you'll know it happened, but it will seem like it happened to someone else."

"Is that how it is with you?" she asked softly. "I mean, all the bad things that happened to you?"

He hesitated. "Yes, in a way. No, in a way, too. So much happened to me. I can't say my whole life was a dream, can I? I met some wild fellows in the Antipodes who do say that. But I don't think so. Still, yes, some of the really bad things do seem like a dream to me now. Some don't."

"How do you live with that?" she asked. "I mean, the regret, the fear, the sorrow?"

"I live with everything. I have to. Now, you, you'll just have a little misadventure to remember. But not now and not tonight. And you still have a chance to mend all. In fact, if you remember this in the future, it can be your one secret grand adventure. You know, something to sit by the fire and have a mysterious grin over, something to make your grandchildren wonder what the old lady was up to when she was young."

She smiled again.

"We'll see what tomorrow brings," he said. "One thing we already know—it will bring the light. Now, just relax."

She fell still, and slowly, he could feel the tension leave her body. He held her as close, as calmly and companionably as if she were a young child, or an old man, or a good friend, or a desperate stranger, or any of the other wretched people he'd had reason to see through a bad night in his tumultuous lifetime.

In time, she dozed.

Then he relaxed. He sat and thought of all the possible ways he could help her, and when he was done with that, he allowed himself at last to dare wonder if he could keep on helping her for the rest of their lives.

Daffyd sat by the fireside with a warm, sweet-scented woman asleep in his arms. He sighed, but carefully, so that the rise and fall of his chest didn't disturb her. The warmth and supple softness of her body felt good against his own. He caught the slightest scent of lemons and flowers that rose from her hair. He felt at peace, and yet felt a need for more. Without thinking, his hand left her shoulder and rose to her hair—and stopped in midair, before he'd touched one silken lock of it. His thin black brows lifted as he looked down at the sleeping woman. He'd surprised himself.

Daffyd carefully placed his hand back on Meg's shoulder, exactly where it had been. He sat quietly, and thought hard.

He wanted her, perhaps more than he'd wanted a female in a long time, and he knew he could have her. That was plain. He'd been teasing her with words, but he knew that was no way to seduce a woman. Words and glances set the stage. Still, the only way to seduce a woman was with touch, and he already knew what his touch did to her, and to himself. He could have her in his bed this very night.

All he had to do was to wake her, place a feathery kiss on her ear, angle his mouth along her soft neck, and whisper soft reassurances as her eyelids fluttered open. While she was still dozy and warm and relaxed, as her lips opened to ask where she was, he could kiss her mouth, deeply, sweetly, and thoroughly. She would rise to him. He didn't even have to take her here, where they sat, though he could. He could put his arms around her and ease her upstairs. He could slowly talk her up the stairs to his room and have her in a wide, clean bed, and show her what pleasure really was, and take his time about it, too.

She already wanted to make love to him. He had only to let her pretend she was still dreaming. Women liked to pretend, that was what seduction was all about. While her defenses were down, he could take her to his bed and have her, and it would be good.

But it would be cruel. With all he was, he tried never to be that. He'd seen enough of cruelty. It would be wrong because she was a one-man woman. And he wasn't that man.

He was a wild gypsy lad, cursed for it in every land he'd ever set foot in. The gypsies didn't want him because he was a bastard of the nobility. The nobility had too many bastards to concern themselves with. He was a Rom and a bastard and a convicted felon and he'd learned that the world considered him useless to everyone but himself.

But he'd also had the incredible luck to live until this hour. Not all of it had been bad. He'd experienced love, or what passed for it among strangers. In fact, he'd known more women than this woman in his arms did, and he'd known most of them carnally. That was because he knew how to get by in hard times, how to take every chance and seize every opportunity. He reasoned that was both the gypsy and the aristocrat in him. Both types only cared for their own, and both had only one aim: to survive. So much as he hated his heritage, he admitted it had kept him alive. He was awake on every suit, and proud of it. He knew a lot.

But he didn't know if he could ever be faithful to one woman. He certainly didn't know if any woman could ever be faithful to him. And for a lifetime? He thought it might be possible for some folk. As for himself? He didn't know, and with all he'd done, he wasn't willing to find out.

He'd had enough of pain. He'd told her only the truth: He meant to live life lightly from now on.

So he looked down at the sweet, dreaming woman in his arms and accepted that whatever became of her, his part in her life would soon be over. And that it would be better that way for him, and certainly for her.

Then Daffyd laid his head back against the settee, planning how to help her one last time, and then move on.

But from time to time, he sighed.

Chapter 15

"The sun's out, the road's dry and hard. The horses are rested and restive. So am I!" Daffyd called from outside Meg's bedchamber door. "Up and out. The hunt is on!"

Meg shot upright in bed and blinked at the sunlight poking through the cracks in the shutters. The last thing she remembered was Daffyd waking her, putting an arm around her, and walking her up the stairs to her bedchamber. No, she thought, with a groan, the last thing she remembered was standing in the hallway outside this room, swaying with weariness, suddenly cold, seeking the warmth she'd felt as she'd dozed beside him downstairs. She'd shivered, and looked up into his dark, dark eyes, hoping he'd take her in both arms and stay the night with her.

He'd looked down at her. Though she'd been fast asleep moments before, she'd suddenly realized she'd never been so awake in her life. She waited.

She'd waited in vain. He'd touched a finger to her nose. "I see you've heard the gossip," he'd said with a laugh. "But don't be fooled. I'm not that easy. I have a reputation to uphold—yours. Go to bed," he'd said, opened her door, and pushed her into the bedchamber. Alone.

Now, she remembered, and her head flopped back down against the pillow. She'd acted on mad impulse. He'd turned her down and she was very glad—and strangely sad.

"Up, up, up!" Daffyd caroled from the hallway. "Its half past dawn. I let you sleep in 'til the sun rose. I'm down to breakfast. If you want to ride on an empty stomach, fine. I don't. I leave in a half hour either way."

She heard his boot steps fading away. Meg scrambled from bed. He was right about the night and what it magnified. He just neglected to mention that it also increased desire and set a woman's body to burning as though a magnifying glass were being held to her heart—and nether regions.

But what she'd wanted in the night had nothing to do with what she had to do today. She looked for the chamber pot and the washbasin, saw them, and popped up out of bed, ready to set about making herself ready to go downstairs.

She hesitated.

She'd see Daffyd by daylight, and maybe see the

knowledge of exactly what she'd wanted to do last night in his eyes. Strangely though, she realized she wasn't embarrassed or ashamed of her nighttime longings. Because she knew that if anyone understood them, it would be Daffyd. She began to dress.

"Are we almost there?" Meg asked again as Daffyd tooled down the road toward the sea in the curricle he'd hired. She could smell a briny scent on the air now, from where she sat on the high driver seat. She hoped that the next turn in the road would show her the ocean and the port city where silly Rosie had landed at last.

"Soon," Daffyd said, as he turned the team around another corner.

Meg had to hang on to her bonnet, and her seat, but she pitched herself to the motion of the carriage and didn't lose her place or her breakfast as they turned. They were going at breakneck speed. She wasn't worried. "You drive well," she said with approval, when she got her breath back.

He glanced at her and grinned. "So that's why you stopped screeching. You like it now."

"I never screeched. I merely gasped."

"Sang like a bird," he said. "It inspired me. But that's the thing about new experiences. If they're any fun they scare you to death at first, yet if you survive you can get to enjoy anything."

"Speed is exhilarating," she said.

"And necessary. It's a fine day with a snapping wind blowing out to sea. I'll wager there are a lot of packets setting off today. We want to get there before they do. Ah," he said, and pointed with the whip. "There it is, there we are. Won't be long now."

Meg held her breath. As they came down the hill the turn showed her a glimpse of the city below. There was a long stretch of coastline and a dizzying array of topmasts and sails crowding the harbor.

"So many boats!" she groaned. "How will we ever find her?"

"Half the ships are fishermen or navy," Daffyd said. "She won't be there. Almost another half are traders, bringing goods in and out. The big ones wallowing in port are those that come and go with passengers as well as cargo. There are fewer of them. I know their names, and their destinations."

Meg's spirits still sank. "And how do we know she's even here?"

"Late in the day to ask that," he said, as he turned another corner. "But this is where I was told they're heading for. It's a seaport for the long haul, with ships heading to the New World: the Americas and Canada."

Meg sighed. "Canada? I remember when Rosie used to talk about the Canadian wilds all the time. They entranced her for a while. She would pick up books when a subject fascinated her, and Canada fascinated her. I couldn't get her mind off the subject. She read tales about the Canadian wilderness and learned more about bears and beavers and fur trapping than she ever did her French or watercolors."

Daffyd slowed the team and turned his head to look at her. "When was this?"

Meg shrugged. "Last Christmas. It was because of Thomas Rackham, her poor fiancé. It was one of his many enthusiasms. He was always getting her fired up with his mad schemes to get rich. The autumn before, all he could talk about was the Caribbean. He wanted to go there with her after they married. He kept talking about the sugar plantation they'd buy and manage until they were richer than anyone they knew. Rosie waltzed around the house for weeks talking about nothing but the tropical fruits and hibiscus and flowers big as horse's heads that she'd have in her garden when she went there. Of course her parents were appalled at the thought of her so far away. Thomas's parents were, too, so the idea was squashed.

"Then it was India and emeralds big as elephant's eyes, or rubies big as elephant's ears, I forget which, that the pair were prattling about. You can imagine the parents' reaction to that! They lectured about wars, savages, and fever, and threatened to disinherit the pair of them, even end the engagement if they didn't come to their senses. That put an end to any Indian adventure before it got further than a few books, maps, and globes.

"Then Thomas was off on his new tangent. All he talked about was a friend of his who went to Canada to make a fortune in rare pelts. Rosie caught fire about that, too. Whether it was the Orient or the North, they spoke about it with the same enthusiasm, as though they expected jewels in the streets and fur pelts laying themselves down on their doorstep."

Meg smiled sadly. "Thomas is a charmer, but the despair of his parents. They wanted him to settle down and look after the little estate his uncle left him, but he was always on about making a real fortune, going abroad and returning a nabob. Rosie played his games, planning fabulous futures as though she believed him. But it must have gotten tiresome. No wonder she finally got weary of him and ran off with . . ."

She blinked, and then stared at Daffyd. ". . . Or did she? But to Canada? *No!* You don't think . . . ?"

"I think," he said, as he raised the whip and set the horses flying, "that you might have remembered this a few weeks ago."

"But she was seen with a redheaded man. . . ."

"And a dark-haired one," Daffyd said grimly, "and a blond. And a man with a big hat. Whenever she was seen with the fellow, whatever wig he had on his noggin, she was always giggling and having a high old time. Like a pair of good old friends as much as lovers, my cousins reported. Did she ever look at another lad before? Did she seem like the type who would get so comfortable with a new man so fast?"

Meg shook her head. "No," she said. "But the reports of Thomas following the pair, riding like a fury?"

"I expect he thought it was a great lark, stowing her at an inn, doubling back and following his own trail partway, before returning to her in disguise again. They probably laughed for hours after."

Meg waited a long moment and then asked, with sinking heart, "So you always thought it was Thomas?"

He nodded. "Seemed likely. Now this flit to Plymouth and a boat to the New World makes a lot more sense. Those who knew the lad said he was a wild man with high imagination, so a midnight dash to the Continent would have been in keeping with his personality. But he didn't go to Dover, he kept heading south and west. I was puzzled. Now, I know why."

"I'm so sorry, I didn't think to tell you, I didn't know it was important, I . . ."

"How could you have known? You trusted her. It doesn't matter. We're here now, or almost."

Meg sighed. "So, at least it looks as though she's not a light-minded cheat. That's a great relief to me. I didn't really think she was, at least, I couldn't believe it. She's not a bad girl, just willful. The way she sees it she's only trying to make her own destiny, with her own true love. I can understand, even if her parents didn't. In fact, I sympathized. I thought we were friends as well as companions. I know that's nonsense, I was being paid to watch over her.

"But we're not that far apart in age. It's true I liked to read, and she liked to talk, and we didn't share much, but we did share laughter, sometimes, and . . . How could I have been so wrong? She knew I liked

Thomas. Why didn't she trust me, why couldn't she tell me?"

"Why? Because you're a nice, decent, law-abiding, moral female with a strong sense of responsibility. She knew that, as well as the fact that you *were* being paid to watch over her. I doubt she ever forgot it. The upper classes seldom befriend those beneath them, though they claim to when they have to. I suppose I'm being unfair. No, I know I am. But I often am. I'm sure you've noticed." He glanced over to see if he'd won a grin.

He hadn't, so he went on, "Anyway, I'll bet your Rosie didn't say anything because she knew you worried about her, with good cause. Of course you'd have told her parents."

Meg was still. Then she asked, in a little voice. "I suppose I would have. It would have been the right thing to do." She hesitated. "Would that have been so wrong?"

He shrugged one shoulder. "Yes. And no. It was your job. You're the type who does her job. It doesn't matter. If you hadn't, you'd have been in just as much trouble as you are now—maybe more. What was wrongest was that she didn't think to leave a note absolving you of blame."

He saw Meg's downcast eyes and added, "Stop blaming yourself. No matter how much she talked about foreign travels you couldn't have known she'd fly off in disguise, because you *are* moral and decent. It isn't a thing you'd have done."

"But I did," she said so quietly he almost didn't

hear her above the sound of the horses and the spinning carriage wheels.

"No," he said, when he understood what she'd murmured. "You chased her to save her. That's different."

"To save myself," she said on a sniffle.

"You're so good at blaming yourself, you leave no room for anyone else to do it. It *is* different. You had to find her. She didn't have to run away. You were earning a livelihood. She wanted adventure, pure and simple. You run for your supper, she's off on a lark. The worse thing is that she could get into trouble. So you were right to follow her, for whatever reason.

"Pelts don't lay in the street," he said, almost angrily. "They grow on wild animals that want to keep wearing them. Canada's a wilderness, and she sounds like the type who can't fend for herself in her back garden. Her man's a boy who acts without thinking. But luck favors lovers as much as the stupid, so she might come out of it without harm. She'll wind up married to the lad, if she isn't already. It's what her parents wanted, and maybe he can protect her, at that. He planned their escape well enough. But I don't trust in a mad young boy's schemes," he said grimly. "And I don't bank on luck. So let's try to get to them in time to give luck a hand."

Meg watched the scenery fly by as they went hurtling down a long curved road that led to the port of Plymouth.

* * *

Meg had been in fishing villages, visited the riverside in London many a time, and once gone to the Billingsgate Market, just to see what it was like. Nothing prepared her for the docks of Plymouth.

It was a city of seafarers. There were men from every land striding along the wooden boardwalks by the sea, or pushing their way through the throngs. There were men of every color and complexion. Meg saw smart naval officers and trim young ensigns, as well as common sailors of all stripes. There were men with beards and long hair, men with more tattoos than teeth, men with bright kerchiefs on their heads who looked like pirates, and boys running messages from the shipping offices to the ships at dock. There were gentlemen, too, along with dockworkers and sailors.

A few women, and those few obviously women of business, could be seen bearing baskets, dealing in mysterious stocks or trades. And of course, there were prostitutes, easily recognized by day or night. Only a few respectable-looking females, surrounded by their servants, could be glimpsed as they hurried to or from the ship's offices or the tall ships at dock.

Daffyd paused and squinted up at the sun. He held a paper in his hand. "Here's today's docket. We'll play the odds and search the ships bound for North America first. There are a lot leaving, trying to avoid the autumn storms. The *Doris* is off to Nova Scotia at the turn of the tide. *Mother's Love* sails for Maryland, and *Black Jack's Dream* is sailing to New York. And no," he said, seeing her expression, "the names mean nothing, no more than in horse racing. We decide by time of departure and destination. The *Wild Rose* is due to leave for Boston later in the day, so we'll see it last. First we visit the shipping offices and have a look at the manifests. Then, and only if we must, we board a ship and have a look 'round."

He saw her expression, and added, "No sane man steps aboard a vessel, even in time of peace, without either a ticket to go and return, or a mighty good reason to risk boarding. England still impresses her navy. America is still not entirely thrilled with Englishmen. Eighteen twelve wasn't that long ago. And too many merchant vessels need able-bodied crewmen and don't care much if they come aboard willing or not.

"I was a convict once. I'll not chance putting my neck in a chain again unless I see no way to avoid it. And forget about asking; a female *never* sets foot on a ship unless she's got a ticket of passage, is looking for bed work, or a pirate's dragged her there. The manifest should give us a good idea who's on board, even if they've given false names. A few coins to the officer in charge of the manifest will give us a better idea. Come along."

But though the stolid clerk who checked the list of passengers for the *Mother's Love* pocketed his coins fast enough, the only suspects he could offer were an elderly couple bound to see their son in the New World.

"I've seen them, sir," he told Daffyd. "And if they're not nearly a hundred years old apiece, I'm a blind man. The others are regular passengers. Sorry I can't be of more help. Have you tried the *Sea Swallow*? She was set to leave yesterday, but the captain had a bellyache."

The *Sea Swallow* had a pair of newlyweds aboard, but they were the captain's own son and daughter-in-law, and it was the captain's head, not his belly that had ached too much after a night of celebration for him to leave on time. There was a lone female, but she was a middle-aged governess, off to New York to work for a noble family.

Trips to the offices of the *Doris* and the *Black Jack* line produced no results either. No redheaded young men, no young lovers, no woman with a lisp had sailed on the last two tides.

The ship's offices weren't close to each other, so Meg and Daffyd had a lot of walking and talking to do. By the time the sun moved westward into afternoon, Meg was footsore and dispirited. Any chance of catching the eloping couple seemed a fantasy.

"Maybe they went to Portsmouth," she said sadly as she watched the *Wild Rose* out of the harbor, and saw the ship unfurl sails so she could fly away from England's shores. "Or Penzance. I was so sure it was Plymouth. But maybe it was another port that began with a P. Maybe I was wrong again."

"Or perhaps, 'Poland'?" Daffyd asked quizzically. "No. Don't doubt yourself about that now. Plymouth it was. My cousins aren't often wrong. And my noble brother almost never is, though please don't tell him I said that. Maybe we'll catch them tomorrow. Three ships leave at first light, two more on the next tide. Let's go to the inn, have a good dinner and a long night's rest, and start again at dawn."

"The inn?" Meg asked dully.

"The same one I've been telling all the pursers about if they want to get word to me. And it's also where my family can find me if need be. I don't just disappear into the ether, Meg; I always leave a trail for those who may have to follow. I'm a lone wolf, but a wise one. No man can ever be completely on his own. We're stopping at the *Old Bucket*, which, in spite of its name, is said to be tolerable. They have fresh linens, soft beds, and serve the best fish pie in England. Come along," he said, offering her his arm.

She looked up at him, the afternoon sun showing her eyes to be as clear as they were bleak. "It's my last day."

"On earth? I doubt it. Here in Plymouth?" His dark brows drew down in a frown. "Yes, I'd forgot. No matter, I've made arrangements. You'll be on a carriage at first light, off to your governess's cottage. Whatever happens, you'll be safe. When I find them, I'll get word to you."

She shook her head. "No. I've decided. I won't go. What's the point?"

"The point," he said patiently, "is your reputation."

"My reputation," she said hollowly, "is no longer

the point, or a point at all. Rosie's been gone too long. I was supposed to watch over her. The baron and his wife won't forgive me for their anxiety during these past weeks, my job was to prevent such things from happening. They'll never give me a recommendation now, and I can't find a decent position if my last employer won't vouch for me. Even if you do find her, I'll have overstayed my leave of absence.

"I won't go back without her," she said firmly, holding up her chin. "So I'll stay and see it through. At any rate, after all this time, it would be too painful not knowing for even more days and nights."

"You'll go, because something may be salvaged from this yet."

"No," she said. "I won't."

"Good," he said. "We'll have nice lively conversation at dinner tonight. And then, you're going," he added, as he offered his arm again.

"No," she said and stood, stubbornly staring at him. "The aunts will take me in no matter what, and so it doesn't matter if I go to them a few days later."

"Look," he said in exasperation, but didn't get a chance to say more.

"Mister? Mister Daffyd?" a young voice asked.

They looked down to see an earnest young boy, cap in hand, staring up at Daffyd.

"Aye," Daffyd said.

"Well, sir, my father, Mr. Greaves, of the *Black Jack* shipping line? Where you was earlier today, and

I saw you? After you left, I said something and my father had a thought, and he asked some questions. He said I'd find you and the lady here on the dock by the *Wild Rose*, and he gave me this note for you. He said he'd be glad to discuss it with you tomorrow, but as his office is closed now and his dinner's a-waiting, he sent this to you now."

Daffyd took a coin from his pocket and gave it to the boy, who bowed, handed over the note, and smiling, raced away.

Daffyd read the note, and his dark brows slammed down. "Damn, damn, damn," he muttered when he was done.

Meg's hands grew cold. "What?" she asked, not really wanting to hear. She was afraid of whatever had upset him.

He handed her the note:

My dear Sir, it said, on elegant embossed Black Jack Shipping Lines letterhead.

Such a couple as you described to me: a young handsome female with a lisp, and a tall thin, young gentleman, very well spoken, left these shores aboard Black Jack's Fancy, *one of the premiere ships of our line, a day past, bound for Halifax. I did not see to the embarkation, as I was busy with the departure of another ship of the line. But my son Jonathan did, as he is learning all facets of the trade. It was the mention of the young woman's speech impedi-*

*ment that triggered my young Jonathan's
memory. He is a likely lad, awake on every
suit.*

*Further inquiry revealed that the young
gentleman bought passage under the name of
Mr. and Mrs. Shaw, but at the last, before they
sailed, it appears that he confessed to the
captain that the manifest should be changed,
as their real names were Mr. and Mrs.
Thomas Rackham. This is not uncommon at
such a time, since some passengers about to
embark suddenly realize the perils of the
crossing they are about to undertake. They
fear that if they are lost at sea, so will their
identity be lost as well. Please do not be distressed. Such a calamity has never befallen
any vessel of our line and we work to ensure
it never does.*

*I have just now found the change of name
documented in a letter sent by the departing
captain, and have made the proper changes to
the manifest. As to the young couple's decep-
tion, we provide only passage. We are not Bow
Street. But if the pair are malefactors, you may
visit the Canadian authorities here in England, so the pair may be questioned when
they disembark.*

*The young couple left various notes to be dis-
bursed to friends and family, which we have not
as yet sent on. Though there is no such missive*

*for you, perhaps the young woman you were
with would like to see if there is one for her.*

> *Your servant,*
> *John Greaves*

Meg put the note down. Her eyes were dry, and
they hurt. She was too upset for tears, and too
numbed to speak. She could only stare out to the
wide sea and watch the fading ripples of the wake
the last ship left behind, and feel her heart grow cold.

"Damn, damn, damn," she whispered.

Chapter 16

◠◡◠

The *Old Bucket* was a clean, nicely furnished, and well-run inn. It was close to the sea, but far enough away for the pervasive sounds and smells of the docks to be muted. Meg only nodded when asked if her large, airy room suited. She looked at it, dull-eyed, and then went silently in to wash and change for dinner.

The private dining room she joined Daffyd in was snug and cheery. He rose to greet her. He'd changed his clothing, and now wore sober evening dress. His hair was damp and freshly brushed, he'd patted spicy scented toilet water on his freshly shaven face. He looked the perfect gentleman of means.

Meg took her seat quietly. She was gowned in lilac

259

and wore a lilac ribbon in her soft curls. Her whole demeanor was tragic and funereal. Daffyd ordered dinner, hoping the fare at the *Old Bucket* would lift her spirits. Food, he'd discovered, usually did.

The fish pie was excellent, but he realized it wasn't to everyone's taste, and understood when she left it untouched. The claret was full bodied, the canary wine light as springtime, the ale was fresh and clean tasting. She only wet her lips with wine, and stared down at her plate.

The soup was thick and delicious. The beef was tender and the fowl fragrant. The ham was juicy and the meat pie savory. The lobster was buttery and the tiny prawns were sauced delicately. Meg didn't eat anything; she only tasted, and that only at Daffyd's repeated insistence.

When she didn't so much as touch a spoon to the plum tart at dessert, even after Daffyd made a show of pouring fresh cream over it, taking a bite and sighing with bliss, he became genuinely alarmed.

"Are you sickening?" he asked.

"I just don't feel like eating," she said.

He drummed his fingers on the table. "So they've done it," he said. "Don't think that doesn't stick in my craw, too. Still, done's done, and they got away with it. It's over. We're not swimming after them. The baron will have a fit when he finds out. But when he calms down he'll realize that at least she's with the man he picked to be her husband. His wife, and the lad's parents, will rail and grouse and blame each other. Then they'll have time to think on it. A lot of time. Absence and worry about the pairs' welfare will make their hearts grow fonder.

"I'd bet they'll even congratulate the couple on their cleverness—in time," he added, "and with a grandchild or two. Maybe the runaways will make a success in the New World. Maybe they'll come home with their tails tucked under. Either way, they'll be forgiven, depend on it."

At last, Meg raised her gaze from her plate. Her eyes were bleak. "Yes, of course, after all," she added bitterly, "there's Rosie's splendidly informative note to absolve me, isn't there?

" *'Dear Meg,'* " she read, taking the crumpled note from her pocket.

" *'Such fun! Tom and I have eloped this time instead of just talking about it, gone to make our fortune! We dressed up and down, and sometimes he sneaked away and pretended to be following us . . . Oh, I know that doesn't make sense, but it was such fun, and we did it! Wish us luck! I know you do!*

Love, Rosie' "

She crumpled the note in her fist again. "I thought I'd taught her to restrain herself with those exclamation points," she murmured. "Her note makes me seem like an accomplice, but yes, if she ever writes more, the baron and his wife may forgive me, in time. I don't have that time. I'm going back to my aunts' tomorrow," she said briskly. "It makes no sense for me to hide at my dear old governess's cottage now. I never was comfortable making her party to a lie, and there's no reason for it now."

She gave him a wobbly little smile that never reached her eyes. "And as you say, in time I might get my recommendation from the baron, and who knows? I may find an excellent position again."

He leaned forward, his expression serious. "Be-damned to that! No 'in time' about it, your time is now. You'll come with me tomorrow. We'll go to my friend and benefactor, the earl of Egremont's, in London. He was a convict, too, but he was never guilty. That's been proved. He's got money and position, and is the most decent man I ever knew. He has decent friends now, too. I know his son Christian does. For that matter, so does my adopted brother Amyas. They'll be sympathetic. We'll get you placed in a good position with good people, so there's no need for you to throw yourself on your aunts' charity."

Now he could see how her eyes glittered as her head came up. He never realized such a piquant face could look so murderous. "And there's no need to throw myself on your charity either!" she said through clenched teeth. "You seem to have forgotten: I traveled the length of England with you, alone. It's not just you—the point is that I traveled alone, with a male, for days and nights on end. I'll not get a good thought from any decent person, and it would be wrong of you to ask the earl for a recommendation saying I'm responsible and moral, *especially* if he's a good man.

"Why, *I* wouldn't believe I was in any way innocent if I didn't know me," she said angrily. "Because even if I did end with my honor intact, there's not a sane person who'd believe it. I scarcely do myself! And what's 'honor'? It's only that I emerged . . . intact," she said, her cheeks growing red as the untouched claret in the glass in front of her. "And only we know it. Besides, that wouldn't be my idea of honor, I can tell you!"

She sat back, bitterly triumphant.

"That kind of honor works for most men," Daffyd said dryly. "It always has, so don't belittle it. Proof of virginity goes for lot on the open market, in marriage . . . or otherwise. I won't go into that. But let me tell you it cost me enough to keep you that way, and that's no lie.

"Now," he said as she gaped at him, "if you don't want to apply to the earl, and I'll bet you will after you meet him, we can ask my brothers. If you don't think they can do enough, I could . . ." He hesitated. ". . . apply to my mother. I failed her by not stopping the runaways. It should please her to do me a favor, even so."

He frowned. "Whatever her reasons, she can do it. She'll find someone highly placed to give you a recommendation. She has no reputation, but it don't matter," he said, his accent becoming rough. "She's got enough money and social standing to ask favors of the Pope. I'll bet she could blackmail anyone in England. But first, we go to London, and the earl."

"No. I'm going home."

"Afraid I'll be proved right? Poor spirited of you," Daffyd said with a nasty smile. "I thought you had more bottom."

She paused, thinking of what to retort.

Daffyd took the opportunity to taunt her again. "Easy to hop on a coach and hie back to your aunts. Nothing simpler: 'I sinned, take me in,'" he mimicked in a high voice, putting his hands together prayerfully. "'Poor me, doomed for eternity.' Ha!" he went on in his usual tones. "Easy. Harder to face the unknown, ain't it? After all, if you dared try something new you might find new insult. Or you could find a solution. That might be worse for you. Then you won't be able to wallow in self-pity." He leaned forward and stared at her, his eyes dark and angry. "I tell you, if I'd had your attitude I'd be a heap of moldering old bones in Newgate's cellars now."

She frowned.

He waited.

She put her spoon into her serving of plum tart, lifted it to her lips, chewed and swallowed. "It is good," she said coolly. "Is there any of that meat pie left? It smelled wonderful."

"It was, and there is," he said.

She ate her dinner. He watched her, and sipped

wine. They never spoke about the next day. They didn't have to. Daffyd had many faults, but they both knew he never gloated.

Daffyd couldn't sleep, and that irked him. He was proud of his ability to sleep anywhere. He'd slept in places people were afraid to die in, he often bragged. But here, in a snug inn, in a wide, clean bed, with nothing but the soft, distant sound of the sea in his ears, he couldn't even doze. He turned over. Again.

Sleep eluded him. Of course, he was annoyed because he'd failed, when he'd been so sure of success. He'd intended to present his mother with her runaway goddaughter, refuse all thanks or reward, then bowing, silently slip away. It would have been a delicious sour victory. He, who had been nothing to her but an inconvenience she'd gladly rid herself of, would have appeared from nowhere to help her, even though she'd never done anything but hurt him. There would have been a reverse sort of joy in it, the only joy he'd ever known from her. Yesterday's outgoing tide had snatched that away.

If it were only that he'd have slept. He was used to disappointment. It wasn't his mother's reaction that kept him from finding a comfortable position in his bed. It was the look on Meg's face that haunted him. She'd looked crushed. That little flower face of hers had been a portrait of sorrow. He'd seen females suffer, of course; both physically and mentally, and had often been unable to help. He'd thought himself impervious to that sort of hurt. He wasn't. That surprised him, and kept him wakeful. *Damn*, he thought, and turned over again.

He was trying to think of all the bad places he'd slept, trying to feel luxurious and grateful for where he was, when he heard a sound at his door. He sat up and reached beneath his pillow for the knife he always kept nearby. His pistol was on the table near the bed, and he was calculating how fast he could get to that, when he saw his door slowly opening. He hadn't thought to bolt it! He silently cursed himself for his unusual lack of foresight. He'd been lulled into carelessness because the adventure was over, he'd had a bit of wine at dinner, too, and the inn had looked so safe. He damned himself for a fool, and tensed.

The door opened further.

"Daffyd?" a small scared voice whispered.

He jumped to his feet, strode to the door, and threw it wide.

Meg stood there in a long white nightshift, looking like a sleepwalking child suddenly wakened. She stared at him, wide-eyed.

"What is it?" he demanded in a rough whisper. "Someone in your room?"

She shook her head in denial, and kept staring. He noticed she was looking at the knife he held, and lowered his arm.

"So what is it?" he asked.

"Well," she said. "I couldn't sleep."

He stared at her.

She looked down at her bare toes.

"You couldn't sleep?" he asked in confusion. Did she want to sit and talk with him?

"Well, no, I couldn't sleep at all," she said. He saw the white fabric at her bosom rise as she took a deep breath, and blurted, "I couldn't because it occurred to me that this is the last time we'll ever be alone together, and as I have no reputation left, and am not likely to have much of a life left, at least not in the sense of free will and adventure, that I'd like to make love with you, if you're still interested."

He kept staring.

"I wouldn't ask if you hadn't always asked," she said in a smaller voice. "I mean, I wouldn't want to be presumptuous. How rude, after all, to ask someone to do something as intimate as that if they really didn't care to, after all."

"Come in," he said.

She stepped inside and stood upright, looking about as seductive, he thought, as the carved wooden figurehead on the prow of a ship. No, he decided, he was wrong. At least the figureheads were usually half draped, and smiling. "Sit down," he said.

She looked around for a chair.

"On the bed," he said. "Saves time. I mean, why start at one end of a room if you intend to end up on the other?" He tried not to smile. But he hadn't been so amused in a long time. He couldn't read her expression clearly in the faint moonlight that came through his window. But he could guess at it from how rigidly she held her shoulders, and then, how slowly she proceeded to his bed.

She climbed the short bed stair and settled herself on the edge of the bed, her legs and feet pressed as close together as a schoolgirl's on a stage.

He closed the door, bolted it, and came to sit beside her. "May I ask if attraction to me plays any part of this?"

"Of course. I wouldn't be here otherwise."

"That's a relief. So, you've decided that you'll never marry?"

"I didn't say that," she said. "Though it's unlikely."

"I see. And if you do, what do you plan to tell your future husband, if there is one, on your wedding night?"

"Well, he won't believe that I'm not experienced after I traipsed halfway through England with you, will he?" she flashed back at him, showing sudden spirit. "And I expect anyone who knew me will have heard about that. He'd have to be an understanding sort if he married me, wouldn't he?"

"You know," Daffyd said quietly, as he just as slowly and quietly placed his arm around her shoulder, "you're making more of this than need be."

She flinched when he touched her, and then quickly recovered, relaxing, with effort.

"You're not a titled lady or a famous courtesan," he said in the same lazy, easy way. He brushed his hand across her flushed cheek. "Your name, if it's bruited at all, will be forgotten. If you stay away from your aunts and the village they live in, I doubt anyone will even remember it in a year or two. Did you ever consider that?

"Not that I'm trying to dissuade you, of course," he added conscientiously. "I like your decision. Very flattering to be told you're desired because you're someone's last chance at having sex on this earth. But I've been told that before," he added thoughtfully. "And I've obliged just for that reason, too. So I'm used to it," he said, frowning as he remembered how true that was.

"Then you understand, I thought you would," she said sadly. "Maybe you're right, maybe they won't remember me and what I did." She turned her head to look him in the eyes and told him the absolute truth that had driven her from her bed to this place. "But I'll remember. And I want to remember you."

That took his breath away. All amusement fled, all sad memories, too. "I see," was all he could say as he looked into her eyes. They were wide, and serious.

He'd been playing with her. He'd intended to send her back to her room after a kiss. It was late and she'd been crushed, and she wasn't used to adventure or failure. But lovemaking wasn't the answer for her, at least, not for the moral and upright Miss Shaw. He knew the consequences of lovemaking, even if she didn't. But he was after all, only human. He reacted. He lowered his head to hers, and kissed her.

All her shyness fled. She wrapped her arms

around his neck and pressed herself to him, and kissed him back with all her heart.

Her mouth was soft and pliant under his, her tongue dared to dart out and seek his. He responded, gathering her closer, drinking more deeply at her lips. One arm was still around her, his other hand went to her breast. He made a sound of annoyance deep in his throat. "No," he whispered into her ear. "You're dressed. We can't do this dressed."

He could feel her stiffen in his arms. Well, that had discouraged her, he thought, and saved him the frustration of doing it later. But he owed her the truth.

"If a man and a woman have the luxury of being alone," he explained. "They shouldn't have to make love fully clothed. It's not fair to you, or me." He drew back, held her shoulders in his hands and looked at her. "Can you do this? You can still change your mind. You can always change your mind. There's only one point where it would be too late. We won't get to that point tonight."

She didn't understand, but she believed him. She reached down and tried to take the hem of her shift in her hands.

"You're sure?" he asked in amazement.

She didn't answer, only tugged and struggled to be free of her nightshift. But she was sitting in deep soft feathers and couldn't manage to raise one end of her shift above her bottom no matter how she tried.

He chuckled, and raising her in his arms, pulled the shift over her head in one swift movement. Then he stopped and looked at her. She froze. He sighed.

There was little on earth as beautiful to him as a naked woman, but even so, she delighted him. If she weren't so inexperienced, he'd have stood her on her feet so he could study the loveliness he'd unveiled. As it was, he looked at her and rejoiced.

He told her why. He thought she needed to know; he knew he needed to tell her, if only to rid her of that fearful look she wore.

"Your breasts are beautiful!" he exclaimed. "Just the right size and shape, uplifted and firm, they look like the breasts on a statue, they're so perfect. But lucky for me, they're not, they're warm and soft." He caressed her breasts as he told her that, and felt her nipples pucker in his palms. "Oh good," he whispered, "you like that. So do I." He bent his mouth to her breast and heard her draw in her breath sharply. "You taste good, too," he said after a moment. "Your skin's so smooth and warm. Your hips swell out, just so, in just the right way. Your bottom's adorable," he said, as he raised her in his arms again. "There, doesn't it feel better when you sit on my lap? Or it would if you'd disregard that annoying stick you feel. Wait, I'll move and it won't bother you."

She knew enough about men to know what was happening, though she'd never experienced such a thing before. He shifted her, and she blinked. Because now she felt his taut rod beneath her thigh, and it felt very much like the end of a broomstick poking her. She thought he must be an enormous size, and felt her courage fail.

But he laughed. "You see, I don't lie. My body

won't allow it. That's just me rising to the occasion, appreciating you. I'm trying . . . there. It's not directly beneath you now. Not to worry. I won't trouble you with it, though it's killing me. Not so," he said when he realized she didn't understand. "Forget it. Concentrate on what you feel. Isn't that good?"

She took a deep shuddering breath. "What about how you feel?"

"Oh, I feel fine," he murmured against her heart.

"But we're alone," she said, and shivered as he tasted her other breast. "And you're still dressed."

"Observant," he said, and drew back. "You want me naked?"

She nodded. "It's only fair."

He blinked, nodded, and immediately pulled his nightshirt over his head. "Done," he said. "Content?"

She surprised him further. She moved away so she could examine him. She placed a tentative hand on his heart. "You're very good-looking," she said. "I mean, your chest is very well muscled. And clean, you smell of soap."

"I grew used to luxury," he said.

"And though you're swarthy," she went on, "you haven't a great mat of hair on your chest. I mean, you have some hair, which only makes sense, because you're a man. But I've seen farm laborers without their shirts, sometimes, in the fields. Some have great bearish chests. You don't. Yours is like a statue's too. A Greek statue. That's very attractive."

"Credit where it's due," he managed to say. "Maybe those old models were bearish too. It's hard to sculpt hair, I think," he said, because the impulse was irresistible. He realized she was trying to do for him in words what he had done for her. She likely thought it was what he expected. He was torn. He wanted to tell her it was unnecessary, but he wanted to hear what else she had to say.

"And you're well proportioned," she persisted valiantly, obviously trying to think of flattering things to say to a naked male. "And your skin is clear and your . . . that is to say . . ." She struggled for words.

He saved her. He pulled her into his arms. "Thank you," he whispered. "But now I don't want to talk. Do you?"

He didn't give her a chance to answer.

She discovered there was nothing she wanted to say. She could only shiver. He kissed her lips until she felt her body begin to flame, and then he drew away and kissed her body until she shook. She was no longer afraid or worried about what he'd think of her, as she'd been when she'd dared come to his room. She no longer cared about anything but discovering where he was slowly and surely taking her.

He knew it.

When she had time to think at all, when he drew back and looked deep into her eyes, she shivered again, this time because she realized again that this night would ruin her. But she'd finish what she'd begun. She'd told him the truth. It was her last chance. She dared reach out and caress him.

"Yes," he said. "Now this." He laid her back against the pillows and followed her there, laying his body over her, holding himself up on his elbows. He kissed her and put his hand on her sex. She instinctively closed her legs. "No," he said, "let me. You'll see."

She took a deep breath, and let him part her. He kissed her mouth as his hand sought her intimately, and she thought she'd die of embarrassment. Then she thought she'd die of pleasure. When he slipped a finger inside her, she gasped into his mouth. When he withdrew and did it again, and then again, and yet again, she shut her eyes tight to hold in the feeling and the shame and the glory of it.

"Yes," he said, and said it again when she finally arched against his hand.

She felt herself ignite, felt the long sweet thrill of it, and rocked against him. She felt such intense pleasure she couldn't hold it together, and she shattered. Then the glorious feeling persisted, differently. It spiraled down, her whole body pulsing and humming.

He withdrew his hand, and lay down beside her.

When her senses returned, she buried her face in his chest. He stroked her hair, and smiled.

She felt his heart still racing, his skin was furnace hot. Then she understood. "But you felt nothing."

"I felt your pleasure," he said.

She sat up. "That's nothing. You cheated."

"Gypsies and convicts and slum lads, those who can't afford much, but who want to give satisfaction, know a thing or three. We know value, for one thing. There are ways you can pleasure a woman without encumbering her or devaluing her, without taking away that precious honor you mentioned," he said. "That was one of them."

"That's not fair to you," she persisted.

He looked at her, and cocked his head to the side. "No, I suppose not. What do you want to do about it?"

"What you did for me. Show me."

He took her hand. "It means you have to shake hands with this fellow," he said, putting her hand on his aroused sex. "I'll understand if you don't want to. It won't dishonor you, but it may teach you more than you want to know."

She closed her hand over his sex. It felt hot and silky and urgent, and for all he tried to appear calm, she could hear breathless urgency in his voice. "Show me," she said again.

He did.

At the end, he suddenly pulled away from her with a groan, and threw himself down on the bed, his face in a pillow, his body arcing into the sheets.

"Thank you," he said breathlessly, after a moment. He moved away from where he'd been. "Now, come here and rest a while with me. You can't stay here all night. But for now, stay with me."

She came into his arms and pressed close to him. He was flaccid now. She felt drained, too, and suddenly, curiously empty. She'd asked to bed him, and he'd taken her. But he hadn't had sex with her. Not really. She should be grateful, and she supposed she was. They'd been intimate in a way, and it had been beyond her expectations. He'd surprised her. After all his enticements and wicked talk, he'd behaved like an experienced gentleman with a gently bred young female. She should be content.

But for all the pleasure he'd shown her and all the pleasure she'd tried to give him, they hadn't exchanged one single word of affection.

"Weeping?" he asked curiously. "But why? I didn't ruin you."

"I know. Thank you. I'm a fool," she said.

"No. It was new to you. But don't worry. You're safe," he said. "No one will ever know."

I will, she thought. *And I'll never forget. But you will.* And then she wept some more.

Chapter 17

Daffyd rose from his chair and smiled at Meg as she came into the inn's sunny breakfast parlor. His smile had no smugness in it, no secrets, not a hint of any hidden message, and certainly not a jot of gloating. Meg let out a shaky breath. He was behaving just as a gentleman ought. But she was sure her own face showed embarrassment, guilt, and confusion.

It did.

Daffyd sat when Meg did, and hid his unease. She looked wary and unhappy, and he knew he was the cause of it. He was also tired; he hadn't slept after he'd taken her back to her room in the middle of the night. He wasn't used to losing sleep over things he couldn't change. It wasn't as though he was sorry for what he'd done, because after all, as he'd kept reassuring himself, he hadn't actually done much. She could still claim innocence; he hadn't altered her future in any way, except perhaps, for changing her expectations of lovemaking, and for the better. She'd enjoyed herself, he knew that. But she'd been unhappy afterward. In fact, she hadn't said one word to him until, at her door, she'd said: "Thank you. Good night."

Not exactly the kind of statement that should have kept him wakeful until dawn. But it was the way she'd said it. She'd sounded lost. Now, in the clear light of day, he wished he'd kept his hands to himself and was grateful that at least he'd kept his body to himself. He was used to merry and mutual appreciation during and after lovemaking. Not despair.

That's what he got for trifling with gently bred females, he thought gloomily. There were enough of the other sort to last him all his life and he'd always been content, no—delighted with them.

He liked Meg. And he enjoyed her company. She wasn't like other females he'd known, but then, he'd only known slum children, criminals, prostitutes, and lately, wealthy and wild women who cared for nothing but their own pleasure. Meg had been fascinatingly different, educated and prim, but with seething fires underneath. He'd had an unexpectedly challenging and eventually fine time with her on their travels.

But he'd made a mistake. He vowed to stay away from gently bred females in future. They took things too seriously, especially lovemaking, even just a kiss and a cuddle. But that was who Meg was, and he'd done what he'd done. It couldn't be changed, but it could be made light of. So he set about putting her at ease.

It wasn't only for her sake. Daffyd thought of his mentor and friend, Geoffrey Sauvage, the earl of Egremont. If he introduced Meg to the earl as she looked now: subdued, chastened, and guilty, Geoffrey would have his ears. The woman looked as though she'd been shamed. Damnation, but looking at her now gave his own heart a wrench, even though he was sure she'd brighten up as soon as she was gone from him, and then she'd consider herself lucky to be shut of him. But given his reputation and the time he'd spent alone with her in the past week, even if the earl didn't know what had happened last night, he'd be sure to guess. Worse, Daffyd thought unhappily, he'd think even worse. Anyone would. And the earl had higher expectations than most men.

The earl had standards. He'd never relaxed them, not even in prison, not even when he'd been in darkest despair. He believed in respecting females as well as males, and treating both decently until and unless they proved unworthy of it. If they were unworthy, then they should be avoided. It had astonished Daffyd how people generally rose to the earl's standards, except for the utter villains, of course.

The earl had been a shining example in Daffyd's darkest hours. Even when he'd been in filthy tatters, beset by hunger and pain, the earl had exemplified grace under fire, acting justly even when justice was nowhere else to be found. There was no one on earth whom Daffyd respected more. He'd taught Daffyd to behave like a gentleman, but more important, he'd taught him to *be* one. Daffyd never wanted to lose the earl's respect, because if he did, he knew he'd forever lose his own good opinion of himself. So he had to set Meg at ease again.

"Did you sleep well?" Daffyd asked her.

She stiffened, and shot a look at him.

"I mean," he said quickly, "you look a little out of sorts."

"Oh, no," she lied. "I'm just tired, I suppose . . ." She hesitated, colored, and added, "I'll be fine as soon as I have some chocolate."

"That," he said with a smile, "we can do." He reached for the pot of chocolate on the table, and poured her a cup.

As he did, she seized the moment and looked fully at him, to study at that fascinating face without him noticing. She noted his long-lashed dark blue eyes, and when he looked up, dropped her gaze to his mouth. She felt herself blushing as she remembered how that shapely mouth had felt against her own. So she looked away and saw his dark hair was slightly damp, and remembered how silky it had felt as it brushed against her naked skin.

She decided it was safest to study the tiny roses on the cup he was filling. Because if he was too much for her in the warm darkness, he was far too much to look at in the broad sunlight.

This morning her gypsy lover was scrupulously clean, dressed soberly and well. He looked a perfect gentleman. He'd been a gentleman last night, too. He'd kept her safe because he'd only played at love. He'd humored her, pleasured her—it had been all for her. The sad thing was that she'd realized it probably wasn't what he did with females who really attracted him.

She knew he didn't love her, but it was painful to realize he didn't even desire her. She'd read novels. She'd heard gossip, knew the old songs, and listened to the stories of sadder and wiser servant maids who'd been compromised. Desire was intense and irrepressible. It was a force, if the poets and the fallen servant maids could be believed, that was overwhelming, like a storm or a flood or any cataclysmic act of nature. It was irresistible. That was definitely not what Daffyd had felt toward her last night.

"Look," Daffyd said now, interrupting her thoughts by leaning forward to whisper, even though the landlord had left them alone. "What happened— it's over. I think nothing of it and neither should you. Just a bit of fun. Someday, in the future, you'll be able to remember and laugh, and maybe even feel a bit sentimental. As for now? No harm done. No shame, neither. No reason for it. I've forgotten it already. You should, too. You are, after all, only human, Meg."

Everything he said was true, and every word chilled her.

Because she was lost. She loved the man, and had, she realized, for quite a while. It wasn't just his generosity to a strange female in distress, or his valor in protecting her, or the amazing uncomplaining way he got on with a life that had been unfair to him from the start. It was the look of him and the taste of him and the sound of his voice. It was the fact that she'd never felt so challenged, and yet at home, as she did when she was with him.

She'd thought she had no future with him because of who he was and what his past had been. Now she knew she'd been an utter fool. It didn't matter what he was born as, or what life had forced upon him, she only knew it had made him the man she wanted to spend the rest of her life with. But she had only days left with him. She didn't know how she'd get on with her life when they parted, and part they would, and soon.

And so, for all that she knew it was stupid and useless and unprofitable, still she didn't want him to think what had happened was nothing. Because it had been everything to her and she knew their careful night of love was all that she'd ever have of love, or ever want, because she wanted no one else but him.

That was, of course, impossible. Not because he was a bastard and a gypsy and a convicted felon. But because he didn't want a woman like her. He wanted light love and easy partners, a life of gaiety and lack of responsibility. He'd said it often enough. He deserved what he wanted, too. She was the one who had erred. Not Daffyd.

Last night had been shocking, thrilling, wonderful—until she'd realized that if he really desired her he wouldn't have been able to stop himself from making love to her, at least not so easily. He'd been amused, utterly in control. It was the knowledge of his charity that destroyed her, not the fact that they'd shared some trifling pleasure in a bed.

But she wouldn't ask for more. She managed a smile. "You're right," she told him. "I'm making a big fuss over very little."

He frowned and eyed her to see if there was a barbed jest hidden in what she'd just said, or if she'd just spoken quickly and was too innocent to see the pun. She did have a fine sense of humor, and he had a lovely, filthy pun to match with it. But he hesitated. It wasn't likely she was trying to be saucy. Not about his body. Though she'd melted in his arms, she was a long way from being able to joke about privy parts.

"So," she went on with forced energy, "how long will it take to get to London? I won't fight you on that anymore. We'll go. But I want to be off to my aunts' before much more time passes. That hasn't changed."

"First, we have to get there," he said. "Then, we have to talk to the earl. Then we'll see about where you go next."

"Correction," she said, raising a finger. "For all I'm grateful to you, Daffyd, I'll see to my own destiny, thank you."

"You're welcome," he said. "Finish your breakfast and we'll get on with it."

*   *   *

Meg didn't move when the coach finally stopped in front of the earl of Egremont's tall gray townhouse in the best section of London, across from the park.

"Coming?" Daffyd asked, extending a hand to her as a footman let down the small stair to their carriage.

"I don't know," she said. "I mean, I know I can't just stay here, but I didn't expect such a grand house. Oh, Daffyd, must I?"

"Yes. He's a very nice man, Meg. Not as cold and imposing as this house. It isn't his, not really, anyway. He inherited it, and doesn't like it above half. Too much like something His Majesty would build to house relics, he says, and he's right. Geoff—the earl—is a much warmer fellow. You'll see. Damnation, Meg," he said as she still hesitated, "if you could face my toplofty half brother in his palace of sin, not to mention sleep like a dead thing in a caravan surrounded by packs of thievish gypsies, why stick now at visiting an earl? Come on, let's go in."

She gave him her hand and followed him out the door and down the carriage stair. She looked up at the house before her. A range of footmen, all in gray and blue livery stood on each step that led up to the house, and a butler stood on the top one in front of the door.

Meg went up the stair with Daffyd, feeling as though she were taking part in some ceremony. That ended when they got to the door.

A man came out. Middle-aged, muscular, and obviously fit, he was dressed like a gentleman of means. He had a full head of brown hair brushed back in the latest fashion, blue eyes, and his strong-featured face was tanned. His teeth were large, white, and even. Meg knew that, because he was smiling so widely she could see almost every one of them.

"Daffy!" he cried, as he embraced Daffyd and thumped him on the back. "You're back, at last, you young dog! I don't even know if you deserve being called that noble beast's name! You only sent me bits and pieces of your adventures along the road. I must hear all . . ." he stopped when he saw Meg where she stood, silent and apprehensive.

"And this must be Miss Shaw," the earl of Egremont said in his deep, rich, mellifluous voice. He gave her a gentler smile. "Such a brave young woman. I commend you for your initiative, so rare these days in well-bred young females. Women are trained to be die-away and fearful of change. But they need courage as much as men do. I was heartened to hear of your bravery, and I'm sorry the runaways eluded you. One thing is sure. They must have been lucky as well as clever to give our Daffy the slip.

"But no harm done," he said briskly. "They're an engaged couple. And as for you, young woman, you're in exactly the right place at last. We'll see that you're not harmed because of their misadventure. But that's later. For now, come in. Wash off the dust from the road, relax, take a nice nap, whatever you wish. My house is yours."

"But first," Daffyd said dryly. "Meg, allow me to

introduce you to my friend and mentor, the earl of Egremont. Earl, here is Miss Margaret Shaw."

The earl laughed, and clapped Daffyd on the shoulder. "You learn fast, and never forget, do you? Excuse me, Miss Shaw," he went on, "My manners flew away in my excitement. But I'm so glad to see you both."

Meg felt a warm glow suffuse her. The earl wasn't a bit haughty or censorious; no one could have made her feel more at home. Her tensed muscles relaxed. Maybe she had found a safe harbor at last.

"Now. All formalities done," the earl went on, "shall we enter my house, before the neighbors fall out of their upper windows trying to see and hear more? I'm a scandal," he confided to Meg as he offered her his arm. He looked up at the surrounding townhouses, and lowered his voice. "They risk their necks trying to see what I'm doing when I so much as step out to get some air, they must be in ecstasies of curiosity now."

Meg's smile slipped. The earl was a paragon of charm and warmth, just as Daffyd had predicted. But the world was as she'd thought, just as she'd feared.

"She's lovely, but I never expected her to be otherwise," the earl said to Daffyd after dinner. Meg had gone to her bedchamber, the house was quiet, and the two men sat in the earl's private study.

The earl looked over his goblet of brandy to see Daffyd's reaction to his comment. His guest was gone.

"Daffyd," the earl said, without glancing around the room. "I'm getting a sore neck tracking you. Sit."

Daffyd came from a far corner of the study, and sat in the chair opposite the earl. "Sorry. You know I pace when I feel cornered."

"I cornered you?" the earl asked in genuine confusion.

Daffyd shrugged. "You assumed she was lovely before you saw her. You think it's all because I couldn't resist a pretty piece."

"She's more than that, and we both know it. Not in the classic style, of course. Not the look of a grand lady, she hasn't the imperious nose or the noble brow. She's got a charming little face, rather like a flower. Winsome. The sort of face that registers emotions, I've no doubt she'll be even lovelier as she ages. And her figure is of course, enticing."

"Indeed," Daffyd said coldly.

"You don't think so?" the earl asked in surprise.

"I'm not blind, of course I think so."

"It's not just my opinion. Nor did I assume a thing. Your brother the viscount wrote to me and told me about her."

Daffyd frowned. "Leland thinks everything in skirts is attractive."

"But she is, remarkably so for a girl who doesn't try to entice."

"The point is," Daffyd said through gritted teeth, "that I don't just help pretty chits."

"I know. Remember Annie Potts and Selma Fisher?"

Daffyd smiled, diverted. "Did you ever see an uglier bit of goods than Selma? Male or female? Gads, I still haven't."

"No, and I hope I never do," the earl said with a smile. "Still you saved her from further abuse from that guard at Newgate. Some men can't help hurting the defenseless. She'd done nothing to deserve his disdain except for being as nature made her. You knew it and it infuriated you. You had only your anger to defend her. Your threats discouraged him. He was afraid of meeting you or me, Amyas or Christian if we were ever out of chains. Especially you, I think. A reputation is as good as a gold coin, you always said, and you were right."

He leaned forward and eyed his guest seriously. "But there's more to your Miss Shaw than looks, obviously. Your brother was much impressed, both with her and with how good you were with her. That last bit bothered him, because he said he'd every intention of stepping in to be her hero if you wouldn't."

"He wouldn't have been any kind of hero," Daffyd said with a dark scowl. "Lee's idea of salvation would be to pay her top price for her company until he got bored with her, then retire her at a nice pension."

"And yours is to bring her here so we can find her a nice position to work at until she gets too old, and then can be retired for a nice pension?"

Daffyd tapped his boot on the floor and looked at

the Turkish carpet as though he were itching to start pacing it again.

"Have you feelings for her?" the earl asked softly. "It would be a very good thing, Daffy, if you did. She seems decent, intelligent, and we know she has courage. She's wellborn and educated, but not filled with airs and graces. It would be a very good thing, indeed."

"You know how I feel about marriage," Daffyd said curtly. "Nothing's changed that. But yes, I like the chit, for all the reasons you said. She's a delight. But she isn't for me."

Daffyd rose, but he didn't pace. He stared down at the earl, his fists knotted at his sides. "Damnation, Geoff, you know me from the old days. I ain't changed that much. I can't," he said, forgetting his manners and grammar in his agitation. "I know Christian and Amyas found lasses to love, but the love was already in them. They needed marriage to feel whole again. It ain't in me. Nor is it in you, neither. I don't see no female ruling this roost. And I don't think I will, at least, not soon. And no one tells you to marry. So I don't know why you're trying to stuff me into the parson's mousetrap just because I helped a female, and an eligible one, at that."

"I don't want to marry because I had a wonderful marriage, and I don't want to ruin my good memories of it," the earl said gently. "It's that simple. How shall I explain it? I have it. You know, when summer's at its peak and you go walking down a country lane and see a bush of ripe brambleberries? You pop one in your mouth. It's warmed from the sun and juicy, and I vow it tastes like all sweet summer in a mouthful. Then, back in London, you get some from a market, or your servant does," he added with a little smile. "They're fresh, they swear. I suppose they are, fresh from a hothouse, or the long journey from Spain or other foreign parts. You pop it in your mouth—and you wonder why anyone in their right mind would eat berries. The sourness makes you forget the joy of the real thing."

"A woman ain't a berry, Earl," Daffyd said.

"A good memory is important," the earl said, "especially when it's all you've got left of a woman. And in case you've forgotten, marriage is forever. I don't need a wife now, because I had the best when I had one and I don't want to sully the memory with inferior goods. But you!"

"I never wanted a wife, remember?"

The earl waved a hand in dismissal. "That nonsense you were always on about wanting to be an uncle? It was funny, but we always knew you were joking. You can be a father and an uncle too. Double the blessing."

Daffy sat down abruptly. His expression was set hard, his eyes deeply troubled. He clasped his hands together hard, and bent his dark head over them. "Look, my lord," he said in a tight voice, "I meant every word of it. I like kids. I like females. But I never saw a good marriage, and happens I don't believe in them. At least, not for me. I never saw ought

but cruelty and meanness, unfaithfulness and deser-
tion come out of one, and that wasn't only in my own
life. I don't want any part of that. I don't like putting
my life and my happiness in someone else's hands. I
don't trust anyone enough, not even myself.

"I like light loving, and variety. Wedlock ain't for
me. And so neither is Miss Margaret Shaw, because
she's proper as a parson, and why shouldn't she be? I
want to find her a good place so I can feel I did right
by her. But that's it, and that's all."

The earl sat and thought. "And Miss Shaw?" he
eventually asked. "How does she feel?"

Daffyd stirred. He looked away. "She's young.
Maybe younger than she ought to be in some ways,
because even though she left her home and was em-
ployed in other people's houses, she's had no experience with men. She isn't like the women I grew up
with, or some of the highbred ones I met after I came
home again. She's got morals as well as manners.
And she doesn't know what love is. Aye, I know how
she feels about me. That's different. She never met
anyone like me before, or if she did," he added with a
humorless smile, "all she ever did was give him a pot
to mend. She'll get over it."

"Can she? I saw her eyes at dinner, whenever she
looked at you."

Daffyd looked up. "'*Can she*?' So meek, my
lord?" he asked mockingly. "So mealymouthed?
That's not like you. Out with it. You want to know if
I ruined her. The answer is no, I didn't. She's impres-
sionable, and there'd never been anyone to impress

her before, that's all. Well, maybe not all. But I didn't sleep with her, not really." He shifted in his seat. "I . . . entertained her, once. She was so damned enticing, and I'm too human. I was trying to get her to forget her worries."

"Certainly a fine way to do it," the earl commented, and hid his expression with his goblet as he took another sip.

"Well, it is. But it didn't go that far, and there was no more and no further, and it's done and over. It was a mistake. It didn't mark her, and it won't mark her future, believe me."

The earl studied him. "There's a lot you know, Daffy. You know more than most people do about their fellow man. There's not a fellow I'd count on more in a scrape, because you know how to fight by the rules, including some I never heard of. You're smart; you soak up knowledge like a sponge. You're funny, loyal to a fault, and compassionate. And you can see through a falsehood as though you could see straight through a person's skull. Impressive. You were invaluable to Christian and me when we were in prison, and I still count you a friend as well as another son I never had. But there's a universe of things you don't know about females and what does mark their hearts."

Daffyd shrugged. "Aye. Another wonderful reason to never marry, wouldn't you think?" He leaned forward and eyed his host. "What I want from you, sir, if you agree, is to help me find a place for her—

and not one in my bed or under my roof. That's firm. Can you do it? Will you?"

"Of course I'll try." The earl sighed. Then he slapped a hand on his knee. "Well, then, let's get on with it," he said briskly. "When I got your note this morning I sent for Mrs. Courtland. She's a widow who lives here in London, and was delighted for a change of scenery. She's already here. She was a friend of my father's. Her own reputation is solid, and she's too old to be of romantic interest to either of us, so the gossips can't even hint at impropriety. We'll put out the word that Miss Shaw, a connection of the family, is visiting, and seeking a proper post in a genteel household."

Daffyd's brows went up.

"Well, you're like a son to me," the earl said imperturbably. "And she's a friend of yours, hence: the connection."

"Playing fast and loose with words is fine with me. But how are you going to get out the word? An advertisement in the *Times*?"

"I'll suffer. I'll accept some invitations. Dine out tonight; go to some clubs tomorrow, the polite world will know in a matter of days. Then prospective employers will descend, count on it. Has she got clothes suitable for the position with her? The gown she was wearing was lovely, but not what is considered suitable for a lady's companion."

Daffyd's dark eyes looked hunted. "Lee secured some for her. There's a lot I'd do, but I'd not try to get her to accept more."

"I would. I'm an earl. She has some fear of me because she doesn't know me yet. Don't worry. She'll accept. After all, I can't get the poor child anything spectacular. She's looking for a position in a respectable household, not going on the Marriage Mart. More's the pity." He saw Daffyd's expression and added, "Not to worry. If I'm not successful, we'll let Christian and Amyas and their lovely new wives try. Too bad they're not in London now. If they can't help," the earl said, looking away, "there's always your mama to consult."

"I'd rather not," Daffyd said quickly.

The study was silent except for the spitting fire in the hearth.

"But if we have to," Daffyd went on wearily, "I will. I don't want to send Meg back to her gloomy aunts so she can feel guilty for the rest of her life. Damn," he said, sitting back at last, laying his head on the back of the chair, "Why is it that the good and innocent people feel the most guilt, and the ones that should be wearing hair shirts, hanging by their thumbs and drinking hemlock, almost never feel any?"

"Hard to drink hemlock while hanging by your thumbs," the earl said thoughtfully. "But I know what you mean. Perhaps because evildoers don't care. And most good people try so hard to be good that it pains them doubly hard when they fail."

"I never try to do good," Daffyd said to the ceiling.

The earl smiled. "I said 'most people.' You, Daffy, are an Original. You just try to do what you think is right, and it turns out good. All right. We begin, to-morrow. I'll invite people who can help your waif. Then it won't be long before the matter is resolved."

The earl sat back and looked content. But Daffyd just tossed the last of the brandy in his goblet down his throat, rose, and began pacing again.

Chapter 18

The earl was wrong. Meg's prospective employers began to call at the earl's townhouse within three days of her arrival there. She'd been having a wonderful time until then.

The earl had been too busy with social engagements to pass much time with her, but when he did he was charming and erudite, and best of all, he gave Meg free access to his enormous library. She only used it when it was time to go up to bed, so she could read herself to sleep, because she spent the rest of her days and evenings with Daffyd. Mrs. Courtland was an amiable old lady, but she was a very old lady indeed, and spent most of her time napping, leaving Meg alone, except for Daffyd.

In the first two days, Daffyd had taken her for

walks in the park, always accompanied by a maid or a footman. He also took her to the sights of London she hadn't visited before. She'd already seen the Palace, theaters, the Tower and the crown jewels the last few times she'd been in London. But she'd never seen Old Bailey and Newgate, and one of the infamous prison ships they called a Hulk, anchored off a grim shore of the Thames. That was when they had their disagreement.

Daffyd stopped the light open carriage he was driving. "No," he said. "Anyplace else. Not there. I couldn't wait to leave, and I won't take you there."

"But I can't go by myself. I'd never find it. And you've talked about it, so I'm curious. If hundreds of people live there, I can certainly be driven though the place."

"Thousands of people live there because they have no choice. You do."

"Exactly!" she said triumphantly. "So take me there. I can scarcely climb into a hack and ask the driver to take me to the slums."

"You could, and you would," he muttered. "And you'd end up in trouble."

"Yes," she said smugly. "So please, Daffyd. I want to see where you came from."

"You did. You even stayed overnight in the same caravan," he added in a lower voice, so the footman standing on the back step of the phaeton couldn't hear.

"I mean, after that. Of course," she said, as thought struck by a sudden thought, "if it's too painful for you . . . Oh, Daffyd, I'm so sorry. I never meant to distress you! Of course you wouldn't ever want to lay eyes on the foul place again. It would make you so unhappy, I do understand. And you've very right to be afraid, too. If it's that vile, then even young Harry, the earl's footman, mightn't be able to keep us safe. And he's a strong lad."

But by then, Daffyd was snarling something under his breath and turning the carriage. He said nothing as they drove on through parts of town she'd never seen. But eventually he took a quick glance at her. She looked smug.

His lips curled up in a reluctant grin. "Gulled by a pigeon," he murmured. "You took me in, wench. Well done."

She laughed, and he drove on.

They entered a district where the houses were closer together. The streets were more crowded with foot traffic and carts, wagons, and pushcarts. They came to a district where the day turned to dusk because the old houses that leaned over the street almost touched and blocked out the sun. It was a pity they couldn't block the stench, Daffyd thought.

He slowed the carriage.

"Here," he said. "I won't take you to a flash ken, because I'm not mad. But this is where I came when I left my grandmother. I ran until I found this place, and I stayed here, because this is where a homeless boy isn't looked at askance. He isn't even looked at, because there are so many like him. Here is where hunger is natural, and thievery is a valid way of life, and the only crime is being caught. I lived in the streets until I found other boys to band with. Here I met Amyas, and called him brother, and we set out as a team so our profits would be higher."

He stopped the curricle at the mouth of the alley where he'd lived in a broken cellar with other boys. He sat and watched her appalled expression as she saw the street where he'd lived. It was just as filthy and stinking as it had been then. Even Harry the footman, lowborn as he was, looked appalled. Daffyd did too, for another reason.

He realized they were not only observing, they were being observed. He scowled. He should have known. Good living had dulled his instincts. They'd attracted a crowd, of course, only half of which he could see. He knew there were more he could not.

Ragged old men and young ones that looked old, the pitifully maimed, crippled and diseased, and those who pretended to be, starving children and gaunt nursing mothers, all came slowly edging toward the elegant lady and gent and the worried footman in their fine, open carriage. The few street vendors Daffyd had seen when they'd arrived were quickly pushing their way out of the vicinity. Their footman tensed and balled his fists. Much good they would do him, Daffyd thought. He knew what was coming, and cursed himself for stopping. He'd lived too well, and had forgotten too much.

As the beggars began to draw nearer, Daffyd raised his whip and stood.

"I ain't no gentlemen," he shouted. "Get back. I

ain't lost neither, and I ain't without weapons. I got a wicked blade and a dandy over and under barker too. I know how to use both. I grew up here. I'm just back to take a look." He turned to Meg. "Enough? I won't be able to hold them off with threats much longer."

She nodded. "Enough," she whispered.

He put a hand in his pocket and threw a shower of coins. As the beggars scrambled for them, they got in the way of the villains who broke from the shadows and ran toward the carriage. But Daffyd's team was already moving, and he drove away as if the devil was after him.

They returned to lunch at home, and their conversation was subdued. Only once, she looked up at him, and whispered, "Sorry."

He shrugged one shoulder, as though deflecting a hit. "No, it was a fair request. Only don't ask again. The last time I was there I had less than they did today. That's the only way you can be safe there."

The earl was making the rounds of his clubs, and accepting invitations to parties, as he said he would. So every night Meg dined alone with Daffyd. Alone, with three footmen and two serving maids present at all times. And dear old Mrs. Courtland, of course, who dozed as soon as she finished the last scraps of her dessert.

Not that they'd needed chaperones.

There'd been no lovemaking, or talk of it, or so much as one longing glance or ribald remark from Daffyd. He was proper as a parson, in fact more so than many clergymen Meg had met. She could scarcely complain because he was acting like a gentleman now. She should have been pleased. He was acting in her own best interests. Now it was obvious to her that she'd been a temptation to him on the road, but no more than that. Maybe it was because she'd been convenient, maybe because he'd been bored; it didn't matter. He was home again, she was there with him, and he no longer cast out lures. Even though she knew she was lucky he didn't, because it was a dangerous attraction that could come to nothing but disgrace for her, she missed the old, seductive Daffyd.

She missed his flirting, and the frisson of danger she'd felt when she'd looked into his dark blue eyes and saw his need for her burning there. That was gone. And yet she often thought she felt his gaze upon her. But whenever she turned her head and met his eyes, there was nothing but polite interest in his own. Still, she was with him and that was enough. If he wasn't watching her, she could certainly gaze at him—and talk to him, and look forward to seeing him each day.

There was no flirtation, but they found they had a lot to talk about: their childhoods, their favorite pastimes, even the people they saw in the streets. They talked and walked together like old friends or friendly siblings; they acted like boon companions. They laughed a lot, too; it was impossible not to laugh when Daffyd wanted to make her merry. Meg thought she'd never been happier, except for the fact that she knew these few halcyon days would end soon, and that Daffyd might not even remember them. Some of the joy in his company was leached out because she suspected he only stayed with her so she wouldn't be lonely, and because she was his responsibility.

She woke on her third morning in the earl's house to find that the maid assigned to her had brought her two boxes of gowns, a gift, she said, from the earl. Meg didn't even look at them. She just jumped from bed, dressed, and immediately requested an urgent audience with him.

She received word he'd see her at breakfast.

The earl stopped talking to Daffyd when she came storming into the breakfast parlor. They both looked up at her.

"My lord," she said quickly, before she forgot all her excellent arguments and the order in which she'd rehearsed them, "I cannot accept such an intimate gift. I have clothing, and . . ."

The earl raised his hand to cut her off. "I'm sorry you don't care for them, Miss Shaw," the earl said, "but please understand I couldn't provide you with garments that were more fashionable."

Whatever Meg was about to say died on her lips.

Daffyd bit his lip, and waited.

"I understand Daffyd's half brother provided you some clothes when you stayed with him," the earl went on. "Of course, you needed them at the time. After all, how could any female pack adequate clothing when she planned to travel light, alone, and at great speed?"

Meg looked down.

"However," the earl said, "now the point is that you're going out for a position. You can't look like a young miss on the Town, or a pampered society female. The viscount has excellent taste, but not for the part you must play now. You must dress as you mean to go on, in more subdued attire."

Meg hadn't even opened the boxes, so she didn't open her mouth either.

The earl nodded approval. Daffyd gazed at him with admiration.

"I'm assured that the garments are perfect for a woman seeking a post as a mentor of young females in a respectable household," the earl said. "Think of the gowns as your livery, my dear, and you'll understand."

Meg faltered. Then she nodded, curtsied, and said, through tight lips. "I see. I will. Thank you."

"Good," the earl said. "Now come join us."

As Meg sat down, he continued. "We can't linger. We're having callers this morning. Now, in the usual way of things, a prospective employee calls on prospective employers. We'll be doing it reverse style."

Meg looked her question at him.

"They're calling on you, instead," Daffyd told her.

Meg blinked.

Daffyd laughed. "It makes perfect sense, Meg, if

you know how things work here in London town if you're a gentry mort. I mean a lady of Society," he translated. "See, fashionable females can't wait to get into this house. They'd trip on the pavement outside so they could come in to get their knees bandaged, if they thought that would work. But they gave up on that ploy months ago. The earl isn't a recluse, but he don't socialize much. Any lady in the *ton* would give an eyetooth just to come here so they can talk about it afterward. It's not that the place is a treasure trove, though it is. The last earl collected as madly as Prinny does. But these females aren't looking for fine art."

"They're not looking for me either," the earl said.

"Well, some are," Daffyd said wryly. "You're a catch, remember? And *all* of them want to see what you've got, since few others have. I'm not just talking about you personally now," he added with a grin.

"Mind your manners around a lady!" the earl said, suppressing a smile. But it's true," he told Meg. "At least, in that they want to see the inside of my house. I don't have guests from the Quality, and so I suppose that makes any invitation from me desirable. In fact, I entertained here just twice: once when my son Christian married, and then when my other boy, Amyas, did. I'm a solitary fellow, at least as concerns the polite world and its endless rounds of dinners, parties, soirees, and balls."

"Aye," Daffyd said. "But you're no recluse; I can drag you out to dinner, and sometimes even to a play."

"And don't forget," the earl told him, "I enjoy riding with old friends, *and* I meet them at my clubs. I like an exciting horse race or a championship mill, and I wager."

"Only with friends," Daffyd corrected him. "You don't go to the clubs for that."

"Why should I?" the earl asked in surprise. "Money's too important to lose to strangers."

"Amen," Daffyd said.

"But the rest of what London Society offers bores me," the earl went on. "And so why do have to entertain the Quality?" He looked at Meg and explained, "I spend most of my time in the countryside. Two of my boys are married and live far from here. And this rascal," he said, smiling at Daffyd, "is as nomadic as a . . . gypsy."

He smiled. Daffyd grinned.

"So, since invitations to this house are scarce as hen's teeth," Daffyd told Meg, "There should be a lot of applicants for the position of offering you a position."

"Yes, I expect a nice turnout this week," the earl agreed. "I'm sure you'll find a position that will suit you, Miss Shaw. Don't worry. I made your abilities and needs clear. And not only is Daffyd vigilant, and almost uncanny in the way he can uncover a secret, I wouldn't let you go to any inferior place with inferior people. I lived among such for a long time, and so you can bet I know what I'm talking about."

There were, Meg discovered again, advantages to throwing in one's lot with convicted criminals.

* * *

Meg was pleased with the gown she wore; one the earl had sent her. It was long at the sleeves and high at the neck, but stylish because of its tailoring and its deep dark rose color. It needed no ornament, which was perfect, because companions weren't supposed to call attention to themselves. Still, the color was ornament enough. Meg admired it, but felt like a fresh fish displayed on ice as she sat on a settee and waited for the earl's guests to come and interview her.

Lady Brower came first, and at the first second of the first hour that it was considered correct to pay a morning call. But no sooner had she gotten her bony body settled in a chair in the grand salon and raised her quizzing glass to study Meg—and the antique porcelain vases on the mantelpiece behind her—than the dowager duchess of Crewe was seen in. The two ladies looked daggers at each other, but were even unhappier when Mrs. Pomfret-Lewes and her talkative daughter arrived. Mrs. Jeffries showed up soon after, as did the honorable Miss Sloan and her mama. Mrs. Franklin and her friend Lady Wickham arrived on the heels of Lady Milton and her subdued daughter. When the last lady to come arrived, it looked and sounded like a party in progress.

By the time it was considered polite for morning visits to end, the parlor was filled, the air stifling, and the scent of attar of roses, violets, lavender, powder, camphor, and sweat was thick in the air. But their time was up, so the assembled ladies of the *ton* had to leave. They did, with many a promise to call again.

Meg curtsied to each of them, hoping her face didn't show the hollow feeling she had in the pit of her stomach.

"They came, all right," Daffyd commented. "Now, can I open a window? I'm used to stenches but it's hard to breathe in here. Almost as bad as Newgate at dawn on a Hanging Monday. Don't the Quality know soap's better than perfume? Don't they use it?"

"Not the old ones," the earl commented "Nor some of the younger ones either. They think perfume covers it."

"Like it would cover a dead dog," Daffyd said. "Smells like something's gone off."

"Well, at least they did," the earl said. "Open the window wide. What did you think, Miss Shaw? I heard at least some of them say they were interested in you."

Meg avoided his eyes. "I know. But in truth, I can't say because I don't know them, after all."

Daffyd flung open a window. "Didn't I tell you?" he asked the earl, and laughed. "The girl's so polite she'd bow to the hangman. Cough it up, Meg. You can do it. You threw your lot in with me after five minutes."

"That was different," she said, stung. "It wasn't five minutes, either. Still, I didn't know how long I'd travel with you, and I knew I could leave any time I wanted to. I was free. This will be my future and my livelihood. A companion is judged harshly if she flits about from job to job. So how can I judge a person I'd have to live with and obey for at least a year on such short acquaintance?"

"Try," Daffyd said, as he perched on the window seat. He wore a teasing smile she knew too well.

"You're among friends," the earl said kindly, but he exchanged a sparkling look with Daffyd.

"Well," she said, "the dowager terrified me, and I don't think I could work for an employer I was afraid of. Nor do I have to. I have a home to go back to."

"The dowager? I wouldn't let you go to that old trout," Daffyd said in bored tones. "And I told you, the aunts aren't a choice."

"But the rest?" the earl asked.

"I don't think many were actually looking for a companion," she said. "In fact, some of them told me they weren't, but that they were looking on behalf of someone they knew."

"Looking for gossip," the earl said, nodding.

"And some," Meg went on, her cheeks turning the color of her gown, "were looking for other reasons."

"Out with it," Daffyd said, with a secret smile. "Come on, Meg, you're not mealy-mouthed."

"Well," she said, looking at the earl, "some of them only wanted to know about you, my lord. I think they were looking for someone to engage, but it wasn't me."

Daffyd exploded with laughter.

The earl looked surprised, but then he laughed, too. "Awake on every suit, indeed," he said. "Was there no one here to employ a companion?"

"Oh, yes," she said quickly. "I liked Lady Sloan, and her daughter, though shy, was charming."

"Well, no need to make up your mind right this

minute. I'll wager the parlor will be stuffed for the next few days once word gets out. And I'll double the wager that you find a position by the end of the week."

"I love a good bet, but I won't take that one," Daffyd commented. "Because I think you're right."

So did Meg, but she didn't smile. Because Daffyd did.

They had visitors for tea, and the parlor was packed with visitors paying a morning call the next day. Even more guests came to call for tea that afternoon. It seemed that the latest craze for the ladies of the *ton* was to come to see the rich, elusive earl of Egremont, and his rich, young, astonishingly attractive ward. Meg agreed with that assessment of Daffyd, which she overheard several ladies making. She didn't have to eavesdrop, either. The earl's guests treated her just as they ought, like a servant applying for a position. So they either talked at her, or over her head to their friends.

Meg thought she was used to that. But her days and nights with Daffyd and his odd, assorted, far-flung family had changed her. It wasn't just the ladies ignoring her that hurt, she suffered when she saw how easily Daffyd fell in with his mentor's highly placed guests. He was charming, and wickedly bright, always staying just this side of scandalous. They loved it. He seemed to enjoy himself as much as they did. And of course, he never spoke to her in company, no more than he joked with her that way at all anymore.

Meg began to think she might have been better off with the aunts, after all. She'd be kept in her place there too, but the only ones she'd have to envy were the sheep.

Still, there was the youthful Lady Sloan, and her poor crushed daughter, Claire. Claire was plain where her mama was ornate, tongue-tied where her mama was facile, and absolutely downtrodden. Meg couldn't help but feel a kinship with her. Ridiculous, of course, she thought, considering the girl was an heiress with a pedigree that coursed through several royal houses. But the lady was kind, and Claire seemed to need a friend as well as a companion.

"So, yes," Meg reported two days later when she sat and talked with the earl and Daffyd at dinner. "I've spoken to all who are really interested, and there aren't that many. But I'm being interviewed by Lady Sloan again tomorrow, at her home. If all works out, I think I might go with them. If neither of you has any objection?"

"I've heard nothing against them, have you?" the earl asked Daffyd, looking from Meg to him.

"No," Daffyd said curtly. "But I'll put an ear to the ground. No time like the present." He flung down his napkin and rose from the table. "I'm off on a ramble. Don't expect me back early, but I'll be home in time to take you to the Sloan house tomorrow, Meg."

The earl shook his head. "I'm promised to Old Doctor Simmons tonight. Remember him, Daffy?"

Daffyd nodded. "Never forget a man who did me a favor. I can't even see that slash he mended."

"Hard to see your back," the earl commented dryly. "But he was a decent fellow. He'd sew up a prisoner as fine as he would a prince, and I've never forgotten our debt to him. I thought you'd like to come along."

"No," Daffyd said curtly. "If it's gossip you want, stay in a parlor. If it's dirt, count on me. I'm off to find out what I can about the Sloans." He hesitated, then looked at Meg. His expression grew softer and his eyes searched hers.

She got a glimpse of the old Daffyd in his gaze: the Daffyd she'd kissed, the Daffyd whose body had once been as intimately held to hers as his gaze was now. She held her breath and waited for what he would say.

Whatever he saw in her eyes surprised him. His expression grew cool, his eyes cold and sapphire bright. His voice was brisk as he looked away and asked, "Mind being alone tonight, Meg?"

She forced a cheerful expression. "No. I found a wonderful book."

"Then, good night," Daffyd said. He paused, and frowned. "I tell you what. I'll get us tickets for a play tomorrow night, sort of a farewell performance."

"An excellent idea," the earl said. "And we'll dine out before. A celebration for Miss Shaw's success, because I'm certain that if she wants something, she'll get it."

"I am, too," Daffyd said. "I'll just make sure she's got something worth celebrating," he added, bowed, and left.

Meg watched him leave the room. She looked down at her lap.

"Sometimes," the earl told her softly. "Things must run their inevitable course. It's difficult for young people to be patient. But I've found, through hard experience, that you can't rush Fate, or Luck, or Time itself. Make yourself comfortable, Miss Shaw. And if there's anything you need—tonight, or ever—please, always feel you can apply to me."

"I do, I will, thank you," Meg said. And hoped he'd leave soon, because she wasn't sure how much longer she could keep her expression calm and contained. After all, tomorrow she might find her place at last, and so be forced to give up all her foolish, dangerous hopes.

Chapter 19

"**M**iss Shaw? How kind of you to come at such short notice," the tall, fair-haired lady said as she glided into the room.

Meg rose from the chair where she'd been waiting. Daffyd had been in a foul mood this morning. She guessed he'd had a late night of drinking, because he'd been heavy-eyed, closemouthed, and brooding. Still, he'd taken her to the Sloan townhouse as promised, and even he'd been impressed by the address.

"Couldn't find anything on them," he'd reported, sounding disappointed. "But the lady's a stick, her husband's hardly ever home, the sons are at school, and the daughter's a clunch. Still," he said, sounding as though he were forced to admit it, "that could be

313

almost any family in the *ton*. They might bore you to death, but I suppose they won't hurt you."

He'd helped her down from his curricle and waited for her to go up the short stair to the door. His eyebrows went up when she headed for the back of the house.

He ran after her, and caught her arm. "None of that," he said, scowling. "You're not going in the servants' entrance."

"But I am one," she'd protested.

"Not if you don't want to be. A companion isn't a scullery maid. You should start as you mean to go on. Apply for a position at the back door and you'll always be taken for a beggar."

"And if they insist?"

"Then you'll find another job."

But to her delight, she'd been expected at the front door. Daffyd left her when the butler offered to show them in. "I'll be waiting," he told her, and stalked back to the carriage.

Now she faced her prospective employer, and once again, Meg was impressed with her. Lady Sloan's pale hair was drawn back and tied simply; this morning she wore a long, slim column of a gown of amber silk. She had the correct bones for such simplicity, and the grace to make it look spectacular. And she had exquisite manners. Meg had been made to feel as though she were just another morning caller by being shown into the parlor, not the kitchens or my lady's study.

Meg sketched a bow, and only then noticed the girl who followed her mother into the room. Dressed correctly in white, Claire, as always, looked like a wan shadow of her lovely mama.

"Do sit down," Lady Sloan said, indicating a chair opposite the divan where she seated herself. Claire drifted over and stood behind her. "I've gone over your letters of recommendation, and am impressed. However," the lady added, "I see there is none from your last employer." She raised a slender hand to cut off any explanations. "I am well aware of the reason for it."

Meg drew in a breath.

The lady smiled at her daughter, and then turned her head to smile at Meg. "More about that later. Let me explain our needs to you first, Miss Shaw. My daughter is to make her come-out next spring. She is woefully unprepared. In fact, the sad truth is that she was long overshadowed by her sister, who recently married." She smiled wistfully. "Such a madcap, our little elf, Emma. But now it's Claire's turn. And there is a difficulty. She does not shine in social situations. In fact, she shrinks from them, shuns conversation, and becomes tongue-tied in front of eligible gentlemen. A problem, to be sure. Therefore, it's necessary for us to give her all the help we can. That is where you, Miss Shaw, come in."

Meg cocked her head to the side.

"We have some time before Claire makes her bows," the lady explained. "We thought to go back to

Somerset and rusticate a while so Claire can get to know you better. Our manor is a delightful place. You're from the countryside, Miss Shaw, I'm sure you'll enjoy it there. And then, we'll return to Town in the new year."

Now Lady Sloan became almost animated. She leaned forward. "I'll be frank. The Season is a brief period in which a young woman must make the greatest impression in the shortest time in a crowd of similar young women, in order to catch the eye of the greatest prizes on the marriage mart." Lady Sloan shook her smooth head. "To be crude, it's no more or less than a mating season. And the truth is that men are like competitive rams; they're only drawn to females other males want. A young woman may be dressed to perfection. She can play the harp and possess a charming singing voice. She may have a tidy fortune and a fine lineage. But if other men don't want her, she won't find a suitable match.

"We have no illusions, Claire and I," she went on, patting her daughter's hand where it lay on the back of the divan. "It's unlikely that she can hone her social skills in time to make a splash in the coming Season. I'd almost given up on bringing her out next year. But then you came to town, and I realized that if Claire is talked about, she doesn't need to talk. If she's noticed, she doesn't have to exert herself to attract attention. And if she is in the company of someone everyone wishes to see, she will be seen. And then, anything may happen."

Lady Sloan looked directly into Meg's puzzled

eyes. "You, Miss Shaw, are the talk of the Town. You ran off from a respectable position to go with that wildly attractive gypsy ward of the earl of Egremont—we saw the gypsy through the window just now. Obviously, since you're seeking a respectable position again, your relationship with him is over, though your friendship is not. Though I can't approve, of course, I can at least understand your reason for straying. He's a striking-looking specimen, with a veneer of civilization that charms, and an undercurrent of wildness that . . ."

The lady paused, and then went on, "You cannot know how many ladies would give anything to have him as a guest. Perhaps he'd come to one of our balls if you ask? I should think so, judging from your past association. We'll leave that for later. The earl of Egremont is himself a man of mystery and fascination. As if your intimate acquaintance with those two fascinating rogues weren't enough, then we hear you passed some time at that delightful rascal, Viscount Haye's, wicked establishment. Now, you come to London, seeking employment.

"The *ton* can speak of little else. For all your wild starts, you're well spoken, and look respectable. Still, you're trying to pass yourself off as untainted goods. Of course, you cannot. Some young women can, even after wilder adventures. That disgraceful Lamb girl was accepted almost everywhere, in spite of her mad exploits. And do not even mention Miss Carrington, last season! Yet she may be seen anywhere these days. But you haven't the necessary fortune or family for that. Still, with the earl's sponsorship, you are acceptable, after a fashion.

"Of course, there's no question of you finding a respectable match. You're utterly ruined, and not in a position to marry well even if you weren't. But if you were to be Claire's companion, every eye would be on you, and so, on her, and she'll have her chance to shine."

"Miss Shaw," the lady continued as Meg sat and gaped at her. "Here is a way for you to earn a decent recommendation, and money, too."

Meg caught her breath. Her hands felt icy even in their gloves, and her heart began a rapid beat. She'd think about what had been said later. Now, she only knew she had to save face. She refused to let this cold creature know how much she'd hurt her. "Aren't you afraid I'll corrupt your daughter?" she asked levelly.

Lady Sloan's laughter was like silvery bells. "Oh, my, no. Claire is incorruptible. She wants only to marry, wisely and well. And actually, your daring might inspire her to go after the gentleman of her choice with more vigor. You see, Miss Shaw, I don't believe you to be unprincipled or lascivious. Did I, you wouldn't now be sitting in my house. I believe you merely made a miscalculation; I should love to hear more about it at some later date."

"Miscalculation?" Meg managed to ask.

"Yes," the lady said smoothly. "The gypsy is very rich, and gossip has it that he's also well connected, if on the wrong side of the blanket. That means he can look higher for a wife, so his children will be freer of taint. So certainly, he will, when he decides to settle down. But how should you have known that? Or that the Viscount Haye never commits to more than above a few weeks? Understandable mistakes on your part, and not so reprehensible as it would have been were you looking merely for pleasure. But I believe you were only seeking to better yourself. Obviously, so do others. The earl may be eccentric and have a shocking past; still, he's widely thought to be an excellent judge of people, and a man of good moral character, and he recommends you highly.

"But that's the past. As for the future? We would hope you don't run off and leave us in the lurch as you did the baron, but I don't think you will. You're too clever for that; you know you need to regain your footing. And so? We will pay well, and there'll be a good recommendation in it for you at the end of your employment."

Meg rose to her feet. "You will, of course, give me time to consider your offer?" she asked in a tight voice. "After all, I have had others, and have more interviews to go on."

The lady's eyes narrowed. "We will meet any price."

Meg bowed. "Understood. Then you'll understand how important it is for me to seek more offers."

Lady Sloan nodded. "Yes, of course. We await your answer and hope it will be in the affirmative."

"Oh, yes!" Claire suddenly blurted. "Please do come work for us, Miss Shaw. Everyone's talking about the gypsy and there he is, waiting for you outside *our* house! It's too exciting. And you stayed with the Viscount Haye! I get shivers just thinking about him, he's so dashing and wicked. And the earl of Egremont! And you knew the runaway heiress! Everyone will envy me having you here, and oh, what fun to have you in our house!"

Meg tilted her head. She looked at Lady Sloan. "Your daughter seems to have no difficulty expressing herself," she said coolly. "Although, I believe it would be better if she learned to elevate the tone of her conversation. Good day."

She marched from the house, head high. She refused to let any emotion show on her face, nor could she. She wasn't sure what she felt, and was afraid that once she did, she wouldn't feel numb anymore.

Daffyd eyed her curiously as he helped her up into the carriage. "So is it to be a celebration tonight, then?" he asked.

"What?"

"The dinner, the theater, tonight. The great farewell party, with the earl," he reminded her.

"Oh, yes, I'd forgot. Yes," Meg said with a tight smile. "Yes. It will be a great farewell."

He gripped the reins, cracked the whip, and they rode back in silence.

Daffyd stared when Meg came down the stair that night.

The earl beamed. "Now that," he said, looking at the gown she wore, "was definitely a present from the viscount, was it not?"

Meg fingered the skirt of her gown lovingly. "Yes. And since I don't know if I can ever wear it again, I thought to have one use out of it, tonight." She hesitated. "It's not too much, is it?"

"It's too little," Daffyd said. "But that's fashion. You look lovely, Meg," he added sincerely.

She let out a breath. She'd finally dared to wear the most beautiful and outrageous gown the Viscount Haye had given her. It was gold cloth, and little else. And Daffyd was right, there was very little of it, at least compared to what she was used to wearing. It was thin, low at the breast, tied under her breasts with a silver ribbon, and clung to her body all the way down to her golden slippered toes. Her maid had done her hair up and topped her ringlets with the delicate gilt coronet that had come with the gown. Meg felt as outrageous, rich, and shockingly sensuous as the gown looked.

"I'm glad you approve," she said, and no longer able to act cool and contained when she was so excited, added, "And there's a shawl that came with it!"

Daffyd took a step forward, but the earl offered Meg his arm first.

"I'll be the envy of every man in London tonight," the earl said. "Come, let's celebrate, although . . ." He paused, and added seriously, "It doesn't have to be a farewell dinner. You don't have to jump at the first decent position offered."

Daffyd grew still, and watched Meg.

"I didn't do that," she said with a curiously sedate smile that made her piquant face look mature and wise. "I just decided to do the best thing for myself."

"Bravo," the earl said.

Daffyd said nothing.

There were no "bravos" offered at the theater that night. The play was outdated, the actors mediocre, and the audience restless. The earl tried to watch the play, Mrs. Courtland dozed, Daffyd often got up to pace the hall or stand in the shadows of their box. Meg enjoyed herself thoroughly.

"Of course you did," Daffyd told her when they got settled into the carriage for the ride home. "The audience made more of a fuss over you than they did over the play."

Meg didn't deny it. "Yes," she said in a curiously brittle voice. "That's true. And before you call me conceited, I know it was because of three things: the earl, you, and this outrageous gown. Lovely ladies in a London theater are as common as mice are in a barn at home. But you two are still the talk of the town. In fact," she went with a small smile, "I was told that just today."

"Speaking of today," the earl said, "shall you tell us your decision now? You said it was too soon in the restaurant, and too noisy at the theater. Come, surely now's the time. I've a bottle of ancient French brandy waiting for your news."

"Let's wait until we get home," she said. "After

all, you did say it was a farewell party, and so it will be. I'll tell my news, and then we'll have a toast, and then to bed. Because I'll be leaving in the morning."

The coach went still.

"In the morning?" Daffyd demanded. "They can't need you that soon."

"I leave in the morning," she said firmly.

"I cannot like this haste," the earl said, sounding troubled. "Are you certain it's necessary?"

"Absolutely," she said. "I'll tell you everything soon enough. Can't we do it my way?"

"Of course," the earl said. "Nothing like a bit of drama."

"But it's nothing like you, Meg," Daffyd said suspiciously.

"Surprise," she said, without a hint of humor in her voice.

They didn't speak again until the coach rolled up at the earl's town house, and Mrs. Courtland's maid had helped her to bed. Then Meg, Daffyd and the earl went into his study.

"Now," Daffyd said, positioning himself by the hearth, hands behind his back, and his back to the fire. "Enough drama. Tell all."

"Not yet!" the earl said as he settled in his favorite chair. "Harris," he told his butler, "we'll have that bottle of '49 now."

They waited until the butler had brought in the brandy, glasses, and a tray of little cakes. When the door closed behind him as he left, both men looked at Meg.

She stood, one hand on the back of a chair, and looked at them solemnly. Her hair had loosened after her evening out, framing her flushed face. Even so, she looked, Daffyd thought, beautiful, though strangely cool and self-composed.

"I went to see Lady Sloan today, as you know," she said. "I was offered the position, and for more money than I've ever been paid."

"Congratulations!" the earl said. He reached for the bottle of brandy.

Meg sighed. "I've written her a note, because I don't want to see her again. You see, I turned her down. There was no other sane thing to do apart from throwing something at her, and I try to be a lady even though I wasn't born one."

Daffyd's body stiffened. The earl's hands paused on the bottle.

"But I can't really be angry at her," Meg went on. "She was only completely honest. She wants me to companion her dreary daughter because I'm the talk of the Town, and my notoriety will bring some notice to the girl, which she wouldn't get any other way. She was perfectly reasonable about it. The more gossip about the notorious companion, the more the gentlemen eye her, the better chance some one of them might notice the poor girl. The thing is, she's right.

"She believes I'm utterly ruined in the eyes of the world," Meg continued, "although I have great value as a conversation piece. Oh, I know I could probably get some better position far from London. But I'd rather not bother. I'd prefer to go home and wait this out. The talk of the Town never stays around Town too long. But it is echoing through London right now. It seems everyone knows what I did, or if they don't, at least know that I did it with Daffyd."

Daffyd opened his mouth to speak, but she raised a hand to stop him. "It isn't just because you're famous, Daffyd, although you are."

"Infamous," he corrected her through tightened lips.

"Well, yes, and no," she said. "You're considered highly desirable, though I'll grant, not just for marriage. All the ladies talk about you. It's not just because of that; you could have been a cobbler or a baker. Except no one would have gossiped about it if you were, and I'd just be considered a common slut and not offered any jobs at all. I'm thought of as an uncommon slut now, which was why I was offered employment.

"The point is that an unmarried woman just can't go coursing across the land in the sole company of a single man. It's just not done. I did it. Moreover, I knew it when I set out. So I'll accept Society's judgment, but not its punishment. I'm going to my aunts' house tomorrow morning," she said, holding her head high. "They'll lecture me. But they always do. They won't beat me, or shun me, or whisper about me."

She raised a hand to silence any protest. "Life will

go on as it did, and in time I'll be able to apply for other positions. Gossip doesn't stay fresh long, and when I'm older it will seem ridiculous, not seamy." She smiled. "Please don't pity me. It was a grand adventure. I was foolish and headstrong, I'll agree with my aunts on that. But now I look back, I don't think I'd have changed any of it for anything. If I'd stayed home, waiting and fretting, I'd be considered a very good girl. But I wouldn't think as much of myself as I do now. I tried to take my fate in my own hands, and I almost did! I gambled, and if Rosie had come home with me, I'd have won."

She cocked her head to the side. "But what would I have won? Only more of the same, a pleasant position for another year. My life wouldn't have changed. Now that I've seen a bit of the world—and more, a bit of myself in the world—I believe I can look forward to better." Her expression grew serious. "I think I now know why women are cautioned to be passive. A little self-respect is a dangerous thing. Once you believe a female can do as well as a male, you find yourself refusing to be downtrodden. That would never do if I chose to stay on in London now. But it will do for me in future, I think. So I'm going home. Thank you for your hospitality, my lord," she told the earl. "I think when you consider it, you'll see I'm doing the right thing."

"Surely not all the ladies in London feel as Lady Sloan does?" the earl asked.

"Oh, I believe they do," she said. "And the gentlemen, too. Otherwise she wouldn't have made the offer. She's a practical woman."

"You can't go!' Daffyd said angrily.

"I can, and I shall," she said firmly. "It won't be so bad. I'll have a roof over my head, enough to eat, and tasks to keep me busy. *You* certainly know there are worse fates for females the world considers sinners."

He fell still.

"So," she said. "May we have that brandy now, my lord?"

The earl sighed. "It's not what I wanted to toast. But yes, I think we should." He poured them each a glass and stood up. He raised his glass. "To a gallant woman," he said, "one I hope knows she'll always have safe harbor here should she ever decide to avail herself of it."

"Thank you," Meg said. "I'll drink to that."

But Daffyd didn't speak, or pick up his glass. He stood glowering as the other two finished their sad toast.

"I'll say good night and good-bye now," Meg said. "I've made arrangements to be at the *Bull and Mouth* early in the morning. That's where my coach will be leaving. Thank you, my lord," she told the earl, "for all your kindnesses."

He took her hand. "I meant what I said," he said soberly. "You can always return here."

"I know," she said, "thank you."

"I'm to bed," he said, glancing at Daffyd. "It's not considered proper to leave you two alone, but we've gone far beyond that sort of nonsense now. You need a private farewell. Good night."

When he'd left the study, Daffyd moved. He strode over to Meg and took her hands in his. "You can't mean to do this."

"I do," she said. She smiled. "The earl's such a clever man. If I couldn't have had a moment alone with you now, I was going to track you to your room later tonight. I'd hate to do that in his house. Now I have a chance to bid you a proper good-bye, Daffyd."

His black brows lowered.

"I want to thank you, too," she said, looking up into his face. "You frightened me, threatened me, teased me, but you always treated me gently, fairly, and honorably, even when you gave me a taste of what lovemaking was all about. In fact, Daffyd, you educated me in a dozen ways, and I thank you for that, too. But I can't stay for more lessons, and you have a life to return to, too. So, let me say good-bye so you'll remember me. I'd hate for you to forget me," she whispered.

She threw her arms around his neck, drew his head down to hers, and kissed him. Her lips opened against some exclamation he was about to make. She tasted brandy and Daffyd, and sighed against his mouth. She pressed close to him and kissed him with all the art he'd taught her, and all the love she felt.

After a heartbeat, he responded. His tension eased, and he enclosed her in his arms, and kissed her with all the passion that she felt. After another long moment, and mutual startled indrawn breaths, they drew back, looked at each other, and kissed again.

Then she pulled away from him. He dropped his arms and looked at her in confusion.

Her face was filled with color, her eyes sparkled. "There," she said breathlessly, "forget that!" Her eyes searched his, and her smile was wistful. "I expect you will. What's a kiss against a lifetime of expert lovemaking? But remember me, Daffyd, at least that. Good night," she said, and went to the door.

She turned when she got there. "I will remember you," she said, "and with gratitude." She hurried from the room before she could say more, or he could see more.

Daffyd took a step after her. He stopped. He ran a hand through his hair. And then he collapsed into a chair, and stared into the hearth. He sat and stared at the fire blazing there until it cracked and crumbled, and deep in the night, fell to ashes.

Chapter 20

"**W**hy don't you just go and get her?" the earl asked the sole occupant of the library in his London townhouse a month later.

Daffyd looked up at him and raised an eyebrow. He'd been sitting staring into space, an unopened book on his knee.

The earl looked troubled. Daffyd's face was darker and drawn, he looked thinner, and his usually lively eyes were dull.

"I know you read," the earl said. "In fact, I taught you to. I know you like books, too. But you've only been using them to decorate your lap for days now."

"I read this one before," Daffyd said gruffly.

"Yes, and it's such a long walk to the bookshelves to get another. Daffy," the earl said. "When are you going to stop this? It's the most tremendous bout of sulking I've ever seen a grown man go through. Either forget the girl or go get her, it can't go on this way. Amyas agrees, he was appalled at your condition when he came to visit the other week."

"I don't blame him. I was drinking then. I'm not drinking now."

"No, you're not doing anything. I'm not sure that isn't worse. Amyas wrote to Christian, and now I've a letter from him that urges me to step in. And before the Viscount Haye left the other day, he said that if I didn't help you win back Meg Shaw, he would."

"That's rich," Daffyd said bitterly, "the Viscount Haye giving advice to the lovelorn."

"So you don't deny it?" the earl asked as he sat opposite him.

Daffyd shrugged. "I've my vices, God knows. Lying to you ain't one of them."

"Then . . ."

"Then why don't I go get her?" Daffyd asked gruffly. "I ain't the marrying sort, Earl. You know that. Never was, never can be. Though I confess she landed me a facer." His sapphire eyes were dark with unhappiness as he looked at his mentor.

"I can't promise to be faithful to her, Geoff," he said, reverting to the way he'd spoken to the earl in the days when they'd first met. "I come from a line of selfish cheats and rovers on both sides. It's in my blood. Neither my mother or father ever loved anything more than they did themselves. How can I know if I'd be different, even if I want to be? I never have been. Love comes too lightly to me. And if I wasn't faithful, it would fair kill her. I'd rather cut off an arm than cause her any hurt. And though I know she'd never be false, still I can't convince myself she'd be faithful to me, neither. That's madness, but so it is with me. I've never seen fidelity.

"Aye, I know," Daffyd said wearily, as though the earl had spoken, "I can see how happy Christian and Amyas and their wives are, and know in my heart neither of them would ever cheat neither. But they've only been married months. I'm talking about the years ahead. It's the wondering that would never leave me. That's no way to live."

"And this is?" the earl asked.

"I'm not happy now," Daffyd said, shrugging. "But it could be worse. This way, I can only regret what can't be, not what I did. I'll get over it."

"Can she?" the earl asked quietly.

"Oh, she'll do. It isn't what I'd want for her, but she's safe, fed and clothed, and better off without me altogether. I couldn't stand poisoning her faith or her love. She's too good for me, earl. It's best this way." He tried a tilted smile. "Not having ain't as bad as losing."

"That isn't what your favorite poet said."

" ' 'Tis better to have loved and lost than never to have loved at all.' " Daffyd quoted. "Aye. And I lost her, so that's that."

"Is it? Daffyd, you're letting the past write your future. If you'd thought that way back then you wouldn't be here now."

Daffyd shrugged.

"You're a good man, Daffy, you've never betrayed any man or woman I ever knew. The woman's in love with you. Any fool could see that, and you never were a fool. Meg Shaw is wholly adorable as well as intelligent. She acted rashly, that is true. But she did so out of desperation, and admits it. She's decent and moral, and, for a wonder, she remained moral even with you to tempt her. Don't tell me you didn't! And don't try to tell me she succumbed. Neither of you would be so unhappy if she had."

Daffyd's thin dark eyebrows rose.

"She's unique and a catch for any man," the earl continued. "You have so much to offer her, too. You possess wit and charm, courage, and tenacity. And now you have great wealth, too. That makes a difference in the social world. I know it doesn't mean a thing to you now, nor to her, but you're already halfway to being accepted everywhere. Your children would be part of Society, if they wished. Where is the impediment, except in your own mind? I've never seen you afraid of anything, this isn't like you."

Daffyd looked up. His eyes flashed. "By God, Geoff, you never spoke so false. I was always afraid. I wouldn't be here now if I wasn't. I took risks because I had to. I gambled because I'd no choice. I was brave, because not being brave would have killed me, and I'd a notion to survive. I still do. Even then, I knew when something was too big for me to try, and I'd let it be. Like now. Let it be, Earl."

The earl put up his hands in surrender. "Let it be?

I'd rather not, but I suppose I must. I can't do otherwise, can I?" He thought a moment and then spoke again, his tone brighter. "So, what are your plans for the day? It's brisk and clear outside. There won't be many fair days left, the last leaves are falling off the trees. Are you going to step out?"

"Clearing out the library? Or just trying to see if I can still walk?" Daffyd asked with a smile. "Don't blame you. The other week, when I was making a tour of taverns, you only saw me carried in. I seem to have grown into this chair now, haven't I? Aye, I guess I'll be moving on soon. Maybe I'll set about finding my other brother, the footloose one. He has his faults too, but he don't moralize like my noble kin is suddenly doing. But first I have to put my ear to the ground. I know a ken where I can get word of the Rom. A little roving might be just the thing to set me right again."

"Indeed," the earl said, though he looked even unhappier. "But before you go, I must tell you: I had a visitor the other day who requested your company. It seems she sent you a note asking the same, but you never answered. At least, you refused to meet with her."

Daffyd put a hand over his eyes and rubbed his forehead. "My mother?"

The earl nodded.

"I thought so. I did send her a note to reply. I told her I bungled it, couldn't retrieve her goddaughter, and offered my apologies and regrets. What does she want? To have me crawl in and say it?"

"I understand it was about something else that she wished to speak."

"What?" Daffyd asked, without moving his hand. But his whole posture was suddenly more alert.

"That, she wouldn't say. She's a charming woman, but she and I are not precisely intimates."

Now Daffyd did move his hand. The earl saw he was smiling, but the smile wasn't a nice one. "Aye, but I bet she wishes you were."

The earl shrugged. "I don't know. Nor am I going to find out. We have little in common. But one thing we do share: a lively concern for you."

Daffyd's smile twisted. "That, I doubt. Not on your part, of course. But on hers? As for her interest in me, she showed none for decades. Then she meets me, raised from the dead or wherever she believed I was, and almost faints on the spot. Then, suddenly, months later, she asks a favor of me. And now she sends a second summons to me? Depend on it, that isn't motherly love. She's got another favor to ask." He sat up straight. "Well, then there's something I can do. And this time, whatever it is she wants, I'll succeed."

"You'll try to please her even though you don't care for her? I confess, Daffyd, I don't understand."

Daffyd looked at him directly then. His eyes were filled with sorrow. "You wouldn't, my lord. You're a thoroughly good man. But me? See, a blighted tree bears twisted fruit. She threw me away. Now she needs me. I could tell her to go straight to hell. But that's too easy. Now, if I show her that she threw away something of worth and then tell her to be damned, *then* she regrets what she did. She sees how wrong she was. It proves my value, Geoff. I want her to see it, I need to have that."

"Ah, Daffyd," the earl said sadly. "If you don't know your value then no one else can ever prove it to you."

"Aye," Daffyd said wearily. "There it is, isn't it? A man who thinks he has no value can never be content, can he? He can't live like a normal fellow, or love like one. . . ." He caught himself, stopped, and muttered under his breath, "Maudlin. That won't do. Listen," he went on in normal tones, "how do you pay someone back for costing you so much? By showing them how wrong they were, that's how."

"I don't know your mother very well," the earl said sadly, "but I'd be willing to wager she never forgets that."

Daffyd rose and carefully placed his book on a table. "That only proves you don't know her at all. But you always were a lucky fellow."

"Mama," Daffyd said, bowing, after the butler had let him into the salon and left. "You sent for me."

The lady stopped pacing. She lifted her head. "I did. Please have a seat. When you pace I get dizzy. And you always pace."

"I'm restless. It's the gypsy in me," he said. But nevertheless he sat in the chair she'd indicated.

She was dressed in icy blue, which suited her elegant looks. But she looked different to him. He eyed her, wondering if she was sick, before he realized it was that she looked unsure and uneasy. He'd never seen that.

"I wanted to speak with you," she said.

"I'm here," he answered. "Wasn't my apology enough?"

She gazed at him in confusion.

"I mean, for not nabbing the runaway. I tried, but I was too late. She isn't in any particular difficulty unless her fiancé, or husband, or whatever he is now, is a total clunch. She isn't alone, nor penniless. I hear he took a heap of cash with him. Clever. For what it's worth, I'm surprised, too. I thought I could catch them. I suppose I let you down again."

"Again?" she asked.

"The first time was when I was born."

He was surprised. He didn't know a pale woman could get that much paler.

"We've never spoken much," she said.

He nodded agreement.

"Indeed, that's my fault, because when I first saw you, last year, at that ball, in the earl's company, I didn't know what to say."

"Makes sense," he said.

"I should have spoken to you then," she said. Now she was the one who rose and paced. "But I was too shocked at seeing you to find my wits. I tried, later. Then you didn't want to talk to me. That's when I be-

gan inventing errands for you to do. I didn't care if
you succeeded or not, Daffyd. I was trying to build a
bridge to you."

He looked bored. "Consider it built. What do you
want? I'll try to oblige you, unless it's some chit you
want me to marry. I'm not in that line no more than
my father was. Or you, for that matter."

She stopped and stared at him. "You look like
him, you know. But you're nothing like. He was
merry, always laughing; it was his carefree air that
drew me to him. You're dark, serious, cold. You have
undercurrents I can't guess at."

"It was impossible to be carefree after I was left
with your merry gypsy," Daffyd said too sweetly.
"Odd, though. He wasn't very merry, as I recall. He
liked to hit more than he liked to laugh, in fact. And
it's hard to be jolly in Newgate prison, Mama. Even
harder when you're stashed on a prison ship on the
way out of England for a time the law hopes will be
no less than forever. The work crews at Botany Bay
are no place for hilarity either. You want me to
smile more, is that it? Is that what you brought me
here to ask?"

"I never meant to leave you!" she cried.

He stilled. Then he smiled. "Ah, *you* want to apologize, is that it? A little late, but fine. Why not?
Apology accepted. Is that it, then?"

"Daffyd,' she said desperately, "I was going to
take you with me the night I ran away from your father, but you were only a few weeks old, and had a
fever. You cried if anyone touched you. Your father's

mother, Keja, said I shouldn't dare. Your father was drunk, he'd fallen deeply asleep, but every time you wailed, he stirred. And Keja had some distant cousins who were passing through, who had agreed to take me away. They were waiting in back of the caravan for me to come out so we could ride. I promised her I'd be back. I meant it. But by the time I returned to my home and could send you for, you and she, and your father, were gone. I could never find you."

Daffyd's smile was gone. He cocked his head to one side. "Fine. I said I understood. What more do you want, madam?"

"You can't understand," she said bitterly. "I ran off with a gypsy, yes. Because he was everything my husband was not. And because I was a foolish, spoiled, and arrogant child. I was not looking for adventure. I sought approval and affection. I was starved for it. My husband was chosen for me. He wasn't a bad man, but he was reserved and prideful, and cold, so cold I froze in his arms. He didn't care for women, and had no conversation for me, no lust either, except for me to bear him an heir. After I did, he left for London, leaving me alone at our country estate. He said I wasn't to come with him.

"I didn't know how to insist. I had no experience of the world, Daffyd! I married young. But I'd been declared a diamond as a girl, and was used to flattery and flirtation. That's when I sought revenge. And that's when your father came whistling down the lane on his way to a country fair near our estate. He flattered me, he teased me, he made me feel beautiful and desirable. More, he taught me what desire was, and what it was for. I stole out at night and danced in the dew with him. I flew from the house and played in the sunlight with him. Then my husband returned and told me he required another heir. I pleaded a headache that night, and eloped with your father the next."

"Foolish, indeed," Daffyd said.

Now her face showed animation, and he got a glimpse of the girl she must have been with his father. "He took me to Keja's caravan, and was pleased with himself for it. Not because he'd gotten me, I discovered, but because he'd stolen a gentleman's wife. He bragged about it every time he got drunk. Which was often. The fact is he grew tired of me before the season changed. And I, of him. He wasn't so merry when thwarted, and he was thwarted easily when he got in his cups. He was free with his hands then, too."

"Well I know that," Daffyd muttered.

"I'd never been physically beaten. I couldn't allow it. I knew my husband had kept my disappearance quiet because he'd hated the thought of a stain on his name. I knew I could return to him. Divorce would be a scandal he wouldn't want to face, and he still needed another heir. But there was a problem."

"Let me guess," Daffyd said. "Me. Or rather, my advent."

She nodded. "I couldn't return carrying another man's child. Even an uncaring husband has limits."

She looked away from him and added, "It was too late for any of Keja's potions to remedy the matter. I stayed, planning to go home after you were born."

Daffyd gave out a crack of laughter.

She looked up, startled.

"I see," he said. "Since I couldn't be prevented, I was going to be presented? You planned to return to your husband, showing him such a winsome babe his heart would melt, is that it?"

"Don't be foolish," she snapped. "I was going to place you with a respectable farm family, and pay for your upbringing."

"Such a pity," he said. "I'd have made such a good thresher, too. Cut line. So you couldn't find me. The old fox was good at hiding his tracks. I believe that. Is that enough for you?"

"No," she said. "But you'll never understand. I was a selfish girl, a cold wife, and a poor mother. Yet I wasn't entirely lost to human feeling. I need you to know that. I kept looking for you, Daffyd."

"Well, you found me," he said as he rose from his chair. "And so?"

"And so," she said, defeated. "That's it. It took all my courage to summon you here and tell you this. Your eyes cut me to pieces. They accuse me and convict me. I don't like disapproval, I suppose. I wasn't a good mother, not remotely so. But I cared what became of you. You don't believe me. It is nevertheless so. Still, you're right," she said as she turned from him. "It is enough."

He stared at her for a moment, this beautiful, cold woman who had given him birth and then given him away. She was right. He'd had enough. He turned toward the door.

"Daffyd," she said.

He turned again. She held out a leather case. "Take this. Go through it at your leisure, I'll trouble you no more. I'm pleased that you and Leland like each other. He's a good judge of character. He's also the image of his father, too, and so I never could warm to him. A pity, because unlike his father or myself, he's a very good person. As for me, I have ever been unfortunate in my dealings with men."

Daffyd took the bulging case, and tucked it under his arm. He bowed. "Good day, my lady," he said.

But it was hours before Daffyd could bring himself to open the case. He took it to his room, placed it on a table, and stared at it. Then, after a long drink he'd poured for himself, he opened it.

There were sheaves of brittle old papers there, some bundles tied with ribbon, some bound with string. He took out the papers and began reading. There were numerous reports from Bow Street, going back many years, stating that the gypsy male known as Johnny Reynard could not be found, nor could his mother or his son.

There were numerous reports from various private investigators over the years, saying the same.

And then Daffyd found a yellowed letter from

Bow Street, reporting that the boy, named Daffyd, had finally been found, and lay in Newgate prison, awaiting hanging for the theft of a pound note.

The document Daffyd found next was hardest to read, because of the tears running down his face. It was the receipt for a huge sum of cash paid to insure that the gypsy boy Daffyd was transported, along with the boy, Amyas, that he'd been sentenced with, rather than to be hanged.

Daffyd's hand shook. He put down the letter. They'd all always known it was the future earl's distant noble relative who had arranged to commute Geoffrey and his son's sentences to transportation. Daffyd and Amyas had wondered how the little money Geoffrey had left had been enough to pay for the bribes necessary to buy the same sentence for Amyas and himself. Now Daffyd knew. It hadn't been enough. It had been his mother who had bought it.

Daffyd sat back and stared blindly into the night. It was too late, of course. And though it had saved his life, it was far too little for her to have done, even so. He didn't know how it could possibly matter anymore. He was a grown man now. His course was set. Nevertheless, he felt warmth in the innermost hidden parts of his heart.

The lady who had birthed him hadn't been much of a mother; he doubted she could be. She was cold and self-centered, and seemed incapable of loving anyone except for herself. He doubted that would ever change. But she hadn't left him like a snake leaves her eggs in the sand. She'd cared if he lived or died.

It wasn't much. But it was more than he'd ever had.

Chapter 21

There was no one on the road on the way to the village, there seldom was. It wasn't much of a road, more a path with pretensions, Meg thought with a smile. She also thought that was a fine pun and wished she had someone to share it with. Her smile faded as she again thought of that someone.

The trees were leafless, the hedgerows were brown, the autumn was fading, readying for the winter. She thought that she was, too. Her hopes were drying up and she was becoming sere in her heart, preparing herself for the long, cold rest of her life. She didn't look for him anymore.

She didn't look up at every birdsong wondering if he was coming whistling down the road, the way she had when she'd first come home. Which was foolish, because even if he was gypsy, she didn't even know if he could whistle. But then, thinking the wind knocking against the door on a restless night was him come to see her was foolishness, too. As was imagining the rattling of the shutters on her bed-chamber's windows was Daffyd, aping Romeo as he climbed to her room in the night. It was a lovely im-age, dramatic and just like him, but she knew it was nonsense. And it was downright stupid to think of him as she did every night as she tried to sleep. But she could no more help it than she could the beating of her heart.

She'd made a fine farewell speech to Daffyd and the earl, and was proud of herself for it. She couldn't blame Daffyd for swallowing it whole, es-pecially since he'd wanted to. And the truth was that it was almost true. She wasn't sorry she'd tried to mend matters on her own, and she did have more confidence in herself since her mad adventure. That inner assurance had enabled her to stand up to her aunts' disapproval and maintain her dignity. It had impressed them, too. They hadn't scolded her again once they'd seen she accepted her fate and didn't regret her actions, only how her quest had ended. And how could she ever regret knowing Daffyd?

All true. But, oh, how she missed him.

She'd left the road and he was gone from her life, and the aunts were right, it was far better this way. But when the wind blew from the east, and she smelled the smoke of faraway cook fires, she thought of him. She thought of him when the sun shone and the rain came or the night fell. She remembered his wit and his touch, his kisses and his laughter. She remembered at night when she was alone, and in the most inappropriate daylight hours as well, though she wondered if there was ever an appropriate time to long for what she could never have again.

It wasn't that there was no one else. For a miracle, after the aunts started speaking to her again, they'd suddenly produced a new neighbor to come calling. She couldn't like him, of course. She couldn't even if he were clever and handsome. George Fletcher was neither. He was a young widower with two children, no conversation, and a face she couldn't place each time she met him again. But there he was, a man to come and sit in the parlor of an evening, take tea with them and comment on the weather and the crops. He'd be a wonderful husband for either of her aunts. Her own heart was already given, and she didn't know how she could ever win it back, so how could poor, dull Mr. Fletcher?

Meg didn't miss the long roads she'd traveled with Daffyd, and didn't pine for London. In truth, she liked the calm beauty of the countryside. She just didn't like being alone. But she knew she always would be from now on. Still, there were things that could distract her.

So she shook the reins. The old horse ignored it. He hadn't hurried for ten years and wasn't about to start now. But she wished he could. Her visits to the village on market day were the most diverting things in her life, and the more time he took the less she had to spend in town. It was like trying to hurry a rock.

Meg sat back and accepted the plodding pace as she had everything since she'd returned to the aunts. She was going over the list of things she'd been sent to get, wondering what she could do with the pennies she'd saved, when the old horse turned round a bend in the road and stopped.

He couldn't go on. Meg caught her breath and her heart raced. There was a caravan blocking the road: a bright gypsy caravan.

It only took a moment for her shocked hopes to fade. Of course. The gypsies often came to market, especially at the turn of the seasons when they took to the road. She was about to stand and call out to see if anyone could move the obstacle from her path, when she saw the profile of a man sitting on the high seat in front, holding the team of horses.

As she stared, two gypsy men hopped down from out of the back of the caravan. She'd never seen them before, and wasn't happy to see them now. They were prototypical gypsies; the sort parents warned children to steer clear of if they didn't want to be stolen away. In her time with Daffyd, Meg had learned that gypsies never stole children, having plenty of their own. But in her travels she'd also learned that some men, from any nation, looked upon lone females as fair game. There didn't seem anything innocent about either of the men looking at her now.

Both were dark, they had on mismatched, blowsy, colorful clothing, and wore bandannas tied around their necks, as well as matching wide and villainous smirks.

Meg tensed. It was broad daylight. But she was alone.

"Lady," one said, pulling off his floppy hat, and sweeping her a deep flourish of a bow. The other grinned.

She couldn't run, and wouldn't scream, because neither would do her any good. But she'd fight, she vowed.

And then another gypsy leaped lightly down from the back of the caravan. He stood in the road, hands on hips, and stared at her. "Took you long enough to get here," Daffyd said.

Meg's hand flew to her mouth.

"It's market day, and we've been here since dawn. Well, but look at what you're driving," Daffyd said scornfully, as he strolled over to her. "It's a wonder you got here at all."

"Naw, that ain't fair, lad," one of the gypsies said as he eyed Meg's old horse. "That plug's got at least another good week in him."

"You can't have him," Daffyd told him. "He goes back to her aunts' with the note. I think they'd miss him more than her. Well," he said, stopping beside Meg's cart and looking up at her, "are you coming?"

She couldn't breathe, much less speak.

"Give the lass a chance," one of the gypsies said as he ran a hand over Meg's old horse's bony back.

"Aye," the other gypsy said disapprovingly. "That's no way to woo a lass. Your father would be ashamed of you."

Daffyd smiled. "But she knows me."

"All the more reason to pour it on," the gypsy chided him.

"Right," Daffyd said. He smiled at Meg. "Meg, my heart," he said, bowing low as the other two had done, "would you please step down from your high perch. And then, run away with me?"

"Whatever are you talking about?" she managed to ask, though she discovered it was hard to say anything because her smile trembled, and she didn't know whether she'd laugh or weep.

"Let me tell you," he said, and raised his arms to her.

She slid down from her seat and into his clasp, and held his shoulders as he lowered her feet to the ground. "You're here," she said in disbelief.

"Obviously. Listen, I've a thing or two to say to you. And not in front of these fellows. Cousins," he said, turning to them, "I thank you for your help. But could you leave us alone for a minute?"

"Have to," the man stroking the horse said. "We got to return this nag. Perry here, he got to help turn the coach so it don't block the road no more. But when I get back, we have to move, and fast."

"Agreed," Daffyd said. He took Meg's hand. She

went with him in a daze as he walked along the road. He spied a stile in a nearby field. "A seat," he explained as he led her through the grasses.

"Now then," he said as he settled her on it, and stood before her. "As quickly as I can say it, and as truly. Meg, my heart, my love, I've come for you. And I ask you to go with me."

The shock of him made it difficult to take in what he said. He wore a white shirt, black trousers and half boots. His black hair shone blue in the sunlight; his deep blue eyes studied her intently. He could be gentleman or gypsy, and today he was dressed like a rover, the sort that could lure a lady from her bower. She steeled herself, because it was literally far too good to be true. And now she had her breath and wits back, she reminded herself that he had taught her that joy was impermanent.

"Then why did you let me go?" she asked seriously. "Are you here because you feel sorry for me?"

"No, because I was sorry for me. Well, and so was everyone who knew me." He reached out and gently lifted off her bonnet. "There, now I can see your eyes," he murmured, and added, with a sad smile, "I tried to drink the thought of you away. I tried carousing too, but it didn't get further than the bottle. You have to be a little bit happy in order to carouse, you know."

"Then why did you let me go in the first place?" she persisted.

His smile faded. "Because I was afraid I'd be bad for you. I'd never seen fidelity, and didn't know if I could learn it. And I wouldn't want anything else for you."

"What changed your mind?"

"You," he said simply. "The constant thought of you. You wouldn't go 'way, though you left me. And some other things too, things that made me think. I realized life is full of surprises and you have to take it as it comes. That's hard for a fellow who thinks he knows everything. But I learned you can't know everything. If you're lucky, only half of what you believe is wrong. You can't even be sure of your next breath, and I didn't want to take many more without you. I love you, Meg Shaw. I'm not worthy of you, but you know that, I've told you often enough. You know all my disadvantages, too. I wouldn't blame you for saying no."

"So you're saying you can't promise fidelity?"

"Damned if I am!" he said angrily. "I'll never stray. But the thing is, I finally saw I was finding excuses, and getting in my own way. I always do, with you. Because I knew I didn't deserve you, and worried you might realize that one day and stray from me."

"Never!" she blurted.

"So, you will?" he asked. "Come away with me? Run off with the gypsy Daffyd?"

She hesitated. She had some pride, and some sense, after all. She'd run away once, and ruined herself. She thought she'd learned her lesson, but here he was, and so here she was, about to utterly ruin herself this time. He'd never actually mentioned marriage.

He saw her hesitation. He'd expected it. "You don't really have a choice," he said gently.

Her eyes flew wide.

"You're being stolen by gypsies. Now, you can come quietly, or be trussed up and carried off neat as a sack of chickens stolen from the henhouse at midnight. You know us gypsies."

She grinned in spite of her surprise. "I'd like to see you truss up a sack of chickens."

"So you would," he agreed. "It's a Romany art. My stealth is a thing of beauty. You wouldn't hear a cluck. So. Docile and dulcet, accepting your fate? Or are you going to make me work?"

She frowned, and thought for a moment.

He nodded, bent, plucked her off the stile where she sat, and slung her over his shoulder.

"Daffyd!" was all she could gasp, because her stomach was across his shoulder and every stride he took pumped the breath out of her.

"My name," he agreed.

"Good," one of the gypsies called when he saw Daffyd and his wriggling burden come marching up to the caravan. "Stow the wench—I mean, the lass— and we'll be off. We're meeting up with Tony down the road, and then we ride."

Daffyd waved his free hand. "I trust you entirely. See you when we get there. Godspeed and good luck."

"Ah, we've gotten out of worse tangles," the fellow said. "By the time an alarm's raised we'll be long gone. Then we travel in company, and I'd like to see the local gentry stop a caravan of caravans, I would!"

"That is, if they raise an alarm at all," Daffyd said, as he swept back the curtain and stepped into the caravan. "I wrote a good note. Carry on!"

The interior of the caravan was dim, but Meg didn't need light to see the blur of vivid colors on the floor, the tables, and the bed. Daffyd lightly dropped her on that bed. She scrambled to her knees and looked up at him. Her hair was down around her shoulders, her face was pink, her eyes flashed with fury and her bosom heaved with indignation.

He sat on the bed beside her and smiled. "You look exactly like a gypsy now," he commented. "Only older than most kidnapped brides."

She was about to shout at him, but that made her pause. "What are your intentions?" she asked.

"Oh, the usual," he said, as he began pulling off his boots. "Rape, dishonor, indignity. You know, the customary."

In spite of her anger, she smiled. "No, really, Daffyd. What is the meaning of this?"

He shucked off his other boot and turned his head to her. "I'm going to ruin you, of course," he said.

"Daffyd," she said quietly. "I am ruined, you know that."

"Oh, not nearly. You don't know the half of it. I mean to be thorough this time."

"Why?"

He didn't answer until he'd pulled his shirt over his head, exposing his lean, tanned chest. Then he smiled at her. "Because I don't want you to leave me again.

And because I really thought this would amuse you." He frowned. "But I may be wrong. I have been before."

He took her hand and looked into her eyes. "Meg, I want you. But I don't trust my intuition anymore and can't be sure you want me. After all, you weren't used to traveling or being on your own, and I was the only male you could count on for days on end. That can addle a woman's perceptions. You may have come to your senses. You do have an independent turn of mind," he added on a crooked smile, "worrisome in a female, as you know."

"Still, my brothers, both those of my blood and those of my heart, kept telling me that you want me, too. And so did the earl, and he's the wisest man I know. If they're wrong, and I was mistaken, I'll take you right back to where you were going. I'll drive you straight to the local market now. You can tell the aunts you escaped my clutches. But if I was right, won't you please stay with me?"

"For how long?" she asked.

"Silly question," he said. He leaned forward and brushed a kiss along her cheek. "Forever, or as long as we have of it."

She shivered, and put her opened hand on his chest. She didn't know if it was to hold him off or so she could feel the living warmth of him again. "But you don't want a wife," she whispered. "You said so. You don't want to be a father. And so much as I love you, I don't want a man who doesn't want to be father to my children, that is, if . . ."

"Oh, no 'if' about it," he said as he tilted her face to his. "But what's this? 'So much as I love you?' You love me?"

"Oh, Daffyd," she said, going into his arms. "How can you ask?"

"Easily," he said seriously.

"But all your speeches about not wanting children? About wanting to be an uncle?"

"Well, I recently heard that's already in train," he said, nuzzling her neck. "My brother Christian and his lady are anticipating. I'm happy for them, but find I want more for myself. I can still be a doting uncle, but you've turned me around, Meg. I want to be a father to your children, and if we can't produce any, than to those we choose to live with us. I want a house full of prim daughters and knavish sons."

He cupped her face in both his hands, tipped a kiss on her lips and gazed at her. "No more games. No more jests. Will you lay back and make love to me now? No one will disturb us. The others are riding up front and beside to protect us. We'll be as private as in any bridal bower until nightfall. Will you?"

And what of after nightfall? she thought in sudden alarm. With all he'd said about babies and forever, he hadn't mentioned matrimony. But she was being greedy. She'd take what he offered, because he'd offered her his heart and his children. What would there be for her if she said no? A dreary life, filled with regrets. And if she said yes? A strange life, filled with regrets? But she couldn't believe he'd ever desert her utterly.

She felt the caravan lurch and begin to move, the room swayed as it rocked slowly down the road. She could still leave. Or she could run off with her gypsy now. If she left him, she suspected it would be for the last time. But she was being foolish again. There was no way on earth she could leave him now.

"Yes," she said. "Please, Daffyd, make love to me. Mind," she added, as she saw his slow smile growing. "I can't promise I'll be very good at it, at least, not immediately. But I want you very much, and I learn quickly."

"Meg," he said as he took her in his arms and lowered her to the bed, "it's not a test or a lesson. It just will mean getting as close to me as your skin. It will be us coming together at last."

She smiled against his lips. And then she couldn't smile for the joy of his kiss. The bed was deep and soft, his body was hot and strong. She stared when he sat up again to peel off the last of his clothes.

He was delighted to see her expression.

"I'm a country girl," she said when she saw his surprise. "I've heard what women prize in their men."

It was her turn to be proud when she saw his face after she'd drawn off her gown. "Oh, Meg," was all he could breathe as he lowered his head to her breast. It was enough for her.

They kissed and touched and tasted. Meg twisted and turned in his arms, warming to furnace heat even as Daffyd did.

But he was more than warm, he was suffering. He hoped she didn't know how difficult it was for him. He'd thought of this for hours, and the feeling of her, so close at last, ignited him. He tried to be careful, restrained, and cautious. Almost impossible, with her body so soft and plaint, supple and willing. It took all his will to keep building her passion at a slow, steady pace, when all he wanted was to quench his desire.

It was the first time he'd ever had to school himself so strictly. Last time they'd made love he hadn't been in love. In truth, at no time when he'd made love had he been in love. Now he ached, his body trembling with the effort to slow down as he discovered how different love made the act of love. Different, and beyond anything he'd ever known.

Meg reveled in his lovemaking. It wasn't only the sensations he brought to her, she could hardly believe she was in Daffyd's arms again, at last, and against all expectation. His body was smooth and strong, lithe and avid. His skin smelled of soap and herbs and spices as well as the wild scent of the forest. She rolled with him in the gently swaying bed as the caravan moved on, attuned to him, calmed by his heartbeat, excited by his nearness and what he was doing.

She felt her body begin to build to unknowable heights. She exulted as she felt the strong hard evidence of his desire against her flesh. She reached out to hold him. This time there was no shame or fear. This was Daffyd, and he was hers at last.

His hand tested her readiness as it entered her, and she opened her eyes. "Daffyd," she gasped, "I thought this time it would be . . . all of it. Us, together, not just for me and then for you."

He moved, holding his body an inch above her. "It will be. But first, let me give you ease," he murmured with difficulty. "It will make it easier for us both."

His hand sought her; she raised her body to allow deeper access, and then was lost as pleasure began to spiral through her. When she gasped with release, she felt his shuddering sigh of relief. Then he lifted her, withdrew his hand and entered her with his body.

She was aware of stretching. A moment's stinging made her tense. Then it was gone, and he filled her, he was with her, in her, part of her. She was astonished and delighted. She clung to him as he began to move without thought or control at last, and smiled against his shoulder, taking her pleasure in the joy of his. She'd known the effort it had taken him to withhold so long; she'd felt it in the dewing on his skin, the pace of his breathing, the tension in his body. This was not the calm, amused lover she had known. So when he closed his eyes and pounded against her, she held him tight and offered herself to him fully even though she was replete, and unaccustomed to this wild passion.

When he thrust hard and groaned as he reached his moment, she clasped him ever closer, and rejoiced.

Because throughout, his hands had been gentle, and his touch never hurtful. And she was his, at last.

They lay twined together as their hearts' frantic beating slowed.

He was the first to speak. "Are you all right?"

"Oh, yes," she said drowsily.

"It improves for females, with time, and practice," he said, as he stroked her back. "It's a shame it isn't bliss the first time."

"Is it bliss for males the first time?"

He chuckled. "Trust you to ask that."

"Ought I not have?"

"Lord, no!" he said fervently, dropping a kiss on her bare shoulder. "Ask anything. I love my free-spoken lass. But as to whether lovemaking's bliss for males the first time? Actually, no. It's astonishment that it was accomplished at all."

Now she chuckled, and buried her face in the crook of his neck.

"But I'm trying to be a gentleman now," he whispered into her ear. "I don't want to talk about my past."

She was silent. "But you do have a past," she finally said. "How was I compared to . . . That is to say, how do I—"

"Meg, my heart," he said, interrupting her. "I'll only tell the truth. You're exactly what I want and need. Forget my past. It doesn't apply. You're my first and only love."

She lay in his arms, content, as the caravan

swayed and rumbled down the road. She'd made her bed, and was lying in it. She didn't know where they were going, or how long he'd stay with her, or what would become of her. She only knew she was with him, and he was her first and only love, too.

Chapter 22

"**T**ime to wake up," Daffyd breathed in her ear.

Meg opened her eyes. The interior of the caravan was still dim, but now from the glow of one lamp. She yawned, and reached for him.

"Oh, no!" He laughed, and danced away from the bed. "I've just dressed. And so should you. We're here."

She sat upright. He was dressed, but no longer in roving gypsy garb. He wore a tight-fitted blue jacket, dark pantaloons, and half boots. His linen shirt was white, she caught a glimpse of a golden waistcoat, and a formal neckcloth was tied round his neck.

She reached for the blanket to cover herself, suddenly feeling shamed.

He sat beside her. His voice gentled. "It's still me. And still you. No need for embarrassment. Just remember that I'm naked under all this finery, and you'll do. Now, get dressed. Your horse and cart, along with a note from me, was delivered to your aunts' house. While he was there, my light-fingered cousin fetched your clothing for you. So put on some finery. We have an appointment. I'll be back soon, but take your time."

He rose and strode to the back of the caravan. He looked at her. "Would you want me to send someone to help with your hair?"

She bridled. "I know I look like a wench tossed in a haystack, but I've taken care of myself for years, thank you. When you return, I'll look proper."

"I want you to look beautiful," he said. "Since that's not hard, I'll leave you, and be back within the hour."

He pulled back the curtain at the back of the caravan and she got a glimpse of the stars before he left.

Meg rose; noticing intimate twinges and aches she hadn't had before. She refused to think about it, threw on her shift, and went to the pitcher and bowl on the table. It was filled with fresh warm water. She washed, and began to brush out her tangled hair. Her hands stopped at their task as she wondered where she was. It was night now. So, they'd traveled all day. He'd said he could send someone to help with her hair. Could they be back in London? She listened close. She heard no traffic, and shook her head at her foolishness. It would be bizarre if they'd taken a gypsy caravan into the heart of fashionable London. It might even be illegal.

Then could they be in some gypsy camp? But he'd said he wanted her dressed well. Could they be back at the viscount's manor in the countryside? She frowned. It was one thing to be Daffyd's lover when they were alone. But if she came to the viscount's pleasure house as his woman, that would set the seal on her disgrace. Meg bowed her head and swallowed hard. This was the path she'd taken, and she had to walk it.

But she wished she hadn't thrown her life away for love.

And she knew she wouldn't have had it any other way, because she'd had no life without him.

Meg found a traveling case and the gowns Daffyd's light-fingered cousin had brought for her. She smiled. Typical. He'd left her simple gowns, and brought only the most extravagant. She chose her coral gown, tied her hair with a matching ribbon, put on her pink slippers, and sat and waited. And worried.

"May I come in?" a familiar voice from outside the curtain asked.

She shot to her feet. "Yes. Of course," she said, because she didn't know how to say no. She ducked her head.

The curtain parted. "Why, you look lovely!" the earl of Egremont exclaimed. "And happy! I'm so relieved. When that madman told me what he was going to do I didn't know in what kind of state I'd find you. He thought carrying you off in a caravan was perfect. I'd my doubts. I should never have doubted you, my dear." He took her hand. "Are you ready?"

He was dressed for an evening in London. His eyes were kind and filled with understanding. But she didn't understand. "Ready for what?" she whispered.

"I shall kill that boy!" the earl said angrily. "Another jest. Or maybe, give him his due, maybe it was just that he wanted me to be the one to ask you. Yes, that makes sense. He's strangely unsure of himself when it comes to you. My dear," he said, "I'm here to ask if I may be the one to give you away."

Her eyes flew wide. Her hand went to her throat. There were too many dreadful things to contemplate at once. "To whom?' she asked in a whisper. "Give me to whom?"

"I will kill him," the earl declared. He shook his head, and looked at Meg. "Give you to Daffyd, in the state of matrimony," he said more softly. "Since you have no father, I'd hoped you would permit me that honor."

She stared at him.

"I've made arrangements for the necessary permits and papers and a special license," the earl said. "I did the moment he wrote and told me what he was planning, and invited me to be part of it. You could wait until you return to London and use them then. But the wretched boy wants the deed done immediately, if not a minute sooner, and he felt it would take too long to get to London. He likes the irony of this, and orchestrated the whole of it. Meg, he wants to marry you here and now."

She digested the information. She raised her head. "I would be proud and honored if you acted as father to me in anything. But I will not marry anyone who hasn't asked me."

"Lord!" he said, "That slow top! Of course. Quite right! I'll tell him." He left, smiling.

Meg paced as she waited.

Daffyd didn't ask if he could enter the caravan. He swept aside the curtain and marched in. "What's this?" he demanded harshly, his voice at odds with his expression. He looked worried. "There's an impediment? The earl said there's an impediment. You changed your mind?"

"I'd nothing to change it from," she said angrily. "You never asked me to marry you, never."

He looked dumbfounded. Then he grinned. And then he laughed. He took her in his arms, and rocked her back and forth. "Did I not?" he asked. "I asked you to run away with me. I told you it would be forever. I told you I loved you. I compromised you thoroughly. Good lord, Miss Shaw, what else do you want of a poor gypsy lad?"

"You never asked me to marry you," she said stubbornly.

"Well, then," he shouted, stepping back and gripping her by the shoulders, "Why the devil did you run away with me? Gads, woman, have you no sense at all?" He shook his head, eased his grip and spoke in calmer tones. "I'm shocked and appalled, Meg," he said, with every evidence of both. "You know better than that. Or should."

"Because I love you so much," she said. "I couldn't bear to have you leave me."

"What a buffle-head you are,' he said tenderly. "What a bad decision." He chided her even as his arms tightened around her. "Running off without a promise of marriage? Lying with me without knowing your future? Didn't the aunts teach you better? Didn't I? What did you think I meant to do with you? Gads. Don't tell me. How could you think it of me?"

"I didn't," she said, burying her head in his neck. "I didn't want to think anymore. I just trusted in you."

"You'd better let *me* see to the raising of our daughters," he said sincerely.

He stepped back a pace, locked his arms around her waist and gazed down at her. "But I'm glad you were a fool for love, because I love you, Meg. I've never said that to a woman, and thought I never would. I know my shortcomings. Heaven help you, so do you. Few men in England had such a dishonorable birth, or led such a disreputable life. But I can learn, and I do. I'll be entirely respectable for you. You took one step already, can't you be just a little more disreputable, for me? Meg, will you marry me?"

She nodded. "Yes, Daffyd, I will."

"Good!" he said, his eyes alight. "Now, I worked on this mad scheme for days. Why wait for London? I thought to marry now, here, just over the border, in Scotland, where it's legal, and take our honeymoon in the caravan. That way you can tell our children how it was when you ran off with a gypsy. It would be a better ending to our story than any of the sad old songs. It might start some new, merrier ones." He sobered. "Marry me, Miss Meg, and now, please."

"You've arranged it so quickly?"

"No, I had a week to plan, and I think I came up with the best for us. Something unforgettable, something amusing and romantic."

She still couldn't get over the fact that she'd been about to leave everything she knew, including respectability, for the sake of love. Now it appeared she could have it all, and Daffyd, too.

He frowned at a sudden thought. "Of course, I'm not a couth fellow. I had no upbringing at all. So, I don't know. It occurs to me now that what appeals to me might seem a clumsy scrambling sort of wedding to you. I suppose it is. What do I know of sensibilities? I could never afford them. But if this is too alien to your feelings, Meg, you don't have to do it. We'll turn right around and go back to London and marry properly, in the eyes of Society. I wouldn't know about that, but you and the earl can arrange it. It's your wedding, and your decision. It doesn't matter, so long as I end up with you."

The reception to celebrate the wedding of the earl of Egremont's ward Daffyd to Miss Margaret Shaw was magnificent. The earl opened his London townhouse to the *ton*, and spared no expense. The bride was dressed beautifully, her gamine charm won over everyone, and the groom was as wickedly attractive as could be hoped. The flowers were profuse, beautiful and out of season, as were the hothouse fruits that graced the exquisite menu. Musicians played; there was a ball, and then an after-midnight supper. The guests varied between the influential and the exotic, and made the event the talk of the town for at least a month.

But some in attendance never forgot the actual wedding of the earl of Egremont's wild young gypsy ward and his lovely bride, the one that had taken place a month earlier.

Not the blacksmith, who married them over the anvil at Gretna Green, though he'd married dozens of runaway couples before. Not the groom's four brothers, two of his blood and the two of his heart, who'd been summoned and came running, and stood beaming throughout the brief ceremony. Certainly not the earl of Egremont, who was as touched by the event as he'd have been were he the bride's real father. Nor the grand lady who stood, silent and veiled, at the back of the blacksmith's shop, to watch her son marry, nor the old gypsy woman who wept where she stood, close to the couple. The other gaily dressed Romany, who came in a string of wagons and caravans to see the event, talked about it for a generation. And the bride's two bewildered aunts, who'd been carried off in a gypsy caravan to be witnesses, never forgot either.

After the wedding there was drinking and eating on the lawn in front of the blacksmith's shop, and dancing under the moon to the tunes of fiddles and drums and squeeze boxes. They drank to the bride and groom, and then to all their friends and family. They even drank to the Baron Osbourne's runaway daughter in Canada, who was toasted as the "greatest matchmaker of the century." The celebration didn't end until dawn.

By then, the wildflower-covered bridal caravan drawn by flower-bedecked horses was long gone down the road.

As the sun rose the next morning, the groom in the bed of the swaying caravan rose up on one elbow and looked down at his bride. She reached up and pulled his head down for yet another kiss.

"Right," Meg sighed. "Oh, Daffy, you're right again. It gets better with practice."

"Good," he said earnestly, as he bent to her. "We'd better to get to it then. We've only got all the rest of our lives, you know."

Avon Romantic Treasures

Unforgettable, enthralling love stories, sparkling with passion and adventure from Romance's bestselling authors

SIN AND SENSIBILITY   *by Suzanne Enoch*
0-06-054325-6/$5.99 US/$7.99 Can

SOMETHING ABOUT EMMALINE   *by Elizabeth Boyle*
0-06-054931-9/$5.99 US/$7.99 Can

JUST ONE TOUCH   *by Debra Mullins*
0-06-056167-X/$5.99 US/$7.99 Can

AS AN EARL DESIRES   *by Lorraine Heath*
0-06-052947-4/$5.99 US/$7.99 Can

TILL NEXT WE MEET   *by Karen Ranney*
0-06-075737-X/$5.99 US/$7.99 Can

MARRY THE MAN TODAY   *by Linda Needham*
0-06-051414-0/$5.99 US/$7.99 Can

THE MARRIAGE BED   *by Laura Lee Guhrke*
0-06-077473-8/$5.99 US/$7.99 Can

LOVE ACCORDING TO LILY   *by Julianne MacLean*
0-06-059729-1/$5.99 US/$7.99 Can

TAMING THE BARBARIAN   *by Lois Greiman*
0-06-078394-X/$5.99 US/$7.99 Can

A MATTER OF TEMPTATION   *by Lorraine Heath*
0-06-074976-8/$5.99 US/$7.99 Can